For Ger Siggins

Should Have Got Off At Sydney Parade

ROSS O'CARROLL-KELLY
(AS TOLD TO PAUL HOWARD)

Illustrated by Alan Clarke

PENGUIN BOOKS

PENGUIN BOOKS

Published by the Penguin Group
Penguin Books Ltd, 80 Strand, London WC2R ORL, England
Penguin Group (USA) Inc., 375 Hudson Street, New York, New York 10014, USA
Penguin Group (Canada), 90 Eglinton Avenue East, Suite 700, Toronto, Ontario, Canada M4P 2Y3
(a division of Pearson Penguin Canada Inc.)
Penguin Ireland, 25 St Stephen's Green, Dublin 2, Ireland
(a division of Penguin Books Ltd)
Penguin Group (Australia), 250 Camberwell Road, Camberwell, Victoria 3124, Australia
(a division of Pearson Australia Group Pty Ltd)
Penguin Books India Pvt Ltd, 11 Community Centre, Panchsheel Park, New Delhi – 110 017, India
Penguin Group (NZ), 67 Apollo Drive, Rosedale, North Shore 0632, New Zealand
(a division of Pearson New Zealand Ltd)
Penguin Books (South Africa) (Pty) Ltd, 24 Sturdee Avenue, Rosebank, Johannesburg 2196, South Africa

Penguin Books Ltd, Registered Offices: 80 Strand, London WC2R ORL, England

www.penguin.com

First published by Penguin Ireland 2006
Published in Penguin Books 2007

6

Copyright © Paul Howard, 2006
All rights reserved

The moral right of the author has been asserted

Set in Monotype Garamond
Typeset by Rowland Phototypesetting Ltd, Bury St Edmunds, Suffolk
Printed in England by Clays Ltd, St Ives plc

ISBN: 978-1-844-88090-4

www.greenpenguin.co.uk

Out 'neath the arms of Cassiopeia,
Where the sword of Orion sweeps,
It's me and you, Rosie, crackling like crossed wires,
And you breathin' in your sleep.
You breathin' in your sleep.
Well there's just a spark of campfire burning,
Two kids in a sleeping bag beside,
I reach 'neath your shirt,
Lay my hands across your belly
And feel another one kickin' inside.
And I ain't gonna fuck it up this time.

'Long Time Comin'', Bruce Springsteen

Contents

What every bird wants more than anything in the world – aport from me, obviously – is to be impregnated. I can't actually remember where I picked up that little, I suppose you'd have to say, fact. I might have read it in a magazine in, like, the dentist's waiting room, or maybe some expert or other said it on 'The Big Bite', but I do remember hearing it, roysh, and that's not me clutching at straws.

It's five o'clock on, like, Christmas morning and I've been awake all night, roysh, torturing myself with the thought that my days as Ireland's answer to Enrique Iglesias could be over when this, like, baby of ours arrives on the scene. It was, like, something Oisinn said last night that got me thinking all, I don't know, intellectually like this. He was like, 'So, you'll be declaring your innings then?' and just as I was about to go, 'Don't kid yourself – these hips'll wear out a few mattresses yet,' Fionn goes and sticks in his two yo-yos worth.

He storts giving it, 'Yeah, no girl is going to be interested in you when they know your wife is pregnant,' which is bullshit, roysh, according to this theory I heard. Want to know the number one quality that birds look for in a goy? It's not good looks, killer bod, personality, sense of humour, or the stamina to last all night long, even though I have all those things. No, what attracts women more than anything else is virility.

See, every bird wants to be up the old Ballyjames. Even the ones who think they don't just haven't realised that they do. It's, like, an animal instinct. And those of us who've proved our virility – and not once, roysh, but twice – are the ones they'll most want to mate with. So I'm, like, worrying unnecessarily. I'm going to be beating them off with a focking cattle prod.

Sorcha asks me if I'm awake. I go, 'Pretty much,' and she turns around to face me and she's like, 'Me too. What are you thinking about?' and quick as a flash I'm like, 'I suppose that little miracle that's growing inside of you,' and in the darkness I can suddenly see a set of teeth, which she's just had whitened, as, like, a Chrimbo present from her old pair.

She goes, 'Ross, I think I know the night it happened,' and I'm like, 'As in . . .' and she's there, 'As in *it!* Oh my God, the *conception!* HELLO? Earth to Ross . . .' and then when the penny finally drops she goes, '*Oh my God*, I know it was that day we drove down to Glendalough, remember? It was, like, SO romantic. Walking hand-in-hand around the Upper Lake. A picnic. Brie and cranberries. Avocados. Focaccia. A nice Chardonnay. We lay down on the grass and when the stars came out we made love on the banks of the water. Oh my God, my body *ached* for you that night . . .'

Now that is the biggest pile of pants I've heard since . . . well, I suppose since the day I made my marital vows. I'm thinking, either I missed the conception or she's, like, dreamt up this whole romantic scene to tell her friends and she's, like, briefing me, just in case anyone asks.

Okay, there is, like, some shred of truth in the story. We did drive to Wicklow, but it was to Greystones, to meet some bird she'd been in college with. We certainly didn't walk hand-in-hand around the Upper Lake. We ended up watching Ireland kick South Africa's orse in The Burnaby – Rog focking *rocked* that day – and the only picnic I remember was a picnic of pints. We did get it on, as I remember, but it was in my BMW Z4 in the cor pork beside the Dorsh station, and if her body ached at all it was because of the jack I left on the back seat after changing the left rear tyre on the N11, just beyond the Loughlinstown roundabout.

But hey, who am I to piddle on her parade?

She goes, 'Merry Christmas, Ross,' and I'm like, 'Roysh back at you, Babes.'

1. Caution – Baby on Board

'Honestly, he's like a child with a new toy,' the old dear goes, already half-pissed on amaretto and apricot daiquiris, the focking soak that she is. You can hear this, like, *whooshing* sound coming from the hall, then the old man's big foghorn voice, going, 'Callaway don't make *toys*, Darling. This is a serious piece of engineering. The new science of distance *with* accuracy, quote-unquote.'

Then the *whooshing* again.

I turn around to Sorcha and I go, 'I knew we shouldn't have bothered our orses coming here,' and she gives me a filthy and goes, 'HELLO? It's Christmas Day, Ross,' as if that means something.

The old man decides to show his face. He comes into the kitchen and he's like, 'Sorcha! Darling!' and it's obvious, roysh, he's been throwing the brandy into him as well. He's giving her a hug and he's going, 'Merry Christmas, one and all,' and then he goes to hug me, roysh, and I go, 'Don't even *think* about it,' but he does anyway.

He puts his driver in the corner and goes, 'How's that nightclub of yours going, Ross – Lillie's, or whatever it's called?' and I could say that it's hopping, roysh, that it was, like, wall-to-wall celebrities last night – we're talking Jenny Lee Masterson, we're talking Isabela Chudzika, we're talking James Kilbane, we're talking Irish boyband ZOO – but I don't. I don't even bother my orse answering him.

I am seriously Hank, though. I could chew a pig's orse through a tennis racquet, but we've got to stand there exchanging pleasantries for twenty minutes before we sit down for nosebag.

'How's that dinner for you, Ross?' the old dear goes after I've had, like, three or four bites and even though it's incredible, roysh – because she's an unbelievable cook – I go, 'I wouldn't serve it to a focking dog,' and then there's, like, total silence until the old man goes to fill Sorcha's wine glass and she puts her hand over the top of it, roysh, and goes, 'Oh my God, not for me, Charles,' and I see this look pass between him and my old dear.

'Not drinking, Sorcha?' he goes, with a big shit-eating grin on his Ricky Gervais and she sort of, like, smiles and looks at me and she's there, 'No, I'm, em . . . going off it for a while,' and the old man's there, 'Well, Fionnuala and I know how much you adore Malbec . . . so *something's* up,' and straight away I go, 'Don't tell them, Sorcha. They'll only make a big deal of it,' but she goes ahead and does it anyway.

'Ross and I have some news,' she goes and you can tell, roysh, that the old pair already know what she's going to say. She's there, 'We're going to have a baby,' and then all focking hell breaks loose, it's hugs and, like, air-kisses and handshakes and all that bullshit.

The old man goes, 'Forget the Malbec, it should be champagne,' and as he's sitting back down the old dear asks Sorcha what date she's due and Sorcha goes, 'Well, you're supposed to take your last period, add one week, then subtract three months – and that's the date you're due. So it should be, like, July 7. Oh my God, it already seems SO close,' and then her and the old dear stort making all these, like, excited noises, the way fifteen-year-old girls do on the Dorsh.

The old man goes, 'Forget the Malbec, it should be champagne,' and I tell him that's the second focking time he's said that, roysh, and that if he keeps on saying it, someone might eventually laugh.

He goes, 'I wondered why the pair of you seemed in especially good form. I suppose if it's a boy, Ross, you'll be naming him after a certain Irish outhalf – and I'm not referring to our friend from Ulster . . .' and I just give him serious daggers, roysh, and I go, 'I already *have* a son called Ronan,' but he doesn't answer me, roysh, just stares into space, like he's blanking it out, which he basically is.

I get up from the table and corve myself a few more slices of turkey and ham and grab a few roasties. Then I go, 'This is focking revolting. I bet I spend all day tomorrow on the shitter,' and I sit back down and wolf it into me.

The old dear dishes up more sprouts for Sorcha and tells her she's looking forward to doing some serious mother-and-daughter-in-law bonding between now and July. The old man sort of, like, gestures towards Sorcha's stomach with his fork and goes, 'I'll put his name down for Portmarnock in the morning. Hennessy will second him,' and Sorcha's like, 'Oh my God, no. It's going to be a girl, Charles. I can, like, SO feel it,' and the old man goes, 'There'll be no Portmarnock if it's a girl. You know our stand on that particular issue . . .'

And the rest of the dinner goes on like that, roysh, basically bullshit. It's nearly five o'clock when Sorcha suggests we hit the road, roysh, because we're going to her old pair's for tea.

On the way out the door, Sorcha asks the old dear how her *little project* is going, roysh, and at first I think they're talking about one of the old dear's bullshit campaigns, like the one to stop newsagents in Dublin 18 from selling scratch-cords because they attract undesirables to the area. But it's not that at all, roysh, because the old dear turns around and goes, 'It's finished,' then suddenly disappears into the old man's study and comes back out with one of those big Manila envelopes, which is, like, stuffed to the gills with something or other and she's like, 'Have a read and tell me what you think.'

Three times in the – what? – ten-minute drive between Foxrock and Vico Road, I ask Sorcha what's in the envelope but she won't tell me. I go, 'I bet it's, like, fliers, calling for poor people to be banned from walking Dún Laoghaire pier on Tuesday afternoons,' but she's giving fock-all away.

As are Sorcha's family when they see me. It's all hugs and kisses for her, roysh, but just a grunt of 'Merry Christmas' for me, which is Kool and the Gang as far as I'm concerned. I know they're not exactly John B. on me – too cool for school, they think – but that's their loss.

I've more than just her old pair to cope with today, though. Sorcha's granny's also in the gaff, which guarantees surround-sound hostility. She hates my guts in a major way, this woman, but then she's a typical old biddy – a big grey afro, an unexplained bandage on her leg and if she's out of the house for more than an hour she's going, '*Ooh, I miss me cup of tea.*'

And she's *always* banging on about the weather. Once I made the mistake of doing an impression of her for Sorcha. It was like, '*Filthy weather, isn't it? Always raining. And what are they doing about it, these politicians? Nothing is right. Sure they're only after your vote. Once you've given it to them, you won't see them from one end of the year to the next . . .*' and it earned me, if I remember roysh, a slap across the face and three nights in the spare room.

I go, 'How the hell are you, Mrs Wells?' which is her name, roysh, because she's Sorcha's old dear's old dear, if that makes sense. All I get back is, 'Huh!'

Sorcha's little sister arrives downstairs then – Afric or Orpha or whatever she's called, the little focking temptress – and of course everyone's, like, staring at me, roysh, to see how enthusiastic my hello is, because they all know I've history there, shameful and all as it is. In fairness to her, she's the only one in the gaff who makes me feel welcome. She goes, 'ROSS!' and throws the lips on me in a major way. She could suck a focking pool ball up a wizard's sleeve, that one.

'Put some clothes on,' the old man goes, obviously not impressed, and Sorcha's sister's there, 'HELLO? What do you call this,' and she points at this, like, top and skirt, roysh, which would basically struggle to cover the palm of your hand. She looks like she's on the way to Bondi – or Wes. '*Put* some clothes on,' the old man goes again and she's like, 'Oh *my* God, I'm *going*,' and she stomps upstairs, with a big-time strop on. Sorcha's just there shaking her head, like she's pissed off with me more than her.

When she comes back, we go into the living room to open our presents. Well, Sorcha opens her presents – piles and piles of them. There's one for me – a book, of all things. Sorcha's old man knows I've never read one in my life, roysh, and I think this bothers him even more than the fact that I'm married to his daughter. It's *Stalingrad* by some dude called Antony Beevor and it looks seriously focking boring.

'Yeah, thanks for that, Mr Lalor,' I go, making the effort because of the day that's in it, and he's like, 'Might educate you,' just staring at me, but I'm, like, SO not rising to the bait.

We move into the dining room. Sorcha's old dear is the worst cook in the entire world. Seriously, roysh, Christmas Day, you'd be better off in prison. It's pretty noticeable that the old man has lost a shitload of weight since Sorcha

9

left home. Of course I'm telling her it's beautiful, roysh, whatever the fock it is we're eating and I can feel Sorcha and her old man staring at me, roysh, because they must know I'm ripping the piss.

'I never liked turkey,' the granny goes. 'If it was up to me, it'd be a nice bit of ox tongue. Or tripe,' and I sort of, like, accidentally let out a snigger, which doesn't go down too well with Sorcha's old man.

Someone's kicked off their shoes and is rubbing their foot up the inside of my leg. It's Sorcha's sister. She does this every time I come to dinner. It's her thing, and now I've a bone on me like Donnacha O'Callaghan's leg. So obviously I end up losing the thread of what's being said, roysh, and I just catch the end of Sorcha's granny saying there's not a song in the charts that you can hear the words to anymore and Count John McCormack was a man who could hold a note.

'Ross and I have some news . . .' Sorcha goes and it's not my imagination, roysh, I can feel the room actually dorken. Then she's, like, straight out with, roysh, going, 'We're going to have a baby . . .' and there's, like, total silence and it's her old man who eventually breaks it, going, 'I thought you were being careful,' and her old dear goes, *'Edmund!'*

Sorcha's like, 'Dad, this baby was *planned*,' which is a lie actually. Sorcha went off the old Jack and Jill for a few months because she said it was the reason she was putting on – *oh my God!* – SO much weight. And that particular night, well, I was supposed to get off at Sydney Parade, and I suppose you could say I missed my stop.

Her old man goes, 'What about your career, Sorcha?' and the old dear's like, 'She can hire someone to look after the shop. Edmund, *stop it*! Sorcha, this is *wonderful* news,' and she gives her a hug and so does whatever the sister's called.

The granny's only contribution is, 'Huh! You're stuck with him now then!' which everyone ignores, roysh, already knowing her feelings on the marriage.

The old man shakes my hand and I don't comment on the fact that he's trying to break my fingers. Sorcha goes, '*Oh my God!* Mum, we can go away on one of those Pregnancy Mini-Breaks. There's a place in England and they have, like, a Dead Sea saltwater pool. And we can have, like, an Indian head massage and – *oh my God* – a body mask,' and maybe it is the drink talking, roysh, but I love Sorcha when she's this happy.

She goes, 'And I'm seriously thinking about having the baby by acupuncture,' and the granny goes, 'They didn't have acupuncture in my day. None of these fancy painkillers either. You put the kettle on, rolled up your sleeves and just got on with it. You had to in them days . . .'

Sorcha's phone beeps. She opens the message and goes, 'Oh my God, it's from Ronan,' and, like, no one reacts. Sorcha's old pair aren't exactly happy bunnies at the idea of me, shall we say, covering another mare, even though I wasn't going out with their daughter at the time. Sorcha's the only one who's actually cool with it, and her and Ronan get on like you wouldn't believe.

So she reads it out. It's like, 'Story, Sorcha? Sorry I can't make it out for your soiree. I'm not allowed to cross the Liffey under the terms of me TR. Just wanted to say Merry Christmas to you and your family. And look after that little brother or sister of mine! X'

And of course I'm just about to say what a great kid he is when the phone beeps again and Sorcha reads it and goes, 'Oh and tell Rosser he's a benny.'

*

11

Being up the Damien gives birds all sorts of cravings. In the last week alone Sorcha's had cravings for a pair of Dolce & Gabbana knee-high boots, a pair of Christian Dior black, rimless shield glasses, an Emilion Pucci faux mink scorf, the new Marian Keyes, an Olympus MJU mini digital camera in pink, a Bodum deluxe cappuccino frother and a tub of Crème de la Mer, as in, like, the large one.

I tell her a couple of times that I'm not rolling in it, roysh, even though that's not strictly true, but she just turns around and goes, 'Oh my God, I cannot *believe* I am *actually* carrying this baby for *you*,' basically trying to guilt-trip me.

So what I've taken to doing is, like, carrying a notebook and pen around with me, roysh, so that when she rings I can, like, scribble down her list of demands, then send Anna, one of the birds who works in the bor – muck, in case you're wondering – across to BTs to pick up everything she wants, then send it up to her in her shop in the Powerscourt Centre.

I mean, this is, like, a typical exchange. The old Wolfe rings. I answer it. It's like, 'Hey, Ross, how are you?' and I go, 'Up to my knackers, Babe. What's the Jack?' and she'll go, 'OH! MY GOD! I am, like, SO bored. Hordly anyone's come in today. I'm just flicking through *Heat*,' and that's, like, alorm bells straight away for me. I'll just be there, 'Go on,' and she'll be like, 'Claire Danes is wearing, *oh my God*, a *gorgeous* pair of Uggs, as in the high ones?' and then out of the blue it'll be, '*Oh my God*, my feet are, like, SO sore today,' and of course not unreasonably I'll go, 'You're only six weeks gone, Sorcha. It's the size of a focking walnut. How heavy could it be?' and she'll be like, 'Don't shout at me, Ross,' which, of course, I don't actually remember doing, roysh, probably because I didn't actually do it in the first place, and then she'll give it, 'The baby gets upset when *I'm* upset,' and of course I just end up going, 'Your personal shopper will be with you in half-an-hour.'

This morning, roysh, I ended up having to send, like, three hundred bills worth of Roberto Cavalli underwear up to her, all because Erika was a bitch to her. I was like, 'But she's like that to everyone. That's what bitches do,' but there's, like, no reasoning with her.

Turns out, roysh, Erika's having a conniption because Sorcha asked Claire – as in Claire from, like, Brayruit, of all places – to be her, like, birthing portner. So Erika calls into the shop this morning, roysh, supposedly to say hello, but actually to give Sorcha this orticle she very kindly printed off the internet, roysh, all about problems that can occur in childbirth, with vaginal and cervical lacerations for some reason sticking in my mind.

Sorcha was in bits, roysh, as you would be, so I rang her half-an-hour after I sent the Cavalli stuff up to her and I was like, 'How are you feeling?' and she goes, 'Fine,' and I was there, 'Why don't you just stay away from Erika in future, Babes? She's a focking wagon,' and – get this, roysh – Sorcha goes, 'HELLO? That *wagon* just so *happens* to be my best friend, Ross!' and she just, like, slams the phone down on me.

According to the January edition of *Pregnancy and Birth* magazine, birds who're up the stick are liable to be moody, irritable and irrational. No focking change there, then.

I'm actually, like, contemplating all this in the office above the club when all of a sudden Oisinn arrives in, full of the joys of Finglas on family allowance day. He goes, 'Some focking Christmas, wasn't it?' and I'm like, 'Are you talking sponds-wise?' and he's there, 'Yeah, you heard how much we took in between Christmas Eve and New Year? Some amount of celebrities in last night as well – Síle Seoige,

Keith Barry, Samantha Mumba's little brother *and* the Corter Twins . . .' I'm thinking, Fair focks to Oisinn. The goy was already pretty much minted before Hugo Boss gave him, like, a million sheets for developing his *Eau d'Affluence* and yet, despite all his success, jetting here, there and everywhere, he's still, like, totally motivated. His new catchphrase is, 'These southside eyes are hungry for the prize.'

There's a knock on the door. It's, like, Fionn and Christian. Fionn's like, 'Are we going to stort?' and I'm there, *'I'm* cool. How many's down there?' and he goes, 'We've got twelve this afternoon. The first is . . .' and he looks at his clipboard − he is such a focking geek − and goes, '. . . Lyudmila Gohr,' and I'm like, 'From?' and he goes, 'Ukraine,' and I'm there, 'Ukraine, I see,' wondering has he just made that up. He goes, 'Come on, she's waiting downstairs,' and I'm there, 'Jugs?' and just as Christian's giving me the thumbs-up, Fionn stops dead in his tracks and goes, 'Please remember, Ross, this is a *job* interview. There are some pretty stringent laws in this area relating to sexual and racial equality,' but Oisinn's there, 'She's got to have tits, though.'

I nod my head in basic agreement. Fionn goes, 'We're looking for *bor staff*,' and I'm there, 'Yeah . . . with decent Walter Mitties. We can't have them all looking like Anna. I mean, where did you find her, Fionn? We're talking Minger the focking Merciless here.'

We needn't have worried. Lyudmila turns out to be a total fun bundle, we're talking Ali Bastian, roysh, except with a bigger rack, not to mention *quality* pins. Me and the goys are, like, sitting in front of her with our mouths open, like the focking frog chorus. She's looking at us all, like, individually, as if to say, you know, is one of you going to ask me a question here?

I go, 'Lyudmila, let me just say at the stort that you've pretty much got the job already. Just a few questions, though . . . Em, how many – I don't know – brothers and sisters do you have?' throwing her a couple of easy ones to, like, break the ice. She goes, 'I hef three seestair – Inna, Tatyana, Nijolé. Also, I hef three bruthair – Dmitri, Viktor, Tonu,' and of course I'm writing this down, roysh, on Fionn's notepad, like it's important and I'm going, 'Three sisters, three brothers. That's *excellent* . . .' and Oisinn goes, 'I don't know about you guys, but I've heard enough. She's perfect for us.'

I just, like, hold my hand up as if to go, Shut the fock up, Oisinn, let the boy wonder here handle it. I'm there, 'Now, what are your *hobbies*?' and Lyudmila goes, '*Oh!*' and makes this face, roysh, like it was the last question in the world she expected to be asked. She's like, 'Em, well, I like to play the badmington. I like also for, uh, to read and to . . . smoke, though perhaps is not so much a hobby. Also I like very much to walk.'

I'm there, 'Okay. That's all great stuff. And just lastly, if at any point in the future our business decided to, shall we say, change direction, would you have any objection to taking off your clothes and performing pole dances for customers?'

Her expression suddenly changes to that of a camper who's not especially contented. Fionn has his head in his hands. She stands up and goes, 'If you are looking for streepers, why don't you say in the ad that you are looking for streepers,' and I'm there, 'I'm just covering bases, Babes. I'm just saying, *if* the nature of our business changed, you would have to be prepared for the nature of your job to change,' and Oisinn goes, 'We're looking for a flexible workforce,' and it takes me about ten seconds to get it. I'm like, '*Flexible*. I like it,' by which time Lyudmila has picked up her bag and is already on the way out the door.

Fionn takes off his glasses, rubs his eyes and goes, 'Christian, will you call in Grete Balzir . . .'

Whiskas is carefully prepared from only the highest quality, most wholesome ingredients . . . to give your cat the taste she naturally deserves. What's going on here? *It also contains the right balance of vitamins and nutrients she needs to keep her healthy on the inside, sleek and beautiful on the outside – and happy all over. What more could she want?*

I know what I want and it's . . .

Seriously weird but . . .

It's just . . .

The way the fork sinks into the meat and the jelly and the way it then collapses into the bowl. And I can almost taste that meaty goodness . . .

I'll tell you how bad it is, roysh. Naomi Campbell's on 'Tyra' and the two of them are, like, patching things up, roysh, after all the shit that went on in the past – they're, like, calling each other 'sister' and talking about closure – and I'm not even *thinking* about what order I'd do them in, like any normal goy. What I'm thinking about is, like, succulent chunks of rabbit and turkey in gravy.

I end up pegging it into the kitchen, roysh, where Sorcha usually keeps a couple of those Whiskas pouches for whenever a cat wanders into the gorden. I check the cupboard under the sink, but she must have used the last one this morning.

Now, anyone in their roysh mind would have, like, copped on to themselves at that point. So I'm clearly not in my roysh mind because I leg it out to the front door and reef it open, just in time, as it happens, roysh, because next-door's cat – this scabby-looking orange thing – is just about to stick his boat race into the bowl Sorcha left on the doorstep before she went to work.

I'm like, '*Get the fock away!*' and suddenly he's pegged it, roysh, like a northsider from a job centre. I pick up the bowl and stort horsing the meat into me, roysh, there on the doorstep, and it tastes every bit as good as it looks on the ad. It's guinea fowl with gravy. And I'm shouting at the cat, even though he's long gone, '*My* lunch! *Mine!*'

And of course I'm too busy feeding my face to notice the postman standing in front of me, looking at me like I'm totally chicken oriental. I'm there, 'What's your focking problem?' and he just hands me the mail – a phone bill and a letter from Amnesty International, which I presume is for Sorcha – then backs out of the driveway, roysh, like he's scared to turn his back on me.

I go back into the gaff. 'Dr Phil' is all about men who experience phantom pregnancies, which sounds pretty boring to me, so I stort flicking through the channels and I accidentally end up on Sky News, roysh, and I notice that loads of people have been killed by a bomb in, I don't know, Iran or Iraq – I can never remember which one – and all of a sudden I notice that I'm crying, as in *actually* crying. Which is weird, roysh, because usually I don't give a fock about what's happening in all those places. I mean, *I'll* never go there, so it's, like, *what*ever. But suddenly I'm wondering what kind of a world me and Sorcha are about to introduce a child to and I'm bawling like a bird who's just been drop-kicked.

I need to lie down.

*

So I'm in Cocoon, roysh, and I am giving serious mince pies to this bird, Kate, who I used to know from Wes, we're talking, like, ten years ago? She went to, like, Muckross, roysh, and she was one of the Johnny Cashes, as we used to call them, or the Orange Blossom Specials – as in, wore shitloads of fake tan. She's grown up to be a serious honey, in fairness to her, a bit like Myleene Klas in the looks deportment, but with a bod on her like Ali Landry. She's with some other bird who's obviously her UBF.

Christian's been wearing the ear off me all night, roysh, about this script he's writing for a new *Stor Wars* trilogy, which he says he might send to George Lucas to see what he thinks. And after living through five hours of it – we're talking battle after battle here – I have to get away from the dude, best friend or not. I turn around to him and I'm like, 'Cover me – I'm going in,' and I'm straight over to the two birds, roysh, and I'm giving it loads, but it's really weird because, for some reason, none of my one-liners are working.

I'm there going, 'I used to say to the goys back in our Wesley days, there's no way that girl could get any better looking than she already is. I'm happy to admit it – I was wrong,' but she pretty much ignores me.

So I stort giving it, 'I would be neglecting my responsibilities as the best-looking goy in this bor tonight if I didn't ask you for your phone number,' and again, nothing. She goes back talking to her mate.

I hate using the line, roysh, but I end up going, '*Sorry*, do you know who I am?' and the mate goes, 'Yes, you're Ross O'Carroll-Kelly. Now will you leave us alone?' and I'm like, 'Oh, the Ugly Best Friend speaks,' which she obviously doesn't appreciate. She goes, 'We're *actually* trying to have a conversation here,' and I just shake my head and go,

'Unbelievable. I remember the days when I'd have had the two of you eating out of my hand.'

Kate goes, 'Ross, you're *married*,' and I'm like, '*So?* You're not prejudiced, are you?' just to let her see what a cracking sense of humour I have. She goes, 'And your wife is, like, *pregnant*?' and I go, 'Bad news travels fast, doesn't it?' and the ugly mate goes, 'Why aren't you at home with her?' and then they both, like, turn their backs on me.

Fionn might be one of the most ridiculous-looking people I've ever seen, roysh, what with his, like, glasses and shit, but there's no doubt the dude is an actual brainiac, and we're actually talking a total one here as well. I mean sometimes, roysh, he even makes me want to get my act together on the whole books and learning and education end of things.

There we are the other night in Kiely's, roysh, wrapping ourselves around a couple of pints of Ken, when he turns around to me out of the blue and goes, 'Do you know where the term *skanger* comes from, Ross?'

I say out of the blue, roysh, but we were actually talking about UB40 coming to Dublin in, like, two weeks time and I just happened to mention that you could probably cut the city's crime rate by, like, ninety per cent if you dropped a focking bomb on the Point Depot that night. It's, like, music for joyriders. According to Fionn, roysh, there's some statistic or other that, like, sixty per cent of stolen cors that are found before they're torched have a UB40 album in the CD player that the owner swears he's never seen before.

I go, 'What *is* this obsession that Ken Ackers have with reggae? I mean – correct me if I'm wrong – but it's basically shit,' which is when he asks me if I know, like, the origin of the word *skanger*. He taps this, to be honest, book that he's put up on the bor, on the *actual* bor in front of him, pretty much advertising the fact that he's a steamer, and he goes, 'According to the *Dictionary of Hiberno English*, a *skanker* is an old Jamaican term for an untrustworthy or dissolute person.'

I'm there, 'Jamaica?' and he's like, 'Jamaica. Which is where what kind of music comes from,' and I knock back a pretty big whack out of my pint, roysh, knowing that he's only getting going now. He's there, 'I have to say, I've always been intrigued myself by this enduring fascination that Dublin's poorer classes have with *Bob Morley*. I used to think it was just the theme of self-pity finding a universal appeal among peasant folk the world over. But that's too facile,' and of course I'm already struggling to keep up here.

He's like, 'You listen to Rastafarian music, Ross, be it the ritual Nyabingi or the more commercial reggae, and in the lower beats you can hear deep structural dissonances that reflect the class conflicts within society. And yet the lyrics demonstrate a clear search for consonance, for hope – *three little birds pitch by my doorstep, singing sweet songs of melodies pure and true*. And *let's get together to fight this Holy Armageddon, so when the Man comes there will be no, no doom . . .*'

I'm like, 'Whoa! You're actually *listening* to that shit now?' and I'm, like, backing away from him, roysh, and looking him up and down, not sure whether I can trust him anymore. I'm there, 'Fionn, that's like, I don't know, focking around with the unknown . . .' and he laughs, roysh, and ends up pretty much gobbing a mouthful of beer all over my new bottle-green Abercrombie.

He goes, 'It's *reggae*, Ross, not voodoo. If you must know, I've decided to do a Masters on it,' and I'm like, 'Fock's sake, you've more degrees than a thermometer. Are you never going to leave college?' which he ignores. I know he was, like, talking about going back to college – he got an offer from Trinity to study, like, anthropology or some shit – but I was thinking, roysh, what with the nightclub going well and everything, why the fock would he want to keep learning shit?

He's going, 'So my Masters is going to be a comparative analysis of the Rastafarians of Kingston and the Skangers of Dublin, comparing and contrasting the cultures, values, rituals, languages and belief systems of these two movements, born out of oppression in the slums of–' and I'm like, 'Are you *actually* focking serious, Dude, or are you, like, yanking my cord?'

He's there, 'I'm serious, Ross. Look, I'm pretty sure this obsession Dublin skobies have with reggae music comes from this dissonance–consonance conflict. Our peasant folk and theirs share this philosophy that, even though life is shit, things will get better. *We'll share the same room, for Jah provide the bread.* It's a phenomenon no-one's yet tapped into.'

I'm like, 'The only thing that they have in common, as far as I can see, is that they spend most of their lives doped off their tits,' and Fionn pushes his glasses up on his nose and goes, 'Yes, the use of marijuana *is* one of the shared rituals I'll be looking into. Take that dumb look off your face, Ross, and I might succeed in educating even *you*.'

He goes, 'Okay, Rastafarianism is a messianic cult indigenous to the Caribbean island of Jamaica. Its members believe that Haile Selassie, the former Emperor of Ethiopia, is the Messiah who appeared in the flesh for the redemption of all Blacks exiled in the lands of the White slavemaster. The movement takes its name from his original title – Ras, which means Duke, and Tafari, which was, like, Haile Selassie's original surname.'

I'm about to go, *'Boring!'* but I stick with it, roysh, because I know it's high time I storted improving my mind and shit?

He goes, 'Anyway, his coronation as Emperor of Ethiopia in 1930 fulfilled, for members of the cult, a prophesy in the Book of Revelations about a black Redeemer. So he became His Imperial Majesty, Emperor Haile Selassie I, King of Kings and Lord of Lords, Conquering Lion of the Tribe of Judah, Elect of God.'

I'm like, 'So who is the equivalent for Dublin skobies?' and he goes, 'Joe Higgins TD, obviously.'

This sounds like total BS to me, but he just carries on. He's like, 'Rastafarians regard Jamaica not as their home but as the place of their enslavement. They were stolen from Africa and put to work on the plantations, just as Dublin's skobies were displaced from *their* homes in the inner city and rehoused in sink estates in the suburbs. They feel similarly dispossessed.'

He goes, 'Rastafarians regard Ethiopia as the Promised Land and consider themselves the first of all men. And it's true that before their enslavement they were the forerunners to one of the world's great civilisations – that of Egypt. Believe it or not, Ross, the Ethiopians and the Egyptians were one and the same people. When we refer to Egyptians these days, we think of a coffee-coloured race of people. That's because of the effect the Persian, Greek, Roman and finally Arab invaders had in diluting the bloodline. I can assure you, Ross, the ancient Egyptians were as black as any sub-Saharan native African.'

I'm like, 'You've pretty much lost me, but go on anyway,' and he's there, 'Well, what I'm trying to explain to you, Ross, is that Rastafarians regard themselves as the Chosen People, the original Israelites. And their entire *raison d'être*, as far as they're concerned, is to be delivered back to

Ethiopia, their Zion, the land where milk and honey flow . . .'

And I'm there, 'Okay, I get it. So what's the equivalent for skobies then?' and he goes, 'Fuerteventura, of course.'

I'm like, 'Oh my God, this is SO the drink talking,' and he calls the borman, gets his round in and goes, 'Maybe it is. But what's the bet I can't argue my way to a Masters?'

And he will.

I'm trying to watch the Leinster match, roysh, but it's pretty much impossible with all the chatter between Sorcha and Claire. In the end, I turn around and go, 'Is there no way you could do whatever it is you're doing in the kitchen?' and they suddenly look up from all the books and notebooks and diaries they've got spread across the dining table. Sorcha goes, 'We *happen* to be making a birth plan, Ross. You remember this baby I'm carrying for you?' which is designed to make me feel like shit.

Claire goes, 'And as Sorcha's birthing partner, it's one of *my* responsibilities to discuss the various options for the birth with her,' and I'm about to say that if I wanted to listen to that ridiculous accent all night I'd have hit Bray Amusements and – as they say down there – *played the slots*, but I keep the old Von Trapp shut.

Claire's, like, scribbling in this diary, going, 'Okay, so it's not going to be a home delivery. You're settled on Mount Carmel. What about pain relief? Do you want Pethidine, Entonox . . . Or what about TENS?' and Sorcha's there, 'Oh my God, we might leave that blank for now, Claire. I *am* veering towards a drug-free birth. I just want to read up on all the various complementary therapies first,' and Claire's like, 'That's fine. Now, what about position?'

Drico's having a focking stormer, as usual, and I'm thinking, but for a bit of bad luck with, like, injuries and shit, that could be me out there. I think *he* knows that as well.

Sorcha's there, 'Well, I know semi-sitting is the most common position, but my instinct would be more towards doing it on all fours,' and Claire goes, 'I think that's a good idea. At least then you can get onto your knees more easily. It says in one of these book that it can help with the dilation of the cervix – just remember to rock your pelvis from side to side.'

That Contepomi is some player.

Like a focking schoolteacher, roysh, Claire's going, 'For the next day, I want you to write down your various thoughts and feelings on the possibility of being induced, of having your waters broken, of having an episiotomy, of having an assisted delivery and of having a Caesarean . . .'

Of course, I can't take anymore. I'm like, 'I'm going to hit The Playwright to watch the rest of this.'

I call into the old pair's gaff, though I really don't know why I focking bothered. Actually, I do. My cor insurance is due, roysh, and there's no way I'm paying three Ks out of my own pocket for it. But I still called to see them, roysh, yet all the old man wants to know about is, like, how Sorcha is and how's that grandchild of theirs coming along. Doesn't give a fock about me basically.

He's in the study, roysh, reading *The Irish Times* and he's, like, making notes in the morgin with his Mont Blanc pen, which only comes out when he's about to get up on his focking high horse about something.

He goes, 'I expect you're here to talk to me about the upcoming Six Nations, or discuss the relative merits and demerits of young Jonny Wilkinson and a certain Mr Ronan O'Gara Esquire for the out-half berth on the Lions team,' and I'm like, 'No,' and I actually have to stop myself from going, I'm actually trying to get focking money out of you, if you must know, you scabby focker.

He goes, 'Well, I'm afraid I've no time to engage with you in one of our world-famous debates this morning, Kicker. Got a rather pressing matter here, with a capital P,' and I'm there, 'And this affects me *how* exactly?' and he goes, 'It seems the Equality Commission – quote-unquote – is stepping up the pressure on Portmarnock. It seems there's going to be some kind of court case,' and of course I'm not even listening to him, I'm just having a nose around, looking for the focker's chequebook.

He's like, '*Women members!* The very idea of it, Ross! I mean, Hennessy's just as upset as I am. Phoned me this morning in an awful state. Said, "If this goes through, Charles, I'm hanging up my Callaway Big Bertha Fusion FT-3 Driver for good." I told him. I said, "Calm down, old chap. You're not thinking straight. Hennessy Coghlan-O'Hara *without* golf? It's absurd. And, more to the point, golf without Hennessy Coghlan-O'Hara?" Well, it'd be an altogether different game, Ross, and it's not just me who thinks it.'

I'm there, 'I can't believe you're actually hiding your focking chequebook these days,' and he goes, 'Still, Hennessy and all his talk of nuclear options did succeed in concentrating my mind on the issue at hand, ie, our right – as members of a private club – to allow whoever the hell we want to join, thank you very much indeed. Excuse me, Ross, I've a phone call to make,' and he picks up the phone, roysh, and actually dials a number and it's like, HELLO? Never mind me!

While it's ringing, roysh, he puts his hand over the mouth-piece and goes, 'Watch this. This'll grab a headline or two,' and then someone answers, roysh, and he goes, 'Hello? Charles O'Carroll-Kelly here, member of Dún Laoghaire-Rathdown County Council, elected on the first count with a surplus of 1,275 votes. Is that the Women's Mini-Marathon office?' and then he's like, 'Yes, I'd like an application form, if it's not too much trouble,' and of course he gives me this big, like, wink, the stupid tosser that he is.

I take down the picture on the wall opposite the desk and try the safe, but the focker's actually changed the combi-nation. He's going, 'No, no – it's for *me*. I'm planning to run in your little race this year. I'm keeping fit. Eating plenty of quote-unquote fruit and vegetables and so forth. And now I'm planning to see if I can't win that little race of yours,' and then after a few seconds silence he goes, 'Ah, repeat that for me, please . . . It's for *women only*. I see. So you're saying that I'm *excluded* from your little event by virtue of the fact that I am a – inverted commas – man . . . Yes, I understand that it's your policy. I just want to let you know that I intend challenging it under the terms of our equality legislation . . .' and before he gets to finish his sentence, roysh, the bird on the other end has got sense and hung up on him.

He slams down the phone and goes, 'They haven't heard the last of this. Oh no, I plan to take my campaign to be permitted to run in the Women's Mini-Marathon to the highest court in the land. *And* to the UN, if needs be,' and I'm there, 'I can't get into the focking safe,' and he goes, 'Oh yes. Sorry, Kicker, I had to change the combination,' and I'm there, 'But it's always been 1, 9, 8, 2,' and he's like, 'Indeed it has, the year of the great Triple Crown win. And I can see what you're doing, Ross, don't think I can't. You're ever so subtly trying to steer me into one of our celebrated debates about how the side of Messrs Campbell, Slattery, Fitzgerald and Duggan would have measured up against your O'Driscoll, D'Arcy, O'Kelly and O'Connell. No time, I'm afraid. I've decided to go to law on this whole inverted-commas *equality* issue. And you know what that means . . .'

I key in 2, 0, 0, 4 and the safe opens, roysh, but it's focking empty. I'm like, 'Where's the focking moolah?' and he goes, 'The what? Oh! Well, your mother and I thought it'd be a good idea if we didn't keep large sums of money around the house anymore. There was €5,000 went missing from that very safe a month ago.'

I'm like, 'It didn't go missing. *I* took it,' and he stops mid-dial, suddenly looking all worried, puts the phone down and goes, '*You* took it? But why?' and I'm there, 'Does it matter?' and he's like, 'Oh, I, em, suppose not,' and I'm there, 'You scabby prick,' and he goes, 'No, it's just that . . . well, your mother got it into her head that Maria took it. You remember that young cleaning girl we got rid of that time. Italian. Well, your mother . . . well, both of us, I suppose, presumed *she'd* taken it, having somehow found out about my secret affection for the great Ireland team of '82 . . .'

I'm there, 'And the old trout sacked her?' unable to keep a straight face, and he goes, 'Yes, I'm afraid so,' and I'm like, 'Well, I actually don't *give* a fock? I need sponds. Four Ks should just about cover it,' thinking it's about time I got a new phone as well. I've had this one, like, three months now.

He goes, 'I have to say – and it's to my eternal shame – that I said a few things to Maria, which, in light of this new information, seem a trifle harsh. About the Italians and their lack of moral fibre. Changing sides in wars and so forth . . .

still, hey ho, I'm sure she'd have stolen something eventually,' and he picks up the phone again and dials a number.

Then, at the top of his voice, he's like, 'Hennessy, it's Charles. I'm ringing with the most wonderful news. You're going to be working on that handicap of yours for a few years yet. Get your wig and gown ready, old boy. We're going to court . . .'

As he's saying this, roysh, he whips open his drawer, pulls out his chequebook and writes me a chicken's neck for four Ks, no questions asked, after leaving me standing there, listening to his crap for, like, twenty minutes. So I grab it off him, give him the finger and, like, get the fock out of there.

Sorcha rings me from the shop and tells me that *oh my God!* she cannot *actually* believe I persuaded her to have that glass of wine the other night and *oh my God!* did I not know that drinking alcohol during pregnancy can cause, like, behavioural problems in children, we're talking ADHD here, as in Attention Deficit and Hyperactivity Disorder and I tell her, roysh, that one glass of Malbec isn't going to turn the kid into a brat and anyway, ADHD only affects *working*-class kids, but she's not, like, listening. She's like, 'I'm beginning to think I'd be better off bringing up this baby on my own.'

So there we are, roysh, we're talking me, Christian, Oisinn and Fionn and we're, like, sitting around in Lillie's, having a few Britneys in the middle of the afternoon and, believe it or not, Fionn's *still* banging on about Ken Ackers and why they're so into their focking reggae music.

I've heard it all before, but the goys are, like, lapping it up. He's going, 'I think I can make quite a compelling argument that the package holiday Meccas of Fuerteventura, Ibiza, Ayia Napa and Playa del Ingles have the same eschatological significance in the life of the average Dublin skobie as Ethiopia does to the average Rastafarian. It's the vision of a homeland, a Zion, a refuge for an oppressed people,' and Oisinn turns around to me and goes, 'I focking love this goy when he's in this kind of form,' but of course that only encourages him.

He's there, 'I mean, just compare the two communities. Two vibrant peasant classes born out of poverty and oppression, whose numbers are multiplying at a rapid rate. One emerged from the tin-house shanties of Kingston, the other from the Council-built Lego shanties of north and west Dublin. Tribal warfare, gun crimes, institutionalised unemployment and police brutality are features of both communities . . .'

It's Christian who says the first sensible thing of the day, which tells you how horrendufied the rest of us must be. He's like, 'What about hash? If you get the Nightlink, you always hear skobies talking about hash. And the Jamaicans are always banging on about *ganja*, aren't they? What's the story there?' and of course Fionn has an answer ready. He always does. That's how he's got qualifications coming out of his focking ears.

He's like, 'During the early, wilderness existence of the Rastafarians, we're talking the thirties and forties, they grew marijuana as a cash crop, as a means of survival. They were determined to be self-sufficient, to live autonomously from so-called respectable society.'

He's like, 'They set up a commune and they called it Pinnacle, suggesting some utopian paradise that was, in fact, at odds with the slum-ridden reality. It's similar to those skobies who call their wilderness commune Tallafornia,' and everyone nods like they understand.

He knocks back a mouthful of Ken, then goes, 'It's interesting that in both instances, the Establishment – through the instrument of the police – has used archaic drug laws to oppress the peasant classes. In Jamaica, they used force to break up Pinnacle on the pretext that the people living there were cultivating a dangerous drug. By the same token, in Dublin some Anto gets three months in prison for possessing a herb that's less harmful to him and to society than this stuff that we are at this present moment in time pouring down our–' and quick as a flash I go, 'Gregory Pecks,' because he's not really up with all the, like, cool sayings.

He's there, '*Exactly*. And in both cultures it performs a similar quasi-religious function – it aids meditation, heightens communal feelings, dispels gloom and anxiety and brings peace of mind to the dispossessed.'

Christian's sorted through the post. He says we've got another batch of CVs: Jadwiga Manoliu. Chen Ping. Nina Kuznetsova. Azuma Ojulah. Zhou Yongyan. Faina Danilova. It's impossible to tell whether they're, like, birds or not. The worst-case scenario, of course, would be calling them all in for interviews and finding ourselves interviewing a roomful of blokes, but *The Irish Times* wouldn't let us put 'Only women need apply' in the ad. Oisinn takes the CVs, roysh, and heads upstairs to Google the names, to see can we get some idea of what we're actually dealing with here.

'Might have known I'd find you hanging out here.' That's the next thing we hear and we turn around, roysh, and who is it only Erika. She's like, 'Have you no lives?' and none of us says anything, roysh, because we're pretty much all knocked sideways by how focking incredible she looks. We're talking perma-horn material here.

She goes, 'Ross, I just wanted to give this to you to give to Sorcha,' and she hands me this stack of, like, thirty or forty pages, roysh, which it seems she's, like, downloaded off the internet.

I'm there, 'So what is this stuff?' and she goes, 'Just something I found on a medical website. All about a woman who was breastfeeding her baby and got a blocked duct. One of her breasts swelled up to three times its normal size. Anyway, there's a picture of it there, look,' and she pulls out one of the pages and she's actually spot on, roysh, this bird has one big knocker and one absolutely focking humungous one, which you have to agree is pretty focking disgusting.

Erika goes, 'Make sure you give it to Sorcha. It's important she knows about these things,' and I go 'Cool. Thanks for, er, pointing it out,' and at the same time I hate myself for not being able to go, Why don't you stop being such a bitch to my bird, wife, even? But that's me, roysh, a sucker for a great boat race – not to mention a great orse.

She turns around to Christian and she goes, 'How are the plans for the wedding coming along, Christian?' and he's like, 'Er, cool,' and he says it really, like, suspiciously, roysh, like he's bracing himself for what's to come. But she doesn't say anything mean. She goes, 'Tell Lauren I found a place in Milan that does that material she wanted for her dress. I'll get it for her. My treat,' and he's like, 'Oh, em, thanks, Erika . . .' and she goes, 'Not a problem,' and she turns around, roysh, and struts out of the place like a catwalk model, which, let's be honest, she could be if she was prepared to stoop low enough as to actually work.

I'm about to state the blindingly obvious – that the girl is basically the biggest focking ride in history – when all of a sudden, roysh, we hear what would have to be described as a kerfuffle coming from upstairs, from the office by the sound of it. So the three of us – we're talking me, Christian and Fionn – leave our drinks there and peg it upstairs to find – unbelievable this – the office turned basically upside-down and Oisinn standing over this, like, total focking skobie he's obviously just decked.

I'm there, 'What the fock . . .' which is when Oisinn turns around and notices us standing there for the first time. He goes, 'Hey, goys, sorry about the noise. Had to subdue our friend here. Came upstairs to find him rifling through the drawers, no doubt looking for money to spend on heroin,' and I'm like, 'I mean, how the *fock* do these people get across the Liffey without being spotted? Surely they should have some kind of border checkpoint on O'Connell Bridge?'

He's your typical creamer: Ben Sherman shirt, untucked, with tracksuit bottoms, Barry McGuigan moustache, mousey-coloured hair, side-ported, ink spot on his left cheek, a serious-looking scor running from his right ear to the corner of his mouth, more sovs than he has fingers and about as much meat on him as a Hare Krishna's breakfast.

Christian goes, 'What are we going to do with him?' and Oisinn's there, 'Ross, hand me that length of rope over there. I've a feeling he'll be sleeping for a while but, just in case, this'll keep him quiet until the Feds arrive,' and when I hand him the rope he storts, like, tying the dude to a chair.

That's when Fionn, totally out of the blue, turns around and goes, 'Let's keep him.'

Of course the three of us turn around and look at him as if to say, What are you focking talking about? I'm there, 'What are you focking talking about?' and he goes, 'I'm just saying, nobody knows he's here. Why don't we keep him?' and I'm like, '*Because* Fionn, we don't know the first thing about keeping a skobie. I mean, what do they eat, for a stort?' and Oisinn's like, 'Anything – once it's been deep-fried first,' and I look at Oisinn, roysh, and I can't believe that he's actually agreeing with Fionn. He's like, 'A skobie, yeah. I mean, it's an unusual one, I'll give you that, but I suppose it'd be like keeping a snake. Or a tarantula.'

I'm there, 'Are you two Baghdad or something? I'm ringing the Feds,' but just as I go to pick up the phone, roysh, Fionn slams his hand down on it and goes, 'Ross, hear me out,' and I'm like, 'What you're talking about doing is basically kidnapping. Christian, back me up on this,' but Christian goes, 'Let's just hear what Fionn has to say first, Ross,' and I'm looking at him, thinking, Yeah, great, some best mate you turned out to be.

Fionn goes, 'Ross, this is just what I need for my research project – a real live Dublin skanger to use as a guinea pig,' and I'm sort of, like, backing away from him, going, 'You *focking* sicko. I mean, I've no conscience at all and even I know that that's basically wrong.'

He's like, 'I'm not talking about chopping him up and experimenting with his organs. I'm talking about, you know, hooking him up to various pieces of equipment to measure his emotional and intellectual responses to various stimuli,' and I'm like, 'I want nothing to do with this. Christian, come on, I think we've both heard enough,' but Christian's like, 'I don't know, Ross, this research Fionn's doing, it can only lead to a better understanding of what makes skangers tick.'

I'm there, 'I don't give fock what makes skangers tick. I'm certainly not spending ten years of my life in prison to find out,' but it's almost like I'm not there.

Oisinn goes, 'Let's find out his name,' and Christian's there, 'How do we do that?' and Oisinn's like, 'Check his tattoos, of course,' and before you can say 'social security' the goys are, like, whipping off the dude's tracksuit, looking at the various bits of ortwork he's got inked up and down his body.

Oisinn's going, 'Mum . . . IRA . . . Aslan . . . Ah, here we are . . . He's called Henrik Larsson,' and Fionn's there, 'I suspect that might be a red herring, Oisinn. Henrik Larsson, I'm inclined to believe, is a football man who once played for Glasgow Celtic, a team that shares a place alongside Bob Morley and The Wailers in the imagination of almost every Dublin skanger. He had dreadlocks as well, you know. That's got to be more than a coincidence.'

Christian's like, 'Here it is – *Marty!*' and Fionn's like, 'Marty?' and Oisinn goes, 'Marty!' and the three of them stand around for, like, ten minutes, saying the name over and over again, like they're seeing who can say it the best. Oisinn goes, 'I don't know about the rest of you, but I like it as a name,' and Fionn and Christian are going, 'Yeah, I like it as well . . .'

Fionn turns around to Oisinn, hands him two fifties and goes, 'Peg it down to the Lido on Pearse Street and get everything on the menu . . . in batter. Oh and some TK lemonade as well.'

2. A Ruffian's Game, Played by Skobies

'It's not like de northside,' Tina's old man is going, looking around him like he's just dropped in from another planet, which I suppose, when you think about it, he has. Apparently, roysh, he hasn't been this side of the Liffey since he saw the Wolfe Tones play the Noggin Inn back in the eighties – 'years befower dis peace-process-me-arse,' he goes.

Even Tina seems, like, embarrassed by him, which is saying something, especially given the way *she's* dressed. Arc ski-pants *never* out of fashion on that side of the city?

The teams run out. Ronan's arguing with a kid off the other team who's, like, pretty much twice the size of him and he's making this, like, gesture with his hand, roysh, which seems to be saying, you know, basically keep talking and you'll see what'll you get. He sees me and he goes, 'Rosser, ya steamer,' and I gave him a little wave, then turn around to Tina and out of the corner of my mouth I go, 'What way are you, like, raising him at all?' and she goes, '*Sarry?*' the way total skobes do.

I'm there, 'Calling me a steamer. I'm his father,' and she's like, 'Ah, dat's just his way of bein' friendlee, so it is,' and I'm looking at her, roysh, wondering how the fock I ever went there.

Her old man goes, 'Never been a fan a dis gayum. Always thought it was for fellas what were a bit . . .' and he gives this little, like, flick of his head and goes, '. . . *funny*, if you know whorramean. You don't see any of dat goin on in de Lee-ig of Oyerlind.'

I just, like, ignore him. Father Fehily sees me and gives me a wave. He's pretty much convinced that Ronan is going to be the greatest Irish rugby player who ever lived. He has him playing at prop-forward today, even though he's, like, one of the smallest players on the field, and I can't believe it, roysh, when his team wins a scrum ten metres inside their own half and he drives the opposition pack – what? – fifty or sixty yords back and when they collapse behind the line Fehily awards him a try. There's not a pick on the kid, roysh, and I've just watched him pretty much single-handedly push eight players half the length of a rugby field.

So I'm clapping, roysh, giving it loads and Ronan gives me the big thumbs-up and I have to say, roysh, I'm pretty proud to be his father, even if I'm ashamed to be whatever I am to Tina and her old man. I mean, he's doing his best to be encouraging, roysh, shouting shit like, 'house, Ronan', 'take it into ye' and 'man on', but they're, like, soccer expressions and I see one or two other parents shooting filthies in our direction and I think I overhear one of them mention the police.

The next thing, roysh, I see Sorcha walking around the field towards where we're standing. She said she'd try and get here. When she arrives she air-kisses Tina on both cheeks, which Tina's old man seems to find pretty strange judging by the way he's looking at her. Tina's going, 'Congrat-ulay-shiddens. Well, you're not showin' yet, in anyway,' and Sorcha's there, '*Oh my God*, not yet. Well, I'm only eight weeks gone.' I can see Sorcha copping sly looks at her, obviously thinking, A belly top in, like, January? HELLO?

Tina goes, 'How are you coping with it but? Any mood swings or anyting?' and Sorcha's there, 'No, funnily enough,' and I can't stop myself going, '*Yeah, roysh!*' and Sorcha looks at me like she's going to tear off my town halls with her bare hands later.

'Howzee ref?' Tina's old man is shouting. The other team have got a try. Ronan does *not* look a happy camper.

Tina goes, 'You'll be wantin' a pram, will ye?' and Sorcha's like, 'Er . . . sorry?' knowing pretty well what's coming next, roysh, but trying to buy herself a few extra seconds to come up with a decent excuse. Tina's there, 'I've Ronan's pram saved. I'll give it ye. I'll let ye have it for half what I paid for it,' and I can tell from Sorcha's face that she's picturing this big focking rusty contraption, like something out of *Angela's Ashes*, a focking bathtub with four wheels and a handle. And at the same time she's thinking about the Bébé Confort Windoo Infant Carrier with air re-circulation system that she's had her hort set on since she saw them in Mothercare, but I can see that she doesn't want to hurt Tina's feelings, roysh, so I decide to step in and save her orse.

I'm there, 'You probably should hang onto it yourself, Tina,' and she looks at me and goes, 'Wha'?' and I'm there, 'You know, in case you end up, you know . . . again,' and of course instead of backing me up, roysh, Sorcha hangs me out to dry. She's like, 'What *exactly* are you saying, Ross?' and I'm there, 'I'm *saying*, you know, think about where Tina's from. Lot of pregnancies out that direction – some of them for the money, some of them for other reasons. All I'm saying is she should always have a pram at the ready,' and Sorcha, the focking backstabber, actually makes me apologise to Tina.

There's, like, a roar from the crowd. The kid that Ronan was arguing with on the way out is lying on the ground, with his hands up to his boat race and Ronan standing over him. Fehily blows the whistle and Ronan's going, 'Think he has a nose bleed, Fadder,' and all the other parents are going,

'He struck him, referee! Send him off!' and Fehily's giving it, 'I didn't see the incident,' lying, of course, just like he used to lie for me.

He goes, 'Did any of you children see what happened?' and of course Ronan's eyeballing them all, daring them one by one to open their mouths. No one says anything, but then the kid that he decked gets to his feet and goes, 'He punched me in the face,' and, like, points at Ronan.

I see Ronan mouth what looks to me like, 'Fooken tout!' and then the kid's old pair arrive over to help him off the pitch. Fehily's going, 'Keeps muttering about someone *hitting* him. He must have concussion,' and a few minutes later I notice Ronan high-fiving Fehily on the sly.

Tina's old man goes, 'What de fook are dey pissin' an' moanin' abou'rover dayer? Is it a man's gayum or wha'?' and I have to actually physically stop him from going over to deck one of the other parents who called Ronan a thug.

'You're gonna have mad stretchmarks,' Tina goes, sounding pretty happy at the idea if you ask me, but Sorcha's there, 'No, I'm already using Bio-Oil,' and I catch Tina looking at her, roysh, as if to say, Who the fock does this one think she is? Sorcha, of course, is totally oblivious to it.

Ronan's, like, screaming at his team-mates, going, 'We can win this! Come on, where's yisser hearts? Where are they? Show me some fooken pride!' and the next thing, roysh, one of them takes a lineout ball he'd no real business taking, Ronan gets the ball in his hands, mills these two goys who were, like, stupid enough to try to tackle him and carries the ball forty yords to put it down under the posts.

Fehily blows the whistle. It's over. A few of the parents are shouting at him that there's at least five minutes left, but he ignores them, roysh, and makes his way over to the sideline where Tina is hugging Ronan and telling him he was great, though I'd hordly call her an expert on rugby. Fehily puts his hand on his head and goes, 'This little one is a force of nature,' and I go, 'Takes after his old man,' hoping it doesn't sound too big-headed.

Tina's old man goes, 'I don't know, Fadder, I tink I prefer sports where–' and I go, 'You're riding a horse around some focking council estate one day and the next you're living in a mock-Tudor mansion with a plasma screen telly on every focking wall?' and he's there, 'Exactly. Took the words ourra me mouth.'

Ronan goes to me, 'Fadder says I'm better than you were at my age, Rosser,' and I just, like, shrug my shoulders and go, 'Not sure everyone would agree with that . . .' and Fehily goes, 'Not just you, Ross. I saw them all. Tony O'Reilly. Jack Kyle. Mike Gibson. The boy O'Driscoll. None of them had what he has. He strikes fear into the other boys – genuine, heart-stopping terror,' and the two of them high-five each other again.

Ronan's face lights up when he sees Sorcha. He goes, 'Did you see me out there?' and she's like, 'Oh my *God*, Ronan, you were, like, SO good,' and I tell everyone to be careful not to give him a big head. He goes, 'How are you feeling in anyway?' and Sorcha's like, 'A little bit tired. But I'm, like, SO glad you're happy about this baby,' and Ronan rubs his hands together, roysh, and goes, 'Every empire needs its foot soldiers, doll.'

We're sitting in, roysh, watching the old Savalas, when all of a sudden Sorcha's phone beeps and I'm like, 'Who's texting you?' though not in a jealous way. She goes, 'It's Claire. She is SO good. She reminds me very two hours to empty my bladder,' and I'm wondering, am I the only one who finds that a bit weird?

So I'm poking around the gaff, roysh, out of boredom more than anything, and at the bottom of Sorcha's underwear drawer I find a big brown envelope, *the* big brown envelope, the one the old dear – the focking cow – gave to Sorcha over Christmas. I pull it out and it's already been opened, roysh, so I put my hand in and whip out what's inside. It turns out it's, like, a big shitload of pages and the top one is like, *Criminal Assets* by Fionnuala O'Carroll-Kelly, and I'm staring at it for a good ten minutes, roysh, before I cop what's going on here. Holy fock! She's *actually* gone and written a focking book, the old bag.

I flick through the first few pages. She's dedicated it to the old man. It's like, '*To Charles, for being an endless source of encouragement and inspiration*' and not a focking mention of me, of course. I turn over the page to the first page of the actual book and I stort reading. It's like:

On mornings like this Valerie wondered whether she had the energy to go on. Her ricotta and sweetcorn roulade, with a chickpea, bulgur and wild rice salad with cumin, lay untouched on the table, as she stared idly through the window at the gardener, tending to his peonies and daylilies, and thought about Richard.

Poor Richard, languishing in Mountjoy Jail, where she doubted they'd ever heard of chickpea, bulgur and wild rice salad, with or without cumin. He looked wretched the last time she visited, nothing at all like the man she married. He was gaunt, his weight spread thinly over his meagre, skeletal frame, his hands slight and bony like a woman's, his hair thinning out to reveal a vast savannah of baldness at the top of his head, his eyes sunken, defeated.

I'm just there, what *is* this shit?

A member of the floor staff was loitering near to her table, trying to determine whether the position of her knife and fork on her plate meant she was finished. 'You can clear this away,' Valerie said airily.

The young service girl, black and pretty – probably from Nigeria or one of those countries, she thought – lifted her plate onto a tray, then her glass.

Suddenly, with nothing in front of her, Valerie was overcome by a sense of isolation, that she had no more business here. 'Can I have a cappuccino?' she asked, inquisitively. 'And a slice of that delicious mixed berry tiramisu I saw earlier?'

'Yes,' the pretty black girl said acquiescently and she smiled in a way that left Valerie feeling quite guilty. Who knew what circumstances had forced her to leave her home in Africa to come to Ireland – the poor girl had probably seen her entire family brutally butchered in front of her eyes by men with machetes – and here she was, bemoaning her lot in life. Still, she couldn't help but think of Richard, that resigned, defeated look on his face as the judge, looking almost reptilian with his sharp, pinched features, pronounced sentence on him – fifteen years for corruption and tax evasion. The last five were suspended, she remembered, but still there was a sting in the tale.

The Criminal Assets Bureau had taken virtually everything. The CAB, established under the Criminal Assets Bureau Act of 1996, was empowered to freeze or confiscate, through court proceedings, assets and other wealth, including real estate, vehicles, cash and other property, which is suspected to derive from criminal activity, including corruption and tax evasion.

Twelve of their bank accounts had been seized, she remembered, as had their home in the well-to-do area of Foxrock, their apartments in Stillorgan, Ticknock and Charlesland, to say nothing of their cars – her Volvo XV90 and his BMW 5 Series, Lexus ES, Audi A6 Avant and, his pride and joy, the 1952 Bentley R-type Continental that he polished to such a shine that he could see his full, healthy face in it. They took the horses, including the three Arabian stallions, to say nothing of the two Jack B. Yeats originals and their 66ft, ocean-going oyster yacht.

She remembered the long hours of interviews, in particular the investigator with the foul-smelling breath, fingernails chewed to the quick, and the benign smile that played upon his lips as he asked her how they could afford five luxury holidays a year on a council planner's salary.

Martinique was a dim memory now, like so much else, she thought wistfully. They'd taken everything, including the man she loved. Richard's old friends from the council – from all political parties, it had to be said – had rallied around and thanks to their kindness she'd been able to buy a modest apartment overlooking Bulloch Harbour in Dalkey and a Peugeot Coupé.

That's all she had now, she thought philosophically. That and her occasional lunchtimes in Avoca Handweavers, where she liked to sit and ponder her old life.

Suddenly, she snapped out of her quiet reverie and noticed a man – early fifties perhaps, but handsome like Harrison Ford – staring in her direction.

I notice that in the morgin Sorcha has written a suggestion. It's like, 'Make him younger and more handsome. I'm thinking Andy Garcia.'

He caught her eye and favoured her with a thick smile. She looked away, embarrassed. She sipped her cappuccino and, with the back of her hand, wiped away the thick moustache of froth it left on her upper lip. She could still feel the weight of his stare.

It wasn't an altogether uncomfortable feeling but she felt her cheeks – those treacherous cheeks – warm to a giveaway blush. She was so hot she thought she might faint. She needed air and she needed it fast. Hurriedly, she got up from the table, made her way out of the restaurant, through the gift shop and out to the garden centre, where she took in great, greedy lungfuls of air. No man had made her feel so adolescently giddy since . . .

Pull yourself together, she told herself, firmly. You're a married woman, she thought, reproachfully.

She re-gathered her composure and, once she was sure she could again trust the mastery of her legs, she walked around, tentatively studying the neat ranks of plants on display – bergamots, African blue lilies, gladioli, bellflowers, rosehips, viola, magnolia and water lilies.

She picked up a packet of tulip bulbs and was studying the instructions closely when she heard a man's voice – deep and resonant – say, 'Beautiful.'

She felt her strength drain inexorably from her body. She was weak as a kitten. Without looking up, she knew it was *him*.

'What?' she heard herself say. It sounded thin, reedy.

'They're lilac perfections,' he said, clearly flirting. 'Double-flowered. Peony-shaped blooms. Tall stems . . .'

'I'm wondering have I left it too late to plant them,' she found the wherewithal to say.

'Those should be okay,' he said, authoritatively. 'They're late flowerers, you see. They're fine to put down, unless they've gone completely soft.'

'Oh,' she said.

'It's amazing how we always associate tulips with Holland. Did you know they originally hail from Persia, where the word means turban?'

'Because of the flower shape . . .'

'That's right.'

'You're interested in flowers?' she asked rhetorically, still determinedly refusing to meet his gaze.

'I'm interested in all *beautiful* things,' he said.

She felt her heart switch up a gear. Beautiful? It had been a long time since she thought of her forty-five-year-old body as such. She began to tremble. She hoped against hope that he didn't notice that packet of bulbs flapping in her hands. But suddenly he stilled them with his big but gentle bear paws.

She took a long, studied look at him for the first time. He was impossibly handsome, with deep, azure eyes, a proud, unapologetic nose, a stiletto smile, like that of some cartoon villain, with perfect piano key teeth, all set above a jawline hewn from granite. 'I expect you have a beautiful garden,' he said.

'A window box,' she said, correcting him. 'I live in an apartment.'

He gave a barely perceptible nod. 'You know,' he said, 'if you like plants so much, you're more than welcome to come to my garden and snip away. Whatever your heart desires. My nerines have to be seen to be believed, you know.'

'Oh,' she said, her head swimming now.

'My details,' he said, proffering a small card, bearing his name in black, embossed letters. Lovell Power, it stated. 'My number's there,' he said, 'Ms . . .'

He let the word hang in the air.

'Amburn-James,' she said. 'Valerie Amburn-James.'

He shook her hand. It seemed an odd note on which

to part, so clumsy compared to the cool slickness of his introduction.

'Just thinking,' he said, as he made to walk away. 'Might be a bit too big for your box.'

'Excuse me?' she said, her voice shrill, yet failing to convey how appalled she was.

'Your tulips,' he said. 'The stems, they grow up to eighteen inches.'

I'm thinking, this shit is so bad it's, like, *actually* funny?

So we're sitting in, roysh, as in me and Sorcha, eating a Chinky and watching 'The X Factor', of all things, when all of a sudden she turns around to me and goes, 'What do you think of the idea of having the baby by hypnosis?' and I swear to God, roysh, I have to bite my tongue to stop myself going, Are we talking you or me? because I have to say, roysh, the prospect of me, like, basically sleepwalking through the – whatever it is – nine months of the pregnancy is, it has to be said, pretty appealing at this stage, as in, like, wake me up when it's all over?

She goes, 'I was talking to Sophie. Her mum's, like, a midwife? *Oh my God*, she is SUCH a cool person,' and I'm thinking she's pretty focking easy on the eye as well. She goes, 'She said that more and more girls are opting for hypnotherapy instead of painkillers as a way of managing the pain of labour,' and I'm like, 'Whatever works for you, Babes.'

Suddenly I'm wondering is she going to eat that last piece of prawn toast. I don't even like prawn toast, roysh, but I want it and we're talking in a serious way here.

She's like, 'You know Belinda, as in, like, Sarah Jane's

sister, as in, like, Sarah Jane who nearly made the Ireland hockey team, was All Ireland Irish Debating Champion two years in a row?' and I'm there, 'Yeah,' and of course I'm there focking drooling like Homer Simpson, imagining the taste of the bread and grease on my tongue as I bite into the prawns and get that, like, aftertaste of, like, sesame seeds.

Sorcha's there, 'Are you actually *listening* to me?' and I'm like, '*Duh!?* Of course, I am. Hockey, debating, go on . . .' and she goes, 'Well, Belinda was – *oh my God*! – terrified by the thought of labour, as in, like, just went to pieces when she thought about the pain. So she asked her about an elective Caesarean and Sophie's mum – who was, like, her midwife – she suggested, like, hypnotherapy. Because if you have a Caesarean, it's like, HELLO? I mean you actually *want* to be conscious to enjoy the whole, like, birthing experience?'

Sorry to go all, like, philosophical on you, roysh, but how can something as small as a sesame seed be SO focking tasty?

Sorcha's going, 'It's not that I'm, like, scared of labour. It's just that, I'd like as natural a birth as possible, in other words no drugs? It's like, *oh my God*, these deep relaxation techniques that Sophie's mum was telling me about, they help you build up confidence in your body's ability to actually *give* birth. And when you approach the whole labour experience without anxiety, your body is better prepared to handle the pain of contractions and it's like, *Oh my God!*'

She *must* be full. She hasn't touched her Kung Po chicken for, like, ten minutes. I *have* to get that prawn toast into my mouth before it goes cold.

Sorcha's still giving it, 'A lot of it is just, like, visualisation exercises? But it can also, like, improve your inner connection with your baby,' and I'm wondering do they, like, deep-fry the bread when all of a sudden, roysh, Sorcha's going, '*Ross!*' but it's like I'm in a trance or something.

She's there, 'Oh *my* God, you're not even listening to me,' and I'm like, 'I am, Babes' and she just, like, follows my stare to the little silver foil tray on the coffee table and she ends up having a total knicker-fit. She's like, 'I'm *trying* to talk to you about *our* baby – AND YOU'RE THINKING ABOUT PRAWN TOAST!' and I'm there, 'I wasn't,' and she's like, 'Look at you! You can't even take your eyes off it!' and I swear to God, roysh, it takes every focking ounce of energy I have to actually turn my head and look at her, which is a mistake, roysh, because I end up getting a slap across the old Ricky Gervais and of course my second mistake is to go, 'Sorry, I didn't realise Munster were playing at home!'

She's like, '*Excuse* me?' and I'm there, 'Nothing,' but she's not going to let it go. She's like, 'Are you referring to *periods*, Ross?' and I sort of, like, look away, not answering her basically. She goes, 'HELLO? I'm *actually* pregnant, Ross. I don't *have* periods anymore?' and she must see the confusion on my face, roysh, even though I'm nodding my head, pretending to know what she's actually talking about.

She goes, '*Oh* my God, is winning a Leinster Schools Senior Cup medal an excuse to go through life totally ignorant of everything?' and of course the answer is yes, roysh, but I keep my mouth shut. She goes, 'When you're pregnant, Ross, the lining of your uterus is needed to nourish the embryo until it has made the placenta,' and that does the trick, roysh, because all of a sudden I don't want that last piece of prawn toast anymore.

*

47

The club was focking hopping last night. We'd, like, Amanda Brunker in, Laura Woods, Brendan Courtney and that focking Ray Shah out of 'Big Brother'. Someone said the blonde one out of Six was in as well, but I didn't see her.

So there I am, roysh, pretty happy with myself, taking a stroll up Grafton Street, watching bird after bird basically check me out and thinking of nipping into BTs for a new Ralph, when all of a sudden who do I see coming out of Morks and Spencers but the old pair. So naturally, roysh, I pretend not to see them, even though they definitely see me because the old man's going, 'Ross! *Ross!*' and I can hear him, like, pushing past people, going, 'Do excuse me, I've just seen my son,' but of course I put my head down and I'm up the street like Jason focking Robinson.

Just before I get to HMV, roysh, I take a sly look over my shoulder and I notice I haven't burned him yet, so I hang a roysh where the flower-sellers are – don't get me storted on them – and I peg it back through the Westbury Mall, hang a left out of there and cross the road into the Powerscourt Townhouse Centre and there I am, roysh, standing at the old Drinklink, thinking what a total focking tosser my old man is, when all of a sudden I get this, like, tap on the shoulder and I spin around and it's him.

He's leaning up against the wall with one hand and – good news – he looks like he's about to have a focking hort attack. He's going, 'Dear, oh dear, I'd quite forgotten how far my rugby-playing days were behind me. Didn't you hear me shouting at you, Kicker?' and I'm there, 'I did. I was trying to get away from you because I hate the focking sight of you,' and he goes, 'I said to your mother, I said, "The chap mustn't have heard me",' and I'm about to ask where *she* is, when all of a sudden I see her coming through the doors, Jackie focking Collins herself, wheezing like a focked hoover and face all red like an inbred kid.

I just give her the finger.

The old man goes, 'I have news for you, young Kicker,' and I swear to God, roysh, for ten horrible seconds I think he's about to tell me about her, about the book, but in the end he doesn't, roysh, he goes, 'You remember I applied to compete in the Women's Mini-Marathon?' and of course I don't even bother answering him, just give him a stare. He goes, 'Well – bit unexpected this – they said yes, I can run. Bit disappointed, if the truth be known. Rather hoped they'd exclude me on the grounds that I'm a man. As you know, Hennessy and I were going to take the case to the Equality Commission and make mincemeat – with a capital M, if you have time – of this, inverted commas, *gender equality* nonsense. A show trial and so forth.'

I go, '*He said rhetorically*,' and I'm looking at the old dear's boat for a response. She cracks on she doesn't know what I'm talking about.

The old man goes, 'It's most inconvenient. Not only that, they've given it to the papers. It's in the *Times*: Controversial councillor Charles O'Carroll-Kelly to become first man to run women's mini-marathon, quote-unquote. So there's no backing out. Not without losing face, which I'm not prepared to do, Ross. Well, the chaps out in Portmarnock would never forgive me.'

I'm there, '*He said with a barely perceptible nod.*'

He goes, 'I've long since come to terms with the fact I'm no longer the dashing young winger who tore up and down the line for Castlerock in the sixties and stole your mother's heart,' and of course I'm like, 'I think I'm going to focking puke.' He goes, 'But your mother's persuaded me. Fifty-three isn't old, Ross. Not by a long chalk. There's no reason why I can't knock this body of mine into shape,' and that's when I look down, roysh, and notice that he's carrying, of all things, a Champion Sports bag. He's like, 'Just bought myself a pair of those *trainers*.'

I'm there, 'You *actually* went into Champion Sports?' and he's like, 'Well, yes,' and I go, 'Are you two never focking done embarrassing me? Did anyone see you?' and he's like, 'Not sure who'd be interested really. What's the problem, Kicker?' and I'm like, 'I cannot focking *believe* you went into that shop. And now you're advertising it. Could you not put that inside a focking BT bag or something? Or an Avoca one?' and before he gets a chance to say something back, roysh, all of a sudden Sorcha's over to us, going, 'Oh my *God*, I *thought* I could hear your voice, Charles,' which is saying something, considering her shop is on the other side of the centre.

Of course it's all air-kisses then – it's like, *mwoi, mwoi* – and they're asking Sorcha about the baby, roysh, and it's, like, fundal height this and oedema that and CTG the other, so naturally, roysh, I just go, 'Okay, goys, I'm out of here,' but before I manage to move a muscle, Sorcha's there, 'Ross, I was going to text you. Will you get me some chocolate?' and I am so tempted to go, 'What's wrong with your focking legs?' because there's, like, a shop just behind us.' Anyway, she must read my mind, roysh, because she goes, 'The Fair Trade one that I like?' and I just stop dead in my tracks. I'm there, 'Babes, I don't care how pregnant you are, I am SO not going into Oxfam.' The last time she sent me in there I ended up scratching for a focking fortnight.

She's like, '*Ross!*' and I'm there, 'Sorcha, I wouldn't be seen dead in a second-hand clothes shop. So build a bridge, Babes, and get over it,' and just as she's giving me a filthy, roysh, the old dear turns around and she's like, 'Charles and

I will go,' and suddenly Sorcha's the most reasonable person in the world. She's going, 'No, I don't want to put you to any trouble, Fionnuala,' and the old dear's going, 'No, we'd *love* to get it for you, Dorling.'

I go, 'Great, Mum! If you're *sure you can trust the mastery of your legs*!' but she ignores me, roysh, and turns around to Sorcha and goes, 'What is it called again? Fair something?' and Sorcha's like, 'Fair Trade. It means the cocoa formers in Ghana get a proper price for their produce,' and of course she missed the look of total horror on the old man's face at that.

She's going, 'They're the *Dork Divine After Dinner Mints*. Oh my God, I have got SUCH a sweet tooth, but I'm trying to make every calorie a good one. Dork chocolate is actually good for you because it's full of, like, antioxidants?' and the old dear's like, 'We might get you some, Charles. Might help get you in shape,' and Sorcha's opening her purse, roysh, and the old dear's going, 'Now don't even think about taking money out of there, Sorcha. This is a treat on Charles and I,' but Sorcha's trying to push the money on her, going, '*Oh my God!* NO way,' and the old dear's going, 'Now don't be silly,' and they're actually storting to draw a crowd, so in the confusion, roysh, I just slip away.

I go down the steps and when I reach the doors I go up to this security gord and I go, 'I don't want to cause any trouble. I mean, live and let live is my motto. But there's a man up there with a Champion Sports bag,' and no sooner have I finished my sentence than the goy is up the steps two at a time, roysh, screaming into his walkie-talkie for back-up.

Birds are like long division to me – we're talking totally focking baffling. I mean, there's Sorcha, roysh, banging on at me for weeks for not being, like, romantic enough, so Vally's Day, roysh, I arrange to have flowers delivered to the gaff, we're talking a large bouquet of spring posies, gay and all as that sounds.

Was she a happy bunny?

Put it this way, she stormed upstairs going, 'OH my God! *Don't* talk to me! Don't *even* talk to me,' and I'm left standing there in, like, pretty much total shock.

I go into the kitchen, roysh, and I notice one of her books, as in like, *How To Be Basically Pregnant*, on the table and I flick through it, roysh, and find this section that's, like, advice for fathers-to-be. It's all, like, make sure you're fully involved and blahdy blahdy blah. But then, roysh, I come across this line and it's like, *Whoa!*

It's like: Wild mood swings are natural during pregnancy. Blame our old friend, the hormonal fluctuations. Remember, don't be always on the defensive.

So I take it on board, roysh. I open a can of Heino, watch a bit of telly downstairs and give her time to calm down. A couple of hours later, roysh, I go upstairs to see how she is – that whole sensitive side of me coming out – and I'm just about to open the door when I hear her on the phone to, I presume, Aoife or Claire or, I don't know, Sophie.

She's going, '*Oh* my God, you will SO not believe what he did tonight,' *he* as in *me* obviously. She's there, 'He ordered me flowers for Valentine's Day. You want to know where from? *Tesco* . . . Yeah, it's free delivery, you see. The florists charge ten euros. Is that the most *oh my God* thing you've ever heard?'

I go back downstairs and crack open another beer. I think she might need a couple more hours.

*

'It's certainly a phenomenon, there's no doubt about that,' Fionn's going, loving the sound of his own voice. He's pointing out one of Marty's tattoos, at the top of his orm, and it's, like, a skull with, like, borbed wire around it and explosions going on in the background and '1916' written underneath it in, like, blood.

Fionn's there, 'I mean, it was a watermork year for both peoples. The year of the Easter Rising, the single most significant date in the establishment of the Irish Republic – its theme of blood sacrifice the lightning rod for the visceral hatred that skobes like our friend here have for the British. And 1916 was also the year that Marcus Garvey told the Jamaican people, "Look to Africa for the crowning of a black king. He shall be the Redeemer,"' and I swear to God, roysh, I could deck Christian when he turns around and goes, 'Who's Marcus Gorvey?' *actually* encouraging the four-eyed focker.

Fionn goes, 'Marcus Garvey, Christian, was one of the original black nationalist crusaders who encouraged people of African lineage to return to their ancestral homeland. Rastafarians consider him the reincarnation of John the Baptist because he prophesied the coming of Haile Selassie,' and as he's saying this, roysh, he's attaching all these, like, electrodes to Marty's head, which he's then hooking up to this, like, machine that he – shall we say – *borrowed* from the psychology deportment in, like, Trinity.

He also has this bird with him, some first year who's going to be, like, his assistant – the *un*lovely Debbie, as Oisinn calls her, because let's just say she's Fionn's usual fare, we're talking red hair, we're talking freckles, we're talking glasses you could get a good focking look at Mars through.

She's also a nerd, roysh, which brings out the worst in

Fionn, because now he's showing off, giving it, 'Marcus Garvey is revered by Jamaica's peasant classes, much as Tony Gregory is in this city,' and now he's making all these, I don't know, adjustments to the machine, pressing buttons and fiddling with knobs, which I'm sure he enjoys, the steamer.

Marty is, like, tied to a chair – *my* chair – and I know he's a Ken Acker and everything, but you'd pretty much almost feel sorry for him. What we're doing feels, I don't know, wrong and I don't know why, roysh, but that long, white lab coat that Fionn's wearing is making me think of *Schindler's List*.

Oisinn goes, 'So, Fionn, explain this to us again like we're a bunch of goys who spent the whole of secondary school throwing a ball around a field and learning fock-all.'

Fionn goes, 'Okay, this piece of machinery is an *electro-encephalograph*,' and I'm like, 'That's easy for you to say,' which deserved a high-five but didn't get one. He goes, 'It's also known as an EEG and it's a non-invasive means of observing human brain activity. The electrodes I've attached to the subject's scalp are meant to pick up electrical impulses in his brain. They are sent down these wires to a series of galvanometers, which detect and measure electrical currents. They, in turn, are attached to a series of coloured pens, which move up and down and give us a read-out on a piece of graph paper.'

I'm like, 'A read-out of *what* exactly?' and he goes, 'Well, I want to measure the subject's emotional responses to a number of stimuli, for the purposes of a comparative analysis. Rastafarians are a very fatalistic people, almost Zen-like in their acceptance of the sorrows of life. Even when Haile Selassie died, there was no great public outpouring of grief in Jamaica. Deep meditation, yes, but no outward manifestation of grief.'

He's there, 'To Rastafarians, you see, death is not a factor, except for the people of Babylon, who, to them, are already dead. Ras Tafari was never an actual Messiah in the flesh, but one in the spiritual body. Like Buddhism, Rastafarianism isn't a series of beliefs as much as an experience, brought about by a liberating ideology.'

He shoves his glasses up on his nose and he goes, 'I want to measure this typical Dublin skobie's response to news of a comparably cataclysmic event . . .' and I'm there, 'Well, can we get on with it because unless it's escaped your attention we actually have, like, a nightclub to run?'

Fionn makes the last of his adjustments, then steps up to the chair where the goy's tied up like a basically turkey. He's out of the focking game. Fionn's going, 'Marty, wake up. Marty, can you hear me? Wake up, Marty,' and you can see the goy slowing coming around, roysh, trying to work out is it labour day, then he remembers where he is and he storts struggling, but there's no point, roysh, because he's tied up tighter than a nun in a brothel.

Fionn goes, 'Marty, sit still for second. I have some terrible, terrible news. You need to hear this . . .' and it takes ages, roysh, but the goy eventually stops struggling and when he's finally calm Fionn turns around and goes, 'Jason Sherlock has been dropped from the Dublin panel. He says he'll never play Gaelic football again,' and, like, ten seconds pass with absolutely no reaction, roysh, but then all of a sudden, the goy just, like, totally explodes. I thought he was actually going to burst the focking ropes. He's, like, kicking and screaming and going, '*Noooooo!*' and calling us all the fooken wankers and doorty-looken doort boords under the sun and the machine is going totally ballistic and we *are* talking totally here. The pens are, like, zigzagging up and down the page like Gordon focking D'Arcy running at the

Scottish defence and I swear to God, roysh, there's actual smoke coming out of the EEC, or whatever it's called.

Fionn goes, 'Hold him down, goys. I'll give him a shot of Morley,' and Oisinn holds onto the goy's orms and me and Christian grab a leg each and all of a sudden, roysh, the room is filled with the sound of Bob Morley singing about a Punky Reggae Porty from this, like, CD player in the corner and Fionn lights up a thing called a spliff – it's, like, drugs for poor people basically? – and puts it in Marty's mouth, and pretty soon the dude is, like, calm again.

I let go of Marty's leg and I go, 'Hey, I want nothing more to do with this,' and Fionn's there, 'What are you talking about, Ross?' ripping reams of focking graph paper out of the machine. He goes, 'Look at these impulses! This is so exciting,' and Oisinn and Christian are looking at the paper in pretty much awe.

Fionn goes, 'This is only the beginning,' and I'm like, 'Not for me, it isn't. It's actually the opposite. As in the end, in other words. What if the focking Feds come looking for this goy? Have you even, like, thought about that?' and Fionn goes, 'Ross, he's a skobie – they'll just presume it's gangland-related, send a couple of frogmen down to search the canals and leave it at that,' and I go, 'They've got something in common with me then, because I'm leaving it at that,' and I don't know why, roysh, but this strange feeling suddenly comes over me and I can actually feel myself on the point of tears. Oisinn's there, 'If there's a Nobel Prize at the end of this, Ross, you needn't think you're coming to Sweden with us for the piss-up,' and then he sort of, like, makes what I can only describe as a breasts gesture with his hands and goes, 'As in, like, *Sweden*?'

And I can actually feel wet on my boat race, roysh, which is when I realise that I'm bawling my eyes out here for no reason at all. Fionn goes, 'Ross, are you *crying*?' and I'm there, 'Don't give me that, I've just got a bit of dust in my eye.'

I asked Sorcha to explain it to me again, roysh, as in the reason she's decided to, like, cut me off until after she's had the baby – as in, like, no sex? She just goes, '*Oh my God*, Ross, I've told you *four* times already. The doctors think I might have a low-lying placenta,' which still sounds like a made-up thing to me, and whether it is or isn't, it was no consolation to me, sitting there with a focking truncheon on me that'd bring order at a GAA match in Wicklow.

She's like, 'Can we actually *not* talk about this now?' because we were in the cor, roysh, sitting outside Mount Cormel hospital where we'd gone to check out this, like, ante-natal class she's thinking of joining when she gets to her final, I don't know, trimester.

I was there, 'You go on in. I'm gonna wait here in the cor,' in other words my BMW Z4. She was not a happy camper when she heard that. She was like, '*Excuse* me? Ross, you're coming in with me!' and I went, 'But what if it's all about, like, childbirth and shit? To be honest, Babes, the old Malcolm's not feeling the Simon Best.'

She goes, '*Oh* my God, you are coming *in* with me!' and she gets out of the cor and slams the door in a way that basically says, Don't bother your orse even arguing.

I was just like, 'Don't say I didn't warn you.'

So I got out of the cor and followed her into the hospital and into this room where there was, like, ten or eleven other birds, most of them with humungous bumps – Sorcha's not showing yet, what with it only being a few weeks – and there's, like, four, maybe five other blokes there.

I sort of, like, shoot them this look, sort of, like, throwing my eyes up to heaven, as if to say, This basically sucks, doesn't it? But I don't get any reaction back, because they're all actually into it, roysh, and I'm thinking there's something NQR about this lot.

The bird in charge of the class was called Stef and I'd have to say, if I was being honest, roysh, I wouldn't touch her with yours, what with her being a ringer for Peter Clohessy and everything. She's focking wetter than Killarney as well, talking to us in a way that reminds me of this Montessori teacher I was boning a few years back.

She's going, 'Now, boys and girls, we have two guests with us here tonight. This is Sorcha, who, as you can probably see, has quite a bit to go yet, but she wanted to sit in on the class tonight, to see what it's all about, just to prepare herself, for when *her* time comes. And this is . . .' and she looks at me, roysh, and either she's pretending not to recognise me or she was in a coma the year I captained Castlerock to the Leinster Schools Senior Cup. *What*ever. I'm not going to rise to the bait.

I'm like, 'The name's Ross,' and she goes, 'You're very welcome here tonight, both of you,' and then she turns to Sorcha and she goes, 'Did you have any trouble persuading *Ross* to come along this evening?' – the shit-stirring bitch – and Sorcha – totally hanging me out to dry again – goes, 'Yeah, it was like, OH! MY! GOD!'

So the next thing, roysh, this Stef one is telling me to stand up, which, like a fool, I end up doing and – this is un-focking-believable – she suddenly storts going, 'Well, boys and girls, it looks like we've got a bit of a grumble-bum in our midst,' and she's saying it in this, like, baby voice.

She's giving it, 'Look at the big grumble-bum, everyone! Look at him! Look at the grumble-bum!' and I'm just stand-ing up, on my focking Tobler, feeling like a total tit, roysh,

60

with pretty much everyone in the room sharing this joke at, like, my expense.

You couldn't blame me, roysh. I ended up just exploding. I was like, 'I COULD BE IN FOCKING KIELY'S WITH THE GOYS, YOU KNOW, WATCHING MUNSTER GET THEIR FOCKING ORSES KICKED, INSTEAD OF STANDING HERE TAKING SHIT OFF YOU WEIRDOS!' which Sorcha seemed to think was a bit on the horsh side of things, but was prepared to put down to, like, hormones and shit? But that was later. At that actual moment, she was ashamed of me. I could tell. She had her hands up to her face and she was going, '*Oh! My God! Oh my God! Oh! My! God!*' giving it the full amateur dramatics.

The rest of the class were just, like, staring at me, shaking their heads, while Stef was totally lost for words. Eventually, roysh, she went, 'Well, you're . . . em . . . very welcome here tonight to the class. This is *the* most exciting time of your life and, hopefully, if you come here, presumably sometime in the final twelve weeks of your pregnancy, we'll help prepare you for it. We all know from our everyday lives – don't we, boys and girls? – that what we fear most is the unknown. Understanding what's happening in the labour process will help you remain calm and relaxed and make you more able to cope with the pain . . .'

She goes, 'I'm presuming, of course, it's your first?' Sorcha's like, 'Yes, it is, Stef,' and I'm there, 'Well, it's *her* first. I've already got one,' and Sorcha's like, 'From a previous relationship,' and I go, 'I'd *hordly* call it a relationship. A quick knee-trembler – no questions asked,' and I only really said it, roysh, to get bit of crack going in the room. I mean you'd see more life in the Leinster pack.

But they're all looking at me in, like, total disgust, even

the goys, and it's pretty obvious that I'm not the only one in the room not getting my Swiss anymore.

Stef turns around to me and goes, 'So were you, em, *present* at the birth?' and I'm like, '*Fock, no!* I mean, the bird involved, my old man paid her fock-off money. I only actually met the kid for the first time last year,' and she's there, 'Oh, I see. Em, well, I have a nice surprise for *both* of you then, because tonight we're going to watch a video of an *actual* birth.'

She turns around, roysh, and behind her, on the wall, is this focking humungous plasma screen telly and before I have a chance to make my excuses, she's switched off the lights and suddenly it's up there – *wallop!* – roysh smack in front of us, taking up forty-eight inches of the wall, we're talking a bird's you-know-what – in other words, vadge, basically – with a focking baby's head sticking out of it.

I can feel my guts do a quick somersault, roysh, and two plates of Sorcha's sauvignon chicken and mushroom filo pie getting ready to leave it. I'm trying not to listen to the commentary, but it's like, '*Childbirth begins with contractions in the uterus, the onset of which may be sudden or gradual. Active labour begins when the contractions occur every two to three minutes and last about sixty seconds in duration, when dilation of the cervix occurs . . .*'

It pretty much goes without saying, roysh, that I love birds – and there's enough of them out there who'll vouch for that. I love them and I love all their basic bits and pieces, roysh, but I have to say, I don't think I could ever feel the same way about . . . *that* . . . after seeing it in this light. Of course, Sorcha's holding my hand, roysh, going, 'Oh *my* God, it is SUCH a miracle.'

The goy on the video's going, '*During contractions, the muscles of the uterus contract, helping draw the cervix up over the baby's head.*

In the transition phase, the cervix will have dilated, in this case to four inches wide,' and I swear to God, roysh, I *am* going to hurl. I can feel, like, acid in my mouth and I'm actually scared to breathe in too deeply at this point.

I was there, 'Babes, I think I need to hit the old TK Maxx,' and she goes, *'Don't you dare!* This is the most important bit,' and though I was trying not to listen, roysh, I can hear the dude going, *'In the second stage of labour, the baby is expelled from the womb through the vagina . . .'*

So I'm trying to think of anything *but* this.

It's like, name the Ireland XV that beat Scotland to win the Triple Crown: The Girvinator, Shaggy, Dorce, Drico of course, Murphy, ROG, Strings, Big Reggie, Shane Byrne, Johnny Hayes, Big Mal, Paul O'Connell, Simon Easterby, David Wallace and . . . Axel.

'During the third and final stage of childbirth, the placenta – which has been your baby's life support during its time in the womb – is delivered . . .'

If you were, I don't know, marooned on a desert island tomorrow, what ten birds would you want with you? Okay. Dido, for storters. Jennie Garth, Keira Knightley, Martina Hingis and Britney obviously. Kirsten Dunst, Neve Campbell, Denise Richards, Claire Danes. One more. Kate Beckinsale. No, Estelle Warren. Fock, did I even say Jessica Alba yet? It's actually hord to choose.

'The squeezing of the uterus separates the placenta from the uterine wall and moves it down into the lower segment of the uterus or into the vagina so you can then push it out . . .'

Okay, *twenty* birds. Davina McCall. Tiffani Thiessen. Isla Fisher. Would the Olsen twins count as one or two?

'Once the placenta is delivered, the vagina can be stitched,' and I'm like, 'Oh my God, I'm gonna borf!'

I swear God, roysh, before I even manage to lift my orse

off the seat I've gone off like a focking volcano, just basically erupted there in the middle of the room.

So there ends up being puke everywhere, we're talking bits of half-digested chicken, button mushrooms and filo pastry – it's also, like, white wine and coriander, in case you're thinking of making it – and it's on the floor and up the walls and, I'm pretty embarrassed to say, all over Stef as well. I mean, there's two birds on the far side of the room who ended up getting their shoes splashed – that's what we're talking here.

Sorcha's going, '*Oh my God! Oh my God! Oh my God!*' as I stand up and make what must be said is a pretty pathetic effort to, like, clean the front of Stef's cordigan using Sorcha's scorf.

I could feel the rest of the room staring at me, giving me total filthies. They were *not* happy bunnies. I looked at Sorcha and she looked back at me like she couldn't believe she'd actually ended up with someone like me, and I don't mean that in a good way. I was like, 'I *told* you I was feeling Moby,' but she didn't answer, roysh, just looked away, while all you could hear in the room at that point was the sound of birds quietly sympathising with her.

And all she said to me in the cor on the way home was that she couldn't believe she ended up married to SUCH a wimp. She was going, 'That was like, OH MY GOD! But that's it, Ross, I've decided – I don't *need* you to have this baby. I've got Mum and Claire for support. So in future, you watch your rugby or whatever it is you want to do.'

We're in Bucks, roysh, and Christian's, like, bending the ear off me as usual, telling me that Sebulba was actually a better Podracer than Anakin, it's just that Anakin's machine had a

Radon-Ulzer engine, which meant it was like a Ferrari, whereas Sebulba was pretty much driving a Jordan – and even then Anakin got lucky. He says it's something he's going to tease out, probably in the second film in his trilogy, and then he goes, '*If* George Lucas goes for it, of course.'

I'm basically throwing the wine into me by this stage and I can't help turning around and going, 'Fock's sake, Christian, can we talk about something else? Birds, for instance?' and of course he gives me the big cow eyes, like I've hurt him, so all of a sudden *I'm* the grinch who stole Christmas.

It's at that point, roysh, that I cop this big-time honey giving me the serious George Hooks from the other side of the bor. And she's, like, well . . . *black*, roysh, and that's not being racist. She's a serious ringer for Tyra Banks and it's obvious from the way she's looking at me, roysh, that she wants me. So I tell Christian to remember where he was in that story, roysh, and I stroll over to her and straight away I'm like, 'Welcome!'

She looks around her, then goes, '*Welcome?*' and I'm there, 'To our country,' obviously thinking she's an asylum-seeker or something.

'What country?' she goes in this, like, total south Dublin accent. 'I'm from Blackrock,' and all of a sudden, roysh, I hear all this laughter behind me and I turn around and it's, like, this gang of birds. Two of them I recognise from the Orts block in UCD. One of them goes, 'Oh *my* God, Lisa, did he *actually* say what I think he said?' and this black one, Lisa, she goes, 'He said, *welcome to our country*,' and they all just crack their holes laughing.

I get it now – they're all friends together.

One of them – I'm pretty sure she went to Cluny – turns around to me and goes, 'You're married to Sorcha Lalor, aren't you?' and then I remember they were on the Leinster

Irish debating team together. I go, 'Maybe,' and she's there, 'I met her mum the other day. Isn't Sorcha, like, pregnant?' which basically translates as, Get the fock out of here.

I'm sitting in the gaff, roysh, watching 'Six One' and the goy, whatever he's called, something Dobson, is going, 'Gardaí have launched an appeal for information on the whereabouts of Martin Coffey, who it's feared may have become the latest victim of a Dublin gangland feud. Members of the Garda Sub Aqua Unit today searched the Royal Canal for the twenty-seven-year-old, who is known to Gardaí and has been missing from his home for five days now,' and then, roysh, the camera switches to this copper – your typical half-acred, woolly-backed, shit-shovelling cabbage-eater – and he's going, 'We would appee-il to inyone wit infer-mayshen to contact de Gyarda confidenchiddle line in tawtle confidence,' and then he gives the goy's description and it's basically like, Last seen wearing expensive trainers, cheap jeans and a focking shedload of jewellery, which could describe ten million people in Tallaght alone.

I'm sitting in the bor, roysh, going through another batch of CVs, ringing some of these birds up and asking them to e-mail us recent photographs of themselves. Some of the birds we called for interview ended up being total hounds. That hour we spent talking to Petra Renk, Ivanka Mollova and Liu Xiuting is an hour none of us can ever get back.

Oisinn comes in and he's, like, on the Wolfe himself, and it's some dude called Hugo – presumably Boss. He's going, 'Nice to hear it, Hugo. You can tell Naomi I'm looking forward to meeting her, too,' and then he storts, like, discussing his itinerary. He's there, 'Oh, New York has been moved forward? It's happening *before* Milan now? So Moscow is when? Okay, cool . . .'

When he gets off the phone, he says he has something he wants to run past me and I cop this, like, black leather pouch that he's carrying under his orm. 'My latest business plan,' he goes and I'm like, 'Well, I'm pretty flattered, Oisinn, but I'm hordly the focking shorpest tool in the box when it comes to, like, thinking and shit,' and he's there, 'Agreed. But you might know what kind of reaction I'm likely to get from JP . . .'

JP? I was actually just thinking this morning how we've hordly seen the dude since he focked off to Maynooth to become, of all things, a priest.

I'm there, 'What's this got to do with, like, JP?' and Oisinn goes, 'I think my idea might be borderline blasphemous, Ross,' and he sits down, unzips his pouch and opens it out on the bor in front of me. It's, like, full of all these, like, drawings of, like, different coloured bottles and all these designs for, like, labels and shit.

He goes, 'Look, it's still in the planning phase, but I don't know why someone hasn't come up with the idea before,' and I'm like, 'What is this shit?' and he's there, 'Perfumed holy water!'

I'm like, 'Perfumed holy water? As in, like, *perfumed*?' and he goes, 'Get this, Ross – *An Exclusive Range of Holy Waters Designed To Revive Your Drooping Spirits!* I've come up with a whole range. There's *Give Us This Day Our Balsam Wood. Take Up Thy Bergamot And Walk. Love One Another As I Have Loved Yuzu . . .*' and I'm like, 'Yeah, I think I'm getting what you're saying about blasphemy. See, they can be funny about that kind of shit. What do you need JP's approval for anyway?' and he goes, 'Well, for it to *be* holy water, it needs to be blessed. And I thought, seeing as we've got a man on the inside now . . . well, he might be my line into the Vatican.'

So there I am, roysh, flicking through all these, like, pages and pages of ideas – I like *Let Him Cast The First Stone He Who Is Without Cinammon* – and I go, 'How many of these things are there?'

He's there, 'Eighty. And that's just the stort of it, Ross. Wait till Scent from Heaven goes international. That's what I'm calling the business by the way,' and I'm there, 'Scent from Heaven? Hey, that's a pretty cool name,' and he's like, 'You'll be able to buy it in the supermarket. I mean, they sell mineral water, so why not *holy* water? Splash a bit on you going out the door in the morning and not only will you feel blessed, you'll smell great too. And the mark-up on this shit is huge.'

I'm there, 'How huge are we talking?' and he goes, 'As in, like, *majorly* huge? I mean, it's basically tap water with two added ingredients – God's blessing and then whatever you're having yourself, wisteria, citronella, honeysuckle, oak-moss, Tonka bean. I can get my hands on *all* that shit easily enough. I could go into production with it next week. Then I'll have a full-time priest in the factory – preferably JP, once he's qualified – to give each bottle the once-over, sign of the cross, blahdy blahdy blah, and the next minute it's on the shelves for, like, four euros a pop.'

I'm like, 'Four *focking* euros?' I'm thinking, This goy is going to be coining it in.

He's like, 'Four euros, my friend. With an exclusive Scent from Heaven holy water font free with three proofs of purchase.'

'Three what?' It's a voice from the past. We both turn around at the same time, roysh, and who is it only JP himself, looking über focking cool, it has to be said, whatever they're feeding him in priest school. I don't care what religion he is, roysh, the dude is getting a high-five. It's, like, I respect his beliefs, but he sure as hell better respect mine and he does, because he responds like the JP of old, high-fiving both of us, while Oisinn turns around to Olga, this Russian bird we hired who is a total ringer for Maria Sharapova, and goes, 'Get this man a Baileys. Make it a focking pint of Baileys.'

JP's like, 'Sweet merciful Lord, no. No, just a short glass is fine,' and he spends the next twenty minutes telling us all about the inner peace he's discovered since he found the Lord and he says he's spent the morning reading Matthew and considering the parallelism of thought and cadence contained in the Beatitudes, to which there's pretty much no answer.

After, like, twenty minutes of banging on about God – as in, like, the real one, not the Ireland number thirteen – he eventually goes, 'So . . . Oisinn, you said you had something you wanted to . . . *run past me?*'

Oisinn's like, 'Oh, er, yeah,' and then he sort of, like, clears his throat and goes, 'What would *you* say to the idea . . . of scented . . . holy . . . water?' and of course JP is, like, stuck for words. He thinks at first it might be, like, a joke. He's like, 'Scented . . .'

Oisinn's there, '*Scented.* As in *perfumed.* Think about the TV ads. *Splash a bit on in the morning and it'll leave you feeling holy – and smelling like a Goddamn miracle.*'

I'm looking at JP for a reaction. The best way to describe it would be, like, total shock.

Oisinn keeps banging on. He's like, 'That's not necessarily going to be the slogan. It could be anything. Could be, *Father, Son and the Holy Ghost – you smell as tasty as a Sunday roast.* I'm thinking in terms of a seven-figure morketing budget . . .' and all of a sudden, roysh, it's pretty obvious from looking at JP just exactly what he thinks.

He's just, like, shaking his head. Then he goes, 'You mean to say, you dragged me away from my studies, all the way in from Maynooth, for *this*?' and before Oisinn can answer he goes, 'Are you familiar with the passage in the Bible where Jesus drove the traders out of the Temple?' and I'm thinking this is *their* argument, and I might actually head up to the Powerscourt Centre, see does Sorcha fancy an early lunch.

JP's like, 'Sit down, Ross,' and I do.

He goes, 'He overturned the tables of the money-changers and the benches of those selling doves. *It is written that my house shall be called a house of prayer. But you have made it a den of robbers.*'

Oisinn goes, 'That's the Bible you're quoting from, yeah? They're free, are they?' and he's like, 'What's your *point*, Oisinn?' and it's already getting nasty. Oisinn's there, 'My *point* is they charge money for the Bible. And for Rosary beads. Lourdes has a gift shop. So does Knock. So does Fatima. My *point* is that everyone's making a buck out of this whole God thing. So, Dude, spare me the focking hypocrisy.'

I'm thinking, it'll be interesting to see what JP comes back at him with. He goes, 'How can you compare them? Bibles and Rosary beads are one thing. *Designer* holy water . . . Do I really need to explain to you why that's sacrilegious? It offends the Second Commandment,' and it has to be said, roysh, it really is fascinating listening to the debate swing backwards and forwards. One minute I think I'm on Oisinn's side, the next I'm thinking I kind of agree with JP.

The dude hasn't touched his Baileys though, which shows how pissed off he is. All of a sudden he's like, 'Why am *I* here anyway? What did you see as my role in this little . . . *enterprise*?' and Oisinn sort of, like, shrugs his shoulders and goes, 'Well, there's no point in having mates on the inside if you're not prepared to use them,' and JP just, like, pushes his drink back across the bor, gets down off his school and goes, 'On the inside? On the *inside*? I'm studying theology with a view to entering the priesthood. You think that gives me a hotline to the Catholic Primate of All Ireland?' who's obviously the head honcho.

But Oisinn's losing the rag as well now. He's going, 'Oh *I'm* sorry, JP, if I mistook you for someone important. You know, you're actually roysh. I'm talking to the monkey when I should be talking to the organ-grinder,' and JP doesn't, like, respond to that.

Oisinn goes, 'I'm actually going to take this to the top man, as in, like, the Pope himself?' and JP sort of, like, sneers at him and goes, 'Yeah, I'm sure the Holy Father is only waiting for your call,' meaning it, like, sarcastically?

But Oisinn, roysh, quick as a flash, goes, 'You seem to be forgetting one thing, JP. I'm on first-name terms these days with Hugo Boss. Guess who's just been given the contract to design the new altar boys' vestments for St Peter's?' JP doesn't answer.

Oisinn goes, 'But thanks for your help, *so-called* friend,' and that's when JP turns around and goes, 'I'm no friend of yours. And you're no friend of mine,' and he storms off, out through the door and down to the street.

We're all out, roysh, in Tonic in Blackrock and I can't remember whether it was, like, Sophie or Chloe, who turned around to Sorcha and went, '*Oh* my God, it's SO true what they say. You really do look glowing when you're pregnant.'

And Erika, roysh, for no reason at all, other than to be a total bitch, goes, 'Yes, your skin *is* very greasy, Sorcha.'

When she reached the mahogany Westminster door with its triple-glazed, bevelled, leaded clustered window set into it, she hesitated, her index finger prevaricating over the bell.

She wasn't looking for anything from this man other than friendship, she reminded herself sternly, so why did she feel like she was being somehow disloyal to Richard?

She immediately banished the thought, pressed the bell and was surprised by the light trill it made in response. She turned around. Her eyes riveted around the garden and she admired his dexterity as a gardener, which was evident in everything, from the perfectly manicured lawns, to the flowerbeds that were a kaleidoscope of different colours and hues. Virginia creepers wainscoted the walls.

She remembered his hands, firm and expert, and his fingers, strong and proficient.

'You seem very interested in my golden rod,' she heard a voice say.

She span on her heel. Lovell was standing there, looking as improbably handsome as he had before, in just a white, tight-fitting T-shirt that showcased his perfect abdominal muscles and fawn-coloured, elephant cords. But she quietly cursed the easy ability he had to unnerve her.

'Your . . . what . . .' she said in puzzled syncopation.

'My golden rod,' he said, a devious glint evident in his eye. 'My Solidago. I must tell you, it's wonderful for a late-summer garden. Adds a dash of colour after all the other flowers have faded. Attracts copious numbers of butterflies. It's wonderful to see you, Valerie.'

She tried to regain her calm. 'You too,' she said. 'Lovell.'

It was the first time she'd said his name aloud since they met a week earlier and she discovered she loved the feel of it in her mouth. It was deep and lusty and hearty and vigorous.

In the morgin, Sorcha's written, 'Really good use of words,' and there's, like, a little red tick beside it and I'm thinking, she SO should have become a schoolteacher, that girl.

He took her coat from her shoulders, then led her down a long hallway to a large, luxury handmade kitchen that looked very like one she'd admired recently in the window of Design House Kitchen Concepts in Dalkey. She couldn't help but notice the range-style cooker with griddle facility and feature canopy with triangular inlay detailing, American-style, two-door fridge-freezer with adjacent open larder, full-size, multi-zone wine cooler, twin dishwasher drawer units and a glass, elevated coffee bar incorporated into the central island, and couldn't but admire the way the natural timbers in the stained walnut cupboards complemented and yet contrasted with the stainless steel and leather-look granite work surfaces.

She thought she could smell tarragon.

'It's spinach, chicken and crème fraiche filo parcels for lunch,' he said. 'I'm sorry, I should have asked you on the phone if there was anything you *don't* eat.'

'No,' she said. 'I really love that. Did you get that from . . .'

'Guilty!' he said, holding his hands up. 'Yes, I ripped off the recipe. God, I *love* Avoca Handweavers . . .'

'I love it too,' she said, all this talk of food making her suddenly flush with excitement again.

She recognised the music. They had so much in common, she mused silently, because she, too, liked, Il Divo.

Sorcha's written, 'OMG! I *love* Il Divo! Ross bought me *Ancora* for Christmas. Which song is it? I think the reader will want to know. Make it "En Aranjuez Con Tu Amor".'

She sat down at the island, which she couldn't help but notice was laden with fresh and exotic fruits – plump Gallia melons, juicy papayas, succulent mangoes, scandalously moist guavas and the most lascivious boisonberries she'd ever set eyes on.

'So,' she said, initiating a new line of conversation, 'what do you do actually? Apart from garden and cook, that is. And listen to wonderful music.'

He laughed heartily. 'Nothing, I suppose. I won't deny it. I'm a wealthy man. Self-made.'

'You're not married?' she said. She hoped she didn't sound hopeful.

'Never had time,' he said airily. 'I was married to my work. Until one day – it was the day of my fortieth birthday – I realised that, well . . . I'd never stopped to smell the roses.'

'What did you work at?' she asked curiously.

'Solicitor,' he said.

Valerie felt her face collapse. Not another solicitor, she thought, remembering that it was the legal profession that had sent Richard to prison.

'Acquisitions and mergers,' he added, brushing the neat, triangular-shaped filo parcels with butter. 'You *are* married. The first thing I did when I saw you was look for your ring.'

'Yes.'

'But you're here now,' he said, a speculative edge entering his voice, 'which must mean . . .'

'He's in prison,' she blurted out. 'I'm not proud of it. He was no saint but . . .' She felt a catch in her chest. 'God damn that Criminal Assets Bureau . . .'

A grim, mordant silence settled on the kitchen, the only sound to be heard the whir of the oven fan, as the spinach, chicken and crème fraiche filo parcels were slowly baked at 180 degrees celsius. Suddenly it felt that temperature in the kitchen as well.

None of my business,' he said briskly, as Valerie composed herself and reset her features into a look of stoic acceptance. 'I'll ... em ... get on with the fruit salad,' he said tentatively, picking up a mango and cupping it in the palm of his big but sensitive left hand. With his other hand he used a Stellar James Martin paring knife to cut away the green and yellow outer peel, deftly following the curve of the fruit, leaving virtually no flesh left attached to the skin. She watched in amazement as he laid it down on its side and, with a cool sleight of hand, sliced it lengthways, then cut the normally stubborn fruit away from stone with the minimum of persuasion. She watched his sturdy, educated fingers carve away the few small pieces of recalcitrant flesh that had attached themselves to the stone and suddenly she found herself having to fend off thoughts, impure thoughts that fixated on those thick, fleshy hands.

Suddenly, unable to help herself, she was imagining them peeling a sensuous black silk dress over her head, then tenderly exploring her body, brushing her skin, then hooking two fingers inside her panties and tugging them down, past her thighs, her knees, her calves, her ankles. Then turning her over ...

Okay, what the *fock* is going on here?

... and entering her from behind.

NO! *No way!*

And their quivering bodies instinctively finding the same rhythm, fast and furious. And both of them gorging on the luscious fruits on the table, sinking their teeth into juicy quarters of Gallia melon and soft, sweet squares of papaya as he took her doggy-style ...

75

What? This is my *old dear* writing this! What kind of a sick . . .

. . . and feeling the waves crashing over her in a tsunami of pleasure.

She snapped out of her lusty fantasy with a sudden start. Down below, she could feel herself moist with anticipation but she knew it was wrong. She could no longer trust herself to stay here. She suddenly jumped off her high stool.

'I have to go,' she said brusquely. For once, Lovell was bankrupt of words. She hurried out of the kitchen and, in one fluid movement, took her coat off the hook in the hall and opened the front door. As she disappeared through the front gate, she heard him call, 'But, Valerie . . . there's pine-nuts in it . . .'

One thing's for sure – if anyone's mad enough to actually print this thing, I am going to have to seriously emigrate.

Sorcha's lying on the bed, roysh, and she pulls out this piece of, like, equipment that looks a bit like one of those bumbags peasants bring away with them on package holidays. She puts this, like, jelly substance all over her Ned Kelly, then straps this thing around and naturally, roysh, I'm thinking, looks like the old Rossmeister General is about to go back into battle.

Saddle up, Dude!

Turns out, though, it's actually a Parental Sound System. I'm there, 'A what?' and she's like, 'A Parental Sound System. You can communicate with your baby by playing comforting music that helps in the bonding and recognition process.'

So I check the CD cover on her locker. It's Natasha Bedingfield.

She obviously cops my boat because she goes, 'You'd prefer if I put on Snoop-whatever he's called. Yes, our baby's first word would be *motherfocker*,' which you'd have to say is bang out of order.

3. Guest of the (Southside) Nation

It's like a scene from focking *Reservoir Dogs*. I push open the door of the office, roysh, and I see Marty there, still tied up and shit, and Oisinn's standing over him, roysh, not chopping his ear off, but doing what I suppose is the next worst thing to him. He's laying out an assortment of mobile phones and iPods on the desk in front of him, roysh, and of course every focking muscle in Marty's body is telling him to steal the things, but of course he can't move his orms or his legs. And all the time, roysh, Oisinn's giving this little commentary. It's like, 'The Nokia 8800 – stainless steel body, fine-pitched scratch-resistant screen, camera, internet access, enhanced graphics, digital music player . . .' and he's got him hooked up to that machine with the pens and they're, like, going ballistic, roysh, pretty much shredding the paper.

Marty's going, 'Will ye fooken lay off me, reet? It's pewer fooken torcher, man!' and Oisinn is just reaching for a black iPod nano when I go, 'What are you doing?' and I swear to God, roysh, he jumps three feet in the air. Of course I end up going, 'Pity you couldn't get up that high in the lineout,' which is probably one of the funniest things I've ever said.

He goes, 'Hey, don't sneak up on me like that,' and I'm there, 'You know, Fionn will have a total conniption if he catches you doing that,' and Oisinn's like, 'It's just a bit of fun, Ross. What are you doing up here anyway?' and I'm there, 'Well, seeing as it's *my* focking office, I shouldn't need an actual reason. But if you must know, I'm looking for those two CVs we got in. Still can't make up my mind about them.'

Oisinn goes, 'Has to be the French one. Evelyne whatever . . . Guenard,' and I'm there, 'But what about . . .' and he's like, 'Heike Bussmann? I'm pretty sure Heike Bussmann is a goy, Ross,' and he whips the CV out of a drawer and hands it to me. I stare at the passport photograph that's clipped to it. I'm there, 'She's got long hair. She's wearing lippy,' and he's like, 'She *also* has an Adam's apple? Seriously, Dude, Heike's a focking tranny,' and I suppose what with Oisinn being mixed up in that whole fashion world, he'd know better than most. He goes, 'The stubble would probably have aroused my suspicion as well,' and I'm there, 'Evelyne it is then . . .'

I'm about to head back down to the bor, roysh, but Oisinn asks me have I, like, got a minute. He has something he wants to show me and says he'll be back in a second. So I'm hanging there, roysh, and I'm just, like, flicking through the address book on his phone, just to pass the time really – I can't believe it, roysh, the dude has got Heidi Klum in his phone. *And* Adriana Lima *and* Gisele Bundchen *and* Else Benitez *and* Loly Lopez – when all of a sudden, roysh, Marty turns around to me and goes, 'How's de baby?'

I don't answer him, roysh, just look at him, wondering how the fock he knows, and he must cop this, roysh, because he's like, 'Ah, sure, I hear evyting up hee-er. I've two meself,' and I'm like, 'Two kids?' and he goes, 'Well, two wit de boord I'm wit now. Shannon and Robbie. Shannon's tree, reet, and Robbie's one,' and there's loads of shit I want to ask him, roysh, but I'm a bit Scooby Dubious about it. This happens in all those, like, hostage films, roysh, where the victim tries to befriend one of the kidnappers.

He goes, 'Sixteen weeks gone, isn't she? Be de size of

yizzer hand now,' and it's amazing, roysh, there's no language barrier at all. I can understand pretty much every word he says – probably from listening to Ronan. I'm there, 'The size of my hand. Really?' and he nods and goes, 'How's *she*? Sorcha, is it?' and I'm like, 'Yeah, em, bit of morning sickness at the stort, but I'd have to say, roysh, the last couple of weeks, everything's been Kool plus Significant Others.'

He nods like a man who's heard it all before. He's there, 'De sickness goes away, reet, as de placenta takes over de production of de hormones,' and suddenly, roysh, whether he's focking with my head or not, I don't care. He knows his shit. I just stort unloading on him, roysh, telling him all about the business with the prawn toast and about me chucking up my guts for no reason and, like, bursting into tears at the slightest thing.

He goes, 'Ah, you're havin' a sympatetic pregnancy, so y'are. De brudder had dat,' and I pull up a chair and sit down, roysh, not just because I'm interested in hearing what he has to say, roysh, but because I've got really bad cramps in my legs and lower back.

He goes, 'See, it's all psychological, man. Dee don't know de reasons for it. Probly yer feelin' sympity for yisser boord, reet, and yisser body starts to copy de symptoms. Are ye constipated, are ye?' and I'm like, 'Yeah, I'm shitting concrete, Dude,' and he nods and goes, 'Same as de brudder. Any mood swings?' and I'm like, '*Serious* mood swings. I'm, like, bursting into tears for no focking reason. I mean, I don't think I've cried since we lost the first Leinster Schools Cup final I played in, although I have to tell you, roysh, I did repeat the following year and we ended up winning. Although I wouldn't say that got much coverage in your port of the world . . .'

Suddenly, roysh, I hear Oisinn coming back up the stairs, so I jump up out of the chair and, at the top of my voice, I go, 'And don't even *think* about trying to escape. Otherwise . . . you'll suffer the consequences,' and Oisinn comes in, going, 'Fock's sake, Ross, it's not Auschwitz. Here, have a snod of this, tell me what you think,' and he hands me this bottle that's got this, like, reddy-brown liquid in it.

He goes, 'That one there is *Happy Are The Myrrh In Spirit*,' and I pull the cork out of the bottle and have a sniff. Smells a bit like trees to me. I'm like, 'Yeah, it's not bad. You're still going ahead with it, then?' and he looks at me as if to say, Why wouldn't I be going ahead with it? I'm there, 'You know, I just thought what JP said might have put you off,' and he's like, 'Shit the bed, Ross, of course it hasn't! Look, JP's only a Paddy Punchclock in the bigger scheme of things. Like I said, Hugo's going to put a word in for me inside. But I do want to get JP back onside . . .'

I'm there, 'Oh?' and it's really weird, but as he's talking, roysh, I stort to feel a bit I suppose *funny*, you'd have to call it? I can't stop thinking about that, I don't know, myrrh, or whatever it's called. It's focked up, roysh, but I just have this, like, urge to drink it.

He takes the bottle back off me, puts it on top of the filing cabinet and goes, 'I'm still going to need someone to actually bless this stuff as it comes off the conveyor belt. So I need to fix things with the Dude,' and I'm there, 'You heard what he said, Oisinn. He wants nothing to do with you,' and Oisinn goes, 'That's where *you* come in . . .'

It's actually thick, roysh, like milk or something. And I know it smells of trees but for some reason – maybe it's, like, the colour? – I've got it into my head that it's going to taste like chocolate oranges.

Oisinn's going, 'I need you to talk to him for me. Make

him see that this idea benefits everyone. If Tesco agrees to stock this shit, it's going to bring religion to the supermorket aisles. Increase the audience. *Flock!* Use the word flock when you're talking to him. A bigger flock for him. A fortune for me. It's a win-win situation, as he used to say himself, back when he was normal . . .'

Sweet and yet tangy. And thick like milk.

He goes, 'And there's fifty Ks in it for you . . .'

I tear my eyes away from the bottle. I'm there, 'You're going to pay me fifty thousand sheets?' and he's like, '*If* you can change his mind, that is. He's going to Lough Derg next weekend, on some retreat or other. You could go with him. You'd have three days solid to work on him . . .'

Marty goes, 'Any chance of gettin' any fooken grub around hee-er, is der?' and Oisinn goes, 'Fionn's gone to the chipper. It's not easy to get curry sauce in this port of town, you know . . .' and then he all of a sudden spins around, roysh, and it's like the dude's got eyes in the back of his head. He goes, 'Ross, put the bottle down,' just as I'm lifting it to my lips. He's like, 'I *knew* it. I knew it from the way you looked at it earlier. You licked your lips.'

I'm there, 'I have to drink it, Oisinn,' but he's going, 'You *don't* have to drink it, Ross,' and Marty goes, 'It's hees moynd playin' tricks on him, so it is. De brudder had it when hees boord was expectin'.'

I'm like, 'It's . . . it's going to taste like chocolate oranges,' and Oisinn just goes, 'Ross, I know what's in it. I can guarantee you, it is *not* going to taste like chocolate oranges. That's *six weeks* of my life in that bottle. Do NOT do this to me, Dude,' and as he's saying it, roysh, he's, like, slowly edging towards me.

I'm like, 'I'm sorry, Oisinn, I'm just not strong enough,' and he's going, 'No sudden movements. Slowly . . . put the bottle down . . . put your hands above your head . . . and, I don't know, lie face-down on the floor . . .' but I'm just there, 'I've got to know.'

In one quick movement, roysh, I throw the bottle up to my lips and knock the whole thing back. Oisinn goes, *'Noooooooo!'* and he throws himself at me, in slow motion, pretty much rugby-tackling me. But it's too late. The empty bottle flies out of my hand and smashes on the floor of the office.

Of course he ends up totally creaming me, the fat focker – I think I might even need a new hip – and the two of us are just, like, lying there in a heap on the floor and he's, like, muttering madly to himself about six weeks of work going down the toilet. Except I didn't actually make it to the toilet?

We'd only just hit the ground when I storted to feel Moby. I'm like, 'I think I'm going to focking borf,' and Oisinn goes, 'You *think*? Have you any idea what you just drank?' and, before I get a chance to say anything back, roysh, I'm throwing my ring up all over the shop, we're talking fifteen minutes of spitting chunks, and we're talking non-stop, and we're talking non-stop in a big-time way.

I'm upstairs in Reynords, roysh, and I end up making a move on this bird who – I am not exaggerating – is the spitting image of Amanda Brunker. It's like, HELLO? How can you *not* be sisters?

I'm giving it loads, roysh, going, 'So, what do you *do*? Aport from give me palpitations, that is?'

She goes, 'I'm a sales rep. for a leading fashion house,' and I'm there, 'I know a bird who's in that game,' and I swear to God, roysh, I end up nearly having a hort attack when she turns around and goes, 'I take it that *bird* is the one you're married to,' and I'm just left there, going, 'Er . . .'

She's like, 'I know Sorcha really well,' and I'm there, 'Sorcha?' and she goes, 'Your wife, Ross? She's one of our best clients,' and of course there's, like, a lull in the conversation then, until she goes, 'How far gone is she now?' and I'm like, 'Em, four months . . .'

I tell her I have to hit the can, roysh, but I don't come back.

I bell the old man, not because I actually *like* him, of course, I'm trying to tap the focker for a couple of grand to get the new Nokia 8810 and a PlayStation Portable, but you can guess the first thing that comes into my mind, roysh, when I hear him – three o'clock on a Wednesday afternoon – puffing and, like, panting for breath. I'm there, 'That woman needs to see someone.'

He goes, 'Woman? I'm on the treadmill, Kicker. All part of this fitness plan a couple of the chaps in the club have put together for me for the big race. Twenty minutes a day.'

I'm there, 'Yeah, *what*ever. Is there any chance of your shutting the fock up for twenty *seconds*?' but of course there isn't.

He's going, 'Running is a science, Ross. Did you know that? Hennessy's coming out here later. Bringing his laptop and that camera he uses to film his swing, to look for glitches and so forth? He's going to have a close look at my carriage.'

I'm there, 'I don't even want to know what that means,' but he's like, 'My bearing, Ross. My posture. My gait. The way I deport myself. It's not pretty, I'll grant you that. A tad ungainly, if the truth be told. But then, as Hennessy said – and he didn't have to say this – it's not that unlike the running style of a certain Mr Ronald Delany Esquire, originally of Arklow Town.'

I'm there, 'Never focking heard of him. I need two grand,' and he's like, *'Never heard of him?* Never heard of the Turkey Trotter, quote-unquote? He won an Olympic gold medal, Ross. Melbourne '56. Fifteen-hundred-metres, thank you very much indeed. Oh, I remember it well. It's, what, fifty years ago? I was just a boy, but I can recall every detail of the race like it happened yesterday . . .'

I'm there, 'Please don't,' but he goes, 'I watched it with my *old dad* as you might say yourself. Nobody expected him to win, of course. *What, this little Irish chap? Go on with you!* He had this funny way of running – Hennessy's right, it *must* be where I picked it up – head back, knees up, arms working away there like pistons. He just about made the team that year, if memory serves. Then he went to Melbourne and ran a terrible heat. Then, to put a top on it, he was *tenth* at the bell in the final. But on the final lap it all came good. Blew them all away. Capital B.'

He's going, 'My apologies. I'm getting more than a few tears in my eyes here, Ross, remembering Dad jumping out of his armchair, shouting, "Here he comes, Charles! Here comes the Turkey Trotter!"' and I go, 'So your old man was penis as well then? It's a focking miracle I turned out alroysh,' and then – forget the lids – I just hang up on the stupid tool.

When I arrive home, Sorcha and Claire are sitting at the table in the dining room, slaving over the books again. I go, 'What's the Jack, are you still working on that birth plan?' but no one answers me.

Claire, who I now notice has a laptop in front of her – stolen would be my guess, given where she's coming from – is full of it, roysh, going, 'Do you want the baby cleaned before it's given to you, or do you want he or she put in your arms immediately?' and Sorcha's like, 'Oh my God, *definitely* immediately,' and Claire types this in and I swear to God, roysh, it's like I'm not even there.

Claire goes, 'After the baby is delivered, do you want an injection to help contract your womb to speed up the delivery of the placenta?' and Sorcha's there, 'Oh my God, yes. And I want the baby to be given a Vitamin K injection. I was reading about blood-clotting disorders in one of these magazines. It's like, *Oh my God!*'

Claire all of a sudden gets up, roysh, and goes, 'You *can't* be comfortable sitting in that hard chair like that, Sorcha,' and she grabs a cushion off the sofa, roysh, and puts it behind Sorcha's back and goes, 'For support . . .' and I'm left standing there, thinking, Hey, that's *my* job.

Claire goes, 'It's probably worth deciding soon how you're going to feed the baby. If you're going to breastfeed, it says here the baby should be put to the breast as soon as possible,' and Sorcha's there, 'I'm *definitely* going to breastfeed,' and I'm looking at Claire's fingers working the keys, roysh, and I end up going, 'That FÁS secretarial course you did is standing to you now, isn't it?' and that's when Claire turns around and goes, 'Sorcha, I really don't feel comfortable doing this with *him* in the room,' and Sorcha goes, 'Ross . . .'

As in, Beat it.

I don't know why, roysh, but I'm actually a bit shocked that they allow trainee priests to *have* mobile phones. JP answers on the third ring and goes, 'Hey, Ross, it's great to hear from you,' which is good for me to hear, roysh, because I didn't know whether he suspected I was in on the holy water thing as well. He goes, 'How's Sorcha doing?' and I'm like, 'Em, pretty well. Lashing the weight on, though I wouldn't say that to her face. Well, not again . . .'

He's like, 'Good. And the club?' and I'm there, 'Going great. We're getting some amount of celebrities in. Last weekend it was, like, Liz Bonin, Anna Nolan, the Irish goy out of Liberty X and Jason McAteer. Oh, and the Corter Twins. But you heard about Vally's night, did you? One F volunteered to do the entertainment and, well, he went and booked this Cher tribute act? As in, like, Cher and Cher Alike?' and JP laughs and goes, 'Good old One F. *His* generation, I suppose,' and I'm there, 'Not exactly our morket, though, is it? The place was empty. It's funny now, though. So what are *you* up to?'

To cut a long story short, roysh, he was reading – of all things – an essay on the theme of cursing and vengeance in the Book of Psalms, so I very slyly use that as my in. I'm like, 'Speaking of God and that whole vibe, I kind of feel like I'm in need of a bit of, I don't know, spiritual guidance at the moment,' and of course he perks up when he hears that. It's like, *Customer!* He goes, 'Ross, this isn't another one of your jokes, is it? Like that time you told me there was a burning bush in your gorden,' and I'm there, 'No, I'm serious this time, Dude. It's probably with the baby on the way and everything, but I think it's time I squared a lot of shit away with Himself. Maybe if there was some, I don't know, *retreat* I could go on . . .'

I let it hang in the air.

He goes, 'Well, *I'm* going on a retreat next week. Well, I say *retreat*, it's more of a pilgrimage,' and I'm there, 'No way . . .' and he's like, 'Yeah, to Lough Derg. I mean, you're more than welcome to join me, if you want,' and I'm there, 'You're shitting me now – you mean there's a place left on the trip?' and he goes, 'It's not an organised trip, Ross. I'm just going up by myself. Recharge the spiritual batteries, so to speak . . .'

I'm thinking, when did he stort saying *so-to-speak*? It's such a priest thing.

I'm there, 'That is SO freaky that I just happened to mention that I was interested in going on a retreat and you just happened to be going on one already . . .' and he's like, 'Well, I think *Himself* might have given you a nudge in my direction,' and then he tells me he has to go but not to worry, roysh, he'll make all the arrangements.

When I hang up, Marty goes, 'You're some fooken man, you are,' and he cracks his hole laughing, but the thing is, roysh, I was actually telling JP the truth. I think I do need guidance. I mean, this business with Marty, it's wrong. Yes, he chose to break into the club and yes, he's a cream cracker, but he's still got the same rights as every one of us. Well, probably not as many as me and the goys, but I'm pretty sure the dude is entitled to his freedom.

And then there's, like, other shit on my mind as well. And Marty can tell. He goes, 'It's a tough toyim in any man's life,' and I go, 'I'm just feeling a bit . . .' and he's there, 'Jealous?' and I'm there, 'Yeah. Left out. I mean, everyone's worrying about how Sorcha is. I feel like I've got nothing to do with it. You know, you're the only person who's actually asked how *I'm* coping and shit.'

He nods. Oh my God, he's SO easy to talk to, this goy.

He goes, 'See, dats how it was in dee old days. You put up de sperm, reet, and dee gave ye a shout from de hospital when de ting was born. Now fadders is more involved, so dee are. Yer apposed to be dare for de mudder every step of de way. But ye have to get involved, man. Ante-natal classes, de foorst scan, de whole shebang,' and I'm there,

'Okay,' and he's like, 'And talk to her abourit. Teller yisser feelings. Udderwise, resentment sets in. I've seen it,' and I go, 'The brother?' and he's like, 'De brudder.'

I go, 'Marty, look . . . I'm sorry about . . . all this,' and I nod at his tied hands. I'm there, 'I mean, if I could, I'd . . .' but he's like, 'Yer game-ball, man. I understand.'

I'm there, 'What about your . . . wife?' and he goes, 'Boord? Ah, she'll just presume I was up to no good. Went off on one of me famous skites till de dust settles. Spayin is where I usually go.'

I pick up the phone. I probably shouldn't, roysh, but I do. I go, 'Do you want to call her?' and he's there, 'You don't moyind?' and I'm there, 'I'm offering, aren't I? What's the number?' and he tells me. I dial it and, like, put my hand over the mouthpiece while it rings. I go, 'Hey, I'm trusting you here. You're not going to pull a fast one, are you?' and he's like, 'You have me woord.'

A woman's voice answers. Definitely Skobe.

I hold the phone up to Marty's ear. He goes, 'Howiya, love . . . Ah, calm down . . . I'm in Spayin . . . Why do you tink? I pulled a job. Waitin' for de heat to come off me . . . Listen, I love ye. Tell de kids I miss dem. I'll see ye in a couple of weeks . . .'

And when I've hung up, roysh, I have to get out of the room, because I don't want Marty to see me crying. He shouts after me, 'Tanks, Ross.'

The doorbell rang. Valerie stepped into the hall. Even through the dulled effulgence of the smoked glass panelling there was no mistaking who was at the door. The broad shoulders. The perfect profile. The thick, lantern jaw. Her heart began to beat in two-four time.

But how had he gotten into the apartment building without

pressing the intercom button? Someone must have been leaving just as he was arriving, she reasoned.

What should she do now? Return to the kitchen and her travails over her Asian-style crab cakes with fruit chutney? Or surrender to the urges crowding in on her to open the door?

Her range of choices suddenly narrowed, because suddenly he could make out her blurry figure through the glass.

Valerie,' he said, plaintively. 'We need to talk.'

She crouched down. 'There's nothing to say,' she said through the embrasure of the letterbox. 'Really. Leave me alone.'

He hunkered down to her level, their eyes meeting, her olfactory senses suddenly overwhelmed by the sharp smell of toothpaste and . . .

And then in brackets, roysh, it's like, 'Sorcha, can you think of a nice aftershave that Lovell might wear?'

And Sorcha's written, 'OMG, it SO has to be Jean Paul Gaultier 2. It's got a kind of soft, woody smell. There's a guy who comes into the shop all the time who wears it.'

I'm thinking, Is there, indeed?

'Please,' he said, beseechingly. 'Open the door.'

She stood up to her full height again. He was right. This was ridiculous. Two adults should be able to control themselves around each other. She turned the catch. As soon as she saw him she felt a stab of lust like a cold steel stiletto.

'I've got something here you might like to put in your box,' he said, holding out his hand and proffering a small, potted azalea.

That cool façade again – she hated it and yet she loved it.

'And make sure not to use too much fertiliser,' he said matter-of-factly. 'Too much nitrogen in the soil tends to encourage vegetative growth at the expense of bud formation. And they like shade but not too much. I have mine planted in diffused light, under some high-crowned trees.'

'I see,' she said, trying to maintain a casual air.

He stepped into the hall.

'You ran out on me,' he said, a disappointed note entering his voice. 'Just before the spinach, chicken and crème fraiche filo parcels were ready . . .'

'I'm sorry,' she said, bowing her head. 'You went to a lot of trouble. I suddenly just felt . . . tired.'

'You don't have to lie,' he said, moving towards her, so close that she was now staring into the firm contours of his broad chest. 'I feel it too, you know. Since that very first day in Kilmacanogue . . .'

'Do you have any tips about wintering azaleas?' she said. Her effort to change the subject was utterly artless. She could feel his eyes boring into her, undressing her. 'Stop it,' she said, reproaching him firmly. 'I'm . . . I'm a married woman.'

It sounded weak, unconvincing.

Suddenly he crushed her with a long, lingering kiss. She put up a perfunctory fight but soon felt herself surrender in his powerful arms. Without even bothering to close the door, he walked her through the hall and into the kitchen, their bodies still pressed against each other. They kissed, long and hard, and groped each other intimately.

She unbuttoned his shirt and his big, robust body made her dizzy with longing. He skilfully shed the rest of his clothes and suddenly she was staring in wonder at his naked erectness.

This is weird shit.

His hands ran leisurely up her spine. He reached for the clips that held her hair up and released her long brown tresses from the furlough of her bun, sending them tumbling free around her shoulders. With his other hand, he expertly flicked open the clasp of her bra and let it drop and she felt him throb with excitement as her bare, white breasts met his healthy, hirsute chest for the first time.

Soon, they were one, making passionate love on the Canadian Maplewood floor, their hips thrusting together, kinetically attuned, arms, legs and tongues entwined, their bodies crackling like crossed wires as she closed her eyes and gave herself up to the moment. She felt the tension of the past few months – the Criminal Assets Bureau and their endless questions, the trial, the invasive media coverage, trying to decide between the apartment in Bullock Harbour and one on Greystones Main Street, then between Venetian and pull-down blinds – rush from her body as he grazed hungrily in the bountiful pastures of her breasts.

Where is she getting this? It's not roysh.

Somehow she knew he'd be a sensational lover but this was so good it frightened her.

She threw her arms behind her head as his thrusts continued until they were soaked with sweat and not even a seawall could hold back the wave of pleasure that was coming. Soon, the perfect breaker arrived and they rode it together, before collapsing into a sticky embrace and savoured every second of the post-coital peace.

Then they went upstairs and did it again.

JP isn't joking. For one minute there, I thought he was, roysh, but he's not.

He's going, 'Ross, it's one of the requirements of the pilgrimage, that it be done barefoot,' and I'm there, 'You *actually* want me to hand over my Dubes? To this dude?' and I nod at this monk, roysh, who's throwing everyone's rhythms into this, like, cloth sack.

JP doesn't answer, so I end up just doing what he says and then on the coach on the way to the gaff where we're staying, roysh, I turn around to him and I go, 'They'll make a movie one day based on this weekend. Called *Not Without My Docksiders*,' and he can't help but laugh at that.

If I was being honest, roysh, I'd say my expectations of the place weren't high, but it's turned out to be an even bigger dump than it looked from the ferry. I turn around and I go, 'Explain to me again why anyone in their roysh mind would come here,' and JP – he's, like, trying to be patient with me – he goes, 'Many reasons, Ross. Some do it as a means of demonstrating repentance. Some to face the same challenges to their faith that St Patrick reputedly faced. Others simply because they've become complacent in their spiritual lives . . .'

I'm there, 'Just *tell* me this place has a Storbucks,' and he looks at me, roysh, his mouth wide open like a Mountie on Senior Cup day. I'm there, 'I'm focking storving,' and he goes, 'That's the idea, Ross. This is a place of fasting,' and I'm just there going, 'Yeah, whatever floats your boat, Dude.'

I go, 'Here,' and I drop a packet of Revels on his lap and I go, 'Don't let the Mother Superior there catch you,' nodding at this old nun who was giving me big-time filthies for eating that BLT on the boat. And what does he do? Pretty much throws them back in my face, roysh, telling me that the challenge of this pilgrimage is great enough without having his own personal devil subjecting him to temptation twenty-four hours a day, the focking drama queen that he is.

He goes, 'Ross, you *wanted* to come. I mean, why are you

doing it?' and I'm like, 'As in . . .' and he's there, 'As in, this pilgrimage. Why have you come?' and I'm there, 'I'm beginning to ask myself the same question. Okay, granted, I knew there'd be, like, praying and stuff? But I also thought there'd be a bit of crack. Although I should have known better seeing as you were going.'

I shouldn't have said that, but he'll forgive me. I suppose he has to in his line of work.

He goes, 'This isn't Playa del Ingles all over again, Ross. This is a place for prayer and introspection. And frugality. Your problem is you have no willpower,' which there's, like, no way I'm taking. I'm like, '*I've* no willpower?' and he's there, 'No, you don't. I doubt you're capable of surviving for three days without the little . . . *accoutrements* of south Dublin life – your Dubes, your mobile phone . . . Look at you, you're already sweating, wondering where your next cappuccino's coming from,' and I'm there, 'It's actually *lattes* I drink? And for your information, I only asked you was there a Storbucks because Sorcha would want a mug. She has them from, like, twenty different countries.'

He goes, 'You're still in Ireland, Ross,' which I pretty much already knew. I go, 'I *have* willpower, JP. And you're going to eat those words,' and he goes, 'Not while I'm fasting, I won't,' and quick as a flash I go, 'That's blasphemous,' basically turning the joke around on him.

We're in, like, a dorm, roysh, with twenty other people. Focking bunk beds. I'm telling you, heaven better not be like this. The old Malcolm O'Kelly's still all over the shop after the boat trip. I'm, like, right on the verge of spewing my ring as we throw our bags into the dorm, roysh, so I leave JP there, meditating or whatever it is he does these days when he's alone in his room and head out for a walk.

I'm already missing Sorcha, weird as that might sound. I know we're not supposed to have any contact with, like, the outside world here, but I whip out the old Wolfe and dial her number. I'm there, 'Hey, Babes,' and she's like, 'Hey, Ross. I'm shopping. With Mum and Claire. *Oh* my God, we have just seen *the* cutest crib in Mothercare, made out of recyclable cardboard,' and in the background I can hear Claire going, 'It *is* fire retardant, Sorcha.'

I'm there, 'How are you, er, feeling?' and she's like, 'Great, except I'm turning into – *oh my God!* – SUCH a blimp. You know, I could hordly close my jeans this morning? As in my early term ones?' and I go, 'Wow,' and I'm waiting, roysh, for her to ask me how I'm doing, but she doesn't. I just hear, '*Oh my God*, Mum, you are SO not paying for that Moses basket,' and she just hangs up on me, roysh, without even saying goodbye.

I'm getting those cramps in my lower back again, roysh, so I make my way over to this little bench where these two old goys, big-time coffin-dodgers, are rabbiting away to each other. One of them, the one with the flat cap, nods at me as I sit down and I'm like, 'Hey, how the hell are you?'

He turns around to his mate and goes, 'How's the arm, Matt?'

I'm trying to place the accent. Sounds like Wicklow: up and down like a first-year BESS student.

The other goy, Matt, goes, 'The arm's great now. Not a bother on it. Offered it up to Saint Amalburga of Ghent . . .'

His mate's like, 'Oh, *she's* very good, isn't she? Very quick. She looks after arm pain, does she? I thought that was Saint Charles Borromeo . . .' and the goy Matt goes, 'No, *he's* abdominal pain. Ulcers and colic, mostly. And apple orchards, starch-makers and catechists . . .' and the other goy's like, '*Ahhh*, I'm glad he got something. He'd a terrible hard life, hadn't he?'

And even though it's, like, one of the funniest conversations I've ever heard, roysh, I'm actually on the edge of my seat here. I never thought of it before, but there seems to be, like, a saint for everything.

I go, 'They really have all the bases covered, don't they?' and Matt turns around and looks at me, roysh, and it's only then that I cop it. I'm like, 'Are you goys . . . twins?' because they're, like, a ringer for each other. I introduce myself and so do they. It's, like, Matt and Eddie. They seem like nice old goys. I suppose Wicklow's not all bad.

I'm like, 'You two seem to know your shit. Sorcha – as in, well, my wife – she's, like, pregnant at the moment. And I'm having one of these, like, sympathy pregnancies? We're talking cravings, we're talking cramps, we're talking constipation, we're talking mood swings . . . Who looks after that deportment? *If* I wanted to pray to someone.'

Eddie takes off his hat. 'Sympathetic pregnancy . . .' he goes and he's, like, mopping his head with a hankie.

'There isn't one,' Matt goes and Eddie's like, 'No, there isn't. But let me think . . . you'd be better off now saying maybe a few ould prayers to Saint Pancras, patron saint of cramps, a few to Saint Bonaventure, who looks after the oul' bowel disorders, and maybe a few to Saint Ursus of Ravenna – fainting – then maybe offer all your suffering up to Saint Brigid, the patron saint of childorden.'

I'm nodding, going, 'But what about the cravings?' and he looks at Matt, then at me, and goes, 'St Quirinus is the patron saint of obsession. I know a fella swears by him. Or even Benedict of Narsia, the patron saint against temptation . . .'

Matt looks him up and down and goes, 'Where are you sending the chap at all? Halfway round the world? No, no, no,' and then he turns to me and goes '*Your* quickest way would be five "Hail Marys" to Saint Ulric, the patron saint against birth complications — see, you're covered for dizziness and stomach upset there as well — then, for the other stuff, maybe a couple of "Our Fathers" to Saint Ubaldus Baldissini — he's the patron saint of possessed people.'

I'm there, 'Fock, I'd hordly call myself possessed! Although that does sound a lot less hassle than the other way. Okay, Ulric and Ubaldus . . . Cheers, goys,' and I get up, roysh, and head across the road to this little, like, church.

Of course I bump into JP on his way out. I'm there, 'Oh, you're up and about then,' and he's looking at me with a big shit-eating grin. He's like, 'Are you going in to pray, Ross?' and it's like I'm caught in the act. I'm there, 'No, I'm just having a sniff around. Checking it out. Seeing what all the fuss is about. You know, God and stuff?'

And just as I'm about to walk away, roysh, Eddie stands up and at the top of his voice goes, 'Oh and have a word with Saint Fiacre, Ross. He's your man for the haemmorhoids . . .'

Sorcha rings me in tears, roysh, and she tells me that Erika rang her — 'OH MY GOD being SUCH a bitch' — and told her about a friend of her cousin, whose perineum — as in the bit of skin between, well, your vadge and your orse basically — actually tore, roysh, and she's still incontinent, as in, like, three years later. Apparently this bird's, like, twenty-nine and she has to wear a nappy. I don't know what Sorcha expects me to say, roysh, but it probably wasn't what I *did* say, which was, 'Fock me! Makes you think, all the same, doesn't it?'

*

Mmmm.

'I'm thinking of having my coffee black in future.'

Well, I'm not actually. I'm just saying it, roysh, just so the rest of this crowd knows it's not getting to me. Coffee with no milk or sugar. It's like, *what*ever! Build a bridge and get over it.

JP goes, 'Try to keep your voice down, Ross. Some people see breakfast as a time to quietly meditate on the day ahead. They don't necessarily want to hear your voice. And here, eat some toast. This is your only meal of the day, remember,' and I'm there, 'Bit burnt, isn't it? Ah well, all part of the challenge, I suppose. That's what we're here for,' and JP shushes me, roysh – as in, *ssshhh!* – and goes, 'Look, Ross, you're not on "I'm a Celebrity, Get Me Out of Here",' and I see this old couple at the end of our table giving me filthies, roysh, and I'm about to tell them to mind their own focking business when JP, obviously picking up on it, suggests we go for a walk.

So the two of us end up sitting on the shore of the lake, roysh, having probably the best chat I've actually had with him since God got to him. The water is, like, so still, roysh, and we're throwing stones into it, then watching the ripples go on pretty much forever.

He goes, 'How was your bed?' and I'm there, 'Pretty focking uncomfortable actually,' and he sort of, like, laughs to himself and goes, 'Even the sleeping arrangements are penitential. You know, St Patrick is supposed to have lived in a cave here during his missionary work in Ireland. During his time here fasting he's said to have witnessed a vision of hell, thus the name often given to the island – St Patrick's Purgatory . . .'

Then he goes, 'Oisinn told you to come, didn't he?' and there's no point in lying to him, roysh. JP's always had this way of seeing straight into your hort. 'How much did he offer you?' he goes.

I'm like, 'Fifty Ks,' and he sort of, like, nods.

I go, 'Would you believe me, JP, if I said it's not just the money? It's not the money at all,' and he looks at me, roysh, eyes boring into me, and he surprises me by going, 'Yeah, I would,' and he nods and goes, 'Yeah,' again.

I throw another pebble into the water. A good distance as well. And I haven't even been working out.

I go, 'It's what you said to him. *You're no friend of his, he's no friend of yours?* You can't just throw that kind of shit around. Whatever happened to Castlerock Forever? We said we'd always be friends, didn't we? Tell me it was about more than rugby, Dude . . .'

He's like, 'Ross, you respect this . . . change of direction I've taken in life. So does Christian. So does Fionn. But not Oisinn. He's still looking for the angle, the opportunity . . .' and I'm there, 'Can I actually remind you that up until a year ago you were working as an estate agent? Remember those days? Who was it who first claimed that Mullingar was within commutable distance of Dublin?' and he laughs and sort of, like, shakes his head at the memory.

He goes, 'I know. I worshipped Mammon, just like our friend. But I think he's losing sight of what's real and what's right,' and I go, 'He's not the only one,' and I swear to God, roysh, I nearly end up telling him about Fionn holding Marty basically hostage. For some reason he doesn't pick up on it.

He goes, 'He's becoming a slave to it now, the lifestyle,' and I shake my head and go, 'You know he's in New York tonight? Having dinner with Scarlet Johannson,' and JP blows hord through his lips. He's obviously still got some urges in that deportment.

I go, 'Look, what I'm trying to say here is, he'd die for

you, JP. And you know it. How many times did he fight battles for you – for all of us – outside nightclubs, on the rugby field? If you were the best full-back in Leinster schools rugby the year we won the cup, it was only because you had Oisinn protecting you.'

And it's true, roysh. As we used to say, the goy was horder than a blind lezzer's nipples in a fish morket.

I think I'm reaching him. He goes, 'You know, for all the bad press you get from people, Ross, you've got more soul than just about anyone I know . . .' and he lets it hang like that, roysh, and fock it, I can feel myself welling up again here.

I don't think he cops it though.

He throws a flat stone and it skids across the surface of the lake seven, eight, nine, ten times until it's too far away to count anymore. He was always good at that, even when we were kids, the little focker.

He goes, 'How's Sorcha doing?' and I'm there, 'Good. Should be having the, er, ultrasound in the next couple of weeks. She thought she felt a kick the other night. It was just wind. A dodgy aubergine.'

He's like, 'What about *you*, Ross? I sense you're not coping quite as well as she is,' and I don't say anything for ages, roysh, and when I do I can hordly get the words out of my mouth because I'm crying. I'm there, 'Look at me! Crying like a focking bird! Seriously, I'm pretty much on the verge of tears all the time and I don't even know why. I'm getting these pains. Then these cravings. It's one of those sympathetic . . .'

He nods and goes, 'It's called couvade syndrome, Ross. I was reading about it on the internet,' and I look at him, roysh, as if to say, Why, for fock's sake? He goes, 'I was talking to Christian. Said he went for a pizza with you. Tuna and blackcurrant jam, I believe,' and I dry the tears from my face. I go, 'Stop, you're making me hungry,' and I laugh.

He puts his orm around my shoulder – but not in a funny way. He's there, 'Apparently, it affects a lot of fathers. They don't know the reasons. Could be just identification with the pregnant woman. Could be jealousy, a feeling of being frozen out of things,' and I'm thinking, now *that* I recognise. He's like, 'Or it could be simple anxiety, about what kind of father you're going to make to this child . . .'

I'm there, 'There's all sorts of shit going on in my head these days. You know my old dear's writing chick-lit now?' But he doesn't seem to see anything wrong with it, roysh, just goes, 'Good for her. We're supposed to lead the world in that now. They're saying it's the new Eurovision,' and I'm like, 'But this is chick-lit with, like, *actual* riding in it? I mean, no one's going to focking publish it, obviously. But it's, like, first that focking yummy-mummy calendar, now this. It's like she's trying to destroy my rep or some shit.'

He laughs. Then he's suddenly serious. He goes, 'Have you sins to tell, Ross?'

It's still hord to come to terms with hearing him say shit like that. A year ago it was all 'brain-storm', 'vertical morket', and 'knowledge base'. Now it's, 'Have you sins to tell?'

I go, 'You know me, I've always got sins to tell,' but he doesn't ask me what they are, roysh, he just goes, 'You're crippled with anxiety. That's how it seems to me. Why don't you have your confession heard while you're here? Unburden yourself of whatever it is before you leave the island.'

I'm there, 'It's weird. I mean, I wouldn't usually have a conscience about most shit . . .' and he goes, 'Perhaps it's being in this holy place. Perhaps God's grace is touching you. Will you think about it, Ross? Your confession?' and

I'm like, 'Yeah,' and he's there, 'And I'll think about Oisinn . . .'

I end up praying, roysh, but not to Ulric or the other dude. I decided, whatever – it's like Oisinn said – might as well go to the boss man. So I just go, 'Dear Father, please let me be basically a good father . . . er, like you are,' and then I say an 'Our Father', or what I can remember of it.

I'm wide awake. I don't know what time it is. I check my mobile. It's, like, four in the morning. I've gone, like, twenty-four hours eating fock-all except burnt toast and I'm so hungry at this stage I'd eat the focking orse off a roadkill badger.

I swing the old legs over the side of the top bunk and get out using the ladder, being careful not to wake JP. I tiptoe out of the dorm and down this long, like, corridor and into the kitchen. It's, like, pitch dork, but I find the fridge handle and pull it open and suddenly there's light. But no food. Unless you count Findus Crispy Pancakes – minced beef flavour – as food, which I usually wouldn't, roysh, but at this moment in time I'd eat my own leg.

I shut the door and suddenly I hear this voice behind me, roysh, and I end up nearly crapping myself, roysh – except there's nothing in my stomach. It's like, 'Well, did you get sorted in the end?'

I whip around and who is it only Matt and Eddie, sitting at the table, in the dork. I'm like, 'Sorted? Er . . .' Matt – or it might be Eddie – goes, 'Obviously not – if you're going to eat those,' and he sort of, like, nods at the packet in my hand. I'm there, 'No, I was actually just . . . em . . . looking at them. Apparently a lot of people on low incomes actually eat these as, like, dinner. Hord and all as that is to believe, with the Celtic Tiger and everything . . .'

Matt – yeah, Eddie's the slightly simple one – goes, 'Is the fasting getting to you?' and I'm like, 'No, actually. Coping pretty well with it,' and out of the blue, roysh, Eddie goes, 'I'd chew the balls off a low-flying duck, me,' which sort of, like, takes me by surprise.

I sit down.

I'm there, 'You goys can't sleep either?' and Matt goes, 'No, we decided to go a night without sleep and offer it up to all the people in the world who's suffering from angina. We do this at least once a week,' and Eddie's there, 'It's not always angina, though. Last week it was wheat intolerance,' and what can I say but, 'All good causes, goys.'

So I get chatting to the two boys, and they're cool, roysh, madder than a pig eating shit, but still sound. To cut a long story short, roysh, they end up telling me their whole life story. Turns out they are from Wicklow and the amazing thing is, roysh, even though they're twins, they didn't talk to each other for, like, forty focking years. Get this, roysh, they fell out over – of all things – a bird when they were both, like, twenty-four, or twenty-five, or something. Eddie was engaged to this bird, roysh, but he was, like, in the ormy and he ended up getting sent to, like, the Congo, wherever that is.

'It was the very first, believe it or not, peacekeeping mission Ireland was involved in after joining the UN,' he goes, though that's not really relevant to the story. While he was away, roysh, Matt was dipping the wick in his brother's ink.

There was, like, murder over it apparently. And that was it, roysh. They lived in the same town, drank in the same battle cruiser and didn't say boo to each other until the summer of 2002, when that little Robbie Keane man scored in the last minute against Germany and – this is their story now – they were both touched by the Holy Spirit, though I suspect the real spirit involved was something else.

Now they're basically, like inseparable. It's an amazing story, roysh, even if it is a bit long.

'I used to go to Mass every day of me life,' Eddie goes, 'and I realised I was wasting me time as long as I refused to forgive. It only takes a small man to carry a grudge.'

And I think about those words, roysh, and how they apply to the whole JP and Oisinn situation and I'm there, 'Say that again. It only takes . . .' and he goes, 'It only takes a small man to carry a grudge,' and I end up ripping the flap off the Findus Crispy Pancakes packet and, like, writing it down.

Ronan rings me at half-eight in the morning – in other words the middle of the focking day over here. I've got a couple of hours of prayers banked already. He goes, 'Rosser, is that a safe line you're on?' and I'm like, 'Ronan, it's my *mobile*. It's the same number you always ring me on. And that's the same question you always ask. And you never have anything to say that anyone would ever want to eavesdrop on . . .'

He thinks about this for about ten seconds, roysh, then goes, 'We'll have to come up with some kind of code, I think . . . Anyways, do you have any Irish, do you?' and I'm like, 'No, but I've got a Leinster Schools Senior Cup winner's medal,' and he's there, 'Yeah, I forget you were thick in school. What about yer man with the glasses?'

I'm like, 'Fionn? Yeah. Irish and about twenty other

languages that are no focking use to him. What a waste of time. Why do you need someone who speaks Irish?' and he goes, 'Ah, Nudger's case is coming up. He got his book of evidence and some of it's in Irish. Thinks Plod might be pulling a fast one. Anyways, stay lucky . . .' and he hangs up.

I can't say when the thought first hit me. Maybe it was always there. Buried.

We were doing the Stations this morning – basically praying at these beds dedicated to various saints, we're talking Brigid, we're talking Patrick, we're talking Davog, we're talking that *whole* crowd – when, mad as it sounds, I realised I was the Messiah.

I don't want to come across as, like, big-headed here, roysh, but I'd always felt like I was a bit, I don't know . . . *special?* Yeah, there was the whole rugby thing. Six points down in injury time, all the goys had to do was give me the ball and I'd look after the miracles. And for as long as I can remember, I've had all these followers – we're talking men *and* women – who believed I *was* an actual God. So I suppose I've always known it on some, I don't know, unconscious level.

JP wasn't ready to hear it, though. At first I put it down to, like, jealousy. He's given the Church – what? – a year of his life and he's still four or five away from getting his collar. Then it turns out that one of his best mates is not only one of the best rugby players Ireland has ever produced but also the Son of God. Of course he's not going to be a happy camper.

He's like, '*What?*' like it's the most ridiculous thing he's ever heard.

Sister Carlotta's giving it, 'Holy Mary, Mother of God,

pray for us sinners, now and at the hour of our death . . .'

I'm there, 'I know you think I'm yanking your chain, but I *am* actually Him,' and he's like, 'As in the Second Coming of Our Lord?' and I'm there, 'Pretty much, yeah,' and he's like, 'And when did this . . . *revelation* happen? This morning, when you were looking for somewhere to watch your *Carmen Electra Aerobic Striptease* DVD?' and I'm there, 'I know it sounds far-fetched, JP, but I think I've always known it,' and he goes, 'Ross, I'm trying to pray here.'

It's, like, six o'clock in the morning, roysh, and we're coming to the end – I hope – of an all-night vigil of prayer, with Father Dennehy and Sister Carlotta, leading us through the last of the 'Hail Marys' and the 'Glory Bes' and the whatever-you're-having-yourselves. That's when it hits me hordest. It's like, *oh my God*, it's me. *I'm* the Saviour they're always banging on about, but I still don't know what to do about it. Do I just stort preaching? Or do I need to get on the same course as JP? And how many points is it, for that matter?

JP's going, 'Give us this day our daily bread, and forgive us our trespasses . . .' and I'm like, 'How old was your goy when He storted?' and JP just, like, shuts his eyes and shakes his head. Then he goes, 'You mean Jesus Christ?' and I'm there, 'Yeah, when did He stort preaching?' and he goes, 'After he was baptised by John the Baptist. They think he was thirty,' and I'm like, 'Ha! I'm only, like, twenty-four. Means I've got a good headstort on him.'

JP goes, 'Ross, you're having a delusional episode, prob-ably brought on by storvation and sleep deprivation. It's not uncommon . . .' and I'm like, 'JP, get *over* yourself, will you? I don't know why *I've* been given these special powers either, but it's a fact now. And you'd better stay on the roysh side of me.' He goes, 'Or what, Ross? You'll smite me down?

Send a plague of locusts?' and I just go, 'Yeah, *whatever*, Dude.'

He gets up off his knees and sits down. The vigil's over. He goes, 'I mean, you heard what Sister Carlotta said. If anyone is struggling with the fasting aspect, they should tell her. She can give you soup if you're feeling weak,' and I sit down then and go, 'I'm not feeling weak, JP. I'm feeling whatever the opposite of weak is – strong, I suppose. Hey, I was thinking, remember that time in the Canaries when I nearly drowned in the pool? I always knew there had to be a reason why I was saved,' and JP's there, 'You were saved because we pulled you out,' and I'm like, 'Oh, yeah, *very* convenient.'

He stands up and goes, 'Okay, loath as I am to put the Lord my God to the test, I'd like to see some proof, please. Any chance you might squeeze a miracle into this busy schedule of preaching you've got planned?' I'm there, 'Yeah, cool by me. What do you want to see?' and he's like, 'Well, you clearly have a special affinity with water . . .' and I go, 'You want me to walk across the lake, don't you? Kool and the Gang,' and I get up, roysh, and he follows me out of the church, roysh, and across the road to this little pier, where I whip off my Ralph and stort unbuttoning my chinos.

JP goes, 'Why don't you leave them on, Ross. I mean, you're not going to get wet, are you?' and I'm there, 'Oh, yeah,' and I button up my chinos again. He's going, 'Go on, demonstrate your supreme power over creation, as in Mark 6:45,' and I'm thinking, Yeah, yeah, thinks he's *it* just because he knows all the focking page numbers – wait'll he gets a load of *this*.

I'm standing there, roysh, psyching myself up for it and it's funny because I actually nearly end up taking five steps backwards and four to the left, like it's the old days and I'm taking a kick, but I end up just going for it. I stort walking. Pretty fast. It's, like, twenty steps to the end of the pier.

Ten steps.

Five steps.

I'm there.

I keep on walking.

And of course I'm like that coyote out of the focking 'Roadrunner'. I stop in mid-air for, like, ten seconds.

Then I plunge to the bottom of the lake.

'What in God's good name was going through your mind?' Father Dennehy's going and I'm there, 'It was the hunger, I suppose. I'd be pretty used to my sleep as well. I'm never actually up before midday. I suppose my mind was, like, playing tricks on me,' and he goes, 'Oh, I see – another one who thought he was the Messiah,' like it happens everyday.

Sister Carlotta – who's, like, a totally cool person – is going, 'Well, it's fortunate I had this soup on. Otherwise I think you'd have frozen to death, the pair of you,' and I look over at JP, who has a blanket wrapped around him and he's wolfing back the soup as well, trying to get the heat back into his body. I'm like, 'Thanks, Dude,' as in for saving my life, and he gives me this big smile and a nod in this real, I suppose you'd have to say, priestly way.

It would be an exaggeration to say that my whole life, like, flashed before me at the bottom of that lake – the last-minute penalty I missed against Michael's to cost us the cup in 1998, the two tries I scored against Newbridge to win it the following year, the time I sold the great Dricster himself a dummy in Stradbrook, the time I wiped Dorce's eye by throwing the lips on some bird he'd spent half the night chatting up in, like, Reynords.

Father Dennehy tops up my mug. He goes, 'Is there something troubling you, Ross?' He's from Northern Ireland. You know the way *they* speak. I'm there, 'Troubling me? As in . . .' and he goes, 'Well, from the moment I set eyes on you yesterday, I thought to myself, now there's a man burdened by a guilty secret,' and I'm there looking at him, then at JP, then at him again and I'm thinking, How do they know this shit? Do they teach them, like, mind reading?

I'm giving JP the big-time daggers, as if to say, Did you focking tell him? Then Father Dennehy goes, 'Shall I hear your confession?' and I look at JP, roysh, and he's, like, nodding at me, so I go, 'Er, I suppose so,' and he brings me into the next room, where there's two big brown leather chairs and we take one each.

I go, 'I think it's only fair to warn you, Father, you could be here for six hours with the shit there is on *me*. I hope the Church pays you good OT,' and he laughs. Then he goes, 'Well, let's just have the big charges against you. Then we can ask for your other offences to be taken into account when it comes to sentencing. Now, do you remember the words?' and I go, 'Bless me Father for I have sinned, it's been . . . I don't know how long since my last Confession. But we're basically talking years.'

He's there, 'So, what are they then? These . . . *sins* that are encumbering you?' And I'm like, 'Well, a lot of casual . . . infidelity, I suppose you'd have to call it. Just playing Jack the Lad. Cheating on Sorcha, who's, like, my wife. Then I suppose kidnapping? And then, well, I wouldn't exactly describe myself as a regular Mass-goer . . . if that's a sin.'

I watch his eyes go wide like saucers. I'm thinking, This dude must have heard a serious amount of bad shit in confession down through the years. It must say something that mine has shocked him. He goes, 'Kidnapping, did you say?' and I'm there, 'Well, yeah, I had a feeling that was the one you were going to focus on. That's why I tried to slip it in there on the sly,' and he goes, 'Kidnapping?' and I'm there, 'Okay, okay, don't go on about it.'

He's like, 'Who did you kidnap?' and I'm there, 'Well, it wasn't *actually* me who did it. It was these, like, friends of mine? A goy broke into our . . . gaff, let's just say. They tied him to a chair and . . . well, they just haven't got around to calling the Feds yet,' and he goes, 'And he's still there? Tied to the chair?' and I'm like, 'Yes! Look, what is this, Twenty Questions?'

He goes, 'What are they doing to him?' and I'm like, 'One of the goys – I don't want to mention names but it's, like, Fionn – he's doing experiments on him. It's for his Masters – he's in Trinity. I don't know if I mentioned that the goy involved is a skobie – not sure that makes any difference . . .'

He goes, 'Ross, I could offer you absolution, but you know what you have to do first. You know the difference between right and wrong, don't you?' and I go, 'A lot of the time, yeah. The funny thing is, roysh, this goy – the skobie – it turns out he's, like, totally sound. And we're talking totally here?'

He makes the sign of the cross in front of me and goes, 'I'm not giving you absolution. I'm giving you my blessing, in the hope that you'll go and do the right thing. *Then* ask for the Lord's forgiveness.'

We're in my cor – as in the BMW Z4 – and we're on the motorway, with the wind in our hair, going home, and I'm showing JP what it can do. I'm doing, like, a hundred and fifty Ks and the goy is seriously impressed. He was always a wheels man, see.

He goes, 'Ross, don't think I'm prying or anything, but Father Dennehy's face, when he left the Confessional . . .' and I'm there, 'Well, you knew I was no saint,' and then I ease off the gas, roysh, because some goy in a Primera coming the opposite way flashed his lights at me, meaning there's probably, like, Feds with speed guns up ahead.

I go, 'I'm sorting it out, JP. The thing I did wrong, I'm going to put it roysh,' and he looks at me, roysh, and goes, 'Good,' but obviously he hasn't a bog what I'm on about.

'Even at your lowest ebb, there's always Saint Jude – the patron saint of lost causes.'

It's Matt. Wicklow's well out of our way, and in normal circumstances I'd say let them take the focking bus, but I'm in cracking form this morning, so I offered.

I go, 'Who would win in a fight between Saint Jude and Saint . . . Patrick,' and for a second I'm worried that someone in the cor is going to tell me it's blasphemous, but then, roysh, all of a sudden Eddie goes, 'Patrick. No doubt about that. Wouldn't even be close,' and out of the corner of my eye, roysh, I can see JP laughing behind his hand, which is good to see.

When we hit Dublin I drop him at his old pair's gaff. As he's getting out of the cor, I go, 'Dude, weird as this sounds, I had a great weekend. A lot of shit's clearer,' and he's there, 'I'm glad,' and I'm like, 'Listen, you won't . . .' and he goes, 'Tell the goys you tried to walk on water? Course I won't. What goes on at sea stays at sea,' and I'm there, 'Lambay Rules, huh?' and I'm suddenly hit with this, like, wave of nostalgia for school and shit.

I go, 'And maybe think some more about patching things up with Oisinn. Remember, it only takes a small man to carry a grudge . . .' I do what I have to admit is a pretty amazing wheelspin, then I'm out of there, watching JP in the old rear-view and he's, like, rooted to the spot, obviously wondering where I got that little nugget from as I disappear into the distance.

When I walk through the door, roysh, it's like I've never been away. There's no, *Welcome home.* No, *Oh my God, I SO missed you.* I'm like, 'Hey, Sorcha,' and from inside the kitchen I hear her go, 'Be careful opening this door, Ross,' so I push it open really slowly and stick my head around it and she's got, like, the table and chairs shoved over against the wall, roysh, and what looks very much to me like a bouncy castle – minus the air – laid out on the floor of the dining area.

I'm there, 'I thought you said we *weren't* having a house-warming?' and she looks at me like I've just shat a lemon, then goes, 'It's a birthing pool, Ross. I've decided to have a water birth,' and as I'm, like, nodding my head, wondering how to react, she goes, 'The contractions are supposed to be – *oh my God!* – SO less painful.'

The only thing I can think of to say is, 'Will the baby not drown?' and she's like, '*Oh* my God, Ross, do you know even the *first* thing about labour?' and what I *should* say is, No, because ever since I spewed my ring at that ante-natal class you've totally frozen me out of, like, everything, but what I *actually* say is, 'No.'

She throws her eyes up to heaven and goes, 'A baby doesn't drown during a water birth because the baby is already in water in the womb. It's going from water *into* water. The lungs are still closed. No water can get in. It's only when she's brought to the surface and her face hits the air that she takes her first breath and her life begins,' but bear in mind, roysh, that she's, like, shouting this at me.

I turn around and go to leave and she goes, 'Ross, I'm

sorry,' and I turn back and she stops whatever it is she's doing with the birthing pool, stands up and gives me a hug. She's like, 'Oh *my God*, I give you SUCH a hord time, sometimes. I'm sorry,' and I'm there, 'Hey, it's cool,' and she goes, 'You can't be expected to know everything. I just forget sometimes that you played rugby at school . . .'

Then she pulls away from me, turns back to the pool and goes, 'It'll be SO less painful this way. *Oh* my God, Erika SO freaked me out with all that talk about my perineum. The water softens the tissue and makes it more stretchy and less likely to tear,' and I'm in, like, nodding overdrive.

She goes, 'I was reading all about it, Ross, in one of my magazines. You wouldn't *believe* the number of psychological problems that can be traced back to the trauma of actually being born. Our baby is going to have – *oh my God!* – SUCH an easy entry into this world.'

Then she takes me totally by surprise, roysh, by wrapping her orms around my waist and going, 'Hey . . . I had *two* orgasms last night,' and I'm thinking, They better be focking cocktails she's talking about. She's like, 'Two orgasms, Ross, *in my sleep*. I am having SUCH x-rated dreams,' and I'm tempted to go, Must be that focking porn my old dear's writing, but I don't.

She's like, 'It's all the oestrogen and progesterone, it makes you SO sensitive . . . *down there*. And you know what it says in one of my books, that orgasms bring about contractions in the uterus, which actually comfort the baby . . .'

I go, 'Great, so everyone's happy . . . except me,' and she kisses me and goes, 'Oh, don't be silly, Ross.'

4. Un Jour Dans Pigalle

I'm driving down Baggot Street, roysh, in the middle of the afternoon, when who do I see sitting on the wall outside the Bank of Ireland, only Ronan. So I pull up, roysh, which is when I notice that he's, like, staring at the front door and he's got, like, a stopwatch in one hand and, of all things, a pen in the other, which he's using to write shit down in this, like, leather-bound diary. I call his name and I swear to God, roysh, the kid jumps six focking feet in the air. He turns around with his hand over his hort and goes, 'Fook me, Rosser. I thought you were Plod.'

He walks up to the window and goes, 'What's the story?' and I'm there, 'I was about to ask you the same thing. What are you doing?' and he's like, 'Looking after me pension plan,' and he opens the door and gets in. He spends a good five minutes looking around the cor, checking it out and I'm like, 'Everything okay, Ro?' and he goes, 'I need a good set of wheels for this job. Don't suppose you fancy leaving it outside your gaff one night, unlocked and with the keys in the ignition?' and I'm like, 'Why aren't you at school?'

He goes, 'Ah, I decided to knock off early. Look, they know the SP. They don't ask me nothing. Means they don't have to tell lies when the jollies come round asking questions. Here, any chance of a lift home, is there?'

I'm like, 'Can we just, like, dispense with the gangster talk for a minute? I'm serious. Why aren't you in school?' and he puts his diary and his stopwatch into his schoolbag and goes, 'We're on a careers day,' and I'm like, 'A careers day?'

as I turn the key and stort her up. I'm like, 'Ronan, you're eight,' and he goes, 'Sure most of the fooken Conors and Tiernans in my class already know what they're looking for in the Leaving. How fooked up is that? They've no childhood, these kids,' and it makes me laugh out loud, hearing him say that.

I'm there, 'So what does this careers day involve, then?' and he goes, 'Jaysus, Rosser, you ask more questions than the filth, you do. Look, we all had to choose a job we might want to do when we leave school. Could be a teacher. Could be a train driver. And then you're sent out on yisser work experience.'

I'm like, 'And Father Fehily knows yours involves casing the Bank of Ireland on Baggot Street?' He storts going through my CDs, roysh, deciding which ones are, like, worth stealing. He's there, 'Fehily knows what I am, Rosser. And he knows where I'm headed,' and I'm like, 'Into a life of crime – he's happy about that, is he?' and he goes, 'I'm not going to be any more of a criminal than the kids who'll end up as solicitors and accountants, know what I mean?' and I'm thinking of Hennessy, roysh, and I can't exactly argue with him.

He goes, 'Jaysus, Rosser, you've some fooken bent CDs here. Who the fook is Katie Melua?' and I'm like, 'It's Sorcha's,' and he's there, 'Better be. Your sexuality is already open to debate, if some of the graffiti I'm reading around the school is anything to go by. By the way, you couldn't lend me a monkey, could you?' and I'm like, 'That depends what a monkey *is*?'

He's there, 'It's five hundrit notes,' and I'm like, 'Five hundred notes? What do you need five hundred notes for?' and he goes, 'It's just this school trip to France, Rosser. It's in two weeks. *Gay Paris*. Be right up your street, wha'?

Anyway, I need a few bob spending money. You know how it is,' and he makes, like, a drinking and then a smoking gesture.

I pull up outside his gaff, whip out a wad of notes and peel off ten fifties and give them to him. Then I peel off, like, four more and give them to him as well. I'm like, 'Here, if it stops you pulling off that bank job . . .'

And he goes, 'Sound man, Rosser.'

I end up crashing and burning with this bird, roysh, and it's a record for me because I don't actually manage to get a single word out. We're in SamSara, roysh, and we're at the bor – we're talking me, One F and Ryle Nugent – and One F turns around to me and goes, 'Kate Groombridge lookalike – six-hundred hours,' and I turn around, roysh, and he's spot-on. I go to open my mouth and the bird goes, 'You should be at home with your wife.'

I can hear Christian's voice from the bottom of the stairs. He's going, 'So Jacen and Jaina Solo – they're, like, Han and Leia's kids, remember – they set off in search of Legger Noghrala, the captain of the Retsniel Kcor, a Thyferran freight ship capable of making the jump into hyperspace. So, along the way, they team up with Lar-Lar Mojo . . .' and then I hear Marty going, 'Lar-Lar Mojo? Hang on, he's not like yer udder fella, is he, Jar-Jar Binks?' and Christian, sounding pretty offended, goes, 'He's a Gungan, yeah.'

I stop and listen at the door. Marty's like, 'See, yer problem dare is, most people fooken hated Jar-Jar, reet? He put people off dat whole foorst filum. Would you not be better off puttin' in an oul' Ewok? Kids love dem,' and Christian's there, 'An Ewok? Hey, you're right. Princess Kneesaa – she was Chief Chirpa's daughter. I mean, she's only ever been conceived of in cartoon form before, but . . . Marty, you're a genius,' and suddenly, roysh, he comes chorging out of the office, not even noticing me standing outside the door, and pegs it downstairs to the bor, where, I noticed earlier, he has his laptop set up.

I go into the office. Marty goes, 'Ah, story, Ross? Christian's after been showin' me his filum idea,' and I'm there, 'Don't worry, Marty, I'm going to get you out of here,' and I stort undoing the ropes around his wrists.

So totally out of the blue, roysh, Marty storts going, '*Don't!* Stop! Stop, will ye!' and I do, roysh, and I go, 'I'm trying to set you free, for fock's sake,' but Marty goes, 'Stall the ball, will ye? Sit down dare for a minute,' and he nods at the chair on the other side of the desk.

I sit down.

He goes, 'Did I ask ye to rescue me, did I?' and I'm like, 'Well, no, but . . .' and he's there, 'But nuttin'. I'm after squarin' de whole ting wi' Fionn.'

I'm not *actually* getting this? He can tell by my boat.

He's there, 'Look, when I broke in here, yous could have called de cops, reet?' and I'm like, 'Roysh,' and he goes, 'Reet, I was only after gettin' out, a year into a tree-year sentence, apposed to keep me nose clean. So if yous had called de cops, I was back insoyid, for anudder two year . . .'

I'm there, 'But if I let you go now, the Feds are never going to know . . .'

He goes, 'Will ye stall it for a minute. Fionn, reet, he's doin' all dees experiments on me, as ye know. Mad interestin' stuff, it is. Jamaica and all dat. Anyway, reet, he's gettin' a grant from somewayer – de EU, I tink – towards hees woork. Twenty tousind. And he's givin' it to *me* . . .'

I'm there, 'Twenty focking grandingtons. No wonder you don't want to go,' and he's like, 'I know what soyid me bread's buttered, man. Two year in de Joy, or a month hee-er, eatin' great food, listenin' to good music and watchin' de horses . . .'

I turn around and see he's been watching the racing on the plasma widescreen opposite my desk. He goes, 'And I leave hee-er after four months wi' twenty grand in me sky-rocket . . .'

The Last King of Scotland won the 3.40 at Haydock. It's Kieran Fallon. Ronan will have had a few squids on him. He loves Fallon, as he calls him.

Marty goes, 'And yiz are a good oul' bunch. Better dan de screws in de Joy. Except dat Oisinn. I'll fooken boorst him when I get out of hee-er. But Fionn's a good lad. Knows hees stuff. And dat Christian, he's from anudder fooken planet, so he is . . .'

I laugh.

He goes, 'How are ye feelin'? Still sick?' and I nod. He goes, 'I'm tryin' to tink what it was de brudder used to swear by – tamatto juice and sumtin else . . .'

I'm like, 'JP – you haven't met him, he's the priest goy – he thinks it's all, like, in my head? Says it's probably anxiety, worrying about what kind of father I'm going to make . . . I met Ronan outside the Bank of Ireland today. You know, he was actually casing the place . . .'

Marty doesn't laugh, roysh, just goes, 'Which Bank of Oyerlind?' and I'm like, 'Baggot Street,' and he just, like, shakes his head and goes, 'The kid's dreamin'?'

Claire has the *actual* balls to ring me the other night, roysh, and go, 'Ross, I'm not sure you're being supportive enough of Sorcha with regard to this baby,' and of course when I hear that, roysh, I'm focking bulling.

I'm like, 'Who the *fock* do you think you are?' and she goes, 'I'm *actually* Sorcha's birth partner. And it's one of my responsibilities to look for signs of tension in her and remind her to relax,' and I'm like, 'She's just come back from Brook Lodge – who the fock do you think paid for that?'

She goes, 'This isn't a *money* issue, Ross. I'm just not sure you're being positive or encouraging enough with her,' and of course I end up throwing a total conniption fit then. I'm like, 'Don't you *ever* focking ring me again! This baby has nothing to do with you! It's mine and Sorcha's!' and she's there, 'Unfortunately for you, Sorcha has *asked* me to be involved. Even during her labour,' and I'm there, 'You are so NOT going to be in the room when the baby's born. Now go and play the focking slots!' and I slam the phone down.

And that's when I notice, roysh, that I'm crying again and – gay and all as it is – it takes me a good hour to actually stop.

She stood in front of the nineteenth-century giltwood mirror, catching her reflection from different angles in the dim light of the room. She had a cool, lascivious sense of herself this morning. Where once she saw small, apologetic boobs and a rapidly burgeoning paunch – and quietly cursed herself for eating that second slice of strawberry meringue roulade – now she saw the robust curves that spoke of a healthy forty-year-old woman in her voluptuous prime.

She smiled a secret smile.

Lovell was still sleeping. They'd been up all night, making fantastic love until the first light of dawn fingered the red, linen curtains.

The night had been a rollercoaster ride, not a cheap, three-euro trip either, the kind one would expect to get in Funderland – which is an abomination, she mused, an eyesore that should be moved to the northside, where it's more appropriate – but the big one, a double-double dipper, full of neck-breaking shunts, loop-the-loops and breathless highs and lows.

She couldn't remember how many times she'd exploded in orgasmic ecstasy.

Who wants to know their old dear has all this sick shit in her head.

She slipped on the pale pink dress that she bought in Sorcha's in the Powerscourt Townhouse Centre the day before, the one *he'd* peeled off her with such forceful manliness she wondered whether she'd have to bring it back to the exclusive fashion boutique the following day, to ask the friendly and helpful staff about their returns policy.

Beside it Sorcha's written, 'Would it be possible to mention the shop's exclusive Chloe and Love Kylie lines?'

Lovell stirred in the bed. 'Honey,' he said, in a half-whisper. 'Is that you?'

'Go back to sleep,' she said softly. 'I have to go out. There's something I must do . . .'

Lillie's is hopping for a Thursday night. We've got that Kian Egan. And Jason O'Callaghan. And Rosanna Davison. Oh and two League of Ireland footballers, though once they were discovered they were obviously focked out.

*

I'm actually in the process of dropping the shopping when the old Wolfe goes, roysh, and what with Sorcha being out with Claire, checking out another class – they're thinking of having the baby by homeopathy now, however that's done – I just let the focking thing ring out. Ten seconds later, of course, my mobile goes off and it's, like, Number Withheld, but I answer it anyway and there's, like, no mistaking the voice.

It's like, 'Hello, my child,' and I go, 'Father Fehily, how the hell are you?' and he's there, 'Oh as well as can be expected of these eighty-five-year-old bones. Although Methuselah lived until he was 969 years old,' and I'm like, 'Er, I don't think he was still teaching at the school when I storted,' and he sort of, like, laughs to himself and goes, 'I'm referring to the Book of Genesis. Methuselah – son of Enoch, father of Lamech, grandfather of Noah . . . if you believe that sort of thing. Did I disturb you? Were you at prayer?'

At *prayer*? He's focking priceless, this goy.

I'm there, 'Er, you could say that. So what can I *do you* for? Hey, if it's about coming back to coach the S again, I'm basically snowed under at the moment, with the nightclub and shit?' and he goes, 'No, listen to me. I'm in Frankreich. *Paris*, to be precise. It's stirring something in me – I've no remorse about saying it. You know, the last time I was on the Champs-Élysées, I stood cheering while they unfurled a banner that covered the entire Arc de Triomphe. *Deutschland siegt auf allen Fronten*, it said. *Allen Fronten! Allen Fronten!*' and I'm there, 'Hey, calm down, Father. Just, like, chillax the kacks for a sec . . .'

He goes, 'Oh, I'm sorry. It's just being here, it's stirring up the sediment of old reminiscence, of a glorious age, when a young man wanted for nothing, save for a bit of *lebensraum* and a solid pair of jackboots as a redoubt against the treasonous damp of the Rhineland . . .'

I'm wondering would it be rude to actually flush this thing.

He goes, 'I travelled here with the pupils of Castlerock Junior School. I admit, as much to indulge that sentimental side of my nature as to supervise. Eighty-four boys we brought here with us. Eighty-three we're taking home in the morning . . .'

A bad feeling suddenly comes over me and it has fock-all to do with the eight pints I tucked away in the M1 last night. I'm like, 'Wait a sec, what are saying?' and he goes, 'Young Ronan. He's gone, Ross,' and I'm there, 'Gone? What do you mean, *gone*?' and he's like, 'Said he had – how did he put it? – *a bit of business*. Might have also mentioned *fish to fry*. Tapped the side of his nose, like he does. Then he was gone. Into the night.'

I can't *actually* believe this. I'm there, 'And you didn't, like, stop him?' and he goes, 'Stop him? Anyone who's ever seen him in full flight on the rugby field would know he's like a Panzer cutting its way through the Ardennes. You're being patently ridiculous.'

I'm there, 'Ridiculous? *I'm* being . . . He's eight years of age. You've got to find him,' and he goes, 'That's where *you* come in, my child.' I'm like, '*Me?* You're yanking my chain, roysh?' and he's there, 'There's only three members of staff on the trip. Ms Milne, well, she's eight months' pregnant and Mrs Gilmore's mother is about to fall off the perch any day now – the liver, by all accounts.'

I'm there, 'And what about you? *You* lost him, Dude. You should find him,' and he lowers his voice, roysh, to a basic whisper and goes, 'I'll let you into a little secret, child. You see, strictly speaking, I should never have set foot in this country again. And if certain *parties* discovered I was here, well, I might end up facing charges for war crimes. Trumped up, naturally.'

I'm there, 'War crimes? What are you bullshitting on about?' and he goes, 'I know that for six years – as long as the War itself, from the day the Wehrmacht crossed the Polish frontier to the day the Americans obliterated Nagasaki – Mr Crabtree attempted to teach you history and with no noticeable success, so I'm not going to attempt it now. Time is short.'

I'm there, 'Hey, you're out of your bin if you think I'm dropping everything to go to France to find a kid who *you* actually lost,' but he goes, 'I've booked you into first class on the 10.00 am flight tomorrow from Dublin to – loath as I am to say the words – Charles de Gaulle . . .'

I'm like, 'Charles de Gaulle? I thought I was going to Paris,' and he sort of, like, sighs and goes, 'You know, I think I'm more fearful for you than I am for Ronan.'

I'm in the country an hour-and-a-half – the time it takes four French baggage handlers to take my bag off the plane and put it on the focking carousel – and I end up getting stung by some big, thick-necked Jo Maxi driver who obviously knows a soft touch when he sees one.

The airport's a focking tip and I'm, like, totally convinced I'll never breathe clean air again when eventually I manage to find the exit – a revolving door that throws me into the open orms of this dude, roysh, who's sitting on the bonnet of a brand new Quarter to Eight, looking happy bo bappy with himself.

'You want transport?' he goes, except the way *they* say it, it's more like, 'Yuwan twans-poor?' and I'm like, 'Roger that,' and I hand him the address of the hotel that Fehily booked me into, roysh – the George V, just off the old Champs-Élysées – and when the goy puts an actual cap on, before he even storts the engine, roysh, I realise there's something NQR about this scene. Turns out the dude's a focking limo driver, not a taxi driver, and if you're wondering what the difference is, it's about a hundred bills in our language.

Doesn't matter, roysh, I'll make sure and get the sheets back off Fehily, who is SO not going to want this story getting out.

Fair focks to him, though, the hotel's a decent enough pile, with a pool and everything, and I end up in a massive room with, like, a balcony and shit?

I get into the scratcher and stort, like, flicking through the big leather-bound book with, like, INFORMATION across the front of it. I hit the button for room service and order two portions of Beluga caviar, a bowl of lobster bisque with croutons, a warm goat's cheese salad, the pan-sautéed fillet of beef in red wine sauce with sautéed spinach and chips, the chocolate tort with vanilla ice cream and pecan nuts, and four bottles of Ken. Then I turn on the old Savalas, see what skin flicks they've got for later.

I'm just wondering could I ring the health and fitness centre and ask for a chocolate body massage without sounding like a total pervert when the next thing, roysh, the old Wolfe goes and it's Sorcha, who's phoned, like, eight times since I landed, though this time I answer it.

The first word out of her mouth is like, '*Well?*' and of course I end up getting the totally wrong end of the stick, roysh, and I go, 'Yeah, it's really nice. Listen to this. *Dressed in restful, muted colours and decorated with Eighteenth Century prints, The Spa offers a true retreat in the vibrant heart of the city. It comes complete with a comprehensive menu of skin and body treatments and therapies, saunas, whirlpools and a pool surrounded by trompe l'oeil garden*. You'd love that, wouldn't you, Babes, especially in your condition? The whole pampering vibe,' but there's, like, total silence on the other end.

And of course, like a tit, I actually carry on reading.

I'm like, '*The Spa also features private treatment rooms, a private VIP room with a whirlpool, sauna, steam bath and two massage beds, and a relaxation room with lounge chairs and private music stations . . .*'

Sorcha flips the *focking* lid. All of a sudden – no warning, roysh – she's screaming down the phone, going, 'I DON'T GIVE A DAMN ABOUT YOUR HOTEL! YOU'RE SUPPOSED TO BE OVER THERE LOOKING FOR YOUR SON!' and in my head, roysh, I'm thinking, 'Probably a touch of the old green-eyed monster,' and then I end up making the mistake of actually saying it out loud to her.

She's like, 'Ex*cuse* me?' and I'm there, 'Look, don't go getting upset. Think of the baby. I'll tell you what, stick on your Ennio Morricone CD, have a nice piece of chocolate cake and just chillax,' but she goes, 'You're already losing the battle to convince me that you're mature enough to be a parent to my child, Ross. What have you done about finding Ronan?' and under pressure, roysh, I end up actually having to lie.

I go, 'Quite a bit, as it happens?' and she's like, 'What *exactly*?' and I'm there, 'I've been basically asking around,' and she goes, 'Asking *around*? Have you contacted the *Gendarmerie*?' but of course I haven't a focking bog what that is, roysh, and after ten seconds of, like, total silence she goes, 'The *police*, Ross? Have you phoned the police?' and I go, 'I have, yeah,' and just as I'm saying it, roysh, there's a big, loud knock at the door and quick as a flash, hopping up off the bed, I go, 'In fact, that's probably them now,' but just as I finish saying it, roysh, the stupid focking tool on the other side of the door goes, 'Rum servees, mees-your,' and there I am wondering whether Sorcha heard it or not, roysh, when all of a sudden the other end of the line goes dead.

How do you find a saucepan lid in Paris? That's what I'm thinking as I tuck into my pan-sautéed fillet of beef. That and, what the fock is caviar – aport from ridiculously expensive, that is?

I'm presuming Paris is a big place, roysh, so – what with it being an emergency and shit – when I've, like, finished the old nosebag, I wander out, get a cappuccino on the Champs-Élysées and bell Fionn, who's been here before and, like, knows his way around. He sounds, like, distracted when I ring. He goes, 'Hang on, Ross,' and I hear Marty talking. He's going, 'I'd be more inta dee early, pelitical stuff, yisser "Signing Off" and yisser "Present Arms". Never liked "Labour of Love". It's a loada me bollix . . .' and Fionn's going, 'It's certainly more commercial, isn't it?' and it's only then he comes back to me and goes, 'Ross, what's up?'

I'm there, 'Fionn, I'm in Paris, as in Paris, France?' and he goes, 'As opposed to Paris Hilton . . .' and I'm like, 'Very funny. Look, Ronan went on this school trip, but he's gone, as in, like, pegged it? I've had to come over and look for him. I mean, Fehily . . .' and he goes, 'Fehily? How did he get into France? He's supposed to be wanted over there. Anyway, Ross, what do you want from *me*?' and I'm there, 'Well, er, my French is actually a bit rusty, not having spoken it–' and Fionn goes, 'Ever . . .' and I'm like, 'Oh, excuse me for concentrating on becoming an unbelievable rugby player,' which shuts him up, roysh, because he knows he wouldn't have a Senior Cup medal if it wasn't for me.

I go, 'Look, I've got a picture of Ronan in my phone, but what I need to know is the French for *I am looking for a young boy.*'

Fionn just, like, cracks up laughing – who focking knows what's going through his head half the time – and then he's like, 'You could try saying, *Je cherche un garçon tres jeune*,' and I sort of, like, scribble it down on the back of my bill, roysh, and then I hear the Unlovely Debbie say something and Fionn goes, 'I've got to split, Ross. We're working here . . .' and he hangs up.

I stare at the piece of paper, roysh, trying to, like, memorise the words. I look around and there's this, like, old couple sitting at the next table and I turn around to them and I say the words, roysh, and before I have a chance to, like, flick through the pictures of Ronan's Communion that I've got on my phone, to get a decent one of him, they actually just get up and, like, walk off, leaving two full glasses of actual wine on the table and looking back at me like *I'm* the one who's Baghdad.

I'm thinking, It is actually true what people say about the French.

So I sit there, roysh, basically chilling, watching the birds go by, we're talking scrious hotties here, and I see this bird coming from, like, fifty yords away and – not being racist here, roysh – but she's black. I swear to God she is SO like Jamelia, roysh, you would swear it *was* her. I catch her eye, roysh, when she's maybe, like, twenty yords away and even from that distance I can see, roysh, that she's checking out the old bod in a major way, thinking, Oh yeah, you could hang your coat on those abs, wouldn't mind that in the sack, or whatever that is in French.

I stand up, roysh, and I go, '*Scuzey mwoi*,' which is pretty much the only bit of the language I remember from school, aport from, like, *café* and *croissant* and shit like that, and she stops next to me and I can smell, I think, *Rive Gauche* by Yves Saint Laurent – I'd have to check with Oisinn – and suddenly she's not the only one thinking all her Christmases have, like, come at once. I've a focking rod on me that could empty Lake Corrib.

I'm looking for a picture, roysh, where Ronan isn't actually giving me the finger and as I'm doing that, roysh, I'm thinking, *Oh my God* this bird is going to big-time fall for the whole, like, caring father act, and in my head I'm already making plans to eat the leftovers of that Beluga caviar out of her bellybutton later on, that's if they haven't taken the trolley away from outside the door.

I show her a picture of Ronan standing next to the bishop and she goes, *'Qu'est que c'est?'* which I don't understand, roysh, and I go, *'Je church un garson trays jun,'* and she sort of, like, pulls away from me and, like, looks me up and down and I have to say, roysh, I really wasn't expecting the literally slap in the face that followed.

I'm there, 'Hey, what's your *focking* problem?' but she just, like, storms off down the road, roysh, stopping only to say something to the waiter, who's straight over, roysh, telling me in English that he wants me to leave.

I whip out a wad of bills, roysh, and push a twenty into his jacket pocket and go, 'Look, I don't want any trouble. I'm just looking for a young boy,' and I show him the picture – actually, that slap really focking hurt – and he goes, 'Pigalle. That ees where you find thees, not 'ere on the Champs-Élysées. Now, you leave,' and I'm like, 'Pigalle – write that down for me, Dude,' and he does, roysh, along with how to get there on the old rattler.

So I walk to, like, Charles de Gaulle-Etoile, roysh, and it's only, like, seven or eight stops from there on the blue line and I walk up the steps out onto the street and, well, it's a bit of a shithole if I'm going to be honest about it, but I'm, like, totally blown away by how easy the birds are here compared to, like, the Champs-Élysées. It would not be an exaggeration to say that four birds basically propositioned me within, like, ten minutes of leaving the station, we're talking majorly forward here in a big-time way. It was, like, straight up to me and like, 'You like to have ze sex wis me?' and I know I'm looking really well at the moment, but I'm thinking, *Oh* my God, the goys are SO not going to believe this.

Of course I'm playing it cooler than a mother-in-law's love, going, 'Later, Babes,' to everyone, until I meet this blonde bird, roysh, who's a total ringer for Hilary Duff, wearing a mini-skirt and the old slut wellies, which I love.

She goes, 'Massage, Monsieur?' and I stop and I think actually, yeah, my shoulder's feeling pretty stiff after the flight and it's never really been the same since that labral tear I picked up against Terenure all those years ago. I'm like, 'Not a bad idea, as it happens,' and I follow her, roysh, down this, like, laneway, roysh, and up the stairs into basically her clinic, which smells of, I suppose, rose petals and candles.

So I strip to my boxers, roysh, and I lie face-down on the bed and there I am, explaining my whole injury history to her, how I'd be pretty much where Brian O'Driscoll is today if it wasn't for the Gick, when suddenly, roysh, my shoulder feels like Martin focking Johnson has just creamed me in a ruck.

I'm like, '*Aaaggghhh!*' and she goes, 'You like softer perhaps?' and I'm like, 'Yeah, just leave it in its socket and I'd be more than happy,' and she goes, '*Je suis désolé.* Sorry, Monsieur,' and I end up having to forgive her, roysh, because she gives me basically the best massage I have ever had.

When she's finished, roysh, she actually says something

that, like, stops me dead in my tracks. She's like, 'You like anyzing else, Monsieur? You like to make sex wiz me? My nem ees Anouk,' and she storts, like, unbuttoning her top, which is when certain things suddenly stort to add up, roysh.

She's the first sports physiotherapist I've ever been to who actually asked for the money upfront, then ran my fifty under an ultraviolet lamp to make sure it was kosher. All of a sudden, roysh, I cop that what I've stumbled into here is basically a knocking shop and that goy in the white vest and the fedora who took the moolah off her isn't a doctor like I thought he was.

I'm there, 'Er, there's been a bit of a misunderstanding, Babes,' and she's like, '*Comment?* You no like me?' and I'm there, 'Hey, I like you. I actually think you look like Hilary Duff. A poor man's Britney. But I don't *pay* for sex, baby. Not being big-headed, but why would I with a face and body like this?' and I can see her looking at me, roysh, thinking, He actually has a point, I knew it was too good to be true, what the fock was I thinking?

She goes, 'So why you come to Pigalle if you no want to make ze sex?' and I'm there, 'I'm actually looking for my son,' and I hand her my phone, roysh, and she straight away cracks up laughing, then calls the dude in the fedora, whose name turns out to be Rick. She hands him the Wolfe and says something to him in French, which I don't catch, and then he cracks up laughing and now I'm wondering did I by mistake show them that picture Ashling – second year Orts, easy like Sunday morning – took of me last Hallowe'en, which didn't do me justice. It was a cold night.

Rick goes, 'Thees ees your son?' and I'm there, 'That's roysh,' and he sort of, like, shakes his head and goes, 'He ees an amazing boy,' and I'm there, 'You've met him?'

and he goes, 'Of course. Rrrunn-ann ees – how he say? – game-ball. *Story, Bud*?' and he cracks up laughing again.

What kind of a focking tool am I? I mean, how did I not cop what kind of a place this is? There's, like, signs everywhere, we're talking neon signs and it's all, like, *Peep Town* and *Supermarché Erotique* and *Live Table Show* and shops that sell, like, lingerie and skin flicks on DVD and there's, like, posters everywhere of birds wearing fock-all, with stuff written in French underneath, like LATEX CUIR and VIENS ME VOIR. Sometimes I'm focking slower than Mass.

Ronan cops me before I cop him, standing at the corner of Boulevard de Clichy and Rue Antoine, roysh, just like Anouk said. All I hear is, 'Rosser, ya faggot!' and I end up having to do a double-take, roysh, because the kid – all four-foot-three of him – is actually dressed like a pimp. I'm like, 'Where the fock have you . . . where did you get that hat?' and he's there, 'Off a fella – Rick. Ah, he's sound as a pound.'

He's got the same white vest on and pair of what, from this angle, look like spats. I'm there, 'Ronan, what are you doing hanging out in a place like this?' and he goes, 'I'm thinking of getting meself a string of bitches when I go home,' and I'm just, like, standing there, totally speechless, and we're actually *talking* totally here?

He goes, 'Take a butcher's at this place, Rosser. Peep shows, strip clubs, clip joints, adult cabarets and general x-rated entertainment, all for the enjoyment and delectation of the pervert community. Twenty-four hours a day this place is buzzing. You'd wanna see the bread changing hands. See, this is the *real* business district.'

I'm like, 'And so this is your latest career idea, is it? From

133

robbing banks to becoming a pimp?' He's even chewing a focking toothpick!

He goes, 'Nah, chill out, Rosser, I'm only busting yer balls. Look, you *know* me – I'm underwurdled troo-and-troo, but I'm not into exploiting vulnerable young birds. Nah, I'm here as an observer. Like an ambassador. Thought it'd be a shame to come all this way and not see how this place works. See, I'm watching . . . and learning.'

I stort to relax. I'm there, 'Well, what's with all the gear then?' and he goes, 'Ah, Rick borrowed me some of his old stuff. Said it'd help me blend in, not look conspicuous. Rick's some fooken man. Owns a massage parlour,' and he gives me a wink, 'down on Avenue Marceau,' and of course I don't mention that I've just spent an hour in there. He's very protective of Sorcha, see.

I'm there, 'Well, you certainly blend in alroysh. You look like a pimp who's been put in a focking spin-drier at the wrong temperature.'

He goes, 'Rick has this boord working for him – Anouk. A *fascinatin'* creature. A fully qualified barrister! And the things she can do with a ping-pong ball . . .'

I'm looking around me and I'm like, 'Look, I really don't fancy spending the next hour standing on this corner discussing the many colourful friends you've made on this street. We need to get the fock out of here – as in *now*?' and he goes, 'Fair enough. Game-ball, me old segosha. But let's get a bite to eat first. What about, *Lily la Tigresse.* Supposed to do a good club sandwich in there,' and I'm like, *'Duh!?* That wouldn't be a strip club now, would it, Ronan?' and he's there, 'Jaysus, you're sharp today, Rosser. Can't blame a bloke for trying but.'

We head back to the Metro station, roysh, Ronan running along to keep up with me while explaining the finer points of clipping, bait-and-switch schemes and other scams he's learned over the past twenty-four hours and is planning to put into practice once we get back to Dublin. 'All part of me education,' he goes. He points to his eyes with, like, two fingers and he's like, 'Watchin',' and then he, like, waves a random finger around the train and goes, 'Learnin'.'

'Where was he?' That's all Sorcha wants to know, roysh. No, *how am I?* No, *fair focks to you for finding him.* It's like, 'Where *was* he?' as if it was me who lost him in the first place, and I'm looking at him, roysh – we're on the actual Metro – and he's, like, fast asleep on my shoulder, we're talking totally out of the game here, and I know I can't tell Sorcha that I found him in the middle of the red light district getting an eyeful of the hookers.

So I go, 'I actually found him at the, em, French rugby academy, of all places,' and she's like, 'Excuse me?' and I'm there, 'The French rugby academy. He was watching all the, em, young pros. Just, like, picking up tips and shit?' which is true, roysh, aport from the bit about the French rugby academy.

She goes, 'OH! MY GOD! That is, like, SO amazing. It's a pity you don't have *half* his ambition. I mean, you never do *anything*, Ross,' and I can't *actually* believe, roysh, that I'm the one who's ending up getting a hord time here.

I'm there, 'Babes, can you lay off me, just for a bit. I've had the weirdest focking day,' and she goes, 'Well, I suppose I *should* be impressed that you managed to find him at all. How is he? I mean, he must have been shocked when you turned up?' And I'm thinking, that's the weird thing, roysh, because he didn't seem surprised to see me at all.

I'm there, 'It was like we'd bumped into each other in The Square. Well, maybe the Frascati Centre. It was like he was *expecting* me.'

Sorcha goes, 'He probably was. We've been so wrapped up in all the changes this baby is going to bring to our lives that we haven't thought of Ronan's feelings at all,' and I'm wondering does *we* mean her and Claire?

She goes, 'Have you thought that maybe his nose is out of joint?' and I'm like, 'In what way?' and she goes, 'Well, ever since you two met, there's been all this fuss over him and now, well, he's suddenly going to have competition and it's like, *Oh my God!* And maybe running away is his little, I don't know, cry for help.'

He's totally out of it beside me. Poor little focker hasn't slept for, like, twenty-four hours. He must be hungry as well. I'm there, 'He definitely needs a good kip. Probably a nosebag as well,' and she goes, 'He needs more than that, Ross. Why don't you stay over there for a couple of days? You two need to bond – find out if this baby business is affecting him.'

I hang up and take the fedora off his head and I can't help but laugh. *A string of bitches!* Where does he get it from?

He moves his head, roysh, trying to get more comfortable and, still half asleep, he goes, 'Where are we, Da?' and I just, like, freeze.

He just called me Da. Before it was just, like, Rosser, or The Ross Lad, or sometimes Steamer, or Benny.

I don't say anything. I'm, like, too in shock and eventually, roysh, his head pops up and he looks at me like I'm Baghdad and he goes, 'Where *are* we?'

I just go, 'Er, not far now. Two more stops.'

One F rings. Wants to know why there's a goy tied up in the office. I know he's a journalist and shit, but he's still, like, a port-owner in the club. They should have kept him in the loop. I'm about to tell him it's fock-all to do with me, when I realise, roysh, that he thinks it's actually a good thing.

He goes, 'Brings me back to Kontum,' wherever the fock that is.

It's ten o'clock in the morning when I wake up, roysh, and I knock on the door connecting me and Ronan's rooms and there's, like, no answer, so naturally I'm assuming, roysh, that I'm going to end up spending the day touring the knocking shops of Paris again, looking for him. Turns out I needn't have worried. He got up early – 'me mind won't rest, Rosser; it's always lookin' for angles' – and hit the breakfast buffet and by the time I arrived down, roysh, he was in the lobby, with a copy of *L'Equipe* under his arm, chatting up these three chambermaids and giving it loads.

I hear him go, 'I'm taking him to that Euro Disney today,' and of course I crack my hole laughing at the idea of *him* taking *me*. He's there, 'He asked me last night did I fancy going and sure what could I say? He seems to have his heart set on it,' and the three birds are, like, rolling around the place laughing.

One of them, roysh, is a total ringer for Jillian Berberie and Ronan obviously has the major hots for her because he's going, 'If I was ten years older, Love . . . You are a – how do you say? – *idole sexuelle*,' and the bird actually blushes, roysh, and the other two stort laughing in that real sort of, like, girlie way and I'm thinking, Yeah, he's my kid alroysh.

I saunter over and I go, 'Hey, Ronan. Hey, girls,' and the three of them, it's actually a bit embarrassing, roysh, but they basically can't take their eyes off me, and one of them – you *would* actually think it was Adriana Lima – I can tell she has a focking serious wide-on for me.

Ronan goes, 'Ah, there you are, Rosser. This is Gabrielle,

Dominique and Bettina,' and I'm there, 'Hey, girls, how the hell are you?' and it's all, like, giggles and then they sort of, like, excuse themselves, saying they've got to do a bit of work. They're like, 'Bye-bye, Rrru-naan,' as they're getting into the elevator and he's going, '*Au revoir*, ladies.'

When the doors have closed, he turns around to me and goes, 'You're some fooken tulip, aren't you?' and I'm there, 'What are you talking about?' and he's like, '*Hey, girls, how the hell are you? Don't* tell me Sorcha fell for *that*?' and I'm there, 'That's actually not a very good impersonation you know,' but he goes '*How the hell are you*?' again and then he's like, 'You're cramping me style, Rosser. Cramping me fooken style.'

I laugh and I'm like, 'You certainly had them eating out of your hand,' and he's there, 'Ah, it's a bit of business, truth be told. I'm gonna see if that Dominique can fix me up with a score or two of them French maid outfits. I've a *contact* – friend of a friend – who runs a toy shop, know what I'm saying? The kind where you have to ring a bell to get in,' and before I get a chance to, like, say anything, he goes, 'Come on, Mickey Mouse'll be wondering what's keeping you.'

Euro Disney is huge, roysh, as in, like, fifty times the size of Funderland, but without the newsprint moustaches and the Elizabeth Duke bling. We actually have a cracking day. We end up doing a shitload of things, roysh – we're talking Phantom Manor, we're talking Big Thunder Mountain, we're talking Adventure Island, we're talking the Orbitron – but of course Ronan insists on giving Sleeping Beauty's Castle a miss ('bent'), not to mention the Pirates of the Caribbean ('bent'), Alice's Curious Labyrinth ('bent'), Dumbo the Flying Elephant ('bent'), Pinocchio's Travels ('bent') and the Paddle Steamers ('Are you pulling my fooken chain or what?').

And at some point in between all that, roysh, we go and grab a couple of burgers in Walt's on Main Street and have the big chats while watching the world go by.

He goes, 'What's on your mind, Rosser?' helping himself to my chips after he's, like, horsed back his own. I'm there, 'What's on *my* mind? It's funny, I was going to ask you the same thing,' and he goes, 'Sure I'm sound as a fooken pound,' and I'm like, 'How do you feel about this, like, baby and shit?' and suddenly he's, like, restless, if that's the word, looking all around him basically.

I'm there, 'Hey, all boys run away from home. I did it myself at your age,' and he goes, 'Did you?' his face suddenly all lit up like a Christmas tree. He's there, 'So where did you end up?' and I'm like, 'Not working a length of pavement in the red light district anyway. Actually, it was me and Christian. I talked him into it,' and he goes, 'So where'd you run away to?' and I'm there, 'Australia,' and he's like, '*Australia!* You are fooken shitting me now!' and I'm there, 'The World Cup was on, you see. I was only, like, seven, but I got this idea in my head that I was going to get a call-up for Ireland,' and quick as a flash he goes, 'You haven't fooken changed much twenty years on then, have you?' and I crack up laughing. He's actually funny.

Of course he didn't lick that up off the ground.

We take a short timeout then to give our full appreciation to this Kristanna Loken lookalike who's just walked in. Then Ronan goes, 'How far did you get but?' and I'm like, 'Actually Dún Laoghaire,' and this time it's him who cracks up laughing. I'm there, 'We were in the Dorsh station looking for Australia on the map. I was convinced it was southside, but Christian reckoned it was, like, somewhere out beyond Killester. One of the goys in the Dorsh station called the Feds and they brought us home.'

He goes, 'So what happened? Did you get sent to a shrink?' and I'm like, 'A shrink? Fock, no, I wouldn't have said we needed a shrink,' and all of a sudden he goes, 'Well I don't either,' and I'm like, 'Ronan, don't get all, like, defensive. Where I found you ... I mean, what kind of father would I be if I just, like, pretended that was normal?'

He doesn't answer.

I go, 'Is it the baby? Are you, like, worried and shit?' and I swear to God, roysh, that little hord man face of his just melts away. It's like someone's flicked a switch, roysh, and for the first time since I met him, he's really eight years old, as in his actual age.

I'm there, 'You *are* worried,' and he sort of, like, shrugs his little shoulders and goes, 'You will still call out, won't you?' and at that moment I just want to pick him up and give him the biggest hug, except I don't, roysh, because I know he'll tell me I'm wrecking his cred, or his buzz, or his vibe.

I'm like, 'Of course, I will. And you'll still come and stay with us. Nothing is going to change Ro,' and he goes, 'Because we have the crack, don't we?' and I'm like, 'Big time,' and he's there, 'Even though you're a fooken tulip sometimes,' and I go, 'Even though I'm a focking tulip,' and he goes, 'And a benny,' and I'm like, 'And a benny . . .' and hearing me say this seems to satisfy him, roysh, because the next thing he says is, 'Are you fit for Space Mountain?'

Of course the answer is no. Ronan has a stomach like a focking goat. Mine isn't built to withstand all that, like, tossing and turning. Well, not *this* kind anyway. They've actually just, like, revamped the whole thing, if that's the word. The original was basically just a rollercoaster, roysh – though I don't even want to think about that particular word since reading that porn shite – but this has got, like, a much faster launch catapult and these, like, high-definition video screens that make you feel like you're actually, like, hurtling through – I don't know – the solar system, I suppose, with all, like, asteroid showers and shit.

So picture the scene. There I am afterwards, roysh, sitting on this, like, bench, next to a life-size Goofy and I am, like, throwing my ring up, we are talking serious spewage here, we are talking splashing the Dubes in a big-time way, and of course Ronan's, like, drawing attention to me by going, 'Nothing to see here! Please move along!' at, like, the top of his voice and he knows, roysh, he might as well be going, 'Roll up, ladies and gentlemen, and see this freak of nature'.

It's at that actual moment my phone rings and I see from my caller ID that it's, like, Fionn. I manage to stop hurling for, like, two seconds to actually answer the thing. It is Fionn. Get this, roysh, the first thing he says is like, 'Ross, are you watching the news?' and I'm there, 'Er, *duh?!*' and he goes, 'Absurd question. I apologise. Ross, Fehily's been arrested,' and I'm like, 'Arrested?' and he goes, 'Yeah, leaving France. He was picked up at Charles de Gaulle. According to Charlie Bird, it's, like, war crimes . . .'

Ronan sits down on the bench beside me and goes, 'What's the story?' and I turn to him and I'm like, 'The Feds have lifted Fehily.'

I go, 'What do you mean *war crimes?*' and Fionn's there, 'Well, we all know of his love for all things related to the Third Reich. Look, I made some calls. Seems he spent most of the War in France. As far as I can gather – and this is just from talking to Brother Ignatius and Father Colm – during the years of the Vichy regime he was a member of the Milice Francaise,' and of course for me it's like being back at school again, roysh. It's like, *whoosh*, straight over my head.

When I don't say anything, roysh, he storts having a

focking huff attack, like the bird that he is. He goes, 'He collaborated with the Germans, Ross,' and I'm like, 'Big swinging mickey. That was, like . . . I don't know how many years ago,' and he's just there, 'Sixty. But he was obviously a senior enough figure that the French police are still interested in him. I really can't understand why he went back. Anyway, Ross, we have to do something,' and I'm there, 'Yeah, I was thinking that – my own instinct is to let him focking rot.'

Ronan's pacing up and down in front of me, muttering some shit to himself – I can make out, *names, pack drill* and *I'm staring down the barrel of a fooken ten-stretch here.*

Fionn goes, 'Let him *rot?* I can't believe you just said that,' and I'm like, 'Look, whatever trouble he's in, it's his shit. Like he pretty much said to me when he lost my kid – it's tough titty,' and he's there, 'I can't believe I'm hearing this from you, of all people. Remind me who was it who lifted the Leinster Schools Cup in 1999? So what happened to *Castlerock boys are we? We shall shy from battle never. Ein Reich, ein volk, ein Rock?'* and I'm there, 'HELLO? We've left school, Fionn,' but of course he loses it with me, storts having a total eppo, and we're talking total.

He's like, 'Castlerock students NEVER leave school! Isn't that what we were taught? That no matter what happened in our lives, no matter where we were, what trouble we were in, the school would bail us out. Do you remember that?' and I'm there, 'Why doesn't Ignatius do something? Or Brother Alphonsus?' and Fionn goes, 'Because they're old. And they're afraid. Ross, whatever it was that Fehily did during the War, he still taught us how to play rugby. What would any of us be today if it wasn't for that?'

The focker's actually playing on my hort strings now. I'm there, 'Skobies, I suppose,' and he's like, 'Well, that senior cup medal around your neck – it wouldn't be there if it wasn't for him.'

I slip my hand inside my shirt and feel the piece of metal.

Fionn's there, 'Now *he* needs *you*. And the question is, where are you?' and I go, 'Sitting on a bench next to Space Mountain. I've actually just vommed,' but of course he doesn't give two focks.

He's like, 'I'm texting you the address of the station where he's being questioned. What you do with it, Ross, is between you and your conscience,' and he hangs up on me, he *actually* hangs up on me, the goggle-eyed freak.

I turn around to Ronan and I'm like, 'What are *you* so jumpy about?' and he goes, 'Let's just get to the cop shop . . . before he starts singing like a box of crickets.'

Five focking hours we're made to wait, roysh, in this, like, reception area, sitting next to, like, hookers, druggies and just plain drunks, many of whom my eight-year-old son is offering free legal advice.

'Been down *that* road before meself,' he keeps telling them, while I'm sitting here, roysh, being made to feel like an actual criminal.

I walk up to the counter and go, 'Hey, Clouseau. It was, like, five o'clock in the day when we walked in here. It's now ten o'clock at night. Pardon my French, but what's the focking Jackanory?' but the dude just goes, 'I am zorry, zir. Your frrrend ees wiz ze inspector. Interview, yes?' and I'm wondering why the fock Drico would even consider moving to a country like this.

Ten minutes later, at long focking last, we're called, roysh, and we're led down this, like, series of dark corridors and into a room with, like, bare white walls, where Fehily is sitting and looking unbelievably relaxed for a goy who's about to get the focking guillotine. Of course, the second he see us he storts with the dramatics.

He's like, 'My children! You came! Just as I was about to cry out in my lonely despair, *Eloi! Eloi! Lama sabachthani!*'

I'm there, '*Eloi* nothing. Do you know how long we've been waiting? It's like focking Store Street out there. So what did you do?' and he goes, 'Sit down, my child. Sit down and listen. You too, Ronan. And don't look so worried, child, they know nothing of your involvement,' and Ronan goes, 'I appreciate that, Fadder. A shut mouth catches no flies,' and I look at Ronan, roysh, then at Fehily and I go, 'Will someone actually tell me what the fock is going on?'

Fehily storts cleaning out his pipe on the table and out of the corner of my eye, roysh, I see Ronan give him the nod.

Fehily goes, 'Well, back in the thirties, Ross, as you may or may not know, I did a bit of travelling. Oh, I can't even begin to tell you now what an exciting place Europe was to an impressionable eighteen-year-old from a rural backwater like Ireland. The colour. The atmosphere. The uniforms. Lines of storm troopers marching in perfect goose-step. You couldn't help but be swept along by it all . . .'

He goes, 'I was in Austria at the time of the Anschluss. I was there to hear the church bells ring when the Furhrer arrived in Vienna – *home!* – standing up in his open-top car, giving the Fascist salute. Couldn't see him through the crowds, of course, though we all pretended we could. There were millions of people – *millions* – on the streets. Women, children, grown men, weeping tears of joy. It seems crazy at – what? – sixty, seventy years' remove, to think that a man with so much . . . evil in him could excite such happiness in people. But history's mistake is too often to divorce events from the context of the times . . .'

I make a point of checking my watch, roysh, to hurry him along.

He goes, 'They had a referendum on the annexation, you know. Ninety-nine per cent in favour. I saw a photograph in a newspaper of Cardinal Innitzer, the Archbishop of Vienna, giving the Nazi salute before going in to cast his vote at a polling station that had Swastika flags hanging from every wall.'

He's like, 'The other business — spring-cleaning, they called it — look, I don't think any of us knew it was going to escalate into an all-out Holocaust. I remember reading about Richard Tauber and Max Reinhardt and thinking it was a terrible shame . . .' and I just go, 'Sorry, do you know how focking boring this is to me. I might as well be back at school. Is there much more of this shit?'

Ronan goes, 'Why don't you hear the man out, Rosser,' and I'm just like, 'Yeah, whatever!' and Fehily goes, 'Tauber was actually a Catholic. Like Hitler. He even considered becoming a priest. His father was Jewish, you see, and he converted. Well, I was an aspiring tenor myself, so not surprisingly I was a big fan. But the Nazis withdrew his passport and his right of abode and he ended up in Britain. Awful. But at the time you don't have the elevation view of events that history affords . . .'

He's like, 'It was in Vienna that for the first and only time in my life . . . I fell in love. Her name was Vianne. She had a sad face. Looked like Constance Bennett,' and I'm just there, 'Never heard of her. We're talking nice, though?'

He goes, 'She was French. From Clermont-Ferrand, not far from Paris. She worked in the box office of a little theatre in Vienna where I auditioned and, well, we fell in love. She took me back to France. It was 1940, not long after the surrender to Germany. Her father was quite senior in the

Vichy regime. Oh, that was the government of the day in France, Ross, during the years of the occupation. They collaborated with the Nazis. He was close to Philippe Petain, Joseph Damand, all those boys. He took me under his wing and I joined the Milice Française.'

I'm there, 'There's a lot of names to remember, isn't there?' and he goes, 'The Milice Française was a paramilitary force set up to fight the French resistance. Well, I was a mere functionary. Vianne had taught me how to type. They gave us each a uniform, a beret and a typewriter and told us to take statements from informers.'

He's like, 'And then, well, I had one of those moments in life when you look in the mirror and see what you've become . . .'

He goes, 'They loved their work, those boys. I mean, they were worse than the Gestapo, worse than the SS. I watched them torture a man – a baker, from Saint Paul, accused of harbouring Jews. He was seventy years old and what they did to him I couldn't bring myself to speak about now. I couldn't stay. I told Vianne. She said she understood . . .'

I'm there, 'You mean she didn't, like, go with you?' and he just, like, stares off into space. He goes, 'We were different people. I had my beliefs. She had hers. We said goodbye.'

I'm like, 'And you never heard from her again?' and he shakes his head and goes, 'I just know what I read years later. Her father was executed after the War, for treason. I was back in Ireland by then. I had, well, a breakdown – a big one. And when I got well again I started studying for the priesthood.'

I'm like, 'Whoa, one thing you need to explain to me – why the fock did you come back here?'

He goes, 'I just wanted to see Paris one more time before

. . . Look, I haven't long left, Child,' and I'm there, 'What are you talking about?' and he goes, 'I have a tumour, Ross. In the brain. It's malignant and inoperable.'

I look at Ronan and from the way he's nodding, it's obvious he already knows.

Fehily goes, 'It'll be a year if I'm lucky,' and all of a sudden, probably just remembering all the great times we had over the years, I can feel my eyes sort of, like, fill up with tears. I'm just there, 'Do *not* talk like that. SO don't. Surely there's, like, shit they can do, as in, like, doctors?' but he just goes, 'Ross, I'm an old man. The Lord is calling me. It's the way of things. But before I went, well, there were things I needed to square in my mind.'

I'm like, 'But if you were, like, on some, I don't know, Most Wanted list, how did you get into the actual country in the first place?' and he's there, 'Let's just say I *obtained* a false passport,' and I go, 'How would *you* get your hands on a false passport?' And all of a sudden, roysh, I see this look pass between him and Ronan.

I'm there, 'I don't focking believe this,' and I turn around to Ronan and I go, 'Where did *you* get a false passport?' managing to sound surprisingly like an actual father. But he just goes, 'Loose lips cost lives, Rosser,' and Fehily laughs, roysh, and I turn around and give him an actual filthy and he ends up going, 'Ronan did a very selfless thing, Ross, to help an old man come to terms with a broken heart he's been nursing all his life . . .'

I'm there, 'Great. You can be cellmates, then,' and he goes, 'He's not going to prison, Ross. No one knows about Ronan and, well, even if they did, he's too young to be charged.'

I'm like, 'So what about you, then?' and he sort of, like, shrugs, then looks up and goes, 'It's in His hands now.

149

Look, I wasn't making decisions or giving orders. I was a low-level functionary. It'll come out at the trial. If there is one. I could be too sick to stand . . .'

He stares off into the distance, roysh, looking like he's about to burst into tears. I go, 'We better make like a couple of bananas and split,' and, after a few seconds thinking about what I said, he goes, 'Oh, I see. Well, thank you for coming to see me. I only wish I was going back with you . . .' and when we get outside, roysh, I turn around to Ronan and go, 'Uncle focking Albert, huh? *During the War* . . .' and Ronan gives me a filthy and tells me to cop myself on.

Sorcha rings me in a panic, telling me – *oh my God!* – she just heard from, like Erika that hair-dye can cause damage to the foetus. It can, like, get through your skin, into your blood stream, across the placenta and cause damage to the baby's genetic material, maybe leading to arthritis, or even cancer later on. Then after three more *oh my Gods* she hangs up on me.

So we're standing at the check-in desk and we're three from the top of the queue, roysh, but some tool wants to bring his focking guitar on as, like, hand luggage and he's, like, arguing with the bird at the desk – who looks a little bit like Sarah Harding – and he's holding everyone up and I am, like, SO tempted to tell him that I've thought of somewhere else he could put it.

Ronan's behind me, talking to some random goy he's never met before, going, 'So the boord asks the punter to buy her a drink and it's only when he's leaving that he realises he's been charged four hundred'n odd quid for a glass of champagne. Of course he's not going to argue, is he, because it's some big fooken gorilla in a tux who presents him with the Jack and Jill . . .'

So eventually, roysh, we check in and we're heading for the departures gate when Ronan turns around and asks me if I'd take his carry-on baggage through for him and he hands me this, like, I don't know, *holdall* is what they call them in those, like, 'Crimeline' reconstructions. I feel bad for saying this, but of course the first question I ask myself is, What the fock is in it? Is it, like, drugs, guns, diamonds, what? You just wouldn't know with Ronan.

I'm like, 'Don't take this the wrong way . . .' and he goes, 'You're wondering am I using you as mule?'

A mule! I mean, where does he get the lingo?

I'm there, 'It's just . . .' and he's like, 'Me arm's sore from carrying it, that's all. I'm a bit hurt to tell you the truth, that you'd think I – yisser own flesh and blood – would be capable of something like that,' and I'm like, 'Ro, I'm sorry . . .' and he's there, 'No, I don't want to hear it,' and I'm going, 'I'm trying to apologise,' and he's there, 'Nah, just leave it, Rosser,' and he goes to walk away with the bag, which is practically the same size as him, and I go, 'Seriously, Ro, I insist,' and he lets me take it from him, roysh, and I'm not surprised he was struggling with it because it weighs a focking tonne.

So we hit the baggage checking area, roysh, and I let him go on through. I actually beep when I, like, walk through the metal detector, roysh, and I have to go back and walk through again, this time after taking my phone out of my pocket and, like, putting it through the scanner. Then I end up getting frisked, roysh, not by this, like, Penélope Cruz lookalike who's standing there, but by Meatloaf's sister, who – I am not bullshitting you – is getting a big-time wide-on patting me down, checking out my abs and pecs and you can tell she's thinking, This is the best job in the world.

So of course I can't wait to get out of there – what with her being a ditch-pig and everything – and I go to grab me and Ronan's bags. But I see the goy working the actual scanning giving her the nod, roysh, and all of a sudden she turns around to me and goes, 'Zees ees also your bag, Monsieur?' and she points at the one Ronan gave me to carry and I'm there, 'Yeah, is there a problem?'

She doesn't answer me, roysh, just goes, 'Can I osk you to open eet, pleece?' so I'm there, 'Yeah, *what*ever,' and I unzip it, roysh, and as she puts her hand into it I turn around to Ronan and give him a shrug, as if to say, I don't know what this is all about.

I end up nearly having a focking hort attrack, roysh, when she puts her hand into the bag and storts pulling out all these, like, French maid outfits. I spin around and look at Ronan, who actually shakes his head, roysh, gives me this disappointed look, then goes on through to duty free, roysh, leaving me there on my focking Tobler.

I turn back, roysh, and this bird's still pulling them out of the bag. There must be, like, a hundred of them in there and of course I'm there sweating bricks. I'm probably going to end up in the same slammer as Fehily.

So she finally gets to the end of the bag, roysh, and all these outfits are, like, piled up at the end of the conveyor belt and other passengers passing by are, like, pointing at me, roysh, and whispering, I presume saying, *Oh my God*, look at that total focking perv.

I go, 'I can explain,' and the bird's like, 'Zare ees no need to explain. You like zis sort of zing, yes?' with a big shit-eating grin on her face. I'm there, 'Wait a minute, they're not *actually* mine? As in . . .' and she goes, 'Zees sings are not illegal, Monsieur. If zis is what – how you say? – float your boat . . .'

She's giving me this look, roysh, which is hord to explain, but it's pretty clear she's gagging for me in a big-time way. Leering, I suppose you'd have to call it. I stort throwing the stuff back into the bag and she suddenly grabs my hand, roysh, and I swear to God, she's got a grip like John Hayes, and she goes, 'I zink I must freesk you one more time.'

5. The Loneliness of the
Long-Distance Tosser

'*Statuesque* – that's the word,' and I'm like, 'What?' and the old man goes, 'My running style – that's the name for it. I told you Hennessy was going to film it, try to break it down and so forth. He's compared it to the style of Michael Johnson, chap who won all sorts of medals, apparently. Black – and that's not being racialist. He defied the laws of biomechanics, if you don't mind. Proved that a high knee-lift isn't essential to attain maximum speed, quote-unquote . . .'

Typical of my luck to be stuck in traffic on the Rock Road, listening to this tosser on the phone. Between him running that race, roysh, and my old dear writing that – well, basically – porn, I'm going to have to go into hiding, like that focking writer goy. Someone tell Bono to get the spare room ready.

He's going, 'The phone hasn't stopped, Ross. Various media outlets and so forth looking for the big scoop. *One man – a golfer – making a stand against the sexual equality Hezbollah, saying, Enough is enough!* There's even talk of a movie, with Gene Hackman playing me. Gene Hackman, if you don't mind!'

At this point, roysh, I have contributed literally one word to the conversation, and that was 'Orsehole'.

He goes, 'Now, Kicker, don't even think about trying to draw me into a debate about whether Wales are the new force in northern hemisphere rugby. I'm a busy man. Twenty minutes on the treadmill, then your mother's going to fix me one of these high carb drinks. After that, TV3 are coming out. Oh it's all go,' and he hangs up before I get the chance to tell him what a total focking tosser he is.

I'm telling Marty all about Paris and he's going, 'See? And you tought you werdent goin' to make a good fadder . . .' and I'm there, 'I suppose that's pretty much *silenced the doubters*, as Wardy might say,' totally forgetting they wouldn't get *The Indo* in his port of town.

I'm there, 'So what are you goys up to?' and Fionn's there, 'We've spent the last couple of days and nights studying Marty's linguistic patterns, to find out how important a role language plays in a skobie's identification with the lyrics of Bob Morley . . .'

The Unlovely Debbie's looking at some, I don't know, computer read-outs maybe. She really is cat.

Marty all of a sudden goes: 'I'll boorst yizzer fooken heads open, yiz bleedin', fooken poshies!' and Fionn laughs and goes, 'Thank you, Marty. They – you might remember, Ross – were the first words that our friend here ever spoke to us.'

Marty's there, 'So we're after been lookin' at dat, reet, and udder shit I say and comparin' it to de way dee talk in Jamaica.'

Fionn's like, 'That's roysh. English, as we all know, is the formal language of both Jamaica and Ireland. However, in both countries the peasant and manual labour classes, who have dropped out of formal education early, speak a creolised, syncopated form of the language, featuring slang words assimilated from other cultures . . .'

While he's saying all this, roysh, Marty's just there nodding his head.

Fionn's there, 'Many of the dialectical elements are identical, such as rhythm, intonation and alliteration – *batter, bleedin', boorst* – though Skobie English contains far less onomatopoeic echoism than the Rasta dialect – and far more violence, probably due to the influence of American gangsterism on the culture . . .'

Debbie looks up and gives Fionn a little smile. Then she says she's going to call it a day and Fionn goes, 'I'll see you tomorrow, then,' as she's heading out the door.

Marty's like, 'Have ye not fooken asked her yet?' and Fionn sits down and goes, 'It never seems to be the right moment,' and Marty goes, 'It's only a bleedin' drink, man. She already knows ye like her. Boords pick up on it.'

I'm thinking, Even Fionn could do better than her, surely?

Marty goes, 'Yiz are all talkers, the lot of yiz. That Oisinn fella's the only one of yiz who gets up off hees arse and goes for it.'

There's, like, a knock on the door, then it opens. It's Christian. He's there, 'Hey, goys, JP's downstairs.'

I'm like, 'Fock, speaking of Oisinn, where is he?'

Fionn goes, 'Oh, he's in the lab,' which is basically an old storeroom in the basement, roysh, where he's set up all his bottles and, like, Bunsen burners? I'm there, 'Well, let's hope he stays down there. We don't those two at each other's throats.'

On the way out the door, roysh, I notice Christian wave this big, brown envelope at Marty and go, 'I did it!' and Marty's there, 'Good man! See, there's hope for yiz all,' and when I ask Christian about it on the way down to the bor he goes, 'He told me I should send my script off to George Lucas. He said it was time I stopped living in a dream world and did something about it.'

'Marty told you that?' I go and my nose feels a bit out of joint, it must be said, because I've thought that about him for years but never, like, said it? He's like, 'Marty really is the best thing that's ever happened to us, isn't he?' and I'm there, 'HELLO? Aport from winning the Leinster Schools Senior Cup?' and he goes, 'Yeah,' but I can tell he doesn't mean it.

JP's dressed totally in black, and I suppose he's got to get used to that kind of clobber. Oisinn comes into the bor. In fairness to JP, roysh, he actually makes the effort, like he said he would. He's like, 'Hey, Oisinn, it's good to see you,' and Oisinn goes, 'Yeah, you too,' but he says it in a way, roysh, that he doesn't mean it.

Oisinn sees we all have, like, pints in front of us and I know what he's thinking. I'm there, 'I was actually going to call you, but I thought you were, like, busy?' and he goes, 'Hey, Ross – ain't no thing but a chicken wing,' which is a new line he picked up while he was away.

He's actually changed since he got back from the States. He's, like, SO up himself, it's unbelievable. There was a story in one of the papers that Eva Mendes threw the lips on him at some porty or other, but Oisinn's giving us that whole real-men-don't-need-to-brag vibe, which I suppose could mean it's total horseshit.

He asks Evelyne for a pint of Ken, then sits down with us. JP goes, 'How was New York?' and Oisinn's there, 'Pretty amazing, actually. It was, like, porty, porty, porty. Met a lot of . . . *influential* people over there. What about you? How's life with the God Botherers?' which is uncalled for, roysh, but in fairness to JP he tries to pass it off as a joke.

He's there, 'Still as rewarding as ever. I've been reading the Book of Psalms . . . And praying hard for Father Fehily, of course,' which sort of, like, strikes a chord with us all. I go, 'Have you, like, heard from him?' and JP's there, 'A letter this morning. And a phone-call during the week. He's in good spirits, under the circumstances. His lawyer's quite hopeful that his age and his health will spare him having to go through a trial.'

There's no doubt we all feel bad for him.

Fionn changes the subject. He goes, 'Ross, did I imagine that report on TV3 last night or is your old man actually running the Women's Mini-Marathon?'

Christian and JP look at me. What a focking tool Fionn is sometimes.

I go, 'You must have, like, dreamt it . . .' and Christian goes, 'Maybe he didn't, Ross. I saw him in Dún Laoghaire last week and he seemed to be . . . *jogging.*'

Fionn goes, 'That must be, er, pretty humiliating for you, Ross,' like the dickhead that he is. Usually, roysh, Oisinn would be weighing in with the slaggings in a big-time way, but he's just, like, hanging on the edge of the conversation, not saying anything but seriously tanning the Britneys. He's knocked back two in, like, twenty minutes and he's already halfway through his third.

I'm there, 'If he wants to run it, let him. Hopefully he'll drop dead of a focking hort attack and I'll be halfway towards my inheritance,' and even JP laughs at that. He knows I hate my old man's guts.

'Hey, goys,' Oisinn goes, all of a sudden, 'I've got a joke for you,' and you just know he's looking for trouble, roysh, because he's staring straight at JP. He goes, 'How do you know Jesus wasn't a northsider?' and Fionn's there, 'Hey, cool it, Oisinn, we're having a few friendly beers here . . .' but Oisinn just goes, 'Because he fell three times and didn't claim once . . .'

JP gets up from the table and goes, 'Sorry, Ross, I tried . . .' and Oisinn, who's actually hammered, stands up as well and goes, 'You never asked me how the water was coming along,' but JP ignores him, roysh, and Oisinn goes, 'I'm working on one at the moment, aimed at the more . . . *senior* members of the flock. Want to know what it's called? Huh? Want to know what it's called?'

Oisinn goes, 'It's called *Make Me A Chanel of Your Peace* . . .'

JP stops and turns around, which is a mistake. All Oisinn's looking for is a reaction. He goes, 'It's not holy water, you're making. It's *un*holy water,' which is a bit weak, you'd have to say. He's got to learn that what's funny out in Maynooth isn't automatically funny to the rest of us.

Oisinn goes, 'I'm going to be meeting your boss soon, as in the Pope,' and JP goes, 'Highly unlikely, Oisinn. The Holy Father is very ill,' and Oisinn goes, 'I'm one step ahead of you, Dude. I'm already working on the new man. The word is it'll be this Ratzinger . . . Southside eyes – hungry for the prize!'

JP goes, 'Well, good luck with that,' but as he's going out the door, roysh, he looks a worried man, because he knows there's pretty much no stopping Oisinn once he puts his mind to something.

What about Amber? That's all I say, roysh, and she gives me this filthy look, like I've just, I don't know, opened my lunchbox at a family dinner.

She goes, 'Oh my *God*, I cannot *believe* you said that,' and I'm there, 'Said what?' and she's like, 'I cannot believe you suggested we actually call our baby Amber. After what happened at the debs?' and it's, like, coming back to me now. I did actually do the dirt on her with a bird called Amber. I'm sure she doesn't want reminding of that every day of her life.

I try to change the subject, of course. I'm there, 'We don't even know if it's going to be a girl yet,' and Sorcha goes,

'It's a girl, I'm telling you. Mothers know their own bodies.'

I'm like, 'Well, what about Chardonnay?' as in the bird with the humungous thrups off 'Footballers' Wives'. Sorcha turns around and goes, 'Chardonnay? Yes, because that would go a long way to explaining how I allowed you to get me in this condition in the first place!' and I don't say anything.

I suppose I should be grateful that she's even involving me in choosing the name. I thought her and Claire would do it, then e-mail me their decision, using Claire's stolen laptop.

Sorcha storts going down through this list she made earlier, crossing shit out. She's like, 'Okay, it's definitely *not* going to be Kyla, Amelia, Fleur, or Aednat. I haven't totally ruled out Tiana, Hermione, Abigail, or Jenna, though. And I'll just put, like, a questionmork down beside Ealga, will I?' and I'm there, 'Yeah, whatever.'

She goes, 'What about Ailbhe?' and I'm there, 'Ailbhe? I mean, is that even a name?' and she goes, 'HELLO? Of course it's a name. It comes from the old Irish word for white. It's Erika's cousin's name,' and I'm like, 'It's just it sounds like, I don't know, a kitchen appliance. As in, will we splash out on the Moulinex or will we just settle for the Ailbhe?' and Sorcha goes, 'Maybe you're right. Ailbhe actually has an attitude problem? Takes after her cousin.'

I go out to the kitchen and grab another Britney and when I sit down again she goes, 'Aoife suggested Etain,' I'm there, 'No, I've actually, er, been with an Etain,' and she goes, '*Oh my God*! we are SO not naming our baby after one of your exes!' and I'm there, 'I know. That's why I focking said it,' and she just gives me this look.

Then she goes, 'Which Etain were you with?' and I'm there, 'Etain Hooper?' and she's like, 'You were with Etain

Hooper? As in, used to be deputy headgirl in Rathdown? As in, made a total fool of herself at the Model UN?' and I'm there just, like, nodding my head, going, 'It was ages ago. It was at, like, Oisinn's eighteenth,' and she goes, 'Oisinn's eighteenth? We were actually going out together then,' and I sort of, like, cleverly cover my tracks by going, 'Must have been some other time then.'

You have to be sharp if you're going to lie to birds.

She's sort of, like, looking at me, roysh, trying to decide if she should believe me or not. Then she goes back to her list. She's like, 'What about Shauna?' and she knows from the big shit-eating grin on my face what's coming next. She goes, 'You've been with a Shauna as well? HELLO? I don't believe this!' and I'm there, 'I'm not doing it on purpose. I was a ladies' man. You knew I'd a past when you married me.'

So she storts reading down through the list, roysh, telling me to stop her when we get to the name of a bird I *haven't* been with. She's like, 'Ailish . . . Beibhínn . . . Madison . . . Alia . . . Sneachta . . . Freya . . . Iona . . . Barbara . . . Adelpha . . . Summer . . . Basanti . . . Alix with an i . . . Ríonach . . .' and it's like my whole life is flashing in front of my eyes. She's going, 'Radha . . . Caireann with a c, an i and an a, n, n . . . Poppy . . . Orlaith with an i . . . Gormla . . . Esperanza . . . Bethany . . . Tori . . . Annis . . . Angharad . . . Anushka . . . Oh my God, Ross, you are a *total* male slut,' I'm there, 'Don't forget, Babes, this is over the course of, like, ten years?'

She goes, 'Muireann,' and I'm like, 'Muireann?' and she's there, 'You've never been with a Muireann, no?' and I'm like, 'Not that I remember. What does it mean?' and she goes, 'According to the book, it means "sea fair" and refers to the legend of the mermaid captured by a fisherman in Lough Neagh in the sixth century. He brought her to Saint

Comghall, who baptised her, transforming her into a woman and then . . .'

I'm like, 'Can I just stop you there? I remember now, I *have* been with a Muireann,' and she sort of, like, throws her eyes up to heaven and goes, 'I think, with your past, Ross, we can pretty much rule out ninety per cent of the actual names in the world. We may need to go for the name of a girl you *have* actually been with, but with, like, a variation on the spelling. What about Georgia?' and I'm there, 'Everyone's called Georgia these days,' and she's like, 'Spelt J, O, R, J, A. Or what about Lisa but spelt L, E, E, S, A?'

I'm there, 'Is that enough Es? Would it look stupid with three?' trying to pretty much lighten the atmosphere, roysh, but she actually writes it out, looks at it from a couple of angles and goes, 'Em, not necessarily. Or what about Susannah, but with an S, O, O, S, A, N, A? Or maybe Jane and a J, E, N and with a little accent over the E,' and she writes it down and looks at it and goes, 'Oh my God, it looks SO nice.'

I'm there, 'We're not in any rush to decide this tonight, are we?' wondering would she flip the lid if I went looking for the remote to try to find out what's going on in Corrie – is Sally going to spread the legs for that boss of hers? – but there's, like, no stopping her now.

She goes, 'What about Emily with an E, M, apostrophe, L, Y? Or Denise with a D, apostrophe, N, E, C, E,' and I'm there, 'I've been with a Denise,' and she's like, 'With an apostrophe?' and I just, like, nod and look at the blank screen, thinking one way or the other I can't believe Kevin didn't give her the old Spanish archer earlier, the focking trout.

She goes, 'What about a semi-colon? D, semi-colon, N, I, C, E. Or a hyphen? Or maybe just D, E, N, I, C, E, with a cedilla under the C. Oh my God, I SO have to have a cedilla,' and I go to get up, roysh, and she's there, '*Sit down!*' and there's pretty much no arguing with that tone. She goes, 'We are coming up with a name for this baby *tonight*. I want to tell everybody at Chloe's barbecue on Sunday,' and she, like, turns to the second page and goes, 'Stop me if you *haven't* been with a girl called any of the following . . . Fabienne . . . Keela . . . Belinda . . . Oonagh . . . Mia . . . Ethas . . . Gundrede . . . Briana . . . Guditta . . .'

I'm in cracking form this morning, roysh, and it's no wonder. It's no secret that Lillie's is once again *the* place to be seen in town. We'd that Kathryn Thomas in last night. *And* Keith Duffy. *And* Simon Delaney. *And* Mondo out of 'Fair City'.

The only, I suppose, cloud on the horizon for me is that I am seriously gagging for my Swiss at this stage. There's nothing else for it. Fionn has a lecture this afternoon. I send Evelyne upstairs to tell the Unlovely Debbie I want to see her down in the bor.

She takes her focking time coming down, it has to be said, and when she finally appears, roysh, she has her nose stuck in whatever it is that's written on her clipboard. She looks up and goes, 'You were looking for me?' and I'm like, 'All work and no play . . .' and it comes out sounding a lot sleazier than I'd intended. I'm sitting at one of the high tables in the bor.

I pour two glasses of red wine and I go, 'Come on – take a break,' and I can tell from her boat race that she's more than a bit Scooby Dubious. She goes, 'I really don't think so. I've got all this to process. I told Fionn I'd have it finished tonight . . .'

I push the glass closer to her and I go, 'Don't be so

uptight. I just think it's a shame that we haven't really taken the time to get to know each other.'

I know Fionn's John B. on her and everything, but fock him. He'd do the same to me if he had the looks to pull it off.

She goes, 'Maybe some other time. We're coming towards the end of our research,' and I'm thinking, this bird is so tight, you'd have a job swiping your Clubcord between her orse cheeks.

I look over my shoulder. Evelyne's getting the till ready for tonight. I reach across the table and take off Debbie's glasses. There's some focking weight in them.

She's not much nicer with them off either.

She goes, 'What do you think you're doing?' and I move closer to her and I'm like, 'There's a chemistry between us. Don't pretend *you* haven't felt it, Debbie,' and all of a sudden she's like, 'Debbie? Who's Debbie?' and I'm thinking, shit, we've been calling her that for so long, I thought it was her actual name.

She goes, 'My name's Janis. Now give me my glasses back,' and I'm there, 'Names are irrelevant,' playing it slicker than an oil tanker leak, the lines just coming to me. I go, 'All that matters is feelings. I've felt something for you since the day I first saw you.'

Yeah, nausea. She really is focking horrendous looking. She's going to come easy, though. Roy Keane's dog.

She goes, 'Give me my glasses back,' and I'm giving it, 'Oh, you want your glasses, do you? Is that what you want?' and I keep offering them to her, roysh, then pulling them away when she goes to take them.

Nothing like a bit of teasing to warm the engine up.

I walk around to her side of the table and I put my orms around her waist and I go, 'You know you want me, give in to your cravings,' which is when – out of nowhere, roysh –

her knee comes up like a focking rocket, and she leaves me in a pile on the floor, thinking this baby that Sorcha's having is definitely going to be my last now.

Ronan answers on the third ring by going, 'Rosser, you doorty-looking drag queen, what's the fooken Johnny McRory?' and I'm like, 'No time for pleasantries, Ro. Do you know anyone with a motorbike?' and he's there, 'Plenty. What's the job?' and I'm like, 'What?' and he goes, 'You're looking for wheels. I'm presuming it's a bank job. Here, it's not my one, is it?'

I'm there, 'Ronan, some of us are already loaded. We don't need to actually rob banks,' and he goes, 'So what's the SP?' and I'm like, 'I just need someone with a motorbike, preferably not stolen. And a spare helmet,' and he goes, 'Gull has one,' and I'm like, 'Which one is Gull again?' and he's there, 'Gull's the best wheels man in the Fermot. Doesn't say much. In and out all his life. Has a sheet like a fooken jacks roll. He'll want paying upfront but.'

I go, 'Just tell him to meet me in Merrion Square on Monday. As in the bank holiday?' and he goes, 'Game-ball.'

I can hear Erika's voice before I've even got the key in the door. And from the way her and Sorcha are talking to each other, you'd never believe that Erika sent her a thirty-eight-page e-mail yesterday on the dangers of ventouse and forceps deliveries.

I open the kitchen door, roysh, and – cool as a fish's fart – I go, 'Hey, girls, how the hell are you?' and I notice that Erika looks unbelievable, as usual. Sorcha goes, 'Hey, where's Christian?' and I'm like, 'Oh, he has a, er . . . *present* for the baby,' and Sorcha looks up from the pot she's stirring and goes, 'A present?' and I'm like, 'He's just getting it out of the cor,' and all of a sudden he appears in the kitchen, holding this, like, stuffed doll of Yoda, which I'm pretty sure our daughter will end up discussing at length in some counselling session – if we were mad enough to actually put it into her crib when she arrives.

The two birds get up and give Christian big air-kisses, which is more than I got out of either of them. Erika asks him how the plans for the wedding are going and he's like, 'Great. There's a bit to go yet, but Lauren's in her element, of course,' and I go, 'It's the stag *we're* looking forward to – Barcelona, here we come,' and I sort of, like, make this I suppose you'd have to say gyrating motion with my hips and out of the corner of my eye, roysh, I can see that Sorcha is not a happy bunny.

He shows Yoda to Sorcha, then holds it out in front of her bump and in this, like, baby voice, he goes, 'This here is Yoda, the greatest Jedi Master of them all, who ensured the rebirth of the nearly vanished Jedi Knights and for more than 800 years, trained people in the ways of the Force . . .' and I tell him he's freaking the shit out of *me*, never mind the baby.

Erika's like, 'Hey, Christian, that reminds me – did you finish your script?' and it doesn't sound like she's being a wagon at all and I'm thinking, since when was *she* interested in *Stor Wars*? Christian goes, 'Yeah. And you know the way you've been at me for ages to send it off to George Lucas . . .' and she's there, 'And you did?' and he sort of goes all, I don't know, shy and, like, nods, and Erika goes, 'That is *amazing*,' and she gives him this hug, roysh, and then she goes, '*I* am going to wear something *amazing* to the Oscars,' and even though I'm laughing along with everyone else, roysh, I have to admit I feel a bit, I suppose, left out of the loop here. Christian told Marty and Erika and God knows who else about George Lucas, but said fock-all to me, his actual best friend, and I'm thinking, maybe I should be a bit more, like, supportive of him in future, instead of, like, ripping the piss the whole time.

Sorcha takes the pot off the hob – it's mixed mushroom and sherry soup – and she goes, 'You two are probably wondering why Ross and I asked you here this evening,' and Erika and Christian look at each other, then at us. Sorcha's there, 'We'd like you to be godparents to our baby,' and I'm looking at them, roysh, and they're in, like, total shock.

Erika goes, 'You'd like me to be godmother? As in *me?*' and Sorcha's there, 'Yeah,' and Erika's like, 'And not Claire?' and I sort of, like, snigger and go, 'No, not Claire. Focking Bray! The *nerve* of that girl,' and I know that Sorcha's not happy with that comment either.

Christian's like, 'Are you goys, like, serious?' and I'm there, 'Of course. Dude, you've been my best friend since we were kids,' and he nods and goes, 'Are you planning to have her midi-chlorian count taken?' and of course I'm wondering what the fock he's talking about. He goes, 'I'm just saying, this baby could be the one to restore balance to The Force,' and I can't resist turning around to Sorcha and going, 'You'd better get your orse down to Blackrock Clinic first thing in the morning then,' and for the first time in ages, roysh, she actually laughs at something I say. Must be the happy hormones I read about kicking in.

Then she goes, 'Excuse me,' and she leaves the room, presumably to drop anchor.

Erika turns around to Christian and goes, 'I'm still going out with Clifford,' as in Clifford Michael Henry Horsburgh, in other words Baron Hacket, the twelfth earl of somewhere or other, who I can pretty much guarantee she didn't meet in Club M. She's there, 'He's at me to marry him, of course, but I just can't make up my mind,' and Christian's there, 'I hope Sorcha's taking it easy. When Leia was pregnant, she nearly ended losing the twins. Mind you, she did have the Noghri chasing her from one side of the galaxy to the other.'

Erika's going, 'I mean, I've no problem with moving to England, but I told him I wanted a title. I was like, "I want to be a Duchess of somewhere. What about Westminster?" Apparently it's already taken. Well, I said it wasn't good enough. Simply was NOT good enough. I got up and left the table. I told him, "Fix it!"'

He's there, 'She never had it easy, I suppose. Whenever she was pregnant, there was always something. When she found out she was expecting young Anakin, she was being held captive with Han and the twins on New Alderaan. They escaped, of course, but she nearly ended up going into labour on the Nespis VIII.'

She's going, 'Do you know what he *actually* had the cheek to offer me? Duchess of Yorkshire (North Riding). I was there, "If you want to get engaged, you'd better come up with something a lot more impressive than that."'

Christian goes, 'A baby Ewok – believe it or not – is called a wokling.'

And I'm sitting there, roysh, listening to the two of them, the two people we're about to entrust our daughter's – what did Sorcha call it? – religious and spiritual upbringing to, these two friends of ours, who are away in their own little worlds, and I'm thinking, Let's hope to fock nothing ever happens to *us*.

*

I think I need a doctor. I've just eaten – in the following order – half a bowl of Golden Nuggets (with water because there's no milk), a spoonful of Dijon muster, a handful of Chinese Five Spice powder, some beans, a packet of Angel Delight Bonkers Butterscotch flavour (just the powder, which was, incidentally, two months past its use-by date), two slices of cold Italian sausage and roasted peppers pizza, a slice of frozen pineapple, four Tuc crackers with ketchup on them and a tub of hummus . . . and I'm not full yet.

The tosser loves the sound of his own voice. There must be, like, fifty reporters crowded around him, we're talking TV cameras, the lot. He's going, 'Ten Ks? I'll run ten Ks! Then I'll run ten more. And ten more after that if that's what it takes to highlight our – inverted commas – struggle.'

He looks a total focking tit of course. He's *actually* going to run in his plus fours and his pink diamond sweater, which is as good as doing it under a neon sign that says, TOOL.

I'm looking around for Gull, but he's nowhere to be seen, roysh, and I'm wondering has he been *lifted* for, I don't know, *selling gear* and then I'm thinking, when did I stort actually *talking* like Ronan?

Some bird from RTÉ asks the old man if he has a time in mind and he turns around and goes, 'What's the course record?' Someone else is like, 'It's thirty-one minutes and twenty-eight seconds,' and the old man goes, 'Is it, indeed? Facts and figures. Well, I'd like to think I could get close to it. I'm not saying I'm going to win today. Top five is as much as I'll predict. I saw Sonia there a minute ago. Looks in great shape . . .'

I shout, 'You're a focking dickhead,' from the back of the big crowd of, like, reporters and a couple of them turn around and, like, tell me to be quiet because they're, like, recording and I end up just giving them the finger.

Some dude from NewsTalk goes, 'Are you saying you think you have a *chance* of beating her?' and he's there, 'Well, I've put in the mileage, you see, as I'm sure she has. But winning today isn't my whole *raison d'être*, if you'll pardon the French. As you're all well aware, I am the first man ever to run the race and I'm doing so to highlight the patent nonsense of the Gender Even-Things-Up-A-Bit Brigade and their campaign against a great institution, *ipso facto*, Portmarnock Golf Club.'

He's there, 'And at this point, I'd like to introduce you all to the man who is my coach, conditioner, solicitor and – I might add, while running the risk of embarrassing him – a man I've taken quite a bit of money from over the years on the fairways . . . Mr Hennessy-Coghlan O'Hara,' and of course Hennessy steps out of the crowd, roysh, wearing a tracksuit, with – of all things – his trilby hat and a big turd of a cigar jammed between his Taylor Keith.

He puts his orm around the old man and goes, 'It's a wonderful thing that this man is doing in the service of golf. As for taking money from me, let's just hope his legs are in better shape than his memory,' and there's all this, like, *haw-haw-haw*, fake laughter from behind him and I notice, roysh, that all their dickhead mates from the club have turned up to support them and they've got all these, like, placards and banners with shit like, 'Equality My Eye' and 'Save Portmarnock' on them.

Even the old dear's carrying one, the stupid wagon.

Where the fock is Gull? Merrion Square is so jammers he might not even find me. There's, like, thousands of birds milling about the place, a lot of them hounds it has to be said. Most of them are those, like, fat birds you see walking the roads at night, swinging their orms and their orses, trying to shed some cargo so they can get a bloke. There's a hell of a lot more of it about than I thought.

The next thing, roysh, I hear this engine revving and I look across the far side of the road and it's, like, the man himself, as in Gull. I wave at him and he comes over and he sort of, like, nods at me. I go, 'About focking time. Here,' and I hand him two hundred sheets, which Ronan told me was the price and he counts it, roysh, then hands me a helmet. Ronan was spot-on – he doesn't say much. He doesn't actually say anything at all. I'm thinking, How do you become friends with someone who doesn't actually talk?

I go, 'This shouldn't be too difficult, even for a man with your background. We're following him over there. He's the only *man* in the race,' and I swing my leg over the bike, roysh, and sit in behind him and he storts up the engine and all of a sudden, roysh, the race is off and we swing a hord roysh onto Mount Street and catch up with him just as he's on the bridge, crossing the canal.

I go, 'Okay, drive slowly,' which Gull does, roysh, and we pull up practically alongside the tosser and he turns, roysh, and looks at me and you can, like, see the look of shock on his face. I reach inside my jacket and he goes, 'DON'T ASSASSINATE ME!' and I end up nearly falling off the bike with the laughter. He's there, 'YOU MIGHT SHOOT ME DOWN – BUT THERE'S A HUNDRED MORE LIKE ME.'

I whip out, not a gun, roysh, but a megaphone, as in the little portable one that Sorcha used to use when she was collecting signatures for Amnesty in College Green, trying to save some Tinpot Tommy from having his block chopped off. There's some focking noise out of it all the same. I hold

the little receiver bit to my mouth and go, 'YOU ARE A TOTAL PENIS, YOU KNOW THAT? YOU ARE THE WORLD'S FOCKING BIGGEST PENIS!' and he looks at me, roysh, and of course, with the helmet on, he doesn't recognise me.

And now that he knows he's not going to be shot, he obviously decides to ignore me, roysh, even though I keep heckling the focker all the way down Northumberland Road.

When we hit Lansdowne Road I tell Gull to pull back a bit – I actually say, 'Stall the ball,' the way I've heard Ronan say it – and we let him go on ahead up the Shelbourne Road and onto Merrion Road, just to give ourselves a breather and lull him into a basically false sense of security.

Then we hit the old pedal and we catch up with him just as he's outside the RDS and I stort giving him dog's abuse again.

I'm like, 'YOU'RE A FOCKING TOSSER!' and – hilarious, roysh – he turns around to me and he goes, 'I don't know who you are, but I'll vouchsafe that you're one of that equality crowd. I'll not rise to your bait, thank you very much,' but I just keep giving it, 'YOU'VE ALWAYS BEEN A TOSSER AND YOU ALWAYS WILL BE! YOU COULD TOSS FOR ACTUAL IRELAND!' and I do that all the way up Nutley Lane, roysh, by which time the dickhead is already out of breath and – this is seriously funny – being overtaken by old dears.

We *stall the ball* again when the race hits UCD. I try to make conversation with Gull by telling him I broke a few horts out this direction in my time, but I'm, like, pissing into the wind. It's like Ronan said: he's not, like, a conversation person.

We let the old man go over the flyover and back up the

Stillorgan Road. When he's just, like, a speck in the distance, we go after him again. We catch up with him just as he's leaving the drinks station, looking – it has to be said – like death warmed up.

And through the megaphone I'm going, 'LOOK AT THE STATE OF YOU, YOU FOCKING OLD WINDBAG! MAKING A TIT OF YOURSELF, LIKE THE DICKHEAD THAT YOU ARE! YOU'RE A FOCKING DISGRACE!'

He stops running, roysh, and Gull has to pull up for us to hear him go, 'You're the one who's a disgrace!'

He's puffing and panting pretty badly now.

He's like, 'I'm doing this . . . to highlight an injustice . . . I should've known I'd be . . . subjected to . . . bullyboy tactics . . . by vested interests . . . Quote-unquote . . .'

I'm going, 'YOU'RE GETTING TIRED, DICK-HEAD! AND YOU KNOW IT!'

But off he staggers, wheezing like a fifty-a-day-man – Ronan, basically – past the bus depot, through Donnybrook and up Morehampton Road, with me shouting abuse at him from the back of the bike, roysh – 'IT'S FOCKING MILES TO THE END! THERE'S NO WAY YOU CAN FINISH THIS THING!' – and him stopping every couple of hundred yords to shout some shit back at me about women and why they shouldn't be allowed to become full members of golf clubs, like I actually *give* a shit?

But it's working, roysh, because all the shouting is actually wearing him out more than the actual running and – un-focking-believable, roysh – there's, like, fun-runners in fancy dress passing the focker out now and his legs look like they weigh, I don't know, a tonne each.

Sonia O'Sullivan's probably back home having a cup of tea by this stage.

It's like watching one of those bullfights, roysh, where they've stuck all those, like, spears in the bull's back and he's lost so much blood that his legs are all over the gaff.

I'm there, 'LOOK AT YOU – YOU'RE OUT ON YOUR FEET! GIVE UP NOW!'

He's not even running in a straight line anymore. He keeps, like, lurching from side to side, like he's hammered, and you can see the stewards, roysh, giving him the once-over, trying to decide whether or not to take him out of the race, because he's basically a danger to the people coming up behind him, including a giant toothbrush and a calculator, who zip past him just at the bottom of Leeson Street.

I'm there, 'YOUR LEGS HAVE GONE! YOU'RE GOING TO GO – ANY SECOND NOW!'

Just before the Burlington, roysh, he storts waving his finger at me again, going, 'It's a private members club and we won't . . . be dictated to . . . by the likes of you! Why don't you just go . . . and live in Pyongyang?' and the next thing, roysh, within sight of the actual finishing line, I see his eyes roll backwards and his knees buckle and I go, 'TIMMMBERRR!' as he finally hits the deck, out of pure exhaustion.

Gull pulls up and I hop off the bike. The St John's Ambulance crowd are pretty much on top of him by the time I make it over. He's, like, totally unconscious.

I'm going, 'I'm his next-of-kin. Take his organs. You have my permission. Even if he's not properly dead,' and the next thing, roysh, I hear all this, like, hysterical screaming and I spot the old dear pegging it down from Leeson Street Bridge, going, *Charles! Charles!*' with Hennessy – in his tracksuit – lagging behind her.

It's time I wasn't here.

I swing one leg back over the bike and I go, 'Okay, Gull, let's see what kind of a getaway driver you really are.'

The happy hormones have officially left the building. Sorcha wakes me up at three o'clock in the morning and tells me she's decided she wants a *doula*.

Of course, there's me, roysh, thinking it's, like, a new Magnum or a *pain au chocolat* or some shit. I go, 'The nearest twenty-four-hour Tesco is Ballybrack. I'm not sure it's safe this time of night. If you're going, I'd say definitely don't take my cor.'

The light goes on then, pretty much nearly blinding me. She goes, '*Oh my God*, you have absolutely *no* idea what a *doula* is, do you?' and I'm thinking, I'm not awake enough to try to bluff this one out. She's like, 'A *doula*, Ross, is someone who offers physical, emotional and informational support to a mother before, during and after childbirth. They're, like, *all* the rage in the States.'

Naturally, I go, 'But you already have a birthing portner – as in Claire. Not that I'd have any qualms about telling her to go fock herself,' and she gives me a serious filthy, roysh, and goes, 'I also need someone who has a lot of experience in childbirth,' and I'm there, 'What about your midwife. Is she not–' and she loses it with me then, roysh. She goes, 'I want a *focking* doula, Ross!' which pretty much stops me dead in my tracks, roysh, because Sorcha never swears.

I go, 'Okay, let me think . . . someone with a lot of experience in childbirth . . . Hey, Tina's from the northside. She's bound to know loads. I'll call her in the morning,' and Sorcha's there, 'What time?' and I'm like, 'Er, nine o'clock,' and she goes, 'Fine,' and she lets me go back to sleep.

So nine o'clock arrives, roysh, and unusually for me I'm wide awake – more out of fear than anything. That and I've suddenly got a craving for liquorice, which I don't even like. I pick up the old Theo and bell Tina who, like every other normal person in the world, is asleep. I go, 'Tina, you're from the other side of the city, roysh?' and she's like, 'Wha'?'

I'm there, 'Look, I don't know how to make it any simpler than that. Coming from where you do, you're bound to know a fair few birds with a lot of experience in childbirth – am I roysh?' but she just, like, slams the phone down on me.

So I'm lying there, roysh, wondering what the fock I'm going to tell Sorcha, when all of a sudden I cop that she's awake and just, like, staring at me. She goes, 'What was that about?' and I swear to God, roysh, it's like our earlier conversation never happened at all.

I'm like, 'You said you wanted a *doula*,' and she goes, 'A *doula*? Ross, I have Claire. *And* a midwife. Why would I need a *doula*?'

Then she goes, 'Was that Tina you just rang?' and I tell her it was and she goes, 'Oh my God, you ring her back and apologise. And do it at a decent hour,' and then she turns her back on me and goes back to sleep.

She pulled a face as she stepped into the visiting room, her nose assailed by the smell of cheap emulsion, while the dull, institution colours brought on what she was certain was one of her migraines.

She hated coming here. Hated having to share the same oxygen as these wretched people in the visitors' waiting area, with their cheap jewellery and their stretch-lycra and their soccer shirts worn as fashion garments. She hated the way the sex-starved inmates leered at her and muttered malevolent threats under their breaths.

Richard had lost weight – if that was possible. He reminded her of a concentration camp survivor. His clothes hung baggily from his shapeless body. His cheekbones looked like they might at any moment burst through his porridge coloured skin. Through his open necked shirt, his breastbones protruded like two little acorns. She would love those, she thought covetously. But that was just about all she wanted from him now.

They sat there saying nothing for twenty minutes.

'Darling,' Richard said eventually, in a barely audible whisper, 'I'm not so sure you should come here anymore . . .'

'Fine,' Valerie said smartly.

'What I mean is, you're still young, you're still attractive – God, you're attractive! – and I think, well . . . I think you should seriously think about finding somebody else.'

'Okay,' she said, offering no argument.

'I know this is difficult for you to hear,' he said plaintively, 'but we're going to have to face facts. It's unlikely my appeal will be successful. I'm going to be here for years. And I think it's unfair for me to ask you to spend that time waiting for me.'

'Good,' she said.

She stood up to leave, the legs of her chair screaming as it dragged across the hard, tiled floor. She afforded him one last look. His face was frozen in shock. Then she turned and walked away, hearing his forlorn cries of, 'Valerie! Valerie!' echoing after her, down the long, cavernous corridors, which she knew she'd never have to walk again.

She could feel her migraine lifting.

'What's that rash there?' Marty's got all these, like, red lumps all over his Gregory.

Fionn goes, 'Some kind of allergy. We've been conducting experiments with various types of food, as part of my overall comparative analysis . . .'

'He's had me eatin' mad stuff,' Marty goes. I notice for the first time that his hands and feet aren't tied anymore.

Fionn goes, 'It's interesting that, when it comes to food, Rastafarians share many of the same taboos as the Jewish and Muslim faiths. Shellfish, for instance, are forbidden, as is pork. Rastafarians won't even use the word. They call it *dat ting*. Incidentally, Ross, notice the dropped Hs. Close your eyes and tell me you're not on the Number 75 heading west.'

I'm there, 'I suppose. So what do they actually eat then, as in, like, Rastas?' like a fool, encouraging him.

He goes, 'Well, all meat is considered injurious to the body, so their diet is for the most part vegetarian. Fish is an important staple, though not big fish. To them, any fish more than twelve inches long is a predator and represents Babylon. They prefer small fish, such as sprat, which, like all Rastafarian food, is cooked without salt and eaten with few, if any, condiments . . .'

He's there, 'Skobies, by contrast, prefer large fish, particularly cod, which is covered in a batter of eggs, flour, cornstarch and baking powder, then deep-fried in fat. Salt, as well as vinegar, are considered essential, as is sauce, either tomato, which is known as red sauce, or curry, which is known as cuddy sauce.'

Marty turns to Fionn and goes, 'Tell him some of de shit you're after havin' me eatin',' and Fionn's there, 'Well, for three days, we've exposed him to a more rich and varied diet, giving him *foie gras*, New Orleans pralines, Scottish wild pheasant, *Brin d'Amour* cheese . . .'

I look down, see the Caviston's bag. I'm like, 'Fock me – he must be costing you an orm and a leg?'

Fionn goes, 'It's all in the name of research, Ross. I've been following the same diet for the past seven days. Two Irish males of similar age and genetic make-up. And I've experienced no ill-effects at all, apart from a little weight gain. It's extraordinary. Marty, show him how far down that rash stretches,' and Marty goes to pull up his T-shirt, roysh, but I'm like, 'It's actually cool, I believe you.'

Sorcha has her nose stuck in – of all things – a book. I'm like, 'Why are you reading?' and she goes, '*Why* am I reading? It's a book about childbirth, if you must know. I'm thinking of having the baby by reflexology,' and I'm there, 'Which in English is . . .' and she goes, 'Reflexology, Ross! It's a form of massage they're using in labour wards now as an alternative to conventional drugs. They work on various points of the feet to help the contractions work more effectively. It says here it increases the production of endorphins and can also speed up labour.'

I'm there, 'Don't be sweating the small stuff, Babes. There's, like, ages to go yet,' and she goes, '*Oh* my God, there is SO *not* ages to go? Of course, you wouldn't know that. You don't have to carry this baby around with you everywhere you go. You can't feel her growing inside you. You can't feel her kicking you . . .'

I'm like, 'Kicking you? When did that stort?' wondering why she never bothered her orse telling me. She goes, 'About two weeks ago,' and I'm there, 'Oh. Did anyone else feel it?' and she's like, 'Claire. And Mum,' and I go, 'Why didn't you tell me?' and she just, like, shrugs her shoulders and she's there, 'It never came up.'

*

I only catch the orse end of the conversation, but Oisinn's going, 'I'm looking forward to meeting you too, Eva,' which presumably means Herzegovina, who's going to be, like, the face of *Eau d'Affluence* in Italy.

Oisinn's been a bit cool with me since I got back from Lough Derg, roysh, and I know why. Of course when he hangs up, roysh, I actually make the effort with him.

I go, 'I hear you're off to Milan in the morning,' and he's like, 'Yep,' and he says nothing more, roysh, just that. So I end up losing it. I'm there, 'What is your *focking* problem, Dude?' and he's like, '*My* problem? Shit the bed, Ross, I would have thought that was obvious. I asked you to do a job . . .'

There's no way I'm listening to this. I'm there, 'I *tried* to get him to change his mind, Oisinn. He's got God on his side, remember? Bit of an unfair advantage,' and he just goes, 'There *is* no God, Ross.'

Of course straight away, roysh, I'm there, 'And this from a man who hopes to make a fortune selling holy water,' but he shrugs, roysh, and goes, 'Quickest way to get rich, Ross, is to give gullible people what they want.'

Evelyne arrives for work. I'm going to make a serious move there unless Sorcha puts out soon.

Oisinn goes back to making notes, probably his speech for Milan. I go, 'If you don't mind my saying so, Oisinn, the last time JP was here, you were like Grant Mitchell's phone, in other words, bang out of order,' and he goes, 'And if you don't mind *me* saying so, Ross, you're so far up JP's hole these days the focker can taste Dax,' and I run my hand through my quiff, roysh, and go, 'It's Trevor Sorbie mg, actually,' and he goes, 'Whatever it is, the goy can do no wrong in your eyes.'

I'm there, 'Maybe I like seeing the goy happy. He has his

beliefs. You've got to respect that. And anyway, you said you didn't need him anymore . . . It's like that old saying, it only takes a small man to carry a grudge.'

But he's not listening to me anymore, roysh. His eyes have gone wide and he's, like, staring over my shoulder at the plasma screen on the wall of the bor. It's, like, Sky News. He grabs the zapper and flicks it off mute.

Kay Burley's going, 'Pope John Paul II, leader of the world's one billion Catholics for the past twenty-six years, has died at the age of eighty-four. The Pope, the third longest-serving pontiff in history, passed away tonight in his private apartment at the Vatican, after a long period of illness . . .'

And Oisinn's there, 'As one door closes . . .'

I can smell something. It smells like boiled sweets. Oisinn says he can't smell anything other than the sandalwood notes he was experimenting with all afternoon. But it's not sandalwood I'm smelling.

In fact, I'm pretty sure I know what it is now.

I hop off the stool and peg it up the stairs. I push open the door of the office and I swear to God, roysh, I'm staring at Fionn and Marty through this, like, fog of cigarette smoke. I go, 'I can't *believe* you're smoking working-class drugs in my office,' and Fionn goes, 'Relax, Ross. It's just *dee 'erb,*' and the two of them, like, collapse into a fit of giggles.

They're smoking the biggest joint ever seen this side of the M50. I'm thinking Fionn must have, like, robbed it off his granny, who's on it for her glaucoma.

I'm there, 'Let me guess – this is research, is it?' and Fionn goes, 'Yes, Ross. Hash plays an important part in the rituals of both subcultures . . .' but he can't keep a straight face, roysh, he keeps cracking his hole laughing.

Marty goes, 'As a means of awakening them to their heritage and their reality,' and I have to say, roysh, it's an

unbelievable impression of Fionn. He has the whole spiel
and everything.

Marty's going, 'The average skobie's life is conditioned
and controlled by forces too complex for him to understand,' and I'm thinking the rest of the goys *have* to hear
him doing this. He's there, 'But like the Rastafarian, he is
no longer capable of seeing himself as he is. To free himself
from these psychic chains – the dole office, the credit union,
the methadone clinic, the courts – he must, as they say in
Kingston, *loose up his head . . .*'

Even I'm laughing now.

Marty's like, 'This is achieved, in both communities,
through use of *dee 'erb* – marijuana in the case of Jamaica
and, in the townships of Dublin, the famous *hashish . . .*'

Fionn is actually on the floor laughing at this point and
I'm not far behind him.

Marty's giving it, 'Only *hashish* can bring about a true
revelation of Skobie consciousness and a proper understanding and appreciation of what it is to be a creamer, disencum-
bering the mind of hang-ups about lack of education, social
status . . .'

Trotting around Mothercare after Sorcha isn't exactly my
idea of a great Saturday afternoon. Once you've messed
around with the motorised breast pumps, there's pretty
much fock-all for a goy to do, though Ronan's in his total
element, roysh, offering Sorcha his opinion on such things
as baby-pink appliqué tops and mitt-and-bootee sets. I even
hear him turn around to one of the birds who works there
and go, 'I take it this snowsuit is *faux* fur, is it?' then turn
back to Sorcha and go, 'They *only* use fake furs apparently.
It's *all* good.'

I am focking gagging for fried eggs, beans and broccoli, all on the same plate, and I'm wondering would it be rude if I slipped upstairs to the Kylemore. Sorcha seems in capable hands. Ronan's going, 'If you're going to buy a bath support, you'd want to be sure it's ergonomic.'

Ergonomic? In fairness to him, he's really into the idea of this baby.

Sorcha's there, 'I suppose. I *like* the terrycloth one? But I suppose this one has contours, which offer better support. Which do you think, Ross?'

Of course I'm caught offguard. I'm like, 'The, er . . . *white* one?' and Sorcha goes, 'Oh my God, they're *both* white!' and then she gives me this filthy, roysh, which basically says, just stay out of my way for the rest of the day, until I ask you for your credit cord.

Ronan's there, 'There's a nice bath mat there, Sorcha. Changes colour when the water's too hot. It's PVC, non-slip, wipe-clean . . .' and she goes, '*Oh* my God, I SO have to have one of those,' and she drops it into the trolley, which I notice is filling up pretty fast.

She goes, 'What about this, Ronan? A shampoo shield,' and he's like, 'Stops soapy water getting in yisser babby's eyes. Yeah, throw one in there,' which she does.

Actually, I'd murder a cheeseburger. No, two.

Ronan's going, 'We've got to start thinking in terms of safety,' and I'm thinking, *we've*? He's like, 'You won't feel the time until she's crawling. Here, look at this,' and he picks up this box. He's there, 'Babyden. *Multi-functional set of five panels and one gate panel to keep toddlers safe from all sorts of indoor and outdoor hazards. Super-strong steel in a choice of three colours.* It's a play den, a safety gate, a room divider and a fire guard, all in one . . .' and no sooner is it said than it's in the trolley.

Sorcha goes, 'We're going to need a safety gate as well

. . . for the top of the stairs. And look at this – a cooker and hob guard,' and Ronan's like, 'You can't put a price on safety,' and I'm thinking, I'd say the bird on the cash register will give it a good shot, though.

Ronan's there, 'Door slam stoppers. You've got to think of her little fingers. We'll need a whole whack of them. And socket covers. Twenty should cover it . . .'

Sorcha's like, 'Look at this, Ronan. It's a glass safety film. You put it over the coffee table and if there's an accident it holds the broken glass in place . . . *Oh my God*, they think of *everything.*'

Yes, they certainly do. Chicken nuggets is what I'd like. And a hamburger – but just for the gherkin.

Ronan's there, 'Corner cushions. You bang these on the corner of yisser tables and shelves. Cover the sharp edges. You can't *not* have them . . .'

Sorcha goes, 'Oh my God, Ronan, what about the cor? We'll need one of these sun shields with a cat's face on it. And a rear-view mirror that lets you keep an eye on what's happening in the back seat. And – OH! MY GOD! – *how* cute is that?' and she holds up this little pink sign that says, Princess On Board.

We don't even know if it's a girl yet, but in it goes into the trolley. And this goes on for another, like, twenty minutes until we've picked up at least one of pretty much every item in the shop. Then they declare their innings.

It turns out you can put a price on safety: €379 is Mothercare's, but I hand over my credit cord without a word, except to go, 'Can we hit Mackie Ds?' and Ronan's there, 'Come on, Sorcha, let's take this fella for a Happy Meal.'

6. Almost outfoxed in Foxrock with a Fox

A lot of people thought Oreanna was Baghdad having anything to do with me again, especially after I killed – in the following order – one, her cat, two, her dog, and three, her cousin's pet snake, all by total accident it has to be said, except of course the snake, which somehow managed to get into our gaff, roysh, and was actually in the process of, like, terrorising Sorcha until I picked up something hord and turned him into a focking draught excluder.

So what with one thing and another, roysh, Oreanna got it into her head that I was totally chicken oriental and got my kicks by basically killing shit and, of course, nothing could be further from the truth. She was one of my old reliables for years, roysh, but the word on the street was that she wanted fock-all to do with me on account of what happened to Simba, Scooby and, last but not least, poor Slinky.

But Oreanna's problem is that she's basically in love with me and she knows she's kidding herself if she thinks she can stay away. So I'm in Café Java in Blackrock, roysh, having a bit of brekky, reading the Sunday papers, getting myself seriously psyched up for the Leinster match, and that's when I notice her, out of the corner of my eye, wrapping her face around a humungous piece of, like, chocolate cake.

I crack on not to see her, roysh, and after a while she cops me. I'm reading Hooky's preview, roysh, wondering why he still hasn't mentioned my name in connection with the problem out-half position – despite certain promises made to my old man over brandies in Riverview – when all of a sudden she's standing over me, going, 'Hi, Ross.'

Sorcha, I should add at this point, has gone off for the weekend, back down to the Brook Lodge Inn with her old dear for another of their pampering weekends, leaving Don Juan here on his Tobler. And I've basically fock-all to do except put together that Provençal cot Sorcha bought ages ago and which is still in flat-pack form, leaning up against the wall in what is going to be the nursery, because I haven't got my lazy orse around to putting it together yet. Her last words to me on her way out the door were, 'I am SO not bluffing, Ross. If that cot isn't together by the time I get back, our marriage is over.'

Oreanna looks well, it has to be said. She has a focking orse on her like two Hummers fighting over a porking space, but she's still a dead ringer for Ivana Hovart.

She goes, 'Can I sit down?' and I'm there, 'I'm surprised you want to. I hear you've been bad-mouthing me around town,' and she's like, 'Please, Ross. I don't want to fight with you anymore,' and she sits down and goes, 'Maybe, on reflection, I'm prepared to believe that it *was* just a series of accidents . . .'

I look up from my paper and go, 'How many times do I have to tell you, I swung the old GTI into your driveway and Simba just didn't move quick enough. Your dog was humping my leg and I shook him off. I couldn't help it if he hit that wall . . .' and she goes, 'Enough, Ross! *Enough!* Please! Let's just forget it. Look, I'm sure they're all up in animal heaven now, looking down on us, having a great laugh . . .'

Fock me. The girl is sadder than a sackful of kittens and a lump hammer.

But like I said, she's a honey, roysh, and a man has needs

and, what with Sorcha not putting out at the moment and me sitting here with knackers like beach balls, it's not long before we're heading back to my gaff for a bit of extramarital fun.

So anyway, roysh, I end up having this idea, which, like pretty much all my ideas, seems incredible at the time. To cut a long story short, I decide to pump up Sorcha's birthing pool, roysh, then fill it up with the sixty bottles of champagne I picked up yesterday from the cash and carry but haven't yet brought into the club.

Of course there's a port of me thinking, that's a bit extravagant, especially given that Oreanna's a sure thing, but then I'm thinking, fock it, I own Lillie's.

Do you think Robbie Fox has never had a champagne bath?

Oreanna's really excited by the idea. She's clapping her hands together in that annoying way that birds do and going, 'This is SO amazing.'

But almost straight away, roysh, we encounter what would have to be described as our first major hiccup. We don't have an actual foot pump. I don't remember ever owning one. I root around under the stairs, then in the garage, for something we might use instead, but Sorcha's hairdryer is the only thing I can find that blows air, and after a couple of attempts I give it up as a bad idea.

So there's nothing else for it, roysh. I find the little rubber tube and I tell Oreanna to get blowing, which she does, while I disappear into the sitting-room to watch the match. I figure it'll probably take her pretty much the whole game to blow the thing up, which suits me just fine.

She's talking to me through the door the whole time, going, 'I had this, like, recurring nightmare that you were a serial killer and you'd, like, worked your way through all my pets and now you were coming after me. That's how I ended up in counselling,' and I'm wondering, Would it be rude if I closed over the sitting-room door, roysh, because I can't concentrate on the game here?

The Dricster's a focking legend – no other word for it. The match is nearly over, roysh, and I'm sitting there thinking what a terrible shame it would be for Irish rugby if we never got to play together on the same team, when all of a sudden I notice that Oreanna's gone unbelievably quiet.

And of course straight away I'm concerned.

I'm there, 'Don't be slacking up out there – this is over in ten minutes,' but there's, like, no answer.

So I go out to the kitchen, roysh, and you can imagine my shock, roysh, when I find her out for the count on the floor. It's pretty obvious, roysh, that she's fainted from all the blowing and suddenly I'm, like, slapping her across the face, trying to wake her up. But it's no good. She's out to lunch.

So being, whatever, call it compassionate, I throw her over my shoulder, which is no mean feat in itself – like I say, she's no stranger to a snack-box – and I carry her up the stairs, dump her on the floor of the nursery, then go back down and watch the last ten minutes of the match.

At exactly the same moment as the final whistle blows, roysh, the old Theobold rings. I answer it and it's, like, Sorcha, going, 'Hi, Ross. It's me. Did you put the Provençal cot together?' and of course I've no choice but to go, 'Last night. Looks pretty good, if I do say so myself. Anyway, never mind me and my DIY adventures, how are *you* getting on?'

She's there, 'Oh my God, we had an *amazing* time,' and obviously I'm like, '*Had?* As in . . .' and she goes, 'We're on the way back. Aoife's back in hospital, so I'm going to have to do the shop tomorrow. We've just passed the Glen of the Downs,' and I swear to God, roysh, I nearly actually shit myself.

I am about to break the flatpack-assembly world record. I slam down the phone, reef the tool box out from under the stairs, grab a hammer and a screwdriver out of it, then take the stairs two at a time. I burst into the nursery and – what are the chances? – it's at that exact point, roysh, that Oreanna wakes up, after having one of her nightmares. And she sees me standing over her, roysh, with a hammer and a screwdriver.

Apparently you could hear her screams as far away as Dundrum.

I arrive at the club, roysh, to find Ronan sitting in the bor with Fionn, who's got what actually looks like a Leaving Cert paper open in front of him. Ronan's got a Coke, but he's, like, pouring something – presumably whiskey – into it from a hipflask whenever Fionn's not looking.

I walk in and go, 'What's the Jack here?' and Ronan goes, 'Ah, there you are, Rosser. 'Member I told you 'bout that bit of bother Nudger was in? Fionn's giving the ould buke of evidence the once-over. These rozzers all have the Gaelic – all boggers, you see. Reading this, you wouldn't know what they were chargin' you with.'

Fionn looks up and goes, 'No, Ronan, this is just an Irish translation of what's on the opposite page. These State documents, they have to give them to you in Irish because it's the official language under the Constitution. But there's nothing hidden in there . . .'

Ronan nods. Then he goes, 'No tricks? No surprises? You sure?' and Fionn goes, 'One hundred per cent,' and

Ronan knocks back the rest of his drink, puts his hand into his inside pocket and whips out an envelope, which he hands to Fionn, then goes, 'A little token of Nudger's appreciation . . .'

And when Fionn opens it, there's, like, five hundred sheets in there.

Valerie loved her Tuesday afternoons in the National Gallery. It was her *me* time. She could exhaust hours walking through its high, airy rooms, admiring seven centuries worth of master-pieces, including works from all the major continental schools. After viewing works by Caravaggio, Titian, Rubens, Monet, Pissarro, Signac, Picasso, Vermeer and Goya, to say nothing of the works of Irish artists, such as Yeats, Hamilton, Lavery and Orpen, there was nothing she liked more than relaxing with a cappuccino, or a Viennese coffee, or even a Caffe Borgia, accompanied by a thick wedge of their Seville orange and passion fruit cheesecake or even one of their ginger and blue-berry crème brûlées.

Applying the finish to her marriage to Richard had been a surprisingly painless business. He had called her mobile phone and her apartment countless times since her last visit. Knowing how strictly the prison authorities rationed phone cards, she felt a slight undertow of guilt at not answering. Sooner or later, she reasoned, he would get the message and he, too, would get on with his life – such as it was now.

Maybe one day he might discover the same kind of happi-ness that she had found.

She felt the soft cream of her coffee greet her lips and felt herself slide into a daydream about Lovell. In it, they were standing naked, in an old oak-panelled study, in front of a fire that smelt unmistakably of apple logs, their bodies curved into one another, her hands exploring his big, Clydesdale shoulders, then entwining in the black thicket of his hair, as he shielded her in his arms and planted a kiss on her quivering mouth.

Through the cloth of her dress she could feel his throbbing manhood.

Throbbing manhood? Who *talks* like that? Actually, I might make myself a bowl of Ambrosia creamed rice in a minute.

Something snapped her from her reverie. A voice. It sounded like Lovell. At first she thought she must have imagined it but when she heard it again she pirouetted around to see him sitting just three tables away.

She felt her blood curdle.

The two men he was eating lunch with were familiar. They were more than familiar. She knew them. After the trial she knew that their faces would be forever branded on her memory. One of them was Larry Leffman, the Criminal Assets Bureau's brilliant young senior counsel, whose questions had rendered her a babbling wreck on the witness stands. The other was the CAB investigator with the bad breath.

For two or maybe three interminable seconds, Valerie wondered what business they had having lunch together.

Then she heard Leffman say it: 'We hired you to find out what he did with the rest of the money . . .'

A chill skittered up her spine. She tried to stand up as quietly as her shaking body would allow but her legs betrayed her. The chair screeched along the wooden floor and in that instant Lovell looked up.

'Valerie!' he said, the colour leaving his face in a hurry.

But she didn't wait for his explanation. She left the restaurant, ran down the steps, through the excellent new Millennium wing and, with Lovell in hot pursuit, melted into the late afternoon throng on Clare Street.

It just gets worse and worse.

So I'm in the gaff, roysh, watching an old DVD of the Dricmeister General ripping the total piss out of, like, France in Paris when the phone rings and who is it only Sorcha, obviously bored off her tits, roysh, with fock-all happening in the shop. Of course this means she's got, like, time on her hands to dream up shit for me to do, as if I'm not, like, busy enough.

She's going, 'Ross, are you even listening to me?' and I'm like, 'Of course I'm listening to you,' and after, like, ten seconds of total silence – during which Dennis Hickie, for me the unsung hero of the match, sprints forty yords to put in a tackle on Dal Maso, we're talking three yords short of the Irish line – she goes, 'I think we should stort getting a hospital bag together,' and I'm like, 'As in . . .' and she's not a happy camper with that.

She's like, '*As in* a hospital bag, Ross! A bag of essentials that I'll need, in case I go into labour unexpectedly and have to be rushed to hospital,' and of course if brains were dynamite, I wouldn't even have enough to blow my nose. Instead of just going, 'Kool and the Gang,' or, 'Ain't no thing but a chicken wing,' or *whatever*, I end up going, 'HELLO? It's only May. The baby's not due for another, like, eight weeks,' and that's her cue to stort totally losing it.

She's going, 'OH MY GOD, JUST TAKE DOWN WHAT I SAY, ROSS, OR YOU ARE SO NOT HAVING ANYTHING TO DO WITH THIS BABY!' and I'm like, 'Okay, okay, just chillax, will you?' and she takes, like, a deep breath and goes, 'The Louis Vuitton Keepall 50 that your parents bought me for my twenty-first is in the wardrobe in the guest room,' and I'm like, 'Cool,' and she's there, 'Now, have you got a pen and paper there. There's a list of things I want you to put into it,' and I'm going, 'Got one here,' which I haven't, of course, because at that stage I'm thinking I'm well capable of remembering whatever it is she wants.

I'm focking gagging for a hotdog here. I wonder is that a craving, or am I just hungry? And peanut butter. I love that shit.

She goes, 'Okay, I want you to get two tubs of that massage body butter that I like – as in the honey olive neroli one? – two tubes of L'Oreal Stretchmork Corrector and Firming Cream and one tube of AVENT Future Mother Indulgent Body Cream,' and I'm like, 'Hey, no probs,' and I'm thinking that I'm in serious trouble, roysh, if she asks me to repeat any of this shit back to her.

I'm there, 'Hey, let's talk about it in more detail tonight,' trying to get her off the Wolfe, but she's like, 'Just keep taking this down, Ross. I need you to go to the chemist and get me a large tube of Retreat Home Spa Revitalising Foot Polish. Aoife says it's, like, SO amazing, but just in case it's not, I'll need a tube of my usual La Source Revitalising Foot and Leg Therapy Cream, and see do they have the Foot Smoother as well, will you? It comes in a tub,' and of course I'm pegging it around the gaff at this stage looking for, of all things, a pen.

She's like, 'Miriam Stoppard NURTURE are supposed to do this – OH MY GOD – *amazing* Refreshing Foot Gel, though you might need to go to BTs for that. Now, there's this spray you can get – you'll probably get it in Boots – called Oramoist,' and I'm there, 'That sounds interesting. Tell me a little bit more about it,' basically trying to buy myself some time, while I'm basically turning the kitchen upside-down, looking for something to write with.

She's there, 'See, all that puffing and panting during labour

SO dries out your mouth and this stuff, like, moisturises and freshens it again,' and I'm there, 'Wow, how *exactly* does it, like, work?' and she goes, '*Oh* my God, you don't *need* to know how it works, Ross. Just get me the vanilla mint one. No, see do they do a chocolate one. No, no, actually vanilla mint is fine . . .'

I'm there, 'Okay,' pegging it up the stairs to see if there's a pen in the bedroom. She's like, 'Now, do you know where my Molton Brown is?' and I'm there, 'Em . . .' and she goes, 'The bottom drawer of my locker. Just grab my Skinfresh Facial Wash, my Skinbalance Toning Lotion, my Active Defence City-Day Hydrator, my Skinboost Twenty-Four-Hour Moisture Mist, my Eye Rescue Ultracool, my Lipsaver, my Heavenly Gingerlily Moisture Bath and Shower Gel – oh! – and my Heavenly Gingerlily Body Lotion, my Ziao Jao Healthy Hairwash and – *oh my God* – my Indian Cress Instant Conditioner . . .' and as she's saying this, roysh, I'm just, like, tipping the entire contents of the drawer onto the bedroom floor and I'm thinking, I know I'm not exactly WB focking Yeats, but what kind of a house is this that we don't even have, like, a pen in it?

Then, roysh, all of a sudden, on top of the locker, I cop one of Sorcha's eyebrow pencils and I grab that and I'm thinking, basically, Kool and the Gang, but now all of a sudden I'm looking around for something to actually write on, but Sorcha's still going, like a Daniel Day into the path of a porked cor.

She's like, 'The Sanctuary Spa Indulgence range is – *oh my God*! – SO amazing. Just get me the Hand Sugar Scrub and the Hydrating Cleanser. Oh and the Foot Soufflé. They don't always have it, but if they do . . . Now, Mothercare. I was thinking, for the baby, we're going to need four pairs of scratch mitts, three light cardigans, six cotton bodysuits,

six sleepsuits, a pack of newborn nappy sacks, baby shampoo, lotion, wipes, cotton wool balls, nappy cream . . . Did
you get that infant carrier car seat yet?' and I'm like, 'Er . . .
not really, no,' and she's like, '*Oh* my God, I told you to do
that, like, a week ago. Am I having this baby on my own?'

Before I get a chance to answer she goes, 'A changing mat,
two packs of newborn disposable nappies, barrier cream, a
baby thermometer, a baby bath, five soft towels – now,
make sure they're Egyptian cotton, Ross – a scissors, a baby
hairbrush and comb, a tub of baby moisturising cream –
and make sure it's unperfumed,' and I'm thinking, probably
the only way out of this is to pretend to have a hort attack
and I'm actually seriously considering it, roysh, as I walk
back into the sitting-room in time to see Strings getting
totally creamed and God scooping the ball up off the ground,
then cutting through the French defence to put the ball
down under the post, a bit like yours truly in his heyday.

I just, like, flop down on the sofa, feeling totally defeated
and she's still going in my ear. She's like, 'Now, while you're
in Mothercare, you'll need to get me three nightdresses –
and make sure they have a front opening for breastfeeding
– a light dressing gown and slippers, four packs of disposable
briefs, twenty-four maternity towels and two packs of breast
pads. Oh and don't forget my digital camera and my spare
phone chorger . . .'

As she's saying this, roysh, I notice the TV guide on the
coffee table and I grab it and get ready to, like, stort taking
down this shit in the morgin using the eyebrow pencil, but
Sorcha goes, 'Oh and three support bras,' and I only manage
to get down the word BRAS on the page before she tells
me that she has to go because a customer has just walked in.

*

I'm out and about, roysh, enjoying a bit of extracurricular fun with this PR bimbo I know called Fearne, who, I swear to God, roysh, is not only a ringer for Jamie-Lynn Discala – except with bad skin – but also drives a Ferrari, we're talking an *actual* Ferrari here, her old man's of course, and I just love revving that little baby's engine – and the cor's as well.

We're out for a spin and, not being big-headed here, but Fearne's hands are, like, all over me, roysh, obviously unable to believe her luck that she's actually scoring *the* Ross O'Carroll-Kelly, but with a set of wheels like this she can look forward to a lot more non-committal fun with me in the future, much as it breaks my hort to keep cheating on Sorcha like this.

Like I said before, though, there's nothing going *on* at home at the moment – except Sorcha's big, grey, don't-even-think-about-it period knickers – and my nuts are like two focking space-hoppers.

Thick and all as she is, roysh, Fearne is loaded. She asks me to pull into the Shell in Stillorgan, roysh, because she needs water for her wipers. She comes back out, roysh, with a bottle of Vittel, and as I'm watching her pour it into the little bottle where the window washer fluid goes, I'm thinking, That is definitely the most Celtic Tiger thing I've ever seen.

So we're back on the road, roysh, and I'm sitting behind the wheel, listening to her blab away about some friend of hers called Melanie who – OH! MY GOD! – sits in the sauna for, like, forty-five minutes before she goes to Weight Watchers, which is, like – HELLO? – SO cheating, even if she is only fooling herself.

Picture this, roysh. We're pulled up at the lights next to Foxrock Church and the next thing, out of the corner of my eye, I see this big gaggle of old biddies getting ready to cross the road in front of us and – I swear to God – they're like the cast of that *Cocoon* that was on the box the other night.

They're obviously coming out of Mass and it's, like, cordigans and walking sticks and shampoo-and-sets everywhere – and I know what they're going to do even before they actually do it.

Bear in mind, roysh, that the light is actually *red* for them and, like, green for me. Doesn't matter to them. They all just, like, spill across the road anyway – this is a focking dualler we're talking about – like a flock of sheep, yapping away to each other, not a focking care in the world, giving it – I don't know – '*I got a lovely bit of meat for me dinner,*' and, '*Cissy swears by that toilet safety frame her eldest had fitted for her.*'

So I end up revving the engine, roysh, basically as a warning, just to let them know that if I actually put this beast into gear, I could end up putting a week's work the local undertaker's way. Of course it doesn't go down well.

Four or five of them actually stop, roysh, and stort muttering about 'disrespect' and of course they all quote me their ages – '*I'm eighty-three, you know*' – but one of them's not saying anything, roysh, she's just, like, staring at me, big focking dandelion puffball head on her . . .

My hort nearly stops beating.

All of a sudden I recognise her and from the way she's looking at me, you can bet your focking orse she recognises me.

I do a pretty smort U-ey, roysh, and I focking lead-foot it back in the direction of Blackrock, we're talking ninety Ks an hour here, and Fearne's there giving it, 'Slow down! Slow down! Ross, *what's wrong?*'

I'm going, 'That was Sorcha's focking granny back there.'

She's like, 'Who's Sorcha?' and I'm there, 'Oh, I mightn't have mentioned it, but I'm, like, married?' and she's suddenly

giving it, 'Oh my God! OH *my* God!' and I'm there, 'I don't want to be rude, Fearne, but I've no time for your focking drama queen act.'

I swing the cor down Newtownpork Avenue, roysh, and pull up outside the gaff, the smell of burning rubber I'd imagine bringing back one or two memories for Fearne from last night.

There's only the one cor in the driveway, roysh – my BMW Z4 – so Sorcha mustn't be home yet. Her and her old dear were in Waterford for the night, checking out some holistic healing centre, which is how I ended up in the Club Shoot your Goo, up to my old tricks, we're talking breaking horts, left, right and centre.

I pull up on the road outside and as I'm getting out of cor, roysh, I notice that Fearne's bawling and when I ask her what the fock is her problem, she goes, 'Last night you told me you loved me,' and I end up just making a W with my fingers and going, '*What*-ever!' because there's no reasoning with them when they're like that.

As I'm opening the door she shouts up the driveway, 'Ross, I'm not leaving here until we've talked this thing through. Maybe your wife would be interested in meeting me,' which is blackmail, roysh, in anyone's language, so I end up having to give it to her with both barrels – put her out of *my* misery basically.

I go, 'You know, you're not even that nice up close? Lookswise, you're alroysh, but you're skin's in focking rag order. Every time I go to kiss you I feel like I'm landing on the moon. You're as thick as whale shit – and that's saying something coming from me. I couldn't pour piss out of a boot if the instructions were on the heel, as Oisinn always says, and I still find you beneath me intellectually. Oh and you're cat in the sack. It's like stuffing sausage meat into a broiler. In fact, if your old man hadn't bought you that cor, I wouldn't have focking touched you with a ten-foot cattle prod,' which seems to do the trick, roysh, because she puts her foot down and focks off.

I feel bad, but I'll make it up to her later.

I peg it up the stairs, whip off the threads and get into the scratcher and – unbelievable timing this – fifteen minutes later I hear Sorcha's cor pulling up outside, roysh, and her stomping up the stairs.

I crack on to be asleep.

She's like, 'Have you been out?' and I'm there rubbing my eyes, going 'What time is it? Have I slept in?' and she's like, 'It's half-ten. And you didn't answer my question. Have you been out this morning?' and I go, 'Of course not. Half-ten? That's practically the middle of the night. What's all this about, Babes?'

She doesn't answer, roysh, just whips out the old Wolfe and bells her old dear.

She goes, 'She *must* have been mistaken, Mum. He's *here*. He's in bed,' and I don't know what her old dear says, but I doubt if it's, like, complimentary, because all of a sudden Sorcha's going, 'Because I *love* him. And I *trust* him. And because when someone you *actually* love tells you something, you can take it for granted that they're telling the truth . . . And anyway I checked his cor – the engine's cold.'

Oh my God, she's like focking Colombo.

Then she's suddenly going, 'You said it yourself, Mum. What about that time she got on the wrong bus in town and ended up at Newgrange with all those American tourists? She *needs* glasses . . .'

When she eventually hangs up, roysh, she kisses me on the forehead and goes, 'I'm sorry for ever doubting you,' and then, probably out of guilt, fixes me a big, fock-off fry-up. I horse it back while watching 'Shortland Street' and about an hour later, roysh, she comes into the bedroom and tells me that her and her old dear are bringing the old bag off to get her eyes tested.

So I decide, roysh, that I *have* to be there to see that. It's, like, payback for ratting me out.

So twenty minutes later, roysh, we're all in my jammer, heading for Dundrum Town Centre and the granny – who's always hated my guts anyway – is going, 'There's nothing wrong with my eyesight. I know what I saw. He was in a red car . . .' and Sorcha's looking at me as if to say, basically, Ah bless!

We hit Specsavers, roysh, and the stupid cow's still giving it loads. She's going, 'I'm not getting my eyes tested if *he's* going to be there, sniggering away at me.'

Sorcha turns to me and goes, 'Ross, would you mind . . .' and I'm there, 'Hey, it's Kool and the Gang with me, Babes. I'll go get a Storbucks,' and she looks at me and goes, 'Thanks, Ross. You're being so . . . *understanding* about all this.' As she's walking away, roysh, I go – really loud, roysh, so the old bag can hear me – 'Make sure and get big focking thick ones for her.'

I swear to God, roysh, I end up nearly focking spitting my white chocolate mocha everywhere when they arrive into Storbucks half an hour later, roysh, with the granny wearing these big focking Coca Cola bottle lenses, basically like the ones the Unlovely Debbie wears.

Sorcha and her old dear go up to the counter, roysh, to get some, I don't know, focking Tazo tea, leaving the old battleaxe sitting with me and, of course, I can't resist going, 'How many fingers am I holding up?' while giving her just the middle one.

She goes, 'You know, I never liked you, from the moment I first met you,' and I stort going, '*Ooh, I think I'll get me nets washed while there's good drying out,'* basically doing an impression of her, which I have to admit is, like, pretty hilarious.

She goes, *'Cheating* on her. And she carrying your child?' and I'm there, *'Ooh, I've got me fuel vouchers but sure I didn't turn the heating on till the fourth of February. THEY ended up owing ME money.'*

She's there, 'Don't you cheek me. I'm eighty-five, you know,' and I'm like, *'Ooh, I'm eighty-five, you know,'* and she's there, 'Oh, you think you're very clever, don't you?' and then she goes, 'Well, I'm going to make sure my granddaughter finds out what kind of a . . . *man* she's got herself mixed up with.'

I just, like, throw my eyes up to heaven and she goes, 'I will, I'm telling you.'

I'm there, 'Oh, so you're stepping up to the plate, Granma? You think you're a match for the old Rossmeister General here?'

And she smiles, roysh, probably for the first time since Count John McCormack was on 'Top of the Pops', and she goes, 'You'll see . . .'

My phone rings. It's Sorcha and straight away, roysh, she's like, 'Oh my God, *what* is your problem, Ross?' and of course I'm there, 'What do you mean?' and she goes, 'I've just called up to Mum's. She asked to borrow our TV guide?' and I'm like, 'Yeah, and?' and she goes, *'And,* you'd written the word bras on it in, like, eyebrow pencil?' and before I can say anything back, roysh, she goes, *'Oh* my God, are you some kind of sicko? You have a *real* problem, you know that?' and then she just, like, hangs up.

*

The doorbell rings and I make the mistake of answering. For fock's sake – it's the old pair. I go, 'Sorcha's not here,' and the old man goes, 'Sorcha? We've come to visit *you*, Ross. Your mother's baked you one of her world-famous lemon curd meringue roulades,' and I'm looking at the two of them, roysh, and it's obvious they want to be asked in.

I go, 'It's a bit awkward, actually – "Kirsty's Home Videos" is about to stort,' but they're not taking that for an answer and – too nice for my own good – I end up inviting them in out of the rain and suddenly, roysh, they're taking their coats off and sitting down and generally making themselves at home.

The old man goes, 'I expect you heard about the mini-marathon,' and I'm there, 'I heard you made a total tit of yourself,' and he's like, 'An assassination attempt. I've no doubt that's what it was, Ross. Tried to induce a heart attack in a bid to silence me. To take me out, quote-unquote. Charlie Bird hinted as much in his report. I think I made my point, though, quite audibly,' and I go, 'By being corted off on a focking stretcher? The only point you made was that you're a focking tosspot and you don't care who knows it. You absolute penis.'

He's like, 'Anyway, we can't sit around here all afternoon debating the wheres and whyfors of my new role as an activist putting his life on the line for golfers' rights. Your mother and I are going away for a couple of days,' and I'm there, 'Where?'

It's her who talks next. She's like, 'Monte Carlo.'

I'm there, 'Monte Carlo? As in . . .' and the old man goes, 'As in, Monte Carlo. As in, Monte Carlo, thank you very much indeed. Bit of a junket actually. Council business and so forth. Don't know if you heard the news, but I'm chairing the Dún Laoghaire-Rathdown County Council Twinning Committee this year. Quite a few of my council colleagues agree that Dún Laoghaire should have that French Riviera ambience. So they're sending your mother and I over on a kind of fact-finding mission, with a view to a link-up.'

He really is a tool.

He goes, 'And – well, it's just a coincidence – your mother and I are interested in a couple of property investments there, *vis-à-vis* setting up a little retirement home out there, *ipso facto* and so forth.'

I'm like, 'Is that the time? Anyway, if you don't mind, I'm pretty snowed under today . . .' and the old dear goes, 'No, wait, Ross. We have other news,' and the old man's there, 'Joyous news,' and for one awful minute I think she might be up the focking Damien herself. Imagine that. Ronan would have an uncle who's, like, nine years younger than him – that is *so* WC.

She has this big, shit-eating grin on her boat. She goes, 'Ross . . . I've written a book,' and I'm like, 'I'm going to cut you off there actually. I don't want to know a focking thing about it,' and she's there, 'But Sorcha's read it, Ross. She really enjoyed it,' and I'm like, '*I've* read it – most of it – and it's embarrassing. You are seriously sexually frustrated, you know that?'

The old man goes, 'Sexually frustrated? Ross, your mother and I enjoy a full and varied–' and I'm like, 'I DON'T WANT TO KNOW! DON'T EVEN *THINK* ABOUT FINISHING THAT SENTENCE. God, I can't believe I'm actually having this conversation . . .'

The old man's there, 'I'm happy to say that not everyone shares your view, Ross. No less a judge than Sinead Moriarty loved it. Think Patricia Scanlan, she said, with a bit of Jackie Collins thrown in,' and he storts laughing. He goes, 'We're thinking of asking that Cathy Kelly to write a little review for the back cover, too.'

I'm there, 'Back cover? Will you two get over yourselves. It's never going to get published, because it's shit!'

The old dear's like, 'Well, actually, Ross, I *have* a publisher,' and I'm there, 'Yeah, some little fly-by-night, backstreet operation, I bet.'

She goes, 'It's Penguin actually.'

I just, like, shrug my shoulders and go, 'Never focking heard of them. I rest my case. And you . . .' I go, turning to my old man, '. . . I can't believe you actually let her write it. What name are they publishing it under?'

The old dear goes, '*My* name, of course. Fionnuala O'Carroll-Kelly,' and I'm there, '*No* way. No *focking* way. You're doing this just to destroy me, aren't you?'

The old man goes, 'Don't be ridiculous, Ross. Everybody remembers *Fionnuala O'Carroll-Kelly* from the famous Yummy-Mummy calendar. Her name has a certain *cachet* – pardon the French – among a particular type of woman,' and I'm there, 'Yeah, other desperate trouts. This isn't happening. I'm telling you now.'

'Well,' the old dear goes, 'I'm afraid the wheels are already in motion.'

Ronan rings Sorcha, roysh, and he tells her he was on the 'net in school and he found some information for her about how far into her pregnancy it was safe to continue working. 'Unless you're on your feet a lot,' he says, 'it's safe to work right up until the due date.' He says he'll e-mail the link. Sorcha turns to me, roysh, and tells me that Ronan is proving to be – *oh my God*! – SUCH a rock to her during this pregnancy, and I know what she's really saying is that I'm not.

We're sitting in The Queen's, roysh, listening to Sophie and Chloe argue over how many points are in an After Eight. Sophie goes, 'It's irrelevant anyway, because you had, like, twelve of them. And you had a Big Mac at lunchtime. That's, like, thirteen points on its own,' and Chloe's like, 'HELLO? It was *actually* a quarter-pounder with cheese?' and Sophie goes, 'Okay, twelve then. All I'm saying is, don't take it out on me just because I'm the thinnest I've ever been.'

I go, 'Yeah, I heard you'd glandular fever,' and she goes, 'Oh my God, yeah,' like it's an actual good thing.

I look at Sorcha and she sort of, like, throws her eyes up to heaven.

Ariande is this, like, Latvian bird who's helping Sorcha out in the shop since Aoife went back into hospital, roysh, port-time basically, the eventual plan being that she's going to be going full-time when Sorcha has the baby. And what with her being a ringer for Ali Bastian and everything, roysh, and what with me getting zero action these days, it pains me to admit that I've storted sniffing around her in a big-time way.

I probably should have learnt my lesson after Fearne, but what can I say, roysh, except that the flesh is weak.

This particular day, roysh, Sorcha's at home – feeling a bit Moby – and I ring the shop and go, 'Hey, Ariande. Er, one or two things I need to talk to you about, just in terms of, like, the shop and shit?' and she goes, 'Everyting ees gude, yes?' the way they talk and I'm like, 'Let's maybe do lunch. Café en Seine? As in, like, one o'clock?' and she's there, 'Em, yes, okay,' playing it too cool for school, obviously not wanting me to see that she's gagging for me even more than I'm basically gagging for her.

She looks unbelievable in this, like, tight black top that does a great job showing off her Walter Mitties, a short black skirt and the old *shlut* wellies and I actually feel a bit, I don't know, sleazy when she sits down at the table beside me and asks me what I want to talk to her about, roysh, and I end up going, 'Your work situation.'

I mean the girl's probably sending most of the minimum wage that Sorcha pays her back home every week to keep five generations of her family. The last thing she needs is sexual harassment from the boss's husband, even if he is a seriously good-looking goy with a killer bod who could be on the Ireland team by the time the autumn internationals come round.

She's like, 'My vurk sitooation?' and I'm there, 'You don't need to be afraid, that's all I'm saying. Of the immigration people. We'll get you a visa, if that's what it takes. I'll get my old man's solicitor on the case. Let's just say we're very happy with the way you're working out. *Me* in particular,' and I actually hate myself at that moment, though that doesn't stop me, like, putting my hand on her leg and giving her knee a squeeze.

Of course I end up nearly choking on my steak sandwich when she turns around and goes, 'But I haf veesa,' and swats me away like I'm one of those Concern collectors with a focking clipboard.

I'm like, 'What?' and she's there, 'I say I haf veesa. How cooed I come to Island wizout veesa?' and I just, like, shrug my shoulders and go, 'Well, I presumed it was in a focking container or something. You know, a couple of thousand of you, packed in there like melons.'

One of the great things about Irish birds is that you always know when you're going to get a slap – or even a drink – across the old Ricky Gervais. 'How DARE you!' is usually your two-second warning and you have a decent chance of, like, ducking or – in the case of, say, a Bacordi Breezer – getting out of the way.

But Ariande hits me like a focking French second-row.

Out of the blue, it's just like, WALLOP! and suddenly – like that focking Fran Cosgrave – I am seeing a lot of stors. Half of focking Café Insane is suddenly, like, staring in my direction.

She goes, 'You are horeeble man,' and off she storms, roysh, leaving her Caesar salad pretty much untouched and suddenly there's all this, like, applause from all around the bor, obviously people who know about my rep in this town and a fair few birds who've been burnt by me in the past.

I'm just like, 'Hey, build a focking bridge and get over it, you lot,' at the top of my voice, roysh, and of course there's a big cheer then.

And just as the noise is dying down, I notice her on the far side of the bor, staring at me, although giving me serious filthies would be more like it.

It's Sorcha's granny.

So naturally I'm in shock, roysh, but I get it together pretty quickly, and by the time she hobbles over to me, I'm playing it cooler than Huggy Bear on a City Break. I just go, 'Are you following me?' and she's like, 'Yes,' straight out with it like that. I'm there, 'Where's your focking glasses?' but she doesn't flinch.

She looks a state. Big grey coat on her. Roy Cropper shopping bag. Big focking tea cosy on her head. I don't even know how she got in here.

She goes, 'Where's your . . . *lady friend* gone?' and I'm like,

'Oh, *I* get it – you're going to tell Sorcha,' and she looks at me all, like, smug and pleased with herself, like the old bird in that ad for the stair-lift.

I go, 'I can't believe you're *actually* following me around, looking for dirt on me,' and she's there, 'I told you, my granddaughter is going to know . . .' and I'm shouting over her, roysh, giving it, '*Ooh, I can't get used to this euro. Very fiddly, isn't it?*' but she just goes, 'My granddaughter is going to know what kind of a person you are.'

I'm there, 'Even if it means our baby has to grow up without a father?' and she goes, 'A girl like Sorcha? I don't think she'd be without a man for long.'

I'm like, '*Them new potatoes is terrible. Very floury. They fall apart when you boil them,*' and she goes, 'In my day, we had respect for our elders,' and I go, 'Yeah? Well, your day's focking gone, Granma. And take my advice – you want to play games, stick to bingo. This is one you're not going to win. Think about it – you tell Sorcha you saw me with another bird again. She's so *not* going to believe you? And I'll totally deny it. It'll be your word against mine.'

She's there, 'You know what day it was yesterday?' and quick as a flash I go, 'Half Price for OAPs day at the hairdresser's?'

She's there, 'No, it was my fifty-fifth wedding anniversary,' and I'm like, 'What are you still focking celebrating that for? Your husband's been brown bread for twenty of those. Got sense and got out, by all accounts,' but she doesn't take the bait.

She goes, 'Young Sorcha bought me a wonderful present. My first ever . . . *mobile* telephone.'

Mobile telephone! *Un*believable.

I go, 'What's that got to do with price of focking stewing beef?'

She's there, 'Amazing thing, technology. No wires. You can ring someone from anywhere in the world,' and I'm like, 'Yeah, get with the programme. That's, like, SO ten years ago.'

But then she goes, 'And would you believe it, this one even has a camera on it.'

And suddenly, roysh, my blood goes focking cold.

I'm there, 'Are you telling me you took a photograph of me with that bird?' and she's like, 'I'm seeing Sorcha this afternoon, you know. She's taking me out for tea,' and she storts putting the old Theobald Wolfe back into her bag.

I go, 'Actually, give us a look at that thing for a sec. I just want to check out how many ringtones are on it,' and she's like, 'You must think I'm stupid,' and I go, 'Seriously, I can also check for you if it's WAP-enabled . . .' but she just smiles at me, roysh, as if to say, basically, Game Over, then hobbles out of the place.

I'm screwed here and I know it.

I decide to ring Ronan. He's bound to know someone who'll focking mug her for me. I'm not talking whacking her around, of course. Just grab her bag and, like, dispose of the phone.

I get his message-minder. It's like, 'This is Ronan. I'm taking care of business. Leave a message.'

I'm sitting there, roysh, pretty much resigned to the fact that this is game, set and match. But then suddenly I'm thinking, Hey, I've got out of bigger scrapes than this before. What if I come clean and come up with a cover story for meeting Ariande for lunch – maybe she was helping me arrange, like, a surprise baby shower for Sorcha?

But knowing the way Sorcha's mind works, she'll probably check. And there's no focking way that Ariande's going to actually cover for me, not after me chancing my orm with her.

So I end up going back to Lillie's, roysh, and spending the entire afternoon in the office trying to come up with an explanation.

And I can't. So the only thing I can do is tell her that it was basically sexual frustration, that it's, like, two months since I had any – from *her*, anyway – a man has needs, blahdy, blahdy, blah.

What kind of bird wouldn't understand that?

Then, if she takes that well, roysh, I might show her this orticle that I read in *Pregnancy – Baby and You*, which I just happened to pick up in the shop, suggesting this position called spoons, roysh, where you both lie on your side and . . . Well, anyway, this basically expert is quoted as saying that doing the bould thing brings on a rush of happy hormones that is actually good for the baby. I get a pen and underline it, roysh, and I'm thinking, This thing could actually end up working out well for me.

Or am I deluding myself?

Half-four, though, Sorcha rings and asks me where I am and she does not sound a happy bunny. I tell her I'm in the club and she tells me she wants me home immediately, roysh, she needs to talk to me, as in *now*?

Ever the optimist, I stick the magazine under my orm anyway and hit the Rock Road but – truth be told – I'm actually kacking myself.

I'm home in, like, half an hour and Sorcha's already waiting at the door, which has to be bad news.

But instead of being met with another slap across the Ricky, she actually gives me a hug, roysh, and I'm thinking it might be wise to cover the old town halls, just in case she's lulling me into a false sense of security before bringing the knee up a bit shorply. I've broken too many horts not to know that move.

But it's not an act at all.

She goes, 'Ross, don't go mad, but I met Gran today for lunch. She had another of her *stories*,' and I'm thinking, Go with this, Ross, and I stort shaking my head, trying to look all sympathetic.

She goes, 'She showed me these,' and she hands me what looks like the granny's Wolfe. It *is* the granny's Wolfe.

I take it off her slowly, not knowing what to expect.

It could still be a trap.

I look at it. I go to Gallery, View Folders, then Images and then I, like, scroll down through the photographs.

There's, like, fifteen of them.

Fock!

I don't focking believe it.

They're all of herself, of her own stupid ugly boat race.

It's hilarious. Big wrinkled face, all screwed up, like it goes when she's trying to concentrate on something. Tea cosy on her ridiculous head.

The stupid old bat was holding the camera the wrong way around.

I'm there, 'What *is* this shit?' cracking on that I don't know. Sorcha goes, 'It's *supposed* to be evidence of you cheating on me. Please don't be mad, Ross. I'm SO sorry. This must be SO hord for you. It must be like, *Oh my God!*' and I'm like, 'Well, it helps to know you understand a little bit of what I'm going through here, Babes,' and I'm thinking now might not be the worst time in the world to bring up that spoons thing.

Before I can, she goes, 'I'm really worried about her. I think she's losing it,' and I sort of, like, stare off into the distance – I really don't know how I live with myself sometimes – and I go, 'I just *hope* she doesn't end up having to go into one of those old people's homes,' just sort of, like, putting the idea out there.

She gives me this big, humungous hug then.

I go, 'By the way, you know that Latvian bird you've got working for you? I think she's stealing from you.'

Fionn's reading the label on Marty's can of Dutch Gold, his fourth, I might add, in, like, an hour. He goes, 'I'm going to try and get this stuff on draught. That way you'll always have your very own tap here,' and the goy is focking dreaming if he thinks that's going to happen. He goes, 'You're welcome here any time, Marty. You *know* that,' and Oisinn's there, 'Maybe don't climb up the fire exit and force a window next time.'

Marty looks at him and goes, 'You, ye doorty-lookin' fooker wi' dem iPods and pho-ins. Torcherin' me,' but he's actually, like, smiling as he says it, roysh, exposing two rows of Taylor Keith that obviously haven't seen Colgate since his Communion.

Fionn goes, 'Yeah, Oisinn, you know that was a breach of the Geneva Convention?' and Oisinn goes, 'Well, you could try the UN, but I suspect Kofi Annan has bigger fish to fry,' and everyone laughs at that, even me, though I'd be lying if I said I got it.

Marty goes, 'I'm gonna miss yiz all but,' and he turns to Fionn and he's like, 'Good luck wi' yizzer Masters,' and he knocks back the rest of his can while at the same time pulling another towards him. 'And that boord – do it, man. You don't want to spend de rest of your life regrettin' it.'

'And you, Ross,' he goes, 'Good luck wi' de rest of de pregnancy. You know, dem wristbands are apposed to be good – same one as ye get for seasickness,' and I'm there, 'Seriously? Oh, thanks . . .'

Fionn goes, 'It's funny, Marty, I always knew the day

would come when I'd have to release you back into the wild. You try not to get attached, but sometimes . . .' and you can see the dude filling up.

Marty's like, 'I'm lookin' forward to goin' home, seein' de kids again. Don't be wreckin' me buzz, man,' and Fionn just nods, like he knows he's being a pussy.

Fionn puts an envelope on the table, which I presume is the twenty Ks. Marty's there, 'Thanks, Bud. Look, yiz'll see me again. I'll be callin' in here all de toyim,' and I don't know whether I should tell him to maybe ring before he does.

The old Wolfe Tone rings. It's, like, Christian. He's at the bottom of Grafton Street in the hire van. I'm there, 'Time to go, goys,' and we all knock back the rest of our pints, roysh, then head down the stairs and out onto the street and Marty's, like, shielding his eyes against the first real sunlight he's seen since he jemmied his way into our lives four months ago.

He lives in one of the townships off the M50. No surprise there. As we're driving through it, roysh, it's the usual scenes of, like, poverty and deprivation. I think it's pretty fair to say that none of us can believe what we're actually seeing out the window. We're talking boarded-up houses and shops. We're talking dogs running wild. We're talking gangs of kids hanging around, looking to make eye contact with you for an excuse to deck you. It would basically come as no surprise to me to find out this place has a Lidl.

Marty's going, 'And yous call out to me de odd time, reet?' and not wanting to hurt the goy's feelings, roysh, I end up going, 'I'll have a good think about it, but I'd see myself as being more southside-based?' and suddenly my attention is grabbed by a man — an actual man — wearing a cowboy hat and riding past us on an actual horse.

Marty's banging on the window, roysh, trying to get the

goy's attention, going, 'Ah, dare's Jesse James Byrne. Must catch up wi'im la'er for a few. Tell 'im I'm not dead.'

Fionn goes, 'It's like Trench Town . . . with rain,' and I'm there, 'Where are we going to actually release him? What about there?' and I point out the window to this patch of, like, waste ground, which has, like, a burnt-out cor and a couple of, like, broken-down cookers and fridges dumped on it.

Christian turns around and goes, 'There's an Aldi up ahead.'

Aldi! I suppose it's as good as a Lidl.

Fionn goes, 'Let's set him free in there then,' so we drive over the cattle-grid and into the cor pork, where Christian pulls over, gets out and opens the side door.

Marty looks at Christian and goes, 'Any word ouda George Lucas yet?' and Christian's there, 'Not yet, no,' and Marty nods like he knows something the rest of us don't know, then he goes, 'Keep believin', Kiddo.'

Then he goes, 'Fionn, it was a pleasure workin' wi' ye,' and he goes to shake Fionn's hand, roysh, but it quickly turns into a hug.

I get out and I'm like, 'Okay, come on, little fellow,' trying to basically coax him out of the van. He doesn't seem to want to go at first. But then none of us wants him to go either.

Slowly, roysh, he gets his confidence up and he puts one foot onto the ground and then, a few seconds later, the other. I'm there, 'Go on, little chap. Off you go. Find your friends,' and after a couple of minutes of, like, standing and staring he just takes off, roysh, without once looking back.

I can see that Fionn's got tears in his eyes. He goes, 'You just don't feel the time going,' and I give him a good firm pat on the top of the orm, instead of a hug – I don't want him to think it's a come-on – and I go, 'Let's go back to the club and get bladdered.'

Christian turns the key in the ignition and I'm just about to ring Sorcha, roysh, to check on her, when all of a sudden I stop dead in my tracks. I'm like, 'Goys, my phone has gone.'

Suddenly the rest of them are, like, patting their pockets as well. Oisinn's there, 'So is mine. And my focking watch,' and Fionn's going, 'Phone, wallet, iPod . . . Fock!'

I'm there, 'My one cost me a thousand sheets,' but I can feel, like, the corners of my mouth turning up into a smile. Suddenly the goys are all smiling too and shaking their heads, basically admiring the cheek of the focker.

We're going to miss him.

I go, 'Let's get the fock out of here before he has the wheels off this thing.'

7. The Unbearable Plumpness of Being

I wake up in the middle of the night, roysh, and realise I'm in the bed on my Tobler. I check the clock and it's, like, four in the morning. I didn't hear Sorcha get up. I swing the old legs out of bed, find the floor and head downstairs. I push open the kitchen door and I'm really not ready for what I end up seeing.

It's dork in the kitchen, roysh, except for the light coming from the open fridge, which illuminates the floor in front of it, where Sorcha's sitting like Buddha, with her legs crossed and her big Malcolm O'Kelly stuck out in front of her, surrounded by what looks to me like every bit of food in the house, which is saying something, considering she shops like there's a nuclear winter on the way.

There's, like, big jellies on plates, roysh, and legs of pork and cakes and bowls of chocolate truffles, roysh, and chicken drumsticks and three tubs of Haagen-Dazs and a whole fresh salmon and a Christmas pudding and different fruits and a platter of cheeses and, like, a half roast duckling and two pizzas and a knickerbocker-glory and a leg of lamb, roysh, and a focaccia and a plate of steaks and a fresh lime cheesecake. And that's only the half of it.

'I thought I'd gotten away with it,' Sorcha goes. 'The cravings, I mean. They're only supposed to affect mothers in the *first* trimester. Now I know what you've been going through.'

She's made some dent in this lot.

'What have you got a craving for?'

And she's there, 'Everything. And in every combination.'

I'm like, 'Can I join you?' and she smiles and goes, 'Of course,' and I sit down on the floor beside her, with my back against the island and I notice how beautiful she looks in the light of the fridge, big and pregnant, with what looks like jam all over her mouth.

'I can recommend the strawberries with black pepper,' she goes and I laugh at that. She feeds me one. She's not wrong. It's an incredible combination. I'm there, 'Is that taramasalata over there?' as she horses into a red pepper as if it's, like, an apple.

'Oh my God, yeah,' she goes, picking the seeds out from between her teeth. 'It's amazing with the smoked salmon. And a little bit of sugar.'

I'm like, 'So what time are you up since?' and she's there, 'One,' which means she's been sitting here, roysh, eating solidly for, like, three hours.

She goes, 'You know, some people believe that the foods we like are determined in the womb,' and I'm there, 'God help this baby then,' and she laughs at that. Then she's like, 'One of the first things we taste in the womb is amniotic fluid. It's the reason why, even as adults, most of us still find comfort in sweet things.'

I'm there, 'Do we have any Grand Marnier?' and she's like, 'There's a bottle in the drinks cabinet. What are you going to have it with?' and I'm there, 'I was going to open a tin of tuna, chop it up with some of that Cherry Garcia ice cream and then pour the Grand Marnier on top,' and Sorcha's there, '*Yuck!* And yet, *Yum!*'

And that's exactly how it tastes. Sorcha's eating raw parsnips with oregano sprinkled on top.

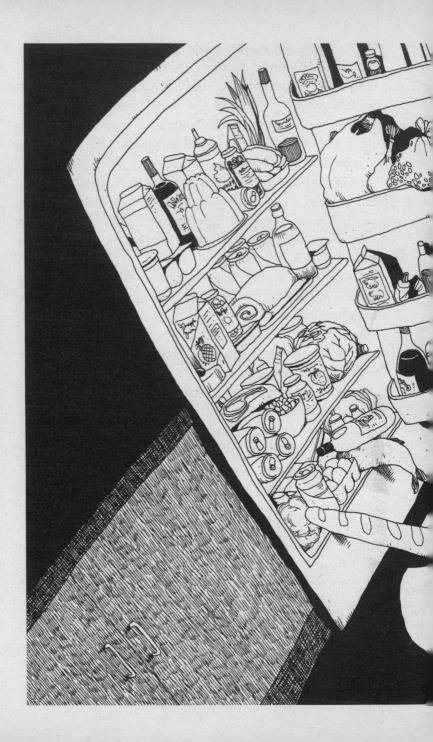

And it's amazing, roysh, because today she's, like, six-and-a-half months into the pregnancy and sitting here on the kitchen floor, stuffing our faces like two bulimics at a Greek wedding, well, it's the first time I've felt like we're actually on the same page.

I go, 'You're beautiful, Sorcha,' and I know she's never heard me use those words to her before. She's like, 'Oh, that's the Grand Marnier talking,' but the thing is, roysh, it's not. Weird as it sounds, roysh, I find the fact that she's carrying my child incredibly arousing.

'Did you ever wonder what farfalle tastes like uncooked?' she goes, but I'm just, like, staring at her. She's there, 'This *is* nice, isn't it? As in, *us* . . .' and I'm about to answer, roysh, when all of a sudden she storts going, '*Oh my God, oh my God, oh my God*,' and she grabs my hand, roysh, and puts it up her nightshirt and lays it flat across her stomach. And that tiny little kick hits me like a bus.

I don't know why I haven't put this thing in the focking bin.

Lovell was persistent – she'd give him that.

Every day now for a month he had turned up outside her building and pushed the button for her apartment. And every day she'd watched him on the green-tinted closed circuit screen – the square of his jaw, his hulking shoulders – and wondered how she could have been so foolish to believe that someone like him could fall for someone like her.

And now she knew the truth. Or rather what a couple of friends from the tennis club had been able to find out by making discreet inquiries in the Law Library.

His name wasn't Lovell Power and he wasn't a solicitor. His name was Kenny Powell and he was a private investigator, hired by the Criminal Assets Bureau to find out where Richard salted away the ten million euros that had yet to be accounted for.

And to think that in the seething heat of their lovemaking, as he spread her olive thighs and she surrendered to the pounding beat of his maleness, he had said that he loved her.

Just doing his job, she thought contemptuously. All in a day's work for Kenny Powell.

Sorcha has circled the word 'pounding' and beside it she's written, 'Thrusting, maybe? Sounds more romantic.'

She stared hard at his image as it filled the screen. Gosh, he was handsome, she couldn't help but feel. Against her better judgement, she pressed the intercom button.

'Go away,' she said curtly.

'Valerie,' he said, saying her name with a voice full of desperation. 'We need to talk.'

'I have nothing to say to you,' she said, reproaching him sternly. 'Except that you're a poltroon, a bounder and a cad of the most unscrupulous kidney . . .'

Beside this, Sorcha has written, 'A bit too Jane Austen. I know you're a fan, but I think she'd be more likely to go: Oh my God, you SO better leave now, or I'll call the Gardaí.

'Okay, I'll go,' he said, resignedly. 'But there's one thing you should know before I do. When I said I loved you . . . well, I meant it. Oh, sure, when I agreed to take the case, it was just another job to me. But from the moment I first saw you, that crazy day in Avoca Handweavers, everything changed. I knew I loved you even then . . .'

She could feel tears well in her eyes.

'That day you saw me in the National Gallery,' he said, 'I was telling them I wanted out, that a conflict of interest had arisen. And that conflict of interest, Valerie, was my feelings for you . . .'

I'm suddenly feeling seriously Moby. I'm not sure if it's the book or the pregnancy.

She felt the dam burst and the tears rush down her face in a salty cascade. Her mind was a jumble of conflicting thoughts and emotions.

'Is that a camellia?' is all she could think to say. She could see that he had brought her a present of a plant.

'Yes,' he said through the intercom. 'I'm going to leave it here for you,' he said, putting it on the ground outside the front door of the apartment building. 'Make sure to plant it in acid soil if you're keeping it indoors. That way it'll thrive even in semi-shaded areas and need only minimal care.'

He was not only sexy, she mused, but also informative – a deadly combination.

'Please, Valerie,' he said, before he moved away. 'Think over what I said . . .'

Sorcha lets out a scream when sees me. I'm, like, running the J. Edgar over the corpet in the sitting-room.

She's like, 'Oh my God! What are you doing?' and I'm there, 'I don't know. It's come over me all of a sudden – this urge to do housework. I was thinking I might hoover in here, then do our bedroom. Then I might *unstack the dishwasher* . . .'

She sort of, like, squints here eyes, roysh, and gives me this suspicious look. She goes, 'Have you been drinking?' and I'm there, 'No, like I said, it was an urge. I mean, we've a baby on the way. I just want the place to be right for her.'

She goes, 'Oh my God! *Weirdo*!'

It was unbelievable, I'm telling Christian. Un-*focking* believable. Weird as it sounds, roysh, it was the first time I thought of it as an *actual* person growing inside Sorcha – *and*, believe it or not, it didn't, like, freak me out? I'm there, 'It was an actual kick, Christian. Can you believe it?'

He goes, 'They had a maternity ward on Bright Hope – as in the transport carrier? – and one time 2–1B delivered this baby,' and I ended up cutting him off, going, 'But that's just a focking movie!' and then I really regret it, roysh, because I can see the hurt in the dude's face.

I'm there, 'Hey, I'm sorry . . . Okay, okay, okay, it isn't just a movie. It's real,' which seems to cheer him up a little bit.

I'm like, 'But I'm telling you, Dude – this baby thing? I swear I'm not going to fock it up this time. This is it for me now. I'm changing my ways. I mean, I haven't looked at another bird all night. And how long are we in here?'

Christian goes, 'Twenty minutes,' and I'm there, 'Twenty minutes! That's a focking famine for me! But the way I look at it is – I can't be a player forever. Even Mr Lover-Lover's got to call it a day sometime. Accept my responsibilities. Okay, sure, a lot of birds are going to be disappointed. And places like this and Reynords are going to see a serious dip in their profits. But there'll be younger goys coming through – obviously not in *my* class, but . . .'

I look up and realise I'm talking to myself here, because Christian's over the other side of the battlecruiser. Lauren's just walked in, roysh, and he's giving her a huge hug, in front of half of Kiely's and I have to say, roysh, it's actually nice to see and I decide there and then that I'm going to stort being a bit more like that with Sorcha – affectionate or whatever.

I ask this lounge girl, who has a serious thing for me, for a vodka and 7-Up, which is what Lauren always drinks. They come over and sit down, roysh, and I ask Lauren how the wedding plans are going, and she says they've decided to have it in Lahinch, in a tiny little church she used to go as a child when she spent summers on holidays at her aunt's and it's amazing, roysh, because I'm actually *listening*, in other words taking an interest in what she's saying, and I'm thinking this is actually the *real* me, the nice goy the public never gets to see.

I go, 'I was just telling your fiancé here that the Ross-meister General has broken his last hort. I'm settling down,' but she doesn't go, 'Congratulations,' or, 'Fair focks,' or anything, roysh, she just gives me this look. Lauren's never had any time for my bullshit, roysh, even though, as Christian's best friend, she's very, very fond of me.

She goes, 'Ross, I would have thought the day you took your wedding vows was the day to *settle down*,' and I don't say anything, roysh, because being given out to by her is like being given out to by a teacher.

I've got my head down, roysh, because she's giving me the big-time filthies, but then, all of a sudden, Oisinn arrives in and that takes the heat out of the situation. As I'm high-fiving him, roysh, I notice that he's here with JP's old man and the two of them look as thick as northside thieves and I'm thinking, What's the Jack there?

Oisinn must cop the look on my Ricky because he goes, 'Mr Conroy has just agreed to become a director of Scent from Heaven,' and it's pretty obvious, roysh, that he's only involving him to piss off JP.

JP's old man turns around to the poor lounge bird – the one who wants me – and goes, 'Hi, I'm Fred Flintstone,' and she's like, 'Sorry?' and he's there, 'My name – it's Fred Flintstone. And tonight . . . I'm going to make *your* Bedrock . . .' and as he's saying this, roysh, he has his orm on her back and he's, like, *actually* trying to undo the clip of her bra through her shirt and it looks like he's playing the double bass.

I turn around to Oisinn, real suspicious, roysh, and I go, 'What do you need him on board for? It's not like you haven't got the shekels yourself,' and he turns around and looks at Mr Conroy, who's very kindly holding the lounge bird's tray while she refastens her bra. He's like, 'Well, it's not just the capital investment he's bringing to the business. There's also his business acumen . . .' and I'm there, 'He's a focking estate agent, Oisinn. Admit it – this is just to get at JP, isn't it?' but he just laughs in my face.

He high-fives Christian then and air-kisses Lauren, who turns around and asks him if it's true that he's going to be on that 'Off The Rails'. He's like, 'Yeah, can you believe that? Shit the bed! They want to come out to the club and do a feature on me – just talking about my style, favourite designers and I suppose general sartorial influences,' and I blurt out, 'It'll be quite short then,' and I don't know why, roysh, but it's probably jealousy.

Oisinn looks at me and gives me this, like, patronising smile. Then he goes, 'I'm sure they'll want to talk about *Eau d'Affluence* and then my new venture as well.'

JP's old man hands me a pint of Ken. He always stands his round, fair focks to him. Oisinn puts his orm around his shoulder and, with a big grin on his face, he offers up a toast, 'To Catholics, who don't just act good – but smell good, too.'

*

Sorcha can't believe I'm being so understanding about her granny, who she and her old dear are now convinced is totally and utterly Baghdad. And for the first time, roysh, she's going, 'Oh my God, I can't believe I've been giving you such a hord time over this baby either. You are SUCH a saint for putting up with my moods,' and I'm there, 'Hey, it's all port of the package, Babes,' playing it cooler than a bricklayer's orse.

Suddenly, it's all, 'No, I realise now it was wrong to exclude you from things. I mean, you couldn't help it if you were sick that night. And I know Claire's been giving you a hord time as well. From now on, Ross, it's me and you, okay?' and I'm like, 'Kool and the Gang.'

So she turns around to me the other day, roysh, and goes, 'Ross, I've an – oh my God! – *huge* favour to ask you. Remember we were supposed to be going to see La Bohème tonight?' and of course I haven't a bog what she's on about. I'm there, 'La, what?' and she's like, 'La Bohème? As in the opera? At the National Concert Hall? You, me and mum?'

And I honestly don't remember volunteering for it, but it sounds like a long focking night to me.

She goes, 'Well, I was going to ask you – now only if you don't mind – could we give your ticket to Gran instead. Maybe if we could just get her out of the house. Even for one night . . .' and I go, 'Hey, that's fine, Babes. Sure I'll see it when it comes out on DVD,' cracking on I'm making this, like, huge sacrifice.

She looks at me, roysh, and she goes, 'I don't know what I did to deserve a husband as wonderful as you,' and of course I'm thinking, This buys me a bit of time and space to relax with the *Davina McCall Extreme Pilates* DVD that Oisinn bought me for Christmas.

Of course it's too good to be true. She goes, 'Ross, I need another favour,' and I'm there, 'Go on,' and she's like, 'Well, she won't go out if it means leaving the house on its own. You know she's paranoid about being burgled. Would you mind house-sitting for her tonight?'

And I'm thinking, Fock this. I'm sitting here with town halls the size of watermelons and someone up there is actually, I don't know, conspiring to stop me having any fun. I won't get to watch anything in Sorcha's granny's gaff. It's well known that she's got the last black-and-white television in Foxrock and she thinks a DVD is God's plague on people who have sex outside the sanctity of holy marriage, blahdy blahdy blah.

So, as you can understand, I'm not in the best of form when I roll up outside her gaff a couple of hours later.

Far from being grateful to me, the old bag actually has a basic conniption fit when she cops me. She's like, 'Not *him*! You said you'd find me someone I could trust to watch over the house. I don't want *him* near my place. Do you hear me?'

And of course the more she loses it, roysh, the more they think she's losing the plot. Sorcha's old dear's apologising to me, going, 'This must be really difficult for you. She's just got this thing in her head,' and I'm like, 'Don't sweat it. A lot of old people go off their cake. I'm just glad I'm big enough to take it,' and when Sorcha and her old dear turn their back on me, roysh, to try to get the granny's coat on her, I stort blowing her kisses and that makes her flip the lid even more.

She's there, 'He's evil! *Evil!*' and I'm looking like I'm hurt but trying not to let it show. But as they're dragging her out, roysh, she goes, 'Don't you bring any of your tarts into this house while I'm gone, because I'll know. Mrs Byrne next door watches all the comings and goings on this street,' and Sorcha looks at me and goes, 'Tarts! I honestly don't know where she gets it from!'

So off they go, roysh, and I end up having a bit of a potter around. It's a typical old dear's gaff. Smells of Marietta biscuits and mince. There's, like, cat hairs, curlers and bits of rolled-up tissue paper everywhere. Cupboards full of empty plastic containers from, like, coleslaw, which she thinks she'll use again. Focking black-and-white telly.

I put my feet up on the coffee table and I have to laugh. She forgot her focking glasses. I think about ringing Sorcha and telling her, just to piss off the old biddy even more, but then I have to be careful not to look like I'm enjoying this. Sorcha's old man is only too happy to believe the stuff she's been spouting. If I stort grand-standing, then she might win over Sorcha's old dear and then I'm totally screwed.

I end up falling asleep watching 'EastEnders' and I have this nightmare where Peggy Mitchell's trying to kill me, roysh – in, like, black and white, of course – and I don't need a psychiatrist to tell me what that means.

I wake up shivering. It's always freezing in this focking house. *I'm not paying money to have the heating on in May. I just won't give it to them.*

You'd almost feel sorry for her, roysh, but I know I've got to keep doing what I'm doing. She's like a dog with a bone with this thing. She's not going to let it go. She'll keep on and on and on about it until something she says will suddenly ring true with Sorcha.

The stakes we're playing for here couldn't be higher. My marriage. My little daughter. I don't want her to grow up seeing me every other weekend, calling some other goy 'Daddy'. I can't let it happen and there's only one way to stop it. Neutralise the enemy, as poor old Fehily used to tell us before we went out on the field.

I go out to the kitchen and grab the kettle. She doesn't have an electric one. It's one of those big metal jobbies that you put on the, whatever you call it, *range*. I look at the microwave – a present from Sorcha that's never been used. The stupid old cow's probably still trying to tune it in to 'Nationwide'.

I open it up, put the kettle inside and close the door. Then I go back into the sitting room and watch the old Savalas until they all arrive back, just after eleven. They come in, roysh, and the old battleaxe glares at me and goes, 'You better not have had any of your tarts in my bed,' and of course I'm cracking on to be Mr Nice Guy. I'm there, 'Could you see the stage without your glasses? I was going to drop them into you,' but she says nothing.

'Picking on a helpless old lady,' she goes. 'I'm eighty-five, you know.'

Sorcha goes out to the kitchen to make tea, roysh, and after five minutes of, like, muttering to herself about not being able to find the kettle, I hear her go, '*Oh my God!*' and of course her old dear goes pegging it out to the kitchen, roysh, to find out what the Jack is and I can make out whispers – we're talking 'danger to herself', we're talking 'supervised care'.

The old cow looks at me and I go, 'You must have accidentally put the kettle in the microwave. You don't know what you're doing anymore, you crazy old bag,' but she turns around, shakes her head and goes, 'They think I'm crazy anyway,' and I'm there, '*Ooh, I remember when this was all fields.*'

She goes, 'Edmund believes me,' and I'm there, 'Big swinging mickey,' and she goes, 'Well, as long as he does, they're not going to pack me off anyway. Believe you me, there's life in me yet,' and I go, 'Not too much, I hope,' and she has basically no answer to that.

I'm on my hands and knees, over the bowl, spitting chunks again, when Sorcha arrives at the door of the bathroom and goes, 'Here, take this,' and I turn around and she hands me this glass of water except it's, like, cloudy and I go, 'What is it?' and she's like, 'Hot water with a spoonful of grated ginger, the juice of half a lemon and teaspoon of honey,' and I knock it back, roysh, then collapse against the wall with my face against the cold radiator, trying to basically cool myself down.

I get it together and follow her into the kitchen, where she's doing what can only be described as a dance while pouring her All Bran into a bowl.

I'm there, 'You should have used the en suite if you were that desperate to go,' but she's just like, 'I'm actually trying to hold it, Ross?' and I'm there, 'Hold it? Why?' and she's like, 'Because a full bladder pushes the womb up closer to the ultrasound camera? You get, like, a clearer picture?'

We've got this Babybond thing this morning, which is, like, a three-dimensional scan? I'm pretty excited about it, roysh, because the baby's, like, twenty-eight centimetres long or something now and, like, fully formed.

So anyway, roysh, this bird meets us in the reception of the ultrasound studio, or whatever it's called, and you definitely would, roysh, because she's a ringer for Jakki Degg, except I don't notice these things anymore.

She goes, 'You must be Sorcha and Ross,' and she's carrying a tray of, like, chocolates and a bottle of wine, which I'm very happy to see, roysh, until the wine turns out to be non-alcoholic and the chocolate turns out to be sugar-free. You might as well be drinking your own piss and chewing the side of the table.

All around the wall there's all these sort of, like, squashed-up babies, presumably still in the womb, and I stort thinking that it's like a gallery for aliens and then I crack up laughing and Sorcha goes, 'You really are excited, aren't you?' and I'm there, 'I suppose I am.'

So eventually, roysh, the bird takes us into this room and it's like a health spa or some shit with, like, flowers and scented candles all over the shop and we're listening to some classical music, which Sorcha immediately recognises as Elvira Madigan's Piano Concerto by – *oh my God!* – Mozart. Then there's, like, a bed and a humungous plasma screen television on the wall.

I sit down in this, like, ormchair in the corner and Sorcha lies on the bed and this goy comes in – he only looks about our age – and he tells us he's our sonographer and of course it's news to me that we actually have one. He obviously picks up on the nerves in the room because he turns around to me and goes, 'Just relax. It's going to be a lot of fun. Are we ready to start now?'

Out of the blue, roysh, Sorcha turns around and goes, 'No, we're just waiting for our guests to arrive,' and before I have a chance to go, 'What focking guests?' I hear his voice – like an elephant – out in reception, going, 'Where's that grandchild of ours then?' and of course I just, like, bury my head in my hands.

He puts his head around the door and goes, 'Hey, Kicker. Hey, Sorcha. All set for the big movie?' and then he gives us one of his big false laughs and the old dear follows him in and it's, like, air-kisses galore for Sorcha, but I don't even bother my orse getting out of my seat. The old man goes,

'We should get some popcorn for the big movie, eh, Ross?' and I'm there, 'Sorry, did anyone laugh at that joke the first time you cracked it?' but he ignores it, roysh, and sits in the ormchair next to me, while the old dear makes a fuss of Sorcha, plumping up her pillows and trying to get her to drink more water.

I hear Sorcha ask her, in a whisper, roysh, how the book's going, so I'm like, 'It's okay, Babes. The secret's out. *Criminal* focking *Assets*. I've read it,' and Sorcha goes, 'That's where my copy went! *You* took it,' and I'm there, 'Yeah, only to have a look at what *she* was writing about,' and I nod at the old dear and go, 'The wizened old filth-bag.'

The old dear ignores this and goes, 'It's coming out at the end of June,' and I'm like, 'Over my dead body.'

The next thing I hear is, 'Is that Mozart I can hear in here?' and the door opens again and it's, like, Sorcha's old man. Of course, Dick Features has to turn around and go, 'Not Mozart, I'm afraid. It's Councillor Charles O'Carroll-Kelly, Independent, Foxrock, and his good lady wife,' and suddenly Sorcha's old pair are in the ward, giving it, 'Charles! Fionnuala! How lovely!' and of course I might as well not exist.

Sorcha's old dear goes, 'Terribly bad luck with the race, Charles. We watched it on the news,' and the old man's like, 'Vested interests. We'll say no more than that. I've no doubt the intention was to kill me,' and Sorcha's old man goes, 'Yes, we saw Charlie Bird's interview with you in the back of the ambulance. You made your points very well. But if I could have got my hands on whoever was on that motorbike . . .' and the old man goes, 'That's what happens when you challenge the liberal consensus in this country. Let that be a warning to everyone, golfers and non-golfers alike.'

The old dear gets in on the act then.

She goes, 'How's Sorcha's grandmother? I hear she's having some ... *problems*,' and Sorcha's old dear goes, 'It's old age, really. And senility runs on our side of the family ...' and I'm thinking, Sorcha kept *that* one from me before she got me up the aisle. Her old dear's there, 'We – very gently, mind you – broached the idea of a retirement village. It didn't go down at all well. We're all going to have to watch her closely, though,' and Sorcha's old man goes, 'Nonsense. There's nothing wrong with your mother,' and I can tell, roysh, from his tone and the way he, like, looks at me that he's actually bought the granny's story. He's always, like, hated my guts.

The door opens again, roysh, and in strolls Claire, as in Claire from Brayruit, of all places, and I go, 'Oh, for fock's sake, no one told me this was going to be, like, a porty,' and I just shoot the girl a look, roysh, as if to say, don't focking steal *anything* in here.

The goy – the sonographer dude? – he asks Sorcha to pull up her top, roysh, and he has more luck than I've had for the past few weeks because she actually does it, showing off this humungous bump, and it's only then that I realise how big she's become.

Sorcha's old man is reminding her of the day she played Mozart on the piano for the very first time – she was only, like, five, according to him, which is probably bullshit – and while they're talking away, roysh, the sonographer has this thing that's like one of those basically cool guns they have for, like, zapping borcodes in the supermorket and he's holding it up to Sorcha's Malcolm, and suddenly the plasma screen is filled with this, like, blurry brown picture.

We're all, like, staring at it, roysh, trying to make out the shape, when it suddenly just, like, snaps into focus and I cannot believe it, roysh, but suddenly we're looking at an actual baby, and it's as if a cold hand has just touched the back of my neck because suddenly I've just, like, snapped forward in my chair.

Sorcha and Claire are probably going, '*Oh my God!*' over and over again, just as the old man is giving it, 'There's the next Ireland number ten.'

It's so tiny and it's sucking its little thumb and then it has this big, like, stretch and Sorcha can actually feel it, roysh, and then all of a sudden, roysh, it turns its back to the camera, like it's suddenly shy or something?

And then Sorcha and my old dear are, like, saying my name and asking me am I okay and I realise, roysh, that I've got, like, tears streaming down my face – bent as that sounds – because suddenly, for the first time, roysh, I'm seeing all this extra weight that Sorcha's piled on as an actual baby and believe it or not, roysh, in terms of, like, emotion and shit, it's up there with winning the Leinster Schools Senior Cup.

We sit there for, like, twenty minutes. I hear and see pretty much nothing else, except this little baby on the screen. Eventually, the goy goes, 'Ross, we're going to give you a DVD of your baby as a souvenir of your visit,' and I try to say thank you, but no words come out.

Then he turns off the screen, roysh, and we're all sitting around, talking about what we've just seen, when all of a sudden the bird who met us at reception comes back in and asks us if we'd like to know the sex of our baby.

I go, '*No!*' at the same time as Sorcha goes, '*Yes!*' and I'm just there, 'Babes, I think we should maybe talk about this?' and she goes, 'We just have, Ross. I want to know,' and the woman smiles at her, then at me, and goes, 'You're going to have a little girl,' and Sorcha just, like, bursts into tears and I give her a hug, roysh, and put my hand on her Ned and when she gets herself together again she goes, 'Oh my God, I can't *wait* to see Erika's face!' and Claire's going, 'Oh my God, neither can *I*.'

I have to go outside. I need some air and a moment alone.

I walk out through the reception area, through the front door and outside, where there's three or four blokes standing around, smoking their brains out and looking pretty much like I feel, basically spaced out of it. One of them sort of, like, looks at me with a sort of, like, half-smile on his face and he just, like, shakes his head at me and neither of us has to say anything, roysh, to know what's going through the other's head: miracle.

All of a sudden I smell cigar smoke. *He's* standing beside me. He goes, 'Bit of a disappointment, eh?' and I just look him up and down and go, 'What?'

He's there, 'I suppose you were hoping for a boy – future captain of the S and so forth. Don't be too hard on yourself, Ross. You and young Sorcha are both fit and healthy. You can always try for another.'

I tell him he's the biggest tosser who ever lived.

You wouldn't think it was actually possible, roysh, but Pamela Flood and Caroline Morahan are bigger rides in real life than they are on actual television. I'm giving it loads, of course. I fix them both a gin and tonic, roysh, and I just happen to mention that if they ever need male models for the show, they should give me a bell.

Caroline goes, 'You've got tickets on yourself, haven't you?' and I'm like, 'Hey, with a body like this, modesty would just come across as, like, sarcastic,' and the two of them look at each other as if to say, I can't believe his confidence, even if he is a really, really good-looking goy.

So of course I decide to, like, hammer the point home. I pull up the old Leinster shirt and give them an eyeful of my six-pack. Suddenly, roysh, their eyes are out on stalks. I'm there, 'I don't care what camera angle you shoot it from, you put that on your programme and you've won the ratings war,' and I swear to God, roysh, they're just about to turn around to me and go, 'We SO need to get that on tape,' when all of a sudden Oisinn arrives in and there their interest in me ends.

They're, like, all over the goy. 'It's an honour to meet you,' Caroline goes. An honour? The stories I could tell that girl if I wanted to . . .

Oisinn's like, 'Ross been keeping you entertained, has he?' and the two birds are like, 'Yeah, you *could* say that,' and suddenly they're all laughing, basically at my expense.

Oisinn goes, 'So where are we going to shoot this thing?' and Pamela's there, 'We've set up the lights and cameras upstairs in the library,' which is the VIP bor, roysh, and Oisinn leads them around to the stairs and then goes, 'After you,' not because he's a gentleman, of course, but because – like me – he wants to get a better look of their orses. And they don't disappoint, in fairness.

So before long, roysh, they've got Oisinn sat on a couch and Caroline's banging out the questions like nobody's business. She's like, 'Now, when people hear the name Oisinn Wallace, they perhaps immediately associate you with Hugo Boss because of the enormous success of *Eau d'Affluence*. But you don't slavishly follow any one designer, do you?'

'No,' he goes, 'I suppose you could say that my sartorial influences are manifold . . . and eclectic,' which for some reason gets a giggle out of the two birds, roysh, and – of course, off-camera – I turn around to the sound engineer and go, 'He doesn't usually talk like that,' and the goy puts his finger up to his lips to tell me to shut up.

Caroline's there, 'For instance, today, you're leaning towards Ralph Lauren. Tell me a little bit about what you're wearing?' and he's giving it, 'Well, this here is just a custom-fit madras-lined Polo shirt in pink, heavily washed for a timeworn vintage look. Obviously, it's got the, er, two-button applied placket, ribbed polo collar and uneven vented hem . . .'

That focker's been on the internet all morning, by the sounds of it.

Caroline goes, 'And obviously the material is a very breathable and durable cotton mesh . . . Tell me about the trousers,' and Oisinn's going, 'Well, these little babies are a classic chino.'

Little! That's the first time I've ever heard a thirty-eight-inch waist described as little. I go to say it to the sound engineer, but he gives me a filthy before I even get a word out.

Oisinn's there, 'The name chino, your viewers might be interested in knowing, is the Spanish word for China, which is where these rather distinctive cotton twill trousers originated. They were first introduced to the States by American soldiers returning to the Philippines after the Spanish-American war,' and Caroline's like, 'No, I didn't know that,' and everyone's delighted, of course, obviously thinking that was educational and unless I'm very much mistaken, we're definitely going to get another series out of this.

Oisinn's there, 'This particular pair are a classic-fitting Hammond chino. Standard rise, double reverse pleats, straight cuffed leg, on-seam pockets . . .' and Caroline's going, 'And split-besom back pockets, I couldn't help but notice,' and Oisinn's like, 'Yeah, the split-besoms have always been a feature of this particular pant,' which, it's fair to say, is one sentence I never thought I'd hear from the mouth of any of my friends.

Then he's like, 'And last but not least, setting off the whole look, I suppose, are the Dubarry Docksiders. These things started out life as a boat or deck shoe but, well, nowadays they're the kind of footwear you can wear any time – and in total confidence. Overall, I'd say my look today is classic – but simple,' and Caroline goes, 'And I can imagine kids all over south Dublin charging out to the shops tomorrow to try to emulate it . . .'

She's unbelievable at her job, it has to be said – not just eye-candy. And I'm actually storting to enjoy Oisinn's whole act when all of a sudden I get this, like, tap on the shoulder and I turn around, roysh, and who is it only JP. And, from the look on his face, he is not a contented temporary tent-dweller.

I'm like, 'Hey, Dude, what's the Jackanory?' and he's like, 'I want word with *that man*,' and he points at Oisinn, who looks over, mid-sentence, and cops JP standing there with a face like a well-slapped orse.

JP's like, 'Did you know that my father was involved in that holy water business of his?'

I can't lie to my friend.

I'm like, 'No.'

Actually, I can.

He goes, 'Yeah. Oisinn sold him shares. One hundred thousand euros worth . . .'

I'm like, 'A hundred Ks? That's some focking bread!' but it's obviously not the money that JP's worried about. He goes, 'Can you imagine the scandal if this was to get out,' and I'm like, 'Actually, you'd want to have a word with One F. He was thinking of writing the story for that *Northside Stor* he works for. "Dad Of Priest In Sacrilegious Scent Scandal" was the actual headline he had in mind.'

But JP doesn't respond, roysh, he's just, I suppose, glowering at Oisinn. And of course what does Caroline go and ask him about at that exact moment? She's like, 'So, tell us about your new venture – perfumed holy water,' and Oisinn goes, 'Yeah, people lead busy lives these days. A lot of them don't have time to put on perfume *and* bless themselves before they go out to work in the morning. So I figured, why not combine the two?' and I swear to God, roysh, he looks straight at JP and winks.

And of course JP's got, like, steam coming out of his ears at this stage. Caroline goes, 'What kind of scents can people look forward to in the range?' and Oisinn's there, 'Well, I'm working on one at the moment that contains white stilton and cheddar . . .' and there's, like, total silence, roysh, and you can feel the tension because you just know there's a one-liner on the way. Caroline goes, 'Interesting. And what's that one called,' and Oisinn looks at JP again and, with a big grin on his face, goes, 'Well, my business portner came up with that one. It's called . . . *One Day At A Time, Sweet Cheeses . . .*'.

Suddenly, roysh, all hell breaks loose. Before I can stop him, JP makes a focking lunge for Oisinn, knocking over a set of lights and, like, totalling them in the process. Now, Oisinn's a big goy, roysh, but JP knocks him on the deck and suddenly there's, like, feet and fists flying and it's, like, ten minutes before the crew manage to pull them aport.

Of course by that stage I'm back downstairs in the main bor with the two birds. Caroline's going, 'That's really weird. I was just about to ask him whether he expected any opposition from religious groups,' and I'm like, 'Do you girls fancy seeing my stomach again?'

'Look at him sitting there. You'd think butter wouldn't melt in his mouth. He's fooling you all. That's what he's doing. But you don't see it. None of you.'

I'm sitting there taking this abuse, roysh, nodding my head, with a sly little smile on my face, knowing that the more of this shit she spouts, the more Sorcha and her old dear are going to think she's lost it — big-time.

She's going, 'I said at the time you shouldn't have married him,' and Sorcha's old dear's going, 'Have another biscuit, Mum. You *like* Arrowroot, you know you do,' talking to her basically like she's six years old, which makes the old bag have even more of an eppo.

She's there, 'He's cheating on you and you can't even see it. He cheated on you when he was your boyfriend, didn't he?'

Uh-oh. Truth alert. There's no denying that one.

Sorcha goes, 'Oh, for heaven's sake, we were kids. He made his mistakes. I made mistakes, too,' which is news to me, though I don't pull her up on it.

The old cow's going, 'Twice, I saw him. TWICE! With my own eyes. And you'd rather take his word. Both of you! *His* word. A proven liar.'

Sorcha's there, 'You saw someone who looked like Ross. I know you've never been mad about him and I do value your opinion, but it's becoming, like, an obsession with you. It's like, *Oh my God!*'

I'm just there still nodding, smug as you like.

Sorcha's old dear, who's not exactly a member of my fan club either, goes, 'Ross is Sorcha's husband now, Mum.

She's going to have his baby,' and Sorcha goes, 'We had the scan the other day, Gran. Oh my God, you are SO going to have to see the DVD.'

The old wagon goes, 'He's a blackguard. Well, he might blackguard you but he won't blackguard me,' and I'm thinking, That's SUCH an old people's word, isn't it? Like *messages* for shopping and *mineral* for, like, Coke or 7-Up.

Sorcha turns to her old dear and goes, 'Mum, I don't think I can take much more of this. It's like, *Oh my God!*' and her old dear goes, 'I think we'll go then,' and the three of us get up, roysh, and Sorcha's old dear goes, 'I really don't know what's gotten into you the last few weeks, Mum. You might need a tonic or something.'

She goes, 'Ask your husband if *he* thinks I need a tonic. He believes me. He knows what this . . . *chap* is. And he won't let you put me away somewhere.'

Like I said before, roysh, one of us is going to have to lose this fight and, with everything to lose, I can tell you, roysh, it is SO not going to be me.

I'm there, 'I need a hit and miss,' and Sorcha's like, 'You can't hold it until we get home?' and I'm there, 'Don't think so,' and she tells me to be quick. I nip into the old TK Maxx under the stairs and pull the two packets of Tramil out of my Henri Lloyd.

One by one, roysh, I pop them out of the silver foil and pull them aport, emptying the actual powder into the sink and keeping the little plastic capsules. I open twenty of them, then I turn on the tap, wash all the shit down the plughole and gather up all the empty shells. I pull the chain, just so they think I *was* actually draining the snake, then I open the door as quietly as I can. I nip into the kitchen, open the little pedal-bin in the corner and put the shells into it, making sure they're on top, roysh, so the old bag sees them the next time she's throwing something out. Then I go back into the sitting-room.

Sorcha goes, 'I said to be quick, Ross,' and I'm like, 'Sorry. Just a bit of, er . . . sickness,' and that makes her feel guilty for rushing me.

Sorcha and her old dear kiss the old cow goodbye, and I go to as well, roysh, just for the crack of it, and she goes, 'Get away from me!' and I look at the other two and sort of, like, shrug, as if to say, basically, What more can I do?

As we're going out the door, Sorcha's old dear is going, 'We might put you back on the Sanatogen, Mum. You might just need more protein.'

'How's that grandson of ours?' the old man goes to me on the phone the other night, just as I'm about to do my usual, which is call him a penis and hang up on him.

He goes, 'How's that grandson of ours?' and of course at first, roysh, I just presume I've, like, misheard him.

Then he goes, 'Young Ronan,' and when he says it, roysh, it knocks me sideways because I've never heard him say Ronan's actual name before.

So I go, 'He's fine,' thinking, it's nice to be nice. Then I'm like, 'What the fock do you care?'

He's there, 'Your mother and I were just saying, it's a terrible shame we haven't been more of a presence in his life,' and I go, 'You haven't been a presence at all. That letter Hennessy sent Tina, warning her away, was your last involvement in his life,' but he's like, 'I said to your mother, it's two grandchildren we'll have, not just one . . .'

8. You Choke, You Learn

I go into our room, roysh, and Sorcha's on the bed, lying on her back, totally naked, roysh, with her knees bent and her orms by her side and, not being crude or anything, but let's just say it's not only my face that suddenly comes alive.

She's like, 'What are you doing?' as I'm kicking off the old Dubes and whipping down the old tweeds and I'm like, 'I knew you'd see sense. I have been GAGGING for it,' and she's like, '*Gagging for it?* Ross, I'm doing my Kegel exercises,' and of course I'm left standing there with my kacks around my ankles, going, 'Your what?'

She's like, 'Kegel exercises,' and she sort of, like, sits up. I go, 'Exercises? But you're not *actually* moving,' and she's there, 'HELLO? I'm, like, moving *inside*?' and I must have, like, a dumb look on my face because she goes, 'Inside, Ross! I'm tensing and then relaxing the muscles around my bum and vagina,' and I'm like, whoa, TMI, thank you.

She goes, 'Sit down, Ross. I've got twenty-five repetitions to do,' and for some reason I end up doing what I'm told.

She goes, 'Ross, you have been SO good about all this business with Gran. Mum wants you kept in the loop about what's happening, since it affects you too,' and I'm there, 'Okaaay?' and she goes, 'The doctor thinks she might be suffering from clinical paranoia, Ross,' and I'm there, 'Oh well, if it's not one thing, it's another, huh?'

She goes, 'That's where all these delusions are coming from. The latest is she thinks someone's . . . *trying to poison her*,' and I'm like, 'Someone?' and I swear to God, roysh,

I'm actually struggling to keep a straight face here. She goes, 'Well, she thinks *you're* trying to poison her, Ross. With tablets, of all things. I'm SO sorry,' and I end up having to go into the en suite, roysh, because I am, like, *cracking* my hole laughing, and in a total way.

Of course, Sorcha thinks I'm crying. I'm sitting on the can, with my face in my hands, sore from laughing and she's outside the door, roysh, giving it, 'Oh my God, Ross, I realise how hord this must be for you. It's like, *Oh my God!*' and then she's going, 'Look, this paranoia about people trying to kill them, it's a common symptom of what the doctor thinks she has. Ross, please, come out,' and I know it's time to, like, get serious. I rub a bit of shampoo into my eyes to make them red, roysh – an old trick of the trade – splash a bit of water on my cheeks, then open the door and walk straight into a hug.

She goes, 'You are the most amazing husband any girl could wish for. You SO don't deserve all the stuff that gets thrown at you,' and then when she pulls away, roysh, she announces that she's going to do her Dromedary Droops.

The next thing I know, roysh, she's down on the ground, on all fours, with her back straight and her head, like, pointing straight out in front of her. It's actually *doing* it for me, believe it or not. She goes, 'Sorry, Ross, this relieves the pressure of the uterus on the spine,' and suddenly it's not doing it for me anymore.

She goes, 'How are your cravings, by the way?' and I'm like, 'Pretty much gone, actually – ever since that tandoori mackerel and lime curd sandwich this morning. But never mind that. What are you going to do about her, as in your gran. God, it makes me so sad to think of her suffering . . .'

She's there, 'I just don't know. We're having, like, a family conference at the weekend. Mum's talking about residential care. Dad ... well, you know what dad thinks. Always prepared to think the worst of you. Oh my God, I probably should apologise for him as well.'

Looks like I spoke too soon about those cravings. I'm looking at Sorcha's papaya and watermelon moisturising lotion, thinking how like Angel Delight it looks.

I go, 'Don't sweat it, Babes. Residential care, though? Well, it's one of those decisions I suppose you can't put off forever. Sooner or later she's going to do damage to herself. She belongs in a home,' and Sorcha suddenly looks at me, all serious, and goes, '*Oh! My God!* It is *not* a home, Ross – it's a retirement village.'

Sorcha's clenching and unclenching something down there and I don't really want to think about what it is.

I go, 'Hope you don't mind me asking, but do you not think maybe you should consider this?' and I hand her this orticle, roysh, that I pulled out of Fionn's *Irish Times* magazine the other day.

Sorcha stares at it and then goes, 'Well, I know she probably needs a break, Ross, but snowboarding? With *her* hip? It's like, HELLO?' and I go, 'Sorry, it's the other side you should be looking at,' and she whips it over, roysh, and suddenly it's the big drama queen act. She's like, 'Euthanasia? *Oh* my God,' and she hands it back to me in total disgust.

I'm there, 'I'm just saying. Might be worth putting on the list of options. Look, it's legal in all these places – Holland, Belgium, Switzerland. I wouldn't even say it's expensive. Listen to this. *A sedative, usually sodium thiopental is administered through an intravenous drip to induce a coma. Once that has been achieved, a muscle relaxant is administered to stop the breathing, thus causing death,'* and she's looking at me in a way no bird has ever looked at me before. Except Oreanna, of course.

She goes, 'OH MY GOD! You are *actually* serious!' and

I'm like, 'I know it's a hord decision . . .' and she's there, 'And it isn't our decision to make, Ross! Euthanasia is entirely voluntary . . . And it's only used as a means of ending suffering,' and I'm like, 'Well, her life isn't exactly a focking picnic, is it? Active Retirement! Mass every day! Up and down to Knock every time she has a runny focking nose!' and Sorcha goes, '*Ross!*' and she sort of, like, screams it, which means she's serious.

Her moisturiser looks so fruity. I have to try it. Just a little bit. On my tongue.

She goes, 'You are talking about my *grandmother*! My mum's mum. The stuff she's lived through, Ross . . .' and I'm like, 'Even more reason to say, you know, you've had a great time, seen a lot of good shit, blah, blah, blah . . . I don't know what the big focking drama is anyway. I mean, she *believes* in heaven, doesn't she? I mean, I wouldn't be a million per cent sure she's on the list, but Mass every day is going to stand to her.'

Sorcha just gets up off the floor, roysh, and goes, 'I don't know *what's* gotten into you but I don't *think* I want to be around you at the moment. Leave me alone. I'm going to do my pelvic tilts.'

On the way out the door, I stop by her bedside locker. I dip my whole hand into the tub of moisturisers and throw a massive glob of the shit into my mouth, then another, then another. I'm like Winnie the focking Pooh cleaning out a pot of honey. Except it doesn't taste like honey. Doesn't taste like papaya or watermelon either. It tastes like moisturiser, and it takes me an hour to wash it out of my mouth.

Dick Features rings the gaff and of course, not having caller ID, I end up answering the phone. He goes, 'Just wanted to make sure you and your good lady wife received your invites for the launch of *Criminal Assets* – quote-unquote. It's just you haven't RSVPed yet,' and I'm there, 'That's because they went straight in the focking bin. And I'm telling you, if I see that pile of shit in even *one* bookshop, you can tell that old bint you're married to that you'll never see me again.'

He goes, 'Now, I know the launch is in the same week as Sorcha's due date, but we'd both love to see the two of you there. *Woman's Way* is already calling it a real page-turner, quote-unquote,' and I'm just about to call him a tosser and hang up on him when he turns around and goes, 'We sent one to young Ronan, too, in that . . . *place* where he lives. We'd love to see him there.'

'What the fook is that?' That's what Tina's old man goes. Sorcha's like, 'It's a sun-dried tomato,' and the goy just stares at it, roysh, stuck on the end of his fork, and goes, 'It's like no tematto *I've* ever bleedin see-in.'

Tina goes, 'I told you, Da, a'thin you don't like, leave it on the side of yer plate,' and I look down at Tina's and she's shoved pretty much everything to the side – we're talking olives, we're talking pine-nuts, we're talking rocket – and she's just eating the fish, roysh, but with a serious focking puss on her. It's like her face caught fire and someone put it out with a flip-flop.

I *told* Sorcha she was going a bit OTT. 'These kinds of people only eat shit that's microwaveable,' I told her, but she'd every cookbook she owns open face-down on the island. I went, 'Suit yourself, but it's like giving strawberries to a focking donkey,' and of course I was bang-on. None of them appreciated all her work – all, that is, except Ronan, who it has to be said is the perfect guest.

He's going, 'You can really taste the majoram, can't you? Is that one of your own, Sorcha?' and Sorcha's like, 'Oh my God, I wish it was. No, it's one of Jamie's,' and Ronan goes, 'Oh . . . Pukkah!' which is pretty funny, you have to give it to him.

Sorcha goes, '*Oh* my God, we are SO going to have to do this more often. I mean, when this baby arrives, we're all going to be, like, family,' which isn't strictly true, though I let it go, because you have to admire the girl for making the effort. I suppose I was the one who brought these people on us in the first place.

Tina's old man gives up on the nosebag. 'Don't know how yiz live on dis side of de bleedin' ci'ee,' is his next effort at dinner-table conversation and as he says it, roysh, his eyes are rolling like two eight-balls, casing the room, doing a quick inventory – if that's the word – of everything we own. Habit of a lifetime, I'd imagine. He goes, 'It's so far away, isn't it?' I'm like, 'Far away? From what?' and he goes, 'Ah, bleedin' everyting. O'Connell Street, for one,' and under my breath I go, 'Amen to that.'

Sorcha's like, 'Thanks for the present. It was, like, SO thoughtful,' and all heads turn to the box in the corner. A focking karaoke machine. Second-hand as well, judging by the state of the packaging. Tina goes, 'You haven't already got one, have ye?' and I'm like, 'I think I can safely say we don't,' and she doesn't, like, pick up on the sarcasm in my voice.

Tina's wearing a pair of hoopy earrings you could put your focking orm through, all the way up the shoulder.

Sorcha goes to stand up, roysh, and I tell her to sit down. I'll clear away the plates and bring dessert. It's that summer fruit-and-prosecco jelly that she makes. As I'm opening the fridge, I hear Sorcha turn around to Tina and go, '*Oh my*

God, it is SO hord to get elderflower cordial in this country, isn't it?' and as I'm scooping the jelly into the bowls I'm thinking, That's, like, one of the reasons I love Sorcha – her total innocence. I mean, I look at Tina and her old man, roysh, and I see two pure and utter skobes who'd steal your focking jaw while you slept if they thought there were gold teeth attached to it. But Sorcha just sees actual people – probably why Amnesty and Trocaire and all that crowd find her such a soft touch.

Sorcha goes, 'Ronan, you never told me about Paris,' and immediately, roysh, the kid turns to me and looks at me sort of, like, suspiciously. I give him a little shake of the head and go, 'I was telling Sorcha that you were, em, checking out the French rugby academy that time,' and Ronan immediately goes, 'Nice cover story, Rosser,' and I think it's, like, the first time he's ever sounded impressed by me. He's like, 'Jaysus, I needn't worry about *you* cracking if Plod pulls you in for a quiet word in your shell-like,' which thankfully goes roysh over Sorcha's head.

He turns to her and goes, 'Paris was great. All the facilities they have . . . Sport's a science over there, you see. Seeing how they do it could only improve me own game,' and he gives me, like, the subtlest little wink.

Tina pushes her dessert to one side, untouched, of course, and whips out a cigarette. I'm about to say something when Ronan turns around and goes, 'Ma, what are you doing? You can't smoke in here,' and he sort of, like, flicks his thumb in Sorcha's direction and goes, 'The girl's eight months pregnant.'

Tina goes, 'Well, I'm not smoking outside,' as if this somehow puts the ball back in our court. There's, like, a ten-second stand-off and eventually Tina's old man goes, 'Let's hit de road, in anyway. Sure, we can smoke on de bus,' and he stands up, roysh, and he's like, 'I don't feel comftible out dis direction. No offence – but it's not de nortsoyid,' and I'm there, 'You wouldn't believe how far from an offence that is.'

So a couple of minutes later, roysh, they're gone and I'm doing a quick scout of the gaff to see if anything's missing, when Sorcha turns around to me and goes, 'Oh my God, I can't believe how well that went . . .'

It's Saturday afternoon, roysh, and we're sitting in Kiely's, the usual suspects, we're talking me, Oisinn, Christian and Fionn, basically chillaxing with a few Britneys, talking about the Lions match this morning and how it would have been a totally different story had I been on the pitch because I would have focking decked Tana Umaga if he even thought about doing that to Drico.

Gerry Thornley, Wardy, One F – any of those goys ring me for a comment and I'm going to, like, say the same thing to them all, which is that Clive Woodward chose not to bring me to New Zealand and, though he probably had his reasons – the fact that I haven't played any rugby for the past few years has to have been, like, a factor – he's basically reaping what he pretty much sowed.

All of a sudden, roysh, who arrives in only JP. He ignores me, roysh – no high-five or anything – walks straight over to Oisinn and goes, 'Can I talk to you for a minute?' and I'm straight out of my seat, roysh, getting ready to step in between the two of them.

Fair focks to Oisinn, roysh, there's no, like, hostility or anything. He goes, 'Sure. Sit down, JP,' which the dude does. Then he goes, 'Oisinn, I owe you an apology. That day in the club, I behaved . . . well, in a way that was decidedly unchristian,' which must be Maynooth for, I acted like a complete focking tosser.

He goes, 'Look, I'm sorry. Not just for physically attacking you like that but also for being so bloody pious.'

Oisinn just, like, shakes his head and goes, 'Don't be so hord on yourself, Dude. I mean, the provocation . . . getting your old man involved like that. I did that just to rub your nose in it. Look, I'm sorry too,' and the next thing, roysh, the two of them are, like, hugging each other and I'm going, 'Get a focking room!'

They laugh and Oisinn goes, 'No, let's get a drink. JP, you'll have a Baileys,' and – this is incredible, roysh – JP goes, 'No . . . I'll have a pint of Ken,' which he hasn't drunk since he ran off with the Catholics.

So while the lounge bird is off getting the round, Oisinn tells JP that he's going to Rome next week to see can he talk his way into an audience with the new Pope, run the idea past him, and JP says that if he can help in any way – contacts, blahdy, blahdy, blah – to give him a shout.

I ask him has he heard from Fehily and he tells me he had, like, a letter from him yesterday. He was doing okay, roysh, although obviously he'd rather not be in the slammer in some way-off country. He's still hopeful that they'll drop the chorges before it comes to trial, on account of how sick he is and shit?

JP goes, 'He asked for you all, especially you, Ross. Why don't you write to him?' and I'm like, 'It's a good plan in theory, but, well, you know me. I'm no good at, like, reading and writing and all that,' and the next thing, roysh, I hear this snigger out of Fionn, who's sitting off on his own reading, of all things, *The Irish* focking *Times* – and not the sport section either.

I'm there, 'What's so focking funny? Another mistake in

the crossword?' which should put him in his place, except it doesn't.

He looks up, roysh, and he goes, 'No good at writing, you say? It seems someone in your family has a talent for it, though,' and I'm like, 'What are you bullshitting on about?' and he's there, 'I'm just reading the books page here. Listen to this. *Loose Leaves. The small and cosy world of Irish chick-lit is set to be shaken to its foundations with the arrival of new talent on the scene. Fionnuala O'Carroll-Kelly's debut novel, Criminal Assets, promises to be a sizzling cross between Patricia Scanlan and Jilly Cooper . . .'*

Oh, *fock!* I decide to play it cool. I go, 'So this woman's got the same name as my old dear? Your point is what exactly?'

He's there, *'The mother of one from Foxrock, who is married to independent councillor Charles O'Carroll-Kelly, is rumoured to have been paid a high six-figure advance for her book, which follows the story of an attractive, forty-something woman from south Dublin, who has to redefine her life after her husband is jailed for planning corruption and tax evasion . . .'*

Shit. That fairly narrows it down alroysh.

I'm there, 'Fionn, I think we're all struggling here to see how this is funny?' which isn't exactly true, roysh, because everyone – even JP – is cracking their holes laughing.

Fionn's there, *'None of the current crop of women's popular fiction writers has dared to write the kind of racy, suspense-filled thriller that has made authors like Cooper and Jackie Collins household names all over the world. O'Carroll-Kelly, who posed nude for a Yummy-Mummy charity calendar a year ago, makes no apologies for daring to embrace the physical. "I'm a very sensuous woman," she says.'*

Focking hilarious, I *don't* think.

But Oisinn's laughing so much he's having trouble catching his breath. Even Christian, my so-called best friend, is having a great old chuckle as well.

Fionn's there, '"*There's nothing in this book that I haven't felt on a very personal level.*" *But how much of the plot is based on the experiences of her husband, who has so far appeared in front of at least two of the country's tribunals, in relation to allegations of corruption and tax irregularities?* "*I won't deny we've suffered,*" *she says,* "*as have a lot of other decent, employment-generating people who've been dragged before these . . . Star Chambers.*" *The book is due to be published in six weeks and comes with a warning to readers to brace themselves for a roller-coaster ride of sex, food and financial intrigue.*'

And as the four of them – my four best friends in all the world – collapse on the floor laughing, I know that my reputation is basically ruined.

'What do you want?' Sorcha's granny goes. She is SO not a happy bunny to see me. I'm there, 'Can I come in?' and she's like, 'You're not getting past this door,' and she goes to shut it in my face. So I stick my foot in it, roysh, then put my shoulder to it, the same one that put the great Gordon D'Arcy on his orse in our school days, so *she* certainly wasn't going to be able to take the power.

She goes, 'There's a nurse on the way around to change the dressing on my ulcer,' and she says it in a threatening way, roysh, but I'm just like, 'HELLO? *Too* much information?' and she's there, 'Any minute she'll be here,' and I'm like, 'Look, I'm not going to hurt you. I'm here because I want to call a truce.'

She shakes her head and goes, 'I'm going to get the Guards,' but as she goes to pick up the Wolfe in the hall I just, like, grab it out of her hand and I'm like, 'Look, I'm sorry for all the shit I caused. I've come because I want to end this thing. Sorcha's about to have a baby, as in your first great-grandchild? Whatever way you feel about me, you can't think it's right for that little girl to grow up without her dad.'

She looks me up and down and goes, 'This isn't about your daughter. And it's not about Sorcha either. You're thinking of you. As usual,' and I'm there, 'You're actually wrong,' and she's like, 'You know who you remind me of, Ross?' and I am so tempted to go, Well, you wouldn't be the first so say Antonio Banderas, but I don't. I don't answer at all. She's there, 'John, Lord have mercy on him,' and I'm like, 'As in your husband, John? What are you banging on about now?'

She grabs the phone out of my hand and hangs it up. Then she goes, 'He was just like you. Had a wandering eye. I never caught him, but oh I knew there were other women . . .'

I'm there, 'So why did you stay with him?' and she's like, 'Because I made a vow before God – till death us do part,' and I go, 'So you stayed with your cheating husband, but you want Sorcha to break up with hers? You said it yourself, you're a big believer in God and all that – why don't you respect *our* vows?'

She doesn't bat an eyelid.

She just goes, 'You know my feelings on that one. Yours never *was* a marriage, not in my eyes. Sorcha could have got an annulment. That business at the reception . . . she should have listened to her father. She still should. Never seen the like of it. Picking on a defenceless old woman,' and I'm there, 'How old are you again?' and she's like, 'I'm eighty-five, you know,' and I end up cracking up laughing in her face.

I'm wasting my time here. I know that now. I shouldn't have come.

I go, 'Hey, there's only going to be one loser in all of this

– and that's you,' and she's there, 'Look at you, bullying a helpless old woman,' and, as I'm opening the front door, I go, 'There's nothing helpless about you. I'm not like the others – I don't *buy* your act.'

As I'm going out the front gate, she shouts at me, 'There's not a bit of goodness in you. You're rotten through and through.'

I get into my cor – BMW Z4 – and I sit there for twenty minutes, just staring into space. I hear the front gate open, roysh, and I see a woman walking up the path to the front door. It must be the nurse.

I get it together and turn the key and point the cor in the direction of home.

I'm in the old man's study, having an old mooch around, roysh, looking for money to steal, if the truth be told. So I'm sitting at his desk, roysh, practising his signature on his jotter-pad, with a view to writing a cheque or two to myself, when all of a sudden I cop this letter, which ordinarily I wouldn't bother my orse reading, roysh, except I cop the stamp and the postmork on it and it's, like, France, and when I open it, roysh, it turns out it's from Fehily – or #1311825 as he is known these days.

So I scan through it, roysh, then I read it again, then again, then again, and suddenly the penny drops.

It storts off, roysh, with all the pleasantries – food's not the best, but the other prisoners and even the screws have been treating him really well, blahdy blahdy blah – and then, roysh, out of the blue, it's like,

'Charles, as a former student of mine, I hope you won't consider it a liberty for me to broach a subject of a rather personal nature. As you know, Ross's son, Ronan, is currently a student at Castlerock College. It's fair to say that, in more than fifty years of teaching, I have never met such an extraordinary child. His grades are consistently astonishing. He's cleverer at eight than Ross was at 18–'

And I'm thinking, that's actually uncalled for.
But I read on.
It's like,

'. . . It's not just academically that he excels. He is a truly outstanding rugby player, so good in fact that, notwithstanding his size, we did consider putting him in the Junior Cup team this year, at scrum-half. Shrewder judges than I – including two former internationals – reckon that he'll play for Ireland one day, without a doubt.'

Then it's like,

'Ronan has a personality that you wouldn't expect to find in a child twice his age – charisma, I think you'd call it. He's funny and a joy to be around. The other children idolise him but he can hold his own for hours in adult company. He's a born leader. The reason I'm writing to you, Charles, is to tell you that I sense a sadness in his heart. Lord knows, it's not my business to pass judgement on what goes on in other people's families, but as your friend, Charles, and as a friend to young Ronan, it would be remiss of me not to tell you, in whatever time I have left, that your non-relationship with your grandson is hurting him. And I know it will upset you to hear that because you're a good man . . .'

*

Sorcha muted 'The OC' the other night, roysh, to tell me that she still feels – *oh my God*! – SO guilty for freezing me out on the whole pregnancy front, and she would SO love if I came to her ante-natal class with her tonight, so I end up going.

Of course, Stef remembers me from before. She's like, 'Ah, Ross – I hope you haven't eaten this time,' and everyone in the class cracks their holes laughing, roysh, which means they've all heard the story.

Stef goes, 'Well, I hope you have the ... *stomach* for tonight's class,' and everyone laughs again. She's there, 'Because we're going to be about pregnancy from the perspective of the father. Now, unfortunately, modern society lacks a clearly defined role for expectant fathers. Most of the books that I'm sure you've read about pregnancy deal with the issue almost exclusively from a female perspective. And yet there's enormous pressure on fathers. You have to be strong when your partner is weak. You have to support without being supported ...'

Sorcha squeezes my hand, roysh, and when I look at her she gives me a smile. She has a great smile, in fairness to her.

Stef goes, 'So as the due date grows ever nearer for you all, we're going to spend some time tonight talking about the role of your equal – but too often neglected – Partner In Reproduction,' and she writes the letters PIR up on the blackboard.

She's there, 'Enormous changes have taken place in social attitudes since your mothers were expecting all of you. And yet despite those changes, the fact remains that pregnancy still takes place within a woman's body. And as a consequence, fathers often wind up feeling left out of the whole process.'

I know I puked on her last time, but I could actually kiss Stef at this moment in time.

She goes, 'So what is your husband or partner thinking? Unfortunately, most of us are too preoccupied to stop and ask. Is he feeling disenfranchised? Are his sexual needs being fulfilled? How is he coping with your mood swings? Is he experiencing any of his own? Does he have anxieties about your health, your baby's health and the changes that this new arrival will bring about in your lives? Is he worried about what kind of father he will make? Is he afraid of watching the labour process? These are the issues you should be talking about with your . . .' and she underlines the letters on the blackboard, '. . . Partner In Reproduction.'

All of a sudden, for some reason, roysh, I look to my left and – I swear to God – I nearly end up shitting myself.

There's a bird sitting four seats away from me, roysh, and it's, like, Lucy Scarne, as in used to be in charge of the school bank in Holy Child Killiney, as in played Winnie Tate the year our two schools did 'Annie, Get Your Gun', as in did French grinds at the Institute? Anyway, roysh, I ended up scoring her one night in the club just after New Year and of course I'm panicking now, wondering did I wear a rain-coat that night.

I don't think I did.

I'm thinking, this *cannot* be happening to me. So I'm sitting there, roysh, trying to catch Lucy's eye, to basically ask her what's the Jackanory.

Am I the . . .

Stef's blabbing away for, like, twenty minutes about fatherhood relationship modules or some shit and then finally suggests we break for coffee.

Out of the corner of my eye, roysh, I see Lucy heading out for a hit and miss and I peg it out after her. I call her, roysh. I'm like, 'Hey, Luce,' and she turns around and, like, gives me the big-time daggers. I'm there, 'Hey, don't look at me like that. I've got a roysh to know,' and she goes, '*Know?* Know what?' and I'm like, 'Am I the father?' and I sort of, like, nod at her bump.

She just, like, looks me up and down and goes, 'The father *happens* to be my husband, Ross,' and I'm thinking, there was no mention of a husband the night we made sweet music together. It's, like, such a relief, though. I try to make light of it, going, 'You're absolutely sure it's not mine? It's just, I'm popping out kids like a focking northsider at this stage.'

She looks me up and down again, roysh, and then gives me this really, I suppose you'd have to say, cruel laugh and goes, 'That would be impossible considering nothing happened the night we were together, what with your little . . . *problem?*' and I end up going, 'Really? Oh. I was pretty much under the impression that I took you to heaven and back that night . . .'

She's like, 'Ha! You couldn't have raised your bus fare that night!' which was uncalled for. She storms into the TK Maxx, slamming the door behind her.

The next thing, roysh, Sorcha comes out of the room, screaming basically blue murder, going, 'Ross, we SO need to talk,' and straight away, roysh – pretty much out of instinct – I go, 'We've had a chat, Babes – don't worry, it's not mine!' but it's not that at all. She just, like, hands me my phone and I notice that I've got a text, which she's very thoughtfully opened and read for me and it's from, like, Oisinn, who's in Rome, and he's telling me he picked up a stack of that porn I asked him to get for me, including the Elona Staler calendar.

So I end making the not unreasonable point that she

couldn't blame *me*, roysh, because the no-sex thing was actually *her* idea.

But she's just there, roysh, staring at the door of the ladies, then at me.

Then she goes, 'What's *not yours*, Ross?' and – cooler than a mullet's mickey – I go, 'Oh, em, that bird Lucy, she thought she accidentally picked up my leaflet on that nurturing and caring module that Stef was talking about . . .'

The old Wolfe rings and I very nearly don't recognise the voice at first. An older man. Sounds pissed off. Of course, it's Sorcha's old man.

He goes, 'Ross, do you remember, not so long ago, you and I, in my office, having a conversation, at the end of which I showed you a gun and told you what I would do with that gun if you ever upset my daughter?' and I'm like, 'Er, yeah, it'd be hord to forget something like that.'

He's there, 'Good. Now, I know you've been baiting Sorcha's grandmother and making great sport of it, by the sounds of it. You paid her a visit a couple of days ago, I hear,' and I'm like, 'I was just trying to straighten shit out before this baby's born because it's upsetting Sorcha . . .' but he just cuts me off mid-sentence.

He goes, 'Ross, I've no doubt in my mind that she saw what she claims she saw. I don't need character references for you. I made up mind about you a long time ago. Unfortunately, my eldest daughter is blind, as is my wife, I'm disappointed to say.'

He's like, 'I'm going to give this to you in plain English, Ross, because I know you failed the subject in your Leaving Cert,' which is bang out of order. He goes, 'Sorcha's grandmother will be going into a nursing home over my dead body. And if I ever hear again that you've tried to bully or intimidate her, or even plain disrespected her, I will shoot you with my gun and bury you in the Wicklow Mountains. Do I make myself clear?' and I'm like, 'Yeah,' and then the line goes dead.

I'm going, 'Where are you?' and Oisinn's like, 'Front row. About ten people from the end,' and I'm there, 'I still can't see you. Oh, hang on . . . JP, do you think that's him there?' putting my finger on the actual screen.

JP goes, 'I'm pretty sure it is.'

It's the new Pope's first meet-and-greet, roysh, and Oisinn's ended up with one of the best seats in the house.

So we decided to surprise JP, roysh – we're talking me, Fionn and Christian – by calling out to his gaff in Maynooth with a shitload of cans – not to mention a lorge bottle of Winter's Tale for him – to watch it on the old Savalas together, with a live telephone link-up to our man in Rome.

I'm there, 'Oisinn, we think we can see you, but we're not sure and shit? Wave your orms around or something,' which he does, roysh, and suddenly I can see him. I'm like, 'Hey, you wore your Castlerock jersey! You the man, Dude!' and suddenly we're all, like, high-fiving each other like there's no tomorrow.

The shot changes to a close-up of the new goy, who I mention looks a bit like the Emperor out of *Stor Wars*, and that's not being blasphemous or whatever.

Fionn goes, 'Oh, Christian, did you bring the letter with you?' and I look at Christian as if to go, What the fock's he talking about, and Christian turns around to me and he's there, 'I got a letter from George Lucas. He read my script,' and I'm thinking, How come he told Fionn about it before me? It's like, Er, which one of us is supposed to be his best friend again?

I go, 'Oisinn, are you hearing this? Christian's got a letter from that focking George Lucas. Christian, read it out,' and Fionn's looking at it over Christian's shoulder, going, 'It's handwritten as well.'

Christian's like,

'Dear Christian. Thank you very much for taking the time to send me your script, which I've just finished reading in a single, three-hour sitting. Let me just say at the outset that it blew me away. I especially enjoyed the plot twist involving Bib Fortuna's brain being transplanted into the head of a Wookie – what a formidable adversary he proved for Han and Leia – and also the love interest for C3PO. You are clearly a very talented screenwriter and your knowledge of the *Star Wars* universe is so vast as to embarrass even me. Unfortunately, as it stands, the *Return of the Jedi* is, for me, the final chapter of the *Star Wars* saga and at this moment in time there are no plans to make a VII, VIII or IX. However, if that situation changes, you can expect a call from me. I would love to talk. In the meantime, keep up the writing. May the Force Be With You.

George.'

JP and Fionn are going, 'That's great, Christian,' and I'm like, '*May the Force Be With You* – that was actually a nice touch. He didn't have to say that,' and I go, 'Oisinn, did you get all that?' and he says he did and he tells me to tell Christian that he's the man, which I do.

Then Fionn goes and spoils the whole atmos by going, 'What about your old dear's *work of art*, Ross? When are we getting copies?' but I don't rise to the bait. I just, like, totally blank him.

Oisinn's going, 'Okay, Ross, the way this thing works is that the Pope will stort at the top of the line and make his way along, shaking hands with people in the first three rows. When he gets to me, I'm going to whip out the bottle . . .'

So we're sitting there, roysh, and we're watching the goy make his way along the line, shaking hands with everyone, and Oisinn goes, 'Ross, this is the moment that's going to change my life forever. Remember, southside eyes – hungry for the prize. I'll ring you after,' and he hangs up on me and we're all sitting there, totally glued to him, roysh, as the Pope, the Holy Father, whatever you want to call him, reaches the point where Oisinn's standing.

And from that moment on, roysh, it all seems to happen in, like, slow motion.

Oisinn shakes his hand, then holds onto it for a few extra seconds – and you can see this, like, look of worry appear on the Pope's face – then Oisinn pulls him close and, like, whispers something in his ear.

The next thing, roysh, all these goys in these, like, blue, red and yellow stripy jumpsuits appear on the scene. They look like they work for focking Statoil or something, but JP says they're, like, the Swiss Papal Guard, in other words, the local Feds.

We watch as Oisinn reaches into the pocket of his Henri Lloyd, roysh, and whips out a bottle, which he uncorks with one hand, and holds it under the Pope's nose. And in that split second, roysh, Oisinn is suddenly decked by, I think, a truncheon and he just, like, disappears under a pile of bodies. With all the colours, it actually looks like a focking circus tent has collapsed on him.

Believe it or not, JP is the first to laugh. The rest of us were probably waiting to see his reaction first. But then I crack up and so do Christian and Fionn.

I'm there, 'Did you see his face when that first goy hit him?' and JP goes, 'It was like when that prop from Mary's hit him that time,' and I'm like, 'Yeah! He looked really hurt!' and we're all cracking our holes laughing again.

So get this, roysh, I'm at this, like, Drinklink? Just off, like, Grafton Street? I stick my cord in and it's like, 'Would you like to do this transaction in a) English, or b) Gaeilge,' and I end up just, like, hitting a), roysh, because there wasn't an actual button for, Are you taking the actual piss?

Emer agrees with me, but then she usually does. I get back to the cor and I'm like, 'What actual country are we, like, living in?' and she's there, 'Em, Ireland?' and I go, 'Focking machine just asked me if I wanted to do the transaction in Gaelic,' and she's there, 'That is like, OH! MY! GOD!' and I go, 'It certainly is, you cracking-looking bimbo,' although I actually said the second port of that in my head.

Emer is this bird, roysh, who's, like, repeating second-year public relations in DBS – Dumb Blonde School, as I call it – and who is a total ringer for Jessica Simpleton and we *are* talking total here.

I've kind of fallen back on my old ways, I have to admit. Alcoholics call it a slip, so I suppose sexoholics call it the same thing.

See, the truth is, roysh, that everyone's getting it at the moment. Christian's getting it off Lauren. Fionn's presumably getting it off the Unlovely Debbie, having finally plucked up the courage to ask the hound out. Oisinn's getting it off half the modelling world, if the papers are to be believed. And even my old pair seem to be getting it, even if it is off each other.

I haven't had any for months and I literally can't take it anymore. So I ended up scrolling down through the numbers in my phone . . .

We're actually driving around, roysh, looking for a place to, like, do the dirty deed and I actually took money out of the Sherman just in case we end up having to get, like, a hotel room. Not that I'm scabby with money, of course. It's just that if we book a room, the pressure will be on me to spend, like, the whole night with her, as opposed to ten minutes of throwing the javelin in some lay-by.

Emer's one of my old reliable's, roysh – total use-and-abuse situation – but the last few times I've been with her, she's been, like, putting the serious squeeze on me, saying she wants more. Of course at first, roysh, I was like, 'More than *ten minutes*?' but she was there, 'No, Ross, I mean more . . . *emotionally*,' and it's that kind of talk, roysh, that frightens goys off.

So she storts this shit again, roysh, while she's driving us around the world and basically, just as I'm about to suggest the cor pork at the back of Dalkcy Hill, she's like, 'Ross, I want more. I *need* more,' and I'm playing it easy like Sunday morning, giving it, 'It's kind of difficult, Emer, what with me being, like, married and shit?' but she goes, 'You told me before Christmas that you were going to leave her,' and though I don't remember *actually* saying it, it is the kind of shit I come up with when I'm hammered and looking for my Nat King.

I actually don't know how I live with myself sometimes, roysh, because I'm there – totally straight-faced – going, 'It's . . . *difficult* at the moment. As in, like, timing-wise? Sorcha may have to . . . go into hospital,' which technically isn't a lie, roysh, even though all she's going in for is to have a baby.

Emer goes, '*Oh my God*, I had *literally* no idea,' and I'm like, 'It's cool,' and she's there, '*Oh my God*, is she going to be okay?' and I'm giving it, 'It's still pretty raw actually. I'd prefer not to talk about it,' and she's going, '*Oh my God*, you *poor* thing,' and I know that I'm pretty much guaranteed my bit now.

I'm thinking that's not an actual bad line to use, roysh, and I must file it away to be used again.

We pull into the cor pork and Emer kills the lights. She's going, 'I just can't wait until there's, like, no more complications and we can tell people about us,' and of course I'm peeling off the old threads while she's making her little speech. The old Henri Lloyd tennis racquet, the Ralph, the Dubes and the chinos are all gone, roysh, and I'm pushing the passenger seat back while she's still blabbing away about 'making it official' and 'no more secrets'.

I'm going, 'Okay, Babes – you're up,' meaning basically, GAME ON! at which exact point, roysh – get this – she reaches down, picks my threads up off the floor of the cor and – before I get a chance to react – gets out, slams the door and then, like, locks it? As in, like, locks me *into* her cor, with the central locking. As in, like, me sitting there only in my boxer shorts?

Of course, I am SO slow on the uptake.

I'm like, 'Hey, what's the Jackanory?' and she's, like, looking at me through the window, going, 'I was sick of it, Ross. I was just, like, SO sick of the lies, it was like, OH MY GOD!' and I'm there, 'Don't go psycho on me, Babes,' thinking she was going to, like, torch the focking cor or some shit.

She's like, '*Oh* my God, you've been treating me like dirt for two years now, not giving a basic shit about my feelings,' and through the window I'm going, 'What makes you think I don't give a basic shit?' and she's like, 'HELLO? You called me a bimbo about ten minutes ago,' and I'm thinking, Fock, I didn't think I actually said that out loud.

I'm like, 'So what are you planning to do? And do NOT say burn me alive,' and she's there, 'Oh, it's worse than that, Ross,' and the next thing, roysh, she whips out her Wolfe, dials a number and tells whoever's on the other end exactly where we are.

I'm sitting there in my total raw, going, 'That better not be a load of Terenure heads you just rang,' thinking, those goys have been waiting a long time to teach me a lesson. But she doesn't answer me, roysh. She just, like, stares off into the distance as I'm trying to, like, reef the door open.

It's no good, roysh, it won't budge.

The next thing, roysh, I hear this, like, *putt-putt-putt* sound and I don't even have to look, roysh, to know that it's, like, Sorcha's granny in her little focking Storlet.

I'm thinking, What in Brian O'Driscoll's name is going on here?

She pulls up beside Emer's Honda Civic – big, shit-eating grin on her face – and the first words out of her mouth are, 'Look at him – like a rat in a trap,' and she's looking through the window at me, roysh, like I'm some sort of animal in a cage.

Of course I'm kacking it now, roysh, but I'm not going to give her the pleasure of, like, letting her know. I'm there, 'Go on, get a good eyeful, you old focking bag. I'd say it's a long time since you clocked eyes on a body like this.'

She goes, 'Emer's grandmother and I are in the Active Retirement together,' and I'm there, '*Oooh, I remember when this was all fields*. You're in Active Retirement together – big swinging mickey. What's that got to do with the price of focking bicycles in Beijing?' and she goes, 'She's been telling me this last two year all about this young ... *pup* who has her granddaughter's heart broken. I said, "I've a grand-daughter the same." It was only yesterday I found out we were talking about the same man. And now look at you! I've waited a long time for this.'

And there I am, roysh, staring at her through the wind-screen as she whips out her phone and I don't even need to ask what number she's about to ring.

But she can't get a signal, the stupid weapon of mass destruction.

Emer's, like, sneering at me through the window of the passenger door and I'm, like, flexing my abs and my pecs, in a last-ditch attempt to basically make her want me, while Sorcha's granny forts around with the phone, roysh, trying to ring Sorcha's number.

She wouldn't exactly be technically minded, the old bag. She tends to call any piece of equipment invented since the sixties a Microwave, and I watch her going at the buttons like she's expecting the thing to explode if she presses the wrong one.

I have a brainwave. I tap on the window and go, 'Do you want to use mine?' thinking that the second they open the door, I can dive out, grab my threads and peg it. Of course, Emer actually goes to open the door until the old battleaxe lets a focking roar out of her and Emer steps backwards with, like, her hands up to her face, going, 'Oh my God, oh my God, I am SO thick sometimes.'

There's no arguments from me on that score.

The granny goes, 'I don't know what's wrong with this blasted phone,' and I sit there for a couple of minutes watching the two of them try to work it out – the blind leading the blonde – and eventually Emer tells her there mustn't be any coverage and they should walk to the end of the hill, where there's usually a good signal.

Emer seems to know her way around Dalkey Hill cor pork pretty well.

So off the two of them go, roysh, and I'm left sitting there in the cor, in the total raw, knowing that the game is over.

I just sit back, roysh, and pretty much resign myself to the idea of my daughter growing up in a one-parent family, like my son, I suppose. And I think about what a balls I've made of things and how being seriously good-looking is a gift I never really came to terms with.

The condemned man decides to listen to a few sounds. I press Play on the CD player and it's that bird that Sorcha likes, roysh, and she's going, '*You live, you learn. You love, you learn. You cry, you learn. You lose, you learn . . .*' and I'm suddenly having one of my real, like, intellectual moments, thinking, Whoa, that shit is, like, SO true.

The next thing I know, roysh, Emer's back and she's, like, screaming and banging on the window and going, '*Ross! Oh my God! Oh my God! Quick!* I think she's had a hort attack!' and, without thinking, I just, like, punch the air and go, 'YES!' and Emer gives me this absolute filthy – though it's nothing compared to the look she gives me when she lets me out of the cor, roysh, and I stort doing the *haka* in the middle of the cor pork.

She's like, 'Ross, are you going to actually help or are you going to, like, let her die?' and I suppose it's that last word that makes me cop onto myself.

I peg it to the bottom of the hill, pulling on my threads as I'm running.

I suppose it only really hits me how serious it is, roysh, when I find her sprawled out on her back at the side of the road, kicking her legs and struggling for breath.

I tell Emer to ring 999, which she does, then turns around to me and goes, 'Which service, Ross?' and I'm like, 'The focking Fire Brigade! Which service do you think?' and after, like, twenty seconds trying to decide whether I was being sarcastic or not, she asks for an ambulance.

As for me, I suppose the adrenalin takes over.

Utter focking wagon and all as this woman is, roysh, at this moment in time, she's basically just an old lady and she's, like, helpless and suddenly, roysh, I don't care whether Sorcha finds out about me and Emer, or me and whoever else. My priority is to save this woman's life and suddenly, roysh, all these, like, episodes of 'ER' are coming back to me and I'm, like, compressing her chest and I'm telling her that help is on its way.

Her face is turning blue.

Emer goes, 'Give her mouth-to-mouth,' and I'm like, '*Excuse* me?' and she's like, 'She looks like she needs oxygen in her airways. Ross, I was in the Order of Malta,' and as I'm kneeling, thinking about this, she goes, 'QUICK!'

And I do it, roysh. I actually end up giving her the kiss of life. I pinch her nostrils closed and, like, breathe into her mouth, one breath every five seconds, twelve per minute, completely refilling my lungs after each breath, like on telly.

I look up and I notice that Emer's got her back to us. I'm there, 'What's wrong?' and she goes, 'I find it really hord to watch you being with someone else,' and I'm like, '*Being* with someone? I'm giving her focking mouth-to-mouth like you told me,' and she goes, 'I know, but it's still, like, *oh my God*, SO hord for me to watch.'

I'm like, 'You're focking unbelievable, you are,' and just as I'm saying it, Sorcha's granny squeezes out a few words and it sounds very much to me like, 'My throat . . . stuck,' which is when I realise, roysh, that she hasn't had a hort attack at all.

I sit her up, roysh, and from behind her, I put both

orms around her waist. Then I give her the old Heinrich manoeuvre.

She gags a couple of times, then splutters and coughs. And out of her mouth shoots what looks suspiciously to me like a Werthers Original.

I collapse beside her and we both lie there on the wet ground for ages, trying to get our breath back, until we suddenly hear the sound of an ambulance approaching. It pulls up and all these goys pile out of it and stort lifting her onto a stretcher.

I go, 'It's okay. It's okay. She just choked on something,' and one of the ambulance dudes looks at her and goes, 'Let's take you in and have a look at you anyway.'

I'm holding her hand as they're loading her into the back, roysh, and I'm, like, reassuring her, I suppose, telling her everything's going to be okay and she sort of, like, smiles at me and squeezes my hand again.

9. Unputdownable

Oisinn's just loving this, and so are the rest of the goys. He's got the book open on the last page and he's going,

> 'The man she now knew as Kenny Powell placed a large brown envelope down on the table in front of her. The other customers looked up from their smoked salmon frittatas, their baked lamb with cardamom and their three-bean salads. 'What's that?' she asked, inquisitively. He raised a cool eyebrow and said, 'Evidence of my bona fides. It's some information that came my way – information that will ensure your husband wins his appeal. And his freedom.'

The goys are all cracking their holes laughing.

> 'Valerie's hand vacillated over the envelope. She looked up at Kenny, studied his sharp cheekbones, his icy cool eyes and panther-like physique and knew she was powerless. She was slippery with longing. Within minutes they were outside, in the car park, making angry love in the passenger seat of his buff-coloured Mercedes, Valerie looking out onto a field choked with figwort and forget-me-nots, savouring every thrust as pleasure crashed over her body like the breaking surf.
> 'When it was over, they lay together for hours, tiring the moon with their sweet whisperings about everything – love, life, whether or not Avoca Handweavers put too much leek in their asparagus, smoked bacon and Gruyère quiche. "What

shall I do with this?" Kenny said, picking the envelope off the dashboard and waving it in front of her. She took it from him briskly, opened the electric windows and dropped it into a litterbin. Il Divo's "Hasta Mi Final" reached its throbbing crescendo. Then they made fantastic love again.'

When he's finished reading, Fionn goes, 'I thought you weren't coming, Ross?' and I just shrug, cracking on it doesn't bother me, and go, 'I'm only here to heckle the stupid bitch,' though the *actual* truth is that if I'm going to have the piss ripped out of me over this for the next ten years, I'd rather be there to see how bad it's going to be.

Still, The Conrad – they're really pushing the boat out for her, this shower.

Sorcha comes up behind me, links my orm and goes, '*Oh! My God!* You must be, like, SO proud of her,' and I'm there, 'It was hord enough to live with the shame of being related to the stupid bitch *before* this,' and Sorcha laughs and pokes me in the ribs, roysh, obviously mistaking this for humour.

I'm there, 'Hey, why aren't you sitting down?' because she's huge at this stage, roysh, and big-time ready to pop. She goes, 'I just wanted to tell you – Gran's here,' and I end up nearly kacking it there on the spot. She's like, 'Now, before you say anything, Ross, just give her a chance. She has been saying – *Oh! My God!* – SUCH nice things about you. It's like she's another person. Mum thinks it might have just been a casein deficiency.'

I go, 'Has she said . . . anything else?' and Sorcha's there, 'Just that she was wrong about you. We don't know what's come over her, but it's like, *Oh* my God! And she is SO looking forward to your mum's book.'

I turn around and catch the old biddy's eye and she just

gives me a nod. No smile, though. I wouldn't think she's any more time for me than she had before, but she probably figured she owed me one.

Sorcha kisses me on the cheek and says she'll see me later and she moves over to Erika and I hear her telling her that I'm still on my housework buzz and that the other night I ruined three of her bras by ironing them.

Fionn's still missing Marty – like the rest of us, I suppose – but he's here tonight with the Unlovely Debbie, who's been filling the gap that was left in his life the day we released Marty back into the wild. And despite a black eye, two cracked ribs and a dislocated finger, Oisinn got a letter from the Vatican saying they're going to give his idea serious consideration. And JP seems, like, genuinely happy for him and shit?

Christian and Lauren are sitting in the corner, all smiles, deep in conversation, possibly about the wedding, but probably about some galaxy far, far away.

And the nicest surprise of all? The old man – penis and all as he is – is chatting away to Ronan, like a proper granddad. He's going, 'I'm hearing wonderful things about you, little chap. Chip off the old block and what-not. Future Ireland number ten, the dispatches say,' and Ronan's going, 'Ah, I haven't properly decided between rugby and football yet,' and the old man pulls a face and goes, 'Good Lord,' but it doesn't matter what he's saying, roysh – the point is that he's acknowledging him. The dickhead.

Then Hennessy pulls my old man aside, sounding worried about something. At first I think it might have to do with Ronan, roysh, but when I look over my shoulder, I notice that he's got a copy of the old dear's book open and he's, like, pointing out passages, going, 'You should have let me read this first,' and the old man's giving it, '*I've* read it. It's fine, old chum,' but Hennessy seems Scooby Dubious about something.

He's there, 'She mentions St Kitts-Nevis. St Vincent and the Grenadines. Sofia. Minsk. If someone was to . . .' but the old man goes, 'Oh, listen to you – Jim Garrison,' and he sort of, like, waves his hand at him.

The next thing, roysh, some publicity dude stands up in front of the microphone and storts, like, introducing the old dear, the stupid focking hag. He's going, 'Fionnuala O'Carroll-Kelly is a woman who manages to successfully combine the roles of housewife, mother, model, campaigner . . .' and I shout, 'Pervert . . .' and all the goys crack their holes laughing, roysh, and a few people – mostly her friends from tennis – turn around and actually shush me.

The goy goes, 'And now . . . novelist. Her book, *Criminal Assets*, is best described as a sexplicit thriller. It's racy. It's steamy. It's full of suspense. Think "Desperate Housewives" meets Torquay Road, Foxrock. Ladies and gentlemen, I have pleasure in introducing to you, the best thing to happen to women's fiction, in my view, since Edna O'Brien . . . *Fionnuala O'Carroll-Kelly*,' and the whole place goes ballistic. There must be, like, two- or three-hundred people in the room.

She looks a state, of course, half of focking Pia Bang hanging off her, and I have to give Oisinn a serious filthy when he puts two fingers in his mouth – we're talking after the applause has died down – and storts, like, wolf-whistling her.

'I'm a very sensual woman.'

They're the five words the old dear manages to get out before basically pandemonium breaks out. Everyone's, like, cheering and clapping – Oisinn and Fionn the loudest, it must be said, though more to piss me off than anything else

– and all of a sudden, roysh, there's a bit of a scuffle going on over to my roysh.

I hear the old man going, 'TAKE YOUR HANDS OFF ME! THIS IS EARLSFORT TERRACE, NOT ALBANIA UNDER HOXHA!' and I look around, roysh, and there's, like, seven or eight goys in suits surrounding him and you can hear one of them go, 'Charles O'Carroll-Kelly, I'm arresting you under . . .' blahdy blahdy blah.

So the whole room goes silent, roysh, and everyone's suddenly turned around, watching this with, like, smiles on their faces, obviously thinking it's a publicity stunt or some shit. But I know from the look on Hennessy's boat – and from the way he's arguing with them – that it's not.

They snap the old bracelets on him, roysh, and the old man goes, 'HOW DARE YOU TREAT ME LIKE THIS IN FRONT OF MY GRANDSON!' and I look at Ronan who, for reasons I don't even want to know about, has his hand up to his face, roysh, shielding it from the Feds.

The old man's going, 'IF IT'S CRIMINALS YOU'RE LOOKING FOR, THE DÁIL IS WHERE YOU'LL FIND THEM! KILDARE STREET, DUBLIN 2,' and it's suddenly dawning on people that the old man really is being hauled off to the can.

It's at that point that the old dear lets out a scream, except she does it into the microphone, suddenly spreading panic throughout the room. So then other people stort screaming at random – a couple of the old hounds she plays tennis with, another bird who's one of her coffee crowd, Angela and Susan from the Funderland campaign. And somehow, through all this noise, I hear this voice going, 'ROSS! *ROSS!*' and straight away I know it's, like, Sorcha.

So suddenly I'm pushing through the crowd, throwing hysterical old biddies out of the way, and by the time I reach her she's lying on the ground, with a space cleared around her. I grab her hand. She's sweating buckets. She looks at me and goes, 'This is it, Ross,' and I'm like, 'You mean *now*?' and she nods and at the top of my voice, roysh, I go, 'SOMEBODY CALL AN AMBULANCE!' and I hear Oisinn go, 'I'm on the case.'

She's actually in labour. I'm timing the contractions like the gynaecologist showed me and the *oh-my-Gods* are definitely getting closer together. Behind me I can hear Ronan clearing the room, going, 'Okay, party's over. Disperse now – or there'll be consequences . . .'

Sorcha goes, 'Oh my God, Ross – you have NEVER known pain like this,' and I'm tempted to mention the time I tore my rotator cuff playing against Belvedere in the junior cup, roysh, but then I remember what Stef said about giving her encouragement, so I end up going, 'I know, Babes.'

I can hear Claire going, 'Sorcha, we never decided between acupuncture and aromatherapy,' and Sorcha goes, 'FOCK ACUPUNCTURE! GET ME PETHIDINE! GET ME DIAMORPHINE!' and Ronan gets rid of Claire and the last few stragglers, going, 'I've been given the authority to crack skulls! OUT! OUT!'

Sorcha looks at me, roysh, with real fear in her eyes and she's like, 'I DON'T THINK WE'RE GOING TO NEED THAT AMBULANCE!' and then she lets out this scream, roysh, which echoes through the empty room. And I'm just on the point of losing it myself when, all of a sudden, something – or someone – hits me from behind, roysh, and sends me flying across the room and I look up, half-expecting it to be Reggie Corrigan.

It's not. It's, like, Sorcha's granny.

I'm rubbing my shoulder, thinking she could be the answer to Leinster's problems up front. She's down on her

knees, having a look. She goes, 'She's almost fully dilated,' and then she looks at me and she goes, 'Are you calm?' and I nod and she's there, 'Good, I'm going to need you at the other end.'

I cradle Sorcha's head in my hands and I tell her how brave she is, roysh, and how much I love her and I remind her about the visualisation exercises she learned and I tell her to think about cascading water as I watch in total awe as Sorcha's granny rolls up her sleeves and – like she said – just gets on with it.

I'm standing at the window, roysh, staring down at her, with just the light of the moon coming in through the window. She's so beautiful. So tiny.

As they were carrying her out of the ballroom on a stretcher, Sorcha said she wanted to call her Honor, and I'm thinking it's more appropriate than she'll ever know.

My phone beeps again. I check it. I must have, like, thirty messages of congratulations from all sorts of people, even Drico and Dorce, who I've not exactly seen eye to eye with in the past. There's too many to answer tonight, though.

I'm grinning to myself, roysh, remembering Ronan's reaction when I handed him his little sister, and I'm thinking it's probably the first time in his life that he's been actually stuck for something to say.

Honor opens her eyes slightly and I lean down into her crib and lift her out. She doesn't make a sound. I whisper to her, 'Your mummy has to sleep now, so you're going to have to put up with your old dad telling you how much he loves you,' and for a minute it frightens me how like Dick Features I sounded just there.

I go, 'We're going to have so much fun together, you and me. So many places to see. So many things to do . . .'

And I'm standing there, roysh, as she drifts off in my orms again and I'm looking at Sorcha, sleeping peacefully in her bed, and Ronan, snoring his exhausted little head off in a chair in the corner, and I'm there thinking, As someone who spent the first twenty-five years of his life focking things up, that here, in this tiny little ward in Mount Cormel, are just about the only three things I ever got roysh.

Acknowledgements

Thanks, as ever, to colleagues past and present, especially Matt, Paddy, Ger, Jim, Deirdre, Maureen, Noirin and Gambling Kenny P. Thanks to my editor, Rachel Pierce. Thankfully, only she and I know what this book would have been without her ideas and input. Thanks for being tough on me. Thanks to my agent, Faith O'Grady, and thank God she's on *my* side. Thanks to Michael McLoughlin, Patricia Deevy, Brian Walker and everyone at Penguin for your enthusiasm and support. Thanks to Mary McCarthy – the woman behind the man behind the man. And to Dad, Richard, Vincent and Mark, and all my friends – there aren't enough words . . .

He just wanted a decent book to read ...

Not too much to ask, is it? It was in 1935 when Allen Lane, Managing Director of Bodley Head Publishers, stood on a platform at Exeter railway station looking for something good to read on his journey back to London. His choice was limited to popular magazines and poor-quality paperbacks – the same choice faced every day by the vast majority of readers, few of whom could afford hardbacks. Lane's disappointment and subsequent anger at the range of books generally available led him to found a company – and change the world.

'We believed in the existence in this country of a vast reading public for intelligent books at a low price, and staked everything on it'
Sir Allen Lane, 1902–1970, founder of Penguin Books

The quality paperback had arrived – and not just in bookshops. Lane was adamant that his Penguins should appear in chain stores and tobacconists, and should cost no more than a packet of cigarettes.

Reading habits (and cigarette prices) have changed since 1935, but Penguin still believes in publishing the best books for everybody to enjoy. We still believe that good design costs no more than bad design, and we still believe that quality books published passionately and responsibly make the world a better place.

So wherever you see the little bird – whether it's on a piece of prize-winning literary fiction or a celebrity autobiography, political tour de force or historical masterpiece, a serial-killer thriller, reference book, world classic or a piece of pure escapism – you can bet that it represents the very best that the genre has to offer.

Whatever you like to read – trust Penguin.

read more
www.penguin.co.uk